Tejas Desai was born in New York City in the early 1980s. He is a novelist, short story writer, blogger, playwright, filmmaker, screenwriter, actor, educator, librarian, publisher, critic of literature, arts, politics and culture, and the founder of The New Wei Literary Movement and Collective. He has won the Wesleyan Fiction Award, sponsored by Norman Mailer, and has been an honorable mention in the Princeton Poetry Contest. He holds both a Master of Fine Arts in Creative Writing/Literary Translation and a Master of Library/Information Science. His novel, *The Brotherhood*, is the first book in *The Brotherhood Trilogy* and was published in September 2012.

GOOD AMERICANS

*

THE HUMAN TRAGEDY

VOLUME 1

*

Tejas Desai

The New Wei

New York

Good Americans

Published by The New Wei LLC in October 2013

Cover Design by Fena Lee

ISBN-13 # 9780988351936
ISBN-10 # 0988351935

"The men American people admire most extravagantly are the most daring liars; the men they detest most violently are those who try and tell them the truth."

- H. L. Mencken

Table of Contents

Introduction

*

Allow me to introduce myself. My name is Ophelia Gibbs Esq. This is what I am known by on my letterhead and in certain emails I send out when I seek to sound important. I am a lawyer by degree but I had made a career representing certain authors. At first I sought to represent black authors, because after all, that is my background. I am African-American, fifth generation. In the Pomonok projects they call me "OG to the NY." I know the ivory-tower liberals might believe that is racist, but we black people know we're just keeping it real— well the ones who don't want to be white and middle class know that. Personally, I am middle class, some might even consider me upper middle class, but I don't go around trying to be it. I am what I am, and I am proud of that.

Coming back to my professional background—I had mentioned that I began my career by trying to represent black authors to the major publishers. But I found such an enterprise was dead to begin with—the only money makers were the Oreos and the romance writers who stuck to tried substance yet acted like they were above it, representing the rising black professionals and such. Well I am a "risen professional" already thank you very much,

I don't need to read about that, at least not exclusively. Still, it gave me an *in*, so I tried to get some clients, but even then I couldn't sell their books: it seems the black literary elite was already held in place, and let somebody try to break that racket!

Finally, after much struggle, I sold some books to small urban fiction labels, those tales that tell the truth from the street in the most riveting ways possible but rely on stereotypes and rarely transcend them. I made some cash on that for a while until I became sick of those writers and was happy when they went independent or jumped to another ship.

I decided to make a switch to genre romance novels, selling authors to Harlequin and the sister publishers, and that was dynamic. I was saying "Yeah, girl!" and "You go, girl!" all the time and it was happening. I was making gravy from these suburban white ladies, and I was secure in my being having a constant stream of royalties pouring into my coffers.

I thought, why not make another change? Why not try the literary crowd? I always wanted my authors to be in the *NY Times Book Review*, and no way urban fiction or romance could end up in those hallowed halls. I decided to put that on my agent website listings, and then I began what was usually the only fun part of my job, actually reading the books that were being published.

I was shocked at what I discovered. These were the most boring, uninteresting books I had ever read, yet the reviews were unanimously positive, creating an ocean's depth out of stream water.

Personally, I had grown up on Richard Wright, Ralph Ellison, William Faulkner, Zora Neale Hurston, Alice Walker, even Dostoyevsky and Dickens, thinking these were the literary writers, the ones who portrayed and challenged society and humanity's conception of itself, but instead, what I found was more ass-kissing of the politically correct, middle class values that were being depicted in the black romance novels I had failed with in the first place. Except these books barely kept my interest at all. Well, I thought, if this is the way it is, then it is this way. By God, I will try it.

I scoured my queries for the blandest books I could find and, while it took me years to set up relationships with editors and publishers in the literary circles, I was eventually able to sell a novel at auction—that legendary editor Sonny Mehta himself signed off on! I was pleased with my accomplishment, but it did gnaw at me that I had hidden my race and pretended to be white. And the book was an utter dud which fetched a relatively small sum given what I had been used to acquiring.

A few days after receiving the completed contact, signed and initialed by the author where the "sign here" post-its indicated, I began to become kind of queasy. I began to take Mylanta for stomach pains. And by the time I received the "on sig" advance payment in the low five figures, far lower than my romance *royalty checks*, I decided from now on I would only pursue the books I was truly interested in.

Easier said than done. Interesting books didn't come around often, even though I sometimes got about 100 queries a day. No way could I read all of them, and often I would never respond. Even the ones I was excited about I knew I couldn't sell. So why try? And when I did try, I realized it was futile. No one would publish anything. The times I was successful were just luck, and again, they usually occurred when I lowered my standards and went bland. I might as well have played the lottery, I would have been more successful with that. And every day I would have my assistant, a gangly Greek kid from Whitestone named Aeneas, tell my clients I wasn't in the office. He lied so often I knew he could use that skill on the street, eventually.

I stopped reading past the first paragraph. That's all it took for me to make a single decision. What did I care? I had my romance royalties rolling in, and I knew the likelihood of selling something was next to nothing.

Then, one day, after buying a bagel w/ cream cheese and cup of coffee from Ahmed at the truck on Sanford Avenue, I received one email, which I opened only because some inner power tugged at me. In bold letters it proclaimed: "QUERY-THE HUMAN TRAGEDY-SERIES OF EPIC COLLECTIONS" and I thought, what, stamp collections? I laughed to myself. The sender had signed "Jester" and I wondered, why didn't spam catch this? And yet, my gmail showed that the email was addressed to me specifically. When I clicked on it, I saw it was from a real email address, which I cannot reveal.

The query intrigued me. This individual claimed that he held a collection of stories written by various authors, depicting certain elements of American society. He would send a batch of them to me, and assuming I could get them published, would continue to stream them in every few years. Well, that intrigued me more than the latest "story about the immigrant experience" or bland short story collection in which everyone speaks in the same way. But I also knew that no other agent would touch this because it was basically impossible to sell. Perhaps in the Golden Age of Fitzgerald and Hemingway, Harold Ober could have sold this book to Charles Scribner or Horace Liveright, but today? No one cared about the truth. No one would publish works of substance and sophistication.

So I decided to take a chance. My email would scan the attachment anyway for viruses, so I didn't worry too much about that. A day after I responded to him, The Jester sent me the attachment, called *Dhan's Debut and Other Stories*. I thought, hmm, we might have to work on that title, for starts. I opened it immediately and began reading the first story, "Old Guido." I was astonished.

Here was a fresh voice from the darkest recesses of the soul, a racist against all races who was aware of his affliction but was unashamed. And then, the relationship he develops with a vicious teenager, the type of nasty individual I ride the bus with every day, seeing her and her friends jump one sweet Asian girl after another. This was truth, brutal truth, the type I would never read about in any literary book.

As a proud woman of Flushing, an African-American of the fifth generation, born and raised in Queens, I knew I had found something I could be passionate about. So I kept on reading. A screwball comedy about academic hypocrisy and racial integration, an epic journey of a prostitute through the South and North, a meditation on America's role in the world, the homecoming of a war veteran injured in Iraq—here was a portrait of a stained and scarred America, full of the guts and glory of our nation: of greed, racism, buffoonery, elitism, false honor, straight out of the pages of a Mark Twain or Sinclair Lewis novel, but set in the 21st century, today. I felt I had gained a window into a messy kind of truth, perhaps incomplete because such truths are never complete, ever. A kind of vision into the state this nation is in, and, perhaps unfortunately, where it is going.

I was pessimistic about my ability to sell this book, and I was correct. Even after changing the title to *Good Americans*, editors laughed in my face at the lunacy of such a project. *The Human Tragedy* seemed so 19th century to them. Literary books are only read by women and the hipster crowd, I was told, and these readers like "satisfying" stories that make them feel good about humanity and reach an understanding which they already agree with. They want short story collections where the stories are as similar to each other as possible and have "subtlety." At least give us a recurring character, I was told. No one wants to learn, to have their perceptions challenged, and certainly they don't want to read about over-the-hill racists, insecure prostitutes or conversations between disaffected elitists. No sir, that is not what the American people crave, let alone the world public!

I realized, then, that I held a truly revolutionary book, and the start of a visionary project. For *Good Americans* is a grand assault against the literature of our time, a mirror to contemporary society, a return to the old days when courageous writers portrayed and attacked the very institutions upon which our society is based.

I may be an old woman now, but I've learned a few things in our time about it. The power of the media to crush and devalue anything that assaults our rigid politically correct notions of how things should be, their tendency to talk endlessly and repetitively about so-called issues on which no one will ever agree, thus deadening the conversation in the process, when in truth a book, film or television show would do a much better job portraying its nuances for discussion by individuals in their homes, in their libraries or on the streets. The tendency of so many people to go along with the prevailing wave of opinion when the nuances of truth are too much work to examine. The cowardice of many of our politicians, academics, and writers to give forthright opinions, always worried about turning off potential constituencies or interest groups or offending the donors who keep them afloat, rather than crusading to reveal truths no matter what the cost.

This is the time we live in, and *Good Americans* is a book of our time that documents it and points backwards and forwards. I'm sure some people will consider it a dirty book, an offensive book, a book whose mirror is skewed to the gross elements of our society. But think, if you look backwards through time, aren't those the truly great works that have ultimately survived?

But no one believes that today. No editor, perhaps not

even Sonny Mehta, though I do not know because my phone call never got past his assistant. No writer or reviewer I knew would blurb it. Apparently, our literary elite believes that Riny Renaldo, Dhan Duval, Tom, Kunal Shah, Malta...that none of these people should be represented in our time.

My only hope was to self-publish *Good Americans*, as the majority of books today must be. I sent The Jester an email about this, and he responded that he didn't have the time or know-how to do so, but he would allow me the privilege.

I thought, I could do it myself, but I am an agent, not an author or a publisher. I searched online for companies that could do it for me, but they seemed to charge an arm and a leg. I could use an aggregator or distributor, but they would take a percentage and wouldn't help design the cover or promote it.

I was resigned to do everything myself, and looked up websites for this purpose. It actually did not seem that difficult, only time-consuming and annoying, and plenty of self-published authors gave advice to the multitudes of hopefuls.

So I prepared for the inevitable, and figured it would be an arduous project that I could make into a fun one. Until I saw a friend suggestion on Facebook for Tejas Desai. Through him I found his blog about The New Wei, a budding publishing collective dedicated to banding together and promoting provocative and dynamic authors who actually had something to say.

It seemed Mr. Desai was trying to build his operation. I decided to contact him, figuring it was worth a shot—he responded right away, in detail and with overwhelming passion. He read the collection and told me, in his deep voice and intense, plodding manner, that The New Wei would publish and promote it, and would release the entire *Human Tragedy* for as long as it was needed, for he believed wholeheartedly urgent works like these should be out in the world, instead of allowing the literary vacuum to be filled with cowardly and undistinguished bores.

And so it came to be. If you happen to be reading this introduction, then the book is published, and you are in for a treat. A glimpse into some of the most fascinating personalities you will encounter in literature, a gateway into the darkest and most compassionate recesses of the human soul, a collection that will make you laugh out loud and which will pierce your heart. A portrait of where this country has been, and where it is going, that will provoke thought in a way that no recent fiction book has. A collection with such a wide range of voices, effects and subjects you will be astonished it is one book. And it is not, for it is just the first step in a long road, a *Human Tragedy* for our time.

Mr. Desai's name is on it—we couldn't put down The Jester's name, for he wouldn't dare expose himself or his associates. In fact, he released himself from the project completely except for his role as messenger for the next batch of stories.

So I am married to Mr. Desai now, jointly responsible for its publication and promotion (who knew, a black woman in her 60s teaming with a brown man in his 30s —the world is a funny place!). But leave no doubt that we are merely vessels for its delivery. Were Chaucer, Shakespeare, Balzac the actual authors of their works? Did Homer or Sophocles exist? Does it matter? Even Faulkner said that his works would have been created anyway, whether or not he had lived. And so *The Human Tragedy* will be released too, for consumption by you.

Faithfully Yours,

Ophelia "Cherry" Donovan Gibbs III, Esquire

Flushing, Queens, New York, New York, USA

October 2013

Old Guido

*

The Italian pizza shop on Main Street is the only place nowadays in Flushing where you can get a goddamn stromboli. Italian shopping's been arm-twisted by the gooks, you gotta go all the way to Howard Beach to buy a decent meatball, and who wants to hang out with those guidos down there? I'm Italian, but hell, I got some pride.

I'm hanging around the pizza shop the other day, drinking some pepsi and eating the best pizza in Queens, when Gino Mellone comes in. It was back in the day in the '50s when we was growing up that we used to run down Oak Avenue together throwing snowballs at the buses. He was drafted in that last draft but he never saw action in Vietnam. I got lucky and I never had to fight those gooks neither, but I didn't know then the gook invasion would come down on me right here in Flushing.

I ask old Gino what he's doin' these days and we start shooting the shit. Apparently he's been a teacher and he's nearin' that retirement. I figure he's been teaching all kinds of kids and he's not prejudiced like me, so I don't say nothing about that. I know I'm prejudiced, I know it's wrong at heart, but I also know facts are facts and there were the good old days when there was community and you knew who your friends were, when folks were celebrating Hanukah and Christmas both and there wasn't no questions about why. Now they got official days off and more and more of those Jew holidays are getting ingrained. It's like they won some battle I never knew was fought and now they're reigning even over the gooks and the Italians just got this pizza shop and the bocce ball court.

Except we don't even got this, because as soon as we start shooting, a crowd of Hispanic kids come in, with this cute white girl. She looks Russian, but I can't tell exactly. She's got that extra pale skin, those thin lips, the cleft chin, the high cheekbones, the slightly squinty eyes. I used to draw girl's faces in art class back in high school, so I know a thing or two about faces—of course there wasn't too many Russian girls back then.

Anyway, I notice them because it's school hours, and they ain't in school, not that it's any surprise, because the schools don't seem to give a fuck. I see these assholes at all hours walking around the neighborhood looking for places to hang out and things to steal, and calling the cops don't seem to work no more, because if the cops come at all it'll be like two hours later. Things don't work like they used to. There just ain't the old values.

I ask Gino why he ain't in school. He says he's taking vacation time, he's got so much saved up it's a joke. He says he usually takes some time before the end of the school year, before the exams start. I'd think he'd want to make a final push to teach these kids so they don't fail, but I guess not. I ask if these kids are from the school he teaches at, but he says no, actually the kids in his school are worse.

They're clustering around one table now, calling each other "nigga" this and yelling "fuck" that. I mean it's ridiculous. I wasn't going around calling myself a guido back in the day, and I wouldn't now neither. And it's funny, these spics are going around acting like they're black, and accusing everybody else of being a racist if they get looked at sideways. Well, I'm prejudiced, but I ain't a racist. I just see things like they are. These kids try to intimidate anyone that's weaker than them, whether they're teenagers or old people. Back in the old days, we wouldn't even talk to each other the way these kids do, let alone to our elders.

Now some of 'em are talking about what to order—at least they got some respect for Italian cooking, not that they know nothing about it. Anyway, I see the Russian girl sit on one of the Hispanic kids' laps, and he's got his hands all over her ass. He's talking to another Hispanic kid about how he fucked her the day before and how wet her pussy was, and she's laughing about that. Then she starts wiggling on his lap and the other Hispanic kid takes out his cell phone and takes a picture.

I look over at Gino.

"This go on in your school?" I ask him.

"And worse. Geez, when we were their age, we had to go to a prostitute to do that."

I nod. I had a couple of prostitutes in my day, before I met Jean and settled down.

I put down my pepsi. I'm nearly finished with the slice except for the crust, which Doctor Patel a few blocks down told me to stay away from on account of my sugar. I've had enough of the animals so I get up and tell Gino to give my regards to his wife, Donna.

"See ya around, Riny," he says, shaking my hand.

I go out to my 1979 Chevy, still working fine, which I've parked at the meter since that's the only way you can get parking close nowadays. I see somebody's leaned a small scooter on it, one of those you can fold up. One of those damn kids, probably. I have a mind to pick it up and chuck it into the street and let some car demolish it, but I was sued ten years back for no reason at all, and I don't feel like going through that again. Seems like you can't do or say nothing in this country no more without some lawyer on your back. So I'm about to pick it up and lean it on a pole, gently, when that Russian girl rushes out of the pizza shop and comes at me.

"Hey, that's my bike," she says, like she's outraged.

"Yeah, and this is my car," I say.

She looks shocked that I've talked back to her.

"Well, don't be touchin' shit that's not yours, white man," she says.

I'm speechless at first. I see the teenage pack males starting to gather in the pizza shop doorway.

"I think you better check out the color of your own skin," I say back, laughing.

She looks shocked again, but I can tell she's checkin' out her brain for a comeback. These kids don't got much going on up there substance-wise, but they're savvy.

She starts saying something, but she holds back. Her face is red now, and she grabs her bike. "Just don't start shit, nigga," she says. "I'll get my boys," she says.

"Do that. I'll call the cops," I tell her. I know the cops won't come, but sometimes, if they aren't that tough, these kids get scared if you say that. I'm already by my driver's side at this point, and I get in. I'm afraid she's gonna key my car or break my window, but I don't wanna act scared. These kids can smell fear. And generally they know if they damage property, there could be hell to pay. I see the Hispanic guys approach the girl, asking her, I guess, what happened. By that time, I've already backed up and merged onto the road.

It wasn't always like this. Way back when, there was respect. In the old days, Flushing was all farmland. My dad didn't know a lot about the history, being he was living on the Lower East Side when I was born, but the old man across the street, Jeffords is his name, he told me all about it: the old style Fords, the quiet pastures, the respect for self and community, the dedication to country. Old man Jeffords served this nation honorably, lost an arm in World War II, and told me about a time he could have killed a gook but chose to spare him instead. I gotta admire him for that. I don't know if I could have done the same.

When I was growing up, there were opportunities but no one forgot about community. They was building new houses and people were moving in, but they was all Italians and some Jews. Even though we were new in the neighborhood, Mr. Jeffords and other folks welcomed us. We was like family. We had fights sometimes, there were bullies and all that, but on the whole folks cared about other folks. There was black folks too, in some of the outer areas. But mostly there weren't too many people about.

Then the gooks started movin' in. First the Chinese, then the Koreans. Slowly they bought up all downtown Main Street and made inroads on Kissena. At the same time, a bunch of other folks, the Greeks, the Indians, the Pakistinians, the Romanians, the Israelis, they just started coming in like a storm. It was chaos and there just wasn't the same togetherness no more. One day I realized that I didn't know nobody on my block except for old man Jeffords and his wife.

Then the drug age came too and Flushing really went south. When you walked in the park you'd find syringes, sometimes even needles on the path. Drug pushers and con artists would approach me on the street. One time a guy who was probably a drug addict, he knocked on my door, claiming to be my next door neighbor. He said his daddy was having a heart attack and could he use the phone, but I knew better. I didn't know most people on my block no more but I had sure seen my next door neighbors, and there was no way this guy fit the bill. I'm pretty sure I wouldn't be here today if I had opened that door.

They started warning parents about vans circling the schools full of molesters trying to kidnap kids. If you walked on Kissena or Main Street after ten at night, you'd get mugged, no doubt. I was even mugged one time on a quiet residential street around here during daytime. In the park sometimes you'd see cops and bagged bodies. Some folks said it was devil worshippers, and I don't doubt they were around, but that was probably the mob's doing. I feel bad about that. They was my people, but those assholes were getting out of Howard Beach and Ozone Park and coming up here to dump folks, and that wasn't right.

Those were bad times. But even then, with all the horror stories on the streets and in the papers, I think kids in the neighborhood, for the most part, showed some respect. Now there's none. Jean and I tried to raise our kids right. They went to decent schools in CUNY and at Hofstra and now they live on Long Island. When our friends were moving out in the late '70s and early '80s, they told us to come with, that New York City was becoming a cesspool of crime and that if we stuck around we'd be drowned in it. But I didn't wanna go. I stood my ground. And I'm proud of it.

Jean was always into gardening. I never liked it as much as her, but we did it to spend time together. We grew tomatoes outside in our garden and basil leaves inside on a large sill. Nowadays, now that she's gone, I do it to pass the time, because I figure it's better to grow stuff I use in salads and pasta myself than to buy it at the Chinese groceries. It's cheap over there, but it's hard to get good stuff.

After I make my food, sometimes if I have leftovers I'll put 'em in a shopping bag and take it over to the bocce ball court in Kissena Park. That's where the old Italian guys hang out, playing bocce all day long. They even got a Korean guy there sometimes, but he's a good old boy. They're always telling me to play with them, but I turn them down, usually. I don't know why, I just don't like playing in groups like that, at least not since Jean died. I kind of like the company of the old guys, but I'd rather be by myself, walking along the paths of the park.

You see a lot of Asian girls walking there. There are one or two young white guys always hanging around, walking with the Asian girls, different girls every time, and the Asian girls let them. I don't know what I woulda done if I had been young now and seen all these nice looking Asian girls around. Maybe I would have done the same thing if I hadn't had Jean. But it's too late now. And it seems kind of pathetic.

I'm looking out the window during the day and I see the same crowd coming down the street. It's one in the afternoon, high time these kids should be in school. In the old days, if an adult saw these kids on the street, they'd come out of their house and yell at them to get back, and usually the kids would listen. Or the adult would call the cops and they'd come and bring them back to school.

Nowadays, you're afraid of getting shot. There's no point of even calling 911. There's no communal action at all. You bring this up at the community board meetings over on Northern Boulevard and you're basically brushed off. There's no organizations no more you can rely on. It's all controlled by the mayor and city hall, and they're probably puppets of the President or something. The people got no voice no more.

I know old man Jeffords, sitting out on his porch all day, might have an idea to tell his wife to call the cops. I know he'd do it. He's lucky enough to still have a living wife, at his age, and he's especially glad because he's only got one arm and it's tough to do things with that. I won't never say that to his face but you better believe it. Jean used to say that a woman is like a man's right arm, and in Jeffords' case it's true literally.

Now I'm still looking out my window, opening my curtain an inch, just to make sure these kids don't mess with my property. What I see is worse than I'd feared, because that Russian girl is looking over the back of my car. I think she recognizes it, or at least she's trying to determine. She's pointing at it now and looking back at the Hispanic kid whose lap she was sitting on. He's waving her over, probably telling her to forget it. But she's jumping up and down now, and this other Hispanic kid is laughing. Then a Hispanic girl, wearing these big loop earrings, runs over and kicks the back of my Chevy. My car's old, but I got an alarm system built into it after the window got broke and my door was graffitied back in the late '80s. I haven't updated it in ten years though, and I don't hear nothing when she kicks it. The kid who was laughing has his hand over his mouth. Then I can hear him say something like "OH! you did that!" but I don't wait to see no more. You can't have no guns in New York

City, but damn right you can have a bat, so I run into the bedroom and get Mighty Matt. That's what I call my slugger. I've had him for thirty years, genuine maple tree lumber. I ain't a violent guy, but you better believe I'm gonna defend my property from a bunch of hoodlums.

I get to the door, take a breath, close my eyes and cross myself, then open it and the screen door and rush out with my bat raised. But it's all for nothing: no one's out there.

I run over to my car to see if there's any damage on the back. Sure enough, there's a dent on the trunk, a small one but present.

"I got 'em to run," I hear a voice yell, and it's old man Jeffords, standing up on his porch across the street. "I yelled and they ran."

I hold up my arm, Mighty Matt in it, a kind of salute to the resolute old timer.

"Goddamn children," he yells. "They don't have any respect anymore."

I look over the dent again, then walk towards the old man, but I gotta stop quick to let a car pass. Then I go forward again into the middle of the street.

"Mr. Jeffords," I say, "you see which way they went?"

He points towards the park, which is only one block from my house. "They went over that way, son," he says. "Don't worry about them now. But we should start calling the cops if we see them, because then they'll make them go to school. They shouldn't be out here on the street."

"The cops don't do nothing," I say. "You know that."

"We have to keep pressing these people," Mr. Jeffords says, his good arm raised. I see his wife is looking out through the window. "That's the only way you get things done. I'm too old now to go to the community board, but back in the day, if we wanted to fight something as a community, we went there and we fought it. They wanted to expand that hospital twenty years back, and we fought it, and we won. We didn't win 'em all. That's what you young people never understood. You can't win 'em all. But you gotta keep pushing."

I nod respectfully, but on the inside I'm a little irked and kind of amused that old man Jeffords would refer to me as a young person, as if it was fifty years back and he was talking to me when I was a teenager. I guess when you reach that age, you're in a time warp, and you see fifty years back as equal to today. And you see every person younger than you as immature and inexperienced.

Later in the afternoon, I decide to pick some tomatoes in the backyard. I also have a whole slew of basil leaves that I cut from plants I have inside, and I put 'em all in a shopping bag. These days, when I'm not looking forward to my disability or social security check, watching some bullshit talk or court show (they're pretty much the same thing), listening to Rush or Don on the radio, or chasing teenagers, I'm prepping to go to the park. It's all you can do when you got a bum knee and you're retired, and got no wife or kids around. Years ago I used to drive out to the country (that's what I call Long Island) to visit my kids, but nowadays that's pretty rare. So far they haven't given me any grandkids and there's only a certain amount of joy a man can get out of spending time with barren young folks.

I put on my Reeboks sneakers, make a cheese and tomato sandwich that I put in my pocket in case I get hungry, and head out with the bag. Sometimes I drive, park near the playground and walk to where the bocce ball court is, but this time I just walk. It'll take me a bit longer than most folks, but that's alright with me.

See, I got knee surgery about five years ago and that's

why I went on disability and why I wasn't able to work construction no more. It sucked especially because not only do I like working fine but the next month after that my wife learned she had cancer. It was a good thing I could still pay my insurance then. But it wasn't easy. You know how these kids are these days, they're just out for themselves. They don't wanna give nothing back to their elders. They don't wanna stick around either, assisting. They'll come on the weekend maybe to the hospital and give their mom a get-well card and their daddy a hug, and meanwhile they expect you to fend for yourself. Or at least they think the nurses in the hospital should do it, and those assistants who come by your house to make sure you haven't fallen in the bathtub and croaked. And when their mom dies, they come to the hospital all teary-eyed and holding cards and flowers, acting like they care, when really they're thinking only about the Jenny Craig appointment they missed or the yoga seminar they've scheduled the next day. That's how it is, on the inside.

At least the old guys at the bocce ball court know what the deal is. They know community. All the guys are responsible for cleaning up, for making sure the court is playable. Even the Korean guy does that. The old men watch, they figure whether a man is worthy by how he respects the court and helps out afterwards with cleaning up. If he seems like a community man, then he can be in. You'd think the values of a bocce ball court would translate to the home, to the church, to the school. But they don't. They haven't, at least, since I was young.

The park is shaped like a pentagon, though it's not a perfect one. It's got baseball fields, basketball and tennis courts, a large pond, a track and the bocce ball court. It's also one-fifth uncut forest on the side closest to my house and the one I walk along right now to get to the court. This is where they found some of the bodies in the '80s and early '90s, where those damn devil worshippers were supposed to have been. There've been a few fires in this forest while I've been around, probably set on purpose by some kids, though they never did find the responsible parties as far as I know based on neighborhood gossip (mainly being old man Jeffords).

Part of the forest was so burned it made huge paths but someone or some committee must have replanted the trees because those paths are filled now. Also, for a long time, there was no pavement on the road next to the forest, so you had to either walk on the other side of the street next to the residential homes or march through dirt and grime and leaves next to a thick barrier, hoping some bad folks wouldn't jump out of the forest and get you. But now there's a pavement. It's nice and new and shiny, and I like walking on it. It's one thing that's improved since the good old days.

Anyway, I'm limping along now (it's not like I'm that disabled or nothing no more, I just walk with a slight limp) and I happen to see a fallen tree in the forest. That ain't uncommon, but it's rare enough for me to notice it, wonder why it went down (lightning? but there hasn't been a thunderstorm in a while) and whether anyone got hurt during the fall. I haven't heard nothing like that, but the truth is, even if someone did get killed, I'd probably never know. Queens only got some bullshit free papers. The paid papers are either from Manhattan and the other boroughs or Long Island. There's no way to know what's really going on locally, except what you see with your own eyes.

Now I do notice something with my eyes, but I'm not sure I'm seeing it right. This part of the forest has an elevated pavement, so that where you're walking and the forest floor ain't at the same level. Basically I'm looking down at the fallen tree, and next to it, sticking out of a bush, I see a pair of legs. Or at least they're pants. I'm thinking maybe somebody just threw a pair of old jeans away, but they seem bulged, like some body or a rod or something long and cylindrical's in 'em. The economy's gone down now, so it says in all the papers and on TV, and maybe the mob's started dumping again. I hope not, I hope to God not, it'd be like the entire world was going downhill again, and it was gonna be like the '80s and early '90s again, but worse.

My kids haven't bought much for me, but they did get me a cell phone (and made me pay the monthly bills). Problem is, I never use it and I left it at home, so there's no way I can call 911 if it is a body. I look around me and there's no one else on the streets, only some cars driving by, and I'm not sure that I trust anyone I would flag down after all the movies that I've seen. I've already passed the residential homes, not that I know no more who lives in 'em, and on the other side of a large road is the fenced off side of a huge golf course. So unless I go home, there's pretty much nothing I can really do about this.

Still, I don't know for sure if it is a body. I can either keep on walking and ignore it, or go back to my house and call the cops and report it, or go down to the forest level on my weak knee and see if it really is what I think it is. I remember all the times I came across bad things twenty years back and just kept walking, knowing how common they were. These days, it seems there ain't as many problems, but I seem to be the one running across the ones there are, and I don't know whether to walk away or not. I didn't follow those kids into the forest, but I did come out with a bat. I hear old man Jeffords' words in my ear, that you gotta keep on pushing, even if you fail. That's what my generation never learned, he said. And thinking about Vietnam, who knows, maybe he was right.

Even before I've made a decision, I'm bending my knees all I can, holding onto tree branches with my free hand and making my way down the slope to the forest level. I almost trip once, and the entire time I'm going down there I'm muttering to myself that this ain't worth doing, that I'm just making a fool of myself. But when I get down to the level I can see much better now, and it's definitely a pair of legs: skinny, female legs. The other thing is, they're moving.

Only slightly, but the knees are bending a bit, up and down, and now they're rising higher. Then the legs move into the bush more, and they come up, bent and lazy, and I can tell the person has sat up. I move closer, carefully, but I'm curious to see what's up with them. Then I see it. The person's groggy and kind of beat up, with these scratches all across her face. She's holding her stomach. Her top's sliced in one place and in other areas there are little rips. Plus one of her hoop earrings is gone.

I come up to her and hold out my hand. She coughs, then shakes her head like she don't want my help. I can't blame her. I'd think I was trying to hurt her too.

"I'm not gonna hurt you," I say to her. "I'm gonna get you some help. You feel okay?"

She keeps shaking her head around. I'm not even sure if it's at me, or if she's so out of it that she doesn't know what else to do.

"I don't care that you kicked my car," I say. "That's not why I'm here."

I say that but I'm not sure I believe it. I can help get an ambulance if she needs it, though I'm not sure how, but damn right I wanna get her too for fucking with my vehicle. Problem with these kids today is that there's no consequences for their actions. Though I guess this girl got some consequence if she was lying here all beat up.

She puts her hand on the ground and gets up on one

knee, slowly, grimacing a bit. She looks up and now she seems to recognize me, to study me.

"Fuck off, old man," she says fast. I almost preferred "white man" to being called "old," even though I am.

"You want me to leave you here?" I ask. "You wanna make it on your own, all beat up like that?"

"I got money," she says, tapping her pockets. But then her eyes go wide.

"They took it, didn't they?" I ask. "Who was it?"

"She took everything, that fucking white bitch took everything."

"The Russian girl?" I ask.

"She Serbian," she says. "Bitch took my metrocard too. Now how am I gonna get home? Can't believe them niggas—"

"Who?"

"Them niggas, Josh and Andre. They violated. And them other niggas. They helped that white bitch out."

"They beat you up too?"

"Them niggas just watchin', son. They been out for the white bitch the whole time. They was just waitin' for me to kick that car—"

"Why?" I ask, not getting it, though nothing surprises me with these kids.

"I cheated, nigga. I fucked that nigga Tony when I be fucking Josh too. And he knew. He knew I be doin' it. Nigga probably holdin' his dick and bragging 'bout that shit in the locker. After he myspace me. Fuck," she says. She falls to both knees now, cradles her stomach and puts her head down to the dirt. I can tell she's crying.

"God, my mama gonna kill me if I don't get home by five. How am I gonna get home?"

"Your mother don't care that you've been mugged?"

She looks up now, her arms out, acting tough.

"I gotten jumped before," she says. "I just put some concealer on my face. My mama don't notice nothin'."

34

"What if she did?"

"Then she beat me. Mista, you glad you not in school. You glad you a white man and not a spic like me."

I'm not sure how to respond to that. I hear these kids call themselves the n-word but this latest comment really floors me. I mean, yeah, I'm glad too. But still.

"Alright," I say, trying to bring this conversation to a close. "Can you walk?"

"It hurts in my stomach and on my face, mista," she says, rubbing her stomach and coughing again. "It hurts bad. But nothing I ain't gotten before."

"So you can walk."

"Them niggas probably waited 'til that bitch got me down and then they took my jewels and my card. Them niggas know I'm transferring. Fucking niggas planned it."

"But you can walk," I say.

She goes silent, looking down again. Then she puts her hand on the ground and lifts herself up.

"Yeah, I walk."

"Then come on," I say. "Come with me. I'll give you some money so you can get on home."

"Really, mista?" she says, looking at me suspiciously. Then she smiles, like a supplicant. They probably taught her that in the school of hard knocks. Seriously, I don't know why I'm doing this. I'm the kind who usually walks away unless it's my person or property being threatened. I can get her a couple of bucks for the bus and the subway, but I've gotta be careful. She could rob me instead. Or if she sees some of Jean's jewelry lying around, she might think it's up for grabs and come back another time with her "homies" to rob and kill me. It happens. It does. And as I'm climbing the slope back up to the walkway, still holding the bag full of basil leaves and tomatoes, I'm regretting this. Especially since it's straining my knee to go up. In fact, I almost trip one time.

"You ok, mista?" this monster says sweetly, as if I'm

gonna fall for that nonsense. I'm half a century older than you missy, I think. I got experience with teenagers too.

"I'm okay," I say back. I make the extra effort and get up the slope and onto the pavement. I'm panting, a little bit short of breath because I'm not used to this kind of exertion, but I'm okay. Now I see her coming up, and she's climbing with her hands in the dirt, like she can't make it up.

"Are you okay? You sure you don't want me to go to a house nearby and call 911?"

"No," she says, shaking her head. "Don't fucking do that, mista. Please don't. I'm okay," she says, coughing again, trying extra hard to get up the slope. I roll my eyes and stick out my hand. She grabs it and after a few runs of the treadmill, blowing dirt around, she climbs up.

I see her face now in the sunlight. Other than those hideous gashes, she looks pretty good for a spic. She's got Jean's olive skin tone, hazel brown eyes, this curvy, smooth nose and apple cheeks. Her hair was in a bun before but now it's scattered, going down her neck. If I was her age and she wasn't from the ghetto, I think I'd ask her out on a date.

But it's now and I'm an old widower. All I can do is walk this brat back to my house and give her two bucks out of Jean's Christian charity. God's money. God.

I start moving and she's following. Even with my limp and me breathing heavy, she's tailing behind. I can tell that after touching my hand she suddenly trusts me. Or maybe she thinks I'm even dumber than she thought before. I better be careful.

"It's nice of you to help me out, mista," she says. "We don't trust white people too much where I'm from. We scared of 'em, anyway."

"You don't have white kids in your school?" I ask.

"Yeah, sure," she says, apparently thinking. "But they not like you, mista. They from the hood too. So they not really white."

"Really?" I say.

"Yeah. Then they got some white kids in the smart classes. But we don't hang with them."

"You don't beat them up?" I ask.

"Some niggas mess with the scrubs. I don't got time for that. Too many bitches lookin' to front, too many bitches snitchin', too many bitches aimin' to get your man. You be walkin' in the hallway in school and some bitch be brushin' against you, all aggressive and shit. I don't got time to be botherin' nobody. I got me to look after."

"Looks like you looked after yourself well," I say.

"I got ganged up, mista. I got caught up with the dick. You can't think about the dick too much. Once it get in your mind, you blocked. Then you in trouble."

"Yeah, you're too young for boys," I tell her, and I remember back when I was saying that years ago to my daughters.

"I old enough," she says, defensively. "I been old. I fucked niggas. What dat say to you, old man?"

"Just because you've had sex doesn't mean you were ready for it," I say, sounding like my wife now.

"I ready, mista. I been ready a long time. Man, what you know anyway?" And she coughs.

"I'm probably forty years older than you," I say back. "How old are you anyway?"

"I'm fifteen," she says, proud.

"Then I'm fifty years older than you. You don't think I know what I'm talking about?"

"It been fifty years since you my age. And what you know about being a girl?"

"I raised two."

"White girls," she says.

She coughs again, this time so hard she has to stop and hold her stomach. We're nearing the edge of the park.

37

"I'm thinking maybe we should go to the doctor," I say.

"No, nigga," she says. She coughs again. "I mean, mista. No. You so nice to me, I'm sorry if I be actin' all hard. I just need that two dollas and I'll be gone, mista." She pauses. "We going to your house?" she asks.

I nod. She smiles. I'm nervous again.

Then I realize old man Jeffords is probably still on his porch, and if I bring this teenage girl into my house, especially the one who kicked my car, he'll get pretty suspicious. He might even raise some stink with the other old timers around the neighborhood, saying I bring young Hispanic girls back to my house, that that's how I deal with Jean being gone. So I stop her and tell her to wait on the corner, that I'll go to my house and get the money and come back. That way, she also won't be able to come in and see what I got there.

She shrugs and says fine, but she doesn't look all that happy about it. I guess she was looking forward to seeing the inside of my house, if not to rob it later, then for the same reason that white women like to look at the inside of houses.

I jog to my front door, still holding the bag of tomatoes and basil leaves. I hear a voice call after me. It's old man Jeffords.

"The boys weren't at the bocce court?" Jeffords yells out.

I turn around. "I forgot something," I say.

"Oh," he yells back. "I thought you came back early."

I shake my head and turn, hoping he won't carry on the conversation. I open the door. As I'm about to close it, I hear old man Jeffords' voice again.

"Say hi to Ernesto for me," he says. Ernesto's one of the founders of the bocce ball court. He pressed Mayor Guiliani to build it in the early '90s.

"Okay," I say, smiling, raising my right arm, then

38

quickly closing the door before Mr. Jeffords can get another word in. I love the old man but he can be a pain sometimes when you need to be getting somewhere. He acts like we still live in the Flushing he lived in when he was young, when this was mostly farmland and life was slow.

I leave the bag near the door, turn around and go into Jean's room. Before she died, she had this bin where she put a dollar in every day and she would donate it to the church on Sundays. I was never religious so I never went to church neither, but since she died, I been putting in a dollar a month to commemorate, even though I haven't gone to church to donate it.

Now I figure I can get two dollars from there to give to this girl, on short notice. It's charity after all. Probably better than giving it to the church, these days.

I keep the bin down under the bed, but when I lift the comforter to look under there I don't see it. I put my hand under, it's dark, and I move it around. Still, I can't locate this thing. Possibly I took it out last time I was putting a dollar in there and absent-minded, I left it somewhere else. So I get up to look around the room when I hear the doorbell ring.

I freeze up. Who could it be? Mr. Jeffords? I hope he didn't see that girl. Maybe he recognized her and came over to let me know. Maybe he called the police. Hope not, though at least then she'd get some ambulance help. I know she don't want it, but...hell, for all she knows, I came in here to call them.

I get to the door, take a deep breath, and open it. It's the girl.

"Took you long enough, mista," she says, coming in, not even asking if she could.

"What the hell you doing here?" I ask, involuntarily letting the lady pass. "I told you to stay on the corner."

"I need to use the bathroom, mista. I can't wait no

more. There aren't no bathrooms on the bus. You want me to pee on the street?"

I shake my head, furious now, but I don't want to lose it. I close the door most of the way.

"Goddamn, did anyone see you come in?"

"How do I know, mista? White folks always peeking out the windows. I got cops called on my ass one time. White folks always callin' the cops."

"Was anyone on the street?" I ask.

"If you askin' 'bout that old man who yelled at us, he went back in his house. I made sure of that. Now, you gonna show me where the bathroom's at, mista?"

I look out the door and sure enough, for once, Mr. Jeffords isn't sitting on his porch.

I close it and without thinking, I point in the direction of the bathroom. As she runs towards it, I remember a couple of imitation gold chains are in the mirror cabinet. They ain't worth nothing but they could serve to whet this delinquent's appetite.

I come up behind her as she goes into the bathroom. As she closes the door, I stick my good foot in and stop it.

"Hold up," I say. "Leave the door open."

"You wanna watch me while I piss, mista? What kinda pervert are you, mista?"

"I..." I'm not sure what to say.

"Damn, mista," she says, "you a different kinda man than I thought. You bring me in here for somethin' else?"

I try to remind her she brought herself in, but I can't get it out.

"Mama always told me don't trust no white people. Daddy thought he was white. He was that kind of spic. That's why he left."

I don't know what else to say. So I turn around and go back into the room where I was looking for the bin. I hear her laugh, then the door close and the lock turn. A couple of imitation gold chains don't mean nothing, right? She'll be out of there in a second anyway. Biggest thing I'll have to worry about is that she won't wash her hands.

I look about five minutes for the bin. I can't find it. I glance back at the bathroom but the door's still closed. Then I go into the kitchen to pour myself some tea.

Lo and behold, on the kitchen counter there's the bin. I must have put it there the last time I put money in— maybe I was making some tea at the same time, I can't remember, and I probably left it there, not even noticing or thinking about it. I open it and take out the two dollars, put it in my pocket next to the tomato and cheese sandwich. Then I figure that I should take the bin back and put it under the bed before the girl comes out and sees that I have a bin full of money.

I peek out the kitchen now and at the bathroom door. It's still closed, and there's still a light on. I can see it at the bottom of the door. I run into the bedroom and hide the bin. When I come out, the door's still closed. She's taking an awfully long time for a piss. Maybe something even happened to her.

I go back on into the bedroom and get a paper clip, which I straighten out. The doorknob's got a hole in it, and you're damn right I've dealt with teenage girls before.

I knock on the door.

"What's taking so long?" I ask.

"Hold on, mista," she says quickly, "it's takin' a while to come out."

I roll my eyes. The things these girls will say to their elders these days. No shame.

"How do I know you're telling the truth, missy? It's been nearly ten minutes."

"I'll be out in like, three," she says. I've got such an urge to use the clip, but I figure what's the worst she can be doing in there? I'll give her three minutes.

I go to the window and look out. Old man Jeffords is

sitting in his usual spot now. He must have gone in for a bathroom break or something. Just in time to not see the girl. Pretty strange.

I take out my sandwich, unwrap the sandwich bag, take a couple of bites, rewrap it and put it back in my pocket. Soon I'm back on the bathroom case.

"It's been three minutes," I say. "What're you doing in there?"

"Hold up, mista," she says. Suddenly I hear the toilet flush. Then she says, "I got another load coming, mista. It's the other kind. Might take a few minutes."

Now I'm getting suspicious. How many loads is this girl gonna have? Is she doing her laundry? And if she is going that many times, there might be a problem with her insides, so maybe I should be calling 911. Except then they might wonder what the hell she's doing in my house. And teenagers, they're trouble. They can make up some messed up stories. And these days, these fucking assholes in authority, they'll believe 'em.

"You shouldn't be going that many times," I say as I fit the clip in. "We should call the ambulance."

"No mista, I just ate a lot."

I hesitate, then open the door.

She's not on the toilet, which is right next to the door. She's standing in front of the sink and staring at the mirror. Except in her hand is a brush and on the sink is a container all filled up with my wife's makeup, with the foundation and concealer open. Worse, there's makeup dust and water all over the sink and the floor.

"Hey!" the girl yells as I charge in, yelling the same thing back to her. She looks at me, scared, ready to say sorry and think up an excuse, but I just react and slap her across the face with the back of my hand. She grabs her face and yells, cowers next to the wall. Immediately I'm regretting what I just did. It came over me, I don't know why.

She starts crying, this tough girl, and I'm next to her now, touching her arms, telling her I'm sorry.

"Damn, mista, you hit me. Get your hands off me, mista. You trying to touch my titties or somethin'? I didn't think you be like this. You a molesta, mista."

She tries to escape but I grab her by the throat and push her against the wall. She's got her hazel eyes wide now, looking at me steady. Her face isn't moving, her bosom's heaving, she's waiting to see what I'm gonna do. I don't know what's gotten over me. I don't wanna do this, but at the same time, if she leaves and starts telling stories, I'm in big trouble.

She's shaking, pretty scared, but calm at the same time, like this has happened to her before.

"I don't wanna hurt you," I say. "I'm sorry for hitting you, I swear. I didn't mean to. I lost it. You shouldn't have lied to me. You shouldn't have used my wife's makeup."

She nods furiously. I guess she's in survival mode now, checking to see how she can get out of this.

I loosen my grip a bit but I don't let go.

"You can't tell nobody that I hit you. Okay? Nobody. Never. You weren't ever in here either."

She nods again. "I won't tell nobody, mista," she says. "I swear. Please don't kill me, mista. I won't tell nobody."

She coughs. I loosen my hold. She breathes, coughs, then tries to bolt. But I catch her by her top and pull her back, and now I've got my forearm on her throat.

"What are you doing?" I ask. She starts crying again.

"Please don't kill me, mista, please don't kill me. I'm too young to die."

I kick the door closed and I take my arm away. She puts her hands over her face and she's shaking her head. Her makeup's coming off. I've got some on my arm and a little on my shirt sleeve.

"Okay, calm down," I say. "Just don't try to leave. I won't hurt you."

She keeps crying.

"Alright, I'm sorry. Listen. Calm down. I'll get you some water. And..." I think. "Listen, if you calm down and don't tell nobody I hit you, I'll do your makeup for you, okay?"

She cries a little bit more, but then looks up at me, strangely. "Do my makeup? What you mean, mista?"

"I used to help my wife sometimes. I used to get the little contours. If I do it for you, your mom won't know you've got all those scratches over your face." And the black and blue eye from my slap, I think.

"Really, mista? You do makeup?"

"I used to help her sometimes," I say. I never did tell none of my friends that. I'd never have heard the end of it if I had. "If I do your makeup, you think you can forget I hit you?"

"I forgot, mista. I been slapped so many times. I forgot that quick, mista. You do my makeup I be happy."

I remember how happy Jean was the first time I helped her with her makeup. She'd had an injury at work and strained her right wrist. I walked by the bathroom one day and saw her struggling to apply it with her left hand. So I offered to help her. She was defensive at first. She'd never even let me watch her doing her makeup. She'd always lock the door, and I'd joke around with my dad about "women's work." My mom had died at that point, my other brother had moved away, and it was just us three there, living like a happy family, except Jean didn't always get along with my dad. He was even more prejudiced than me, except it was against women, faggots and black folks. She didn't see eye to eye with that. She was a Christian girl.

Anyway, I think that time she left the door open was on purpose, to allow me to peek. Because when she gave in and let me help, she seemed to trust me. True, my dad wasn't there that day, so maybe she felt more at ease. And when I started doing it, I felt at ease too. Even after her wrists were okay, she let me do it, and it was like making love. Because soon after that, we had kids, and we stopped making love for real, but at those rare times when my dad wasn't around and the kids were asleep, we got around it by me doing her makeup.

In the beginning I didn't know the difference between foundation and concealer and fondue, and still I don't know much, but when I'm putting on this girl's makeup, I just feel it. Her skin's awfully like Jean's, and I know exactly what to put where. I get a stool from the kitchen, trusting the girl for a few seconds not to run away, and I know she won't, because she needs it. I guess she'd put on makeup to cover scratches plenty of times, but it don't seem like it from the mess in the bathroom. I know she needs the guidance. She still seems like she's a little on edge, especially when I touch her face, but she seems to enjoy me putting it on. So I try to imagine it's Jean's face, and I remember all those times we had together. But I can't get away from this girl's beautiful face, its crevices, its secrets.

She seems happy with the job. I can't see no scratches or a black eye, anyway, and I even put some on her neck. Afterwards, I change my shirt in my room, again trusting her not to run, then I take the bag of basil leaves from next to the door and put it on the counter. Putting a couple of leaves into a pot, I make tea for her and then we sit in the kitchen. She moves the stool back and sits on that, and I'm right across from her. The blinds are closed, so I'm comfortable.

"Thanks for doing this for me, mista," she says. "You a really nice man."

"Not a problem," I say.

"Your wife at work, mista?" she asks.

"No," I say, carefully. "She's not on this planet."

She pauses. "She an astronaut?"

I laugh. I can't help it. "No, she's dead."

"Oh. I'm sorry, mista. My daddy dead too."

"How'd he die?"

"He was in the army," she says vaguely.

"I'm sorry about that."

"I got a stepdaddy. Nigga's a slavedriver."

"He beats you too?"

"Worse, mista."

"What's worse than that?"

For once, she's at a loss for words.

"In the morning," she finally says, pointing to her face, "this might come off, right, mista?"

I think. "I guess you can take the makeup with you. I'll give you a bag. As a matter of fact," I say, feeling generous at that moment but regretting it right after I say it, "why don't I drive you home?"

"Really, mista?" she asks, excited. "You really gonna drive me in that nice car, mista?"

I don't know what the hell I'm doing. After hitting this girl and covering her up, I should give her two bucks and tell her to take a hike. But it almost feels like buying somebody off, or paying a hooker. And I feel like I've gotta protect my artwork, make sure it survives the ride to its destination. Plus I gotta admit, I wanna see too if it's gonna get this girl off the hook with her folks.

"What's your name, anyway?" I ask. "I should have asked you before."

"Taina," she says. "Sorry for kicking your car before,

46

mista."

"It's okay, Taina," I say back, trying to get used to this name. "I'm Riny. Where do you live?"

"Corona."

"And you come to Flushing to go to high school?"

"Niggas come from all ove', mista. We got niggas from the South Bronx. They the craziest niggas. One time this nigga brought a gun—"

And I thought some part of the neighborhood that I couldn't see had changed. Truth was that the gooks still dominated. These spics were just coming on over from different neighborhoods. Must have been the mayor and city hall. No way the community board would allow this on its own. Mr. Jeffords was wrong. Even if you fought, you still got beat in this new world.

I finish my tea.

"Alright, Taina," I say, trying to pronounce it right—I think of a "tie" and a "hyena." "Why don't you grab your makeup and let's get going."

She smiles, gets up, heads to the bathroom. I realize she might not be able to gather all the makeup right so I go over and help her. I give her a shopping bag to put the makeup in. She rolls it up and tries to fit it in her pocket but she can't. She's worried that her mom will see it when she comes in, but she thinks and says she can probably find a hiding spot before she heads into her apartment. I ask if the boys took her schoolbag too.

"Schoolbag? I don't got no schoolbag."

I remember now that she didn't have a schoolbag on her when she kicked my car.

"Your mom doesn't care?"

"Guess not," she says.

I realize that her top's shredded too, so I look inside my younger daughter's old room and find one of the same color and give it to her. It's a little big but she says she don't think her mom will notice. Also her jeans have dirt on them. She says they were already like that, but I wet a cloth and wipe most of it off. Then I think I can find a similar pair in my daughter's room, but she tells me it's okay.

Finally the earrings. She's missing one. I tell her we can go back to the park and try to find it. She shrugs her shoulders and checks the time. It's 4:30.

"Fuck," she says. "I got half an hour, mista."

She looks around frantically. I tell her to calm down. She takes the earring off and puts it in my hand. "Maybe my mama won't notice I was wearing it," she says. "Can we go now, mista?"

I put the earring in my pocket. Then I tell her to wait at the side door. I'll pull my car up the driveway and pick her up there, so Mr. Jeffords won't see her.

I go around to the front. Mr. Jeffords is still on his porch. I wave to him.

"Going back to the park in a car, eh, Riny?" he asks as I go around to the front door of the Chevy.

I nod and smile. "My knees ain't so good no more, you know," I say.

"Take it easy, Riny, take it easy," he says. "You don't want to go under the knife again."

"Thanks pops." Sometimes I call him that. It feels weird after I say it but when I'm saying it, it just comes off the tongue.

I get in my Chevy and pull it further up my driveway and next to my side door. Normally I don't pull it up this far because I don't want it to block the door and plus I'm lazy and don't wanna waste the gas. I don't usually gotta worry about teenagers kicking it neither.

I put it in park but I leave the engine on, get out and come around the back. I see the small dent on the trunk. I guess I could live with it. It's an old car anyway, and I'm an old man.

I get to the side door. A tree on the street blocks Mr.

48

Jeffords' view from the porch, at least it did last time I was over there and looked back at my house.

I knock. I don't hear nothing. Guess you can't trust a teenager to even know how to open a door.

I put my key in and open it. She's not there. I call out and she's running over, in a flash, holding the bag.

"Thought I told you to stay here," I say. She laughs, then tries to get past me and to the car, but I stop her with my arm.

"Hold up," I say. "We gotta sneak you inside so Mr. Jeffords don't see."

I tell her to bend down and crawl out. I open the car door and lower the seat so she can slide in. I tell her to lie on the floor and she does. Then I go inside my house again and get Mighty Matt. I put him in the driver's seat. I haven't been to Corona in a decade and what I do remember don't make me feel easy. I guess I can still get out of this, put two bucks in this girl's hands and drop her off at the bus stop. She's already got the makeup on her face. But I told her I would take her and Riny's a man of his word.

I pull out of the driveway and back up right. I see Mr. Jeffords stand.

"Needed to put something in your car?" he asks.

"Just forgot the tomatoes and basil," I say.

"That's some good eating, Riny. You better bring some of that by here sometime."

Corona isn't too far. It's a few exits down on the LIE. But once you get onto the streets, it can be tough finding your way. Taina's sitting up now in the back seat. I'm like her chauffeur. I guess she must like that.

She knows her address but don't know all that much

about how to get over there by car, so I'm driving slowly through the streets, making random turns here and there, something I don't particularly enjoy since the houses are so run down. I was carjacked once in the '70s, and I didn't particularly like that. I haven't read about no carjackings recently but you've always gotta be vigilant.

I make a left and I notice it's the street Taina told me she lived on. I'm afraid I might have to make a u-turn or three rights and a left in case I gotta go the opposite way, but I see the numbers on the houses are going down and they're approaching the address she gave me.

Taina's excited and she's pointing now. Then she dies down again. I guess she's apprehensive.

It's a quiet, residential street, with a series of attached three-story apartment buildings. I try to find a parking spot here, but I don't see one, so I double park instead. I feel like going inside and making sure she's okay. I wanna see if she beats the rap from her mom. But there's no way I could do that. There's no way I should. I feel stupid for even thinking about it.

I put on my blinkers and open my door. I get out and lower the car seat. I tell Taina she can get out. But she don't move.

"You gotta go," I say. "It's the end of the line," I add, trying to sound tough. She hesitates. Then she jumps out, the bag in her hand.

"Thanks mista," she says, smiling at me. Then she laughs crazily. She runs towards her house and into a small, crowded driveway. She stops suddenly, looks both ways, puts the bag of makeup behind a bush. Then she's at the door and I stop staring. I've got an uneasy feeling, so I get in my car and go.

The next morning, I come back. I haven't been out driving this early in a long time. Usually I sleep 'til about eight or nine, but it's 6:30 right now. Just yesterday I was terrified of this neighborhood, sick of being among the spics, but I'm feeling a sense of community and calm about this place. I don't know why. I can't explain it. Maybe it reminds me about the old times. But it's something different from being in that house across from Mr. Jeffords, or walking toward that bocce ball court, I can tell you that.

I'm double parked where I was last time. I guess that's kind of conspicuous. But I don't care though. I could park somewhere far away and hide in the shadows waiting but I don't feel like being that kind of guy. I'd rather be straight. I have no idea if she'll be out this early, or if she already left, or if she's going to school at all today, but I wait. See, I got nothing else to do.

Ten minutes later, I see her. She's hurrying. She runs towards the bush and takes out the bag. Looks like she's about to go back in, but she notices me and I wave at her. I've got the window open. It's a little chilly this time of morning but that's alright with me.

She comes over. The bag's in her hand. She's looking backwards, then at me.

"What you doin' here, mista?" she asks. I see now her makeup's gone, she's got those scratches on her face, and there's this black and blue mark over her eye too. I get scared, thinking it's from me, but then I realize she's got a lighter one over her other eye too, and only one of them can be mine.

"What happened? Did she see the scars?" I ask.

Taina shakes her head. "No, mista. What you doin' here?"

"I didn't bring you home too late, did I?" I ask.

"No, mista. What you come here for?"

"You need to put on the makeup again, right? I can do

it for you."

"I wanted to put it on before my breakfast," she says.

"Is your mom gonna beat you if you don't eat?" I ask. I know my mom would have done that. But times have changed. "Can you skip it?" I ask.

She hesitates. Her eyes dart toward the second-floor apartment, then back at me.

"I guess so. My mama's asleep. I eat my cereal by myself, but sometimes she wakes up and comes out to make coffee. Sometimes she sleeps."

"I'll make pancakes for you. You like pancakes?"

"Yeah, mista."

"And I'll put on your makeup. Then I'll drive you to school."

She looks back at the apartment again. Her arm with the bag in it's trembling.

"You have your stuff? Come on," I say. I open the car door and lower the seat. "Get in," I say.

She looks at the apartment again, one last time, then kisses me on the cheek for some reason, and gets inside.

I take pride in doing her makeup. I love feeling her scratches and her pores, and covering them to make her presentable. She makes painful noises sometimes, like when I brush over her bruises. She tells me her mom didn't see the scratches, that she hadn't been late. Her mom had slapped her because she saw her get out of my car, thinking she'd hitched a ride or worse. She would have beat her more but her mom's boyfriend had stopped her. Maybe he wasn't that bad a guy after all, unlike what she'd been suggesting.

But I guess I am. A bad guy I mean. First I hit her, then I get her hit. But I finish her makeup, I make her pancakes, I drive her to school. When she gets out, I tell her to come to the corner of my block at three-thirty so I can pick her up and drive her home, where I drop her a block from her house. Before she left for school, I told her to let me know if those kids were giving her trouble, but she said it wouldn't matter because this was the last day of school for her (she said she don't take exams) and that she's transferring to another school next year. When I'm driving her later, she says they were there but she ignored them, even after they snickered at her. In the past, I like to think before she met me, she probably would have jumped the white girl in the hall, because what'd she have to lose anyway? But she'd restrained herself, for once in her life. She didn't figure it was worth it, unless the white girl fought first. She'd expected her to, but she hadn't.

She says she needs a favor from me. The white girl had stolen her cell phone. It was just her safety phone: her mom never called her on it unless Taina was late and she had to. Then she'd beat her because she had to waste the extra minutes, even though her mom was on the phone all day herself. If her mom found out she'd lost the phone, she'd get into even more trouble, maybe even with her mom's boyfriend, who had bought it for her.

So the next day, early on a Saturday morning, I pick up Taina. I bring the makeup with me and after I park near Queens Boulevard I apply it while sitting in the driver's seat, her in the passenger's. I'm really getting the hang of it now.

Afterwards we head over to a cell phone store near the Queens Center Mall where she bought the phone. Apparently her mom's boyfriend knows the owner, so he got a discount on it. She's kind of worried, in case the owner recognizes her or her number. I tell her we can go to a different store. I don't really know any others but I guess I can call one of my kids or look in the yellow pages. But she insists on going to that one.

The owner isn't there. Instead, it's some smart aleck twenty-year-old. I don't wanna say it, because it sounds like Taina's generation, but he's a goddamn guido. He talks in this monotone that no one can understand. It's guys like these that irritate me more than the immigrants.

"We need to buy a phone," I keep insisting. "She lost her phone."

"You got insurance? Because, you know, we have this deal..."

"I don't know if we have any goddamn insurance," I say, pretty angry. "Can't you check under her name? Don't you have something on that damn computer?"

That bullshit goes on for a while. I might not know shit about cell phones, or any technology generally, but I know when I'm getting the run around and when you gotta stick up for yourself and your money. A lot of things get old but that don't. I swear, I feel like punching this kid for ending up in this kind of sleazy job instead of making something out of himself. Us Italians gotta get out of the pizza shop and the bocce ball court, the construction and the sales and the mob. It's no wonder we ain't produced no Presidents.

An hour later, my voice is almost dry, but she's got a new phone that looks exactly like the old phone, except it's new.

"Mista, should I put a few scratches on it?" she asks as we walk out of the store.

"If you think that's better, do it," I say. "Did you lose anything else you need replaced?"

I see her think. "Let me see, mista. I got an Ipod..."

"Don't you lie to me, Taina," I say. "You didn't say nothing about that before." I pause, thinking. "But maybe I'll buy one for you. As a late Easter present."

She perks up, and I'm happy now. Then she loses her smile. I look ahead and see a skinny, short Hispanic man approach us.

"Hey, senorita," he says to her. "¿Que pasa?"

"De nada," she says. She stands there awkwardly, and I stop too. He looks at her happily, with familiarity. Then he looks at me, strangely. I wonder if maybe this is her mom's boyfriend.

"¿Donde esta tu mama?" he asks her.

"En su casa."

"Bien," he says. He keeps on looking over at me, then back at her. We're standing in the middle of a crowded street, right in front of the Queens Center Mall.

"¿Quien es viejo?" he says to her.

"Mi profesor," she says. He looks at me and smiles, nodding his head, up and down, holding out his hand to me. I shake it back.

"Nice to meet you," he says in English. He seems to speak it fine. I thought maybe he only spoke Spanish.

"Vamos a tomar lecciones," she says to him. He nods enthusiastically and turns to me and shakes my hand again. I can't help but laugh.

"Diga hola a su madre," he says to her. Then he turns to me again. "Nice meeting you, sir. Bye." He waves to me, still smiling, and then he's gone, to the other side of the street and toward the subway.

"Who was that?" I ask.

"My uncle, mista."

"That was your uncle? I thought maybe it was your mom's boyfriend."

She laughs. "Nah, nigga," she says, and stops herself from that talk. "Nah mista, that's just my uncle. He's my mama's brother. He used to live with us but now he lives in Rego Park."

"What'd you say to him? Did he ask you who I was?" I ask, even though I got some of it from the little Italian I know.

"Yeah. I said you was my teacha, mista. And I guess

you are, mista."

"I'm your makeup artist," I say to her. "And I buy you things."

"That's like a teacha, right, mista?"

I don't wanna say nothing to that. I don't even wanna think. I lead her into the mall to see if I can buy her an Ipod, and maybe a wallet too.

All that time I was afraid of taking her back home, because I knew she'd want me to teach her something else too. And I get it was gonna happen no matter what, as soon as I came back to pick her up.

Of course she starts and I try to resist it, but there's no way a man can resist it. I swear, I didn't mean for this when I went back. I really did want to help this girl. I liked doing her makeup so much. I guess it made me feel close to another human being. For once, since Jean died.

This is so wrong, I think, as she undoes my pants and puts my cock in her mouth. I pull her out by her hair, but this turns her on even more. She's like a hungry animal, and she's at it again, and I don't stop her. Seems like she's experienced, and good. Jean wasn't all that good, though I never minded. I still remember those prostitutes from way back when, and they knew how to suck cock. But I don't want to think of Taina as a prostitute.

When she don't have my cock in her mouth, when she's not licking it, she keeps on telling me how hard I am, and it's true. I haven't had this kind of erection since I can remember. It's been so long since I was even thinking about sex. I guess I just thought my life was over except for picking tomatoes and heading down to the Italian joints and hating the kids and minorities I passed. But this is an amazing rush, and I almost come too fast, it's been so long. Somehow I hold on, taking her head off my cock when I'm close, and finally she gets out, saying she wants to drink my cum but she'd rather take off her clothes and let me fuck her. I wonder if she learned these things from the internet, or in other ways.

She's got a nice body. I never thought I'd say that about a Hispanic, but I have to say it. She bends over doggy-style, a position I never even tried with my wife, because I knew it would offend her. And it seems like she wants me to put it in her asshole. Because when I tell her I'd rather do it missionary, she gets scared.

"Really?" she says.

"Yeah. Why? You don't like that?"

"I'm just afraid it'll hurt."

It turns out she's a virgin there. Guess she's used to taking it in the ass from whoever. And I'm starting to get an idea who that whoever, or at least one of them, is.

I'm having second thoughts now about doing this, but suddenly, she gets excited about losing her virginity, and she talks me into it. So I get some really old, expired condoms from my drawer, and I pray to God they won't break. But before I stick it in, I decide I shouldn't take the chance, so I go over into my younger daughter's room and look in her drawers, in case she left some there from the last time she stayed over with her husband. It's been a long while, but you never know.

By luck, I find some in her sock drawer. These are expired too, but they're newer than mine. So I go back in and use one. It's really tight, and it hurts me, and I come pretty fast. It hurts her too, and she bleeds. Afterwards, I feel like real, real scum, and I think of Jean, and how she'll throw me into hell fast.

Taina's sitting in the kitchen. I'm standing, making her a burger. She's reading this book she brought along. It's got a bunch of scary black people on the cover. I guess they call that Black Experience at the library. What an experience.

Some of the makeup on her face has smudged a little and I can see clearly a couple of the scars. I look back at the burger and I feel my stomach churning a little.

"Wonder what them niggas at Newtown is like," she says.

I'm not sure how she expects me to answer something like that. She usually doesn't use that kind of language around me, and it makes my stomach even more sick. I'm flipping the burger but I feel like throwing up.

"You hear me, mista? Riny, right?"

I try to nod. I put down the spatula.

"Mista?"

Then it's off to the bathroom and I'm throwing up in the toilet. It gets even worse because I notice the bloody towels in the garbage can next to the toilet, the ones I used to wipe up the blood from her popped cherry. When I finally get out (I have to move the garbage bin away from my eyes to keep from throwing up even more), she's sitting there laughing, like losing her cherry was like nothing to her.

"Mista, you feelin' sick, mista?"

I give her a cold look, wipe my mouth, and go back to the spatula and the burger on the frying pan. She keeps on laughing.

"You niggas all be the same, son," she says. "Didn't think white men be like them niggas in Corona."

I turn around, angry.

"What do you mean?" I try to say, but it comes out kind of muddled.

"You niggas fuck us n' then you actin' all guilty and wrong and shit. Your dick hurt or somethin'?"

"No, I just..."

"Yeah, you liked doin' it, right? Niggas like fucking tight pussy, what I hear."

"That was your first time, right?" I say.

"In there, nigga. Ain't no man fucked me in there yet. Niggas don't wanna use no rubber. They like it wet. I like it too."

"Damn," I say. "How many times...have you done it like that?"

"What? In the ass? Why mista, you jealous? You can fuck me in the ass. No problem with that. I just thought you feel special to fuck me in the pussy. You be the first, mista."

"Not sure I wanted to be," I say. I go back to the pan, holding the spatula and thinking.

"You was, mista. I know you don't wanna have no baby. That's why I don't let niggas fuck me in the pussy 'less they wear a rubber. But no nigga wants to do that. 'Cept white men all about that."

"It was wrong," I say, and I'm about to say that it was a crime. But in case she don't know that, I don't wanna say nothing.

"It's okay, mista. I don't mind no rubber."

I'm shaking my head now. I can't believe it.

"How many guys have you had sex with like that?" I ask.

"Why you wanna know, mista?" she asks, her voice sounding defensive now.

"I just want to," I say, turning to her now.

"I fuck mad niggas."

"How many?"

"Why? You wanna fight a nigga be fucking me?"

"I wanna know if you have AIDS," I say, forgetting myself. She doesn't say anything at first. Then she starts cracking up.

"You think that's funny?" I say. "You wanna die? Do

59

you know what AIDS is?"

She stops laughing. She's staring down at the table.

"Well, do you?" I ask.

"Yeah, mista."

"You ever think you might get it from one of your...homies?" I ask.

She swallows and shakes her head.

"Well, maybe you should," I say. Then I think. "God, those condoms were expired," I say out loud, and then I think again, the HIV could have seeped in through the condom.

I drop the spatula. I'm afraid. I'm an old man but I don't wanna die yet.

"God," I say.

"Sorry, mista," she says.

"God," I say again. "When's the last time you were tested?"

"I never been tested," she says.

"Goddamn," I say, slapping my thigh. Then I'm in my daughter's room, digging out another condom, reading the back of it to see what could happen after the condom expires. But I don't see nothing about that.

Taina's in the doorway. She's looking around the room, at the dolls and the pink wallpaper, then at a picture of my daughter.

"That your daughter, mista?" she asks.

"God," I say yet again, and I sit on the bed and I start crying. I don't know what the hell's gotten into me, but I'm bawling and I'm scared.

"I'm sorry, mista," she says, coming up to me and holding me, then kissing the side of my nose. Maybe she learned that from her mom.

I'm okay with it for a few seconds, but then I shrug her off and stand up.

"I think you've gotta go home now," I say.

"What about my burger?"

"I don't care," I say, angry. Then I calm down a little. "Take it with you if you want."

"You ain't making it for me?"

"Why don't you fucking do it yourself?" I ask.

"Damn, nigga," she says. "What you getting like this for?"

"Isn't it obvious, you idiot spic," I say. "Don't you get it? You wanna fucking die or something?"

"Fuck you, nigga. Fucking white folks."

"Look," I say, digging into my pocket. "Here's five bucks. Take the bus and you've got money left over to buy a burger or a pizza or something. Just get out of here."

"You ain't gonna drive me, mista?"

"No. Just get out," I say to her. She looks at me, sad and mad at the same time. I can't tell exactly. Though I'm not really thinking about her feelings.

"You cold, mista," she says to me. "You a cold nigga. Maricon," she says. She grabs the five dollars, spits in my face, and runs into the kitchen. I hear the spatula hitting the wall and something breaking.

I yell as I wipe my face but I hear her running to the door. I come out to the kitchen and then to the door but she's gone. I peek out the door and I see that Mr. Jeffords is on the front porch, so I don't go out. I close the door and think. A few minutes later I go back into the kitchen. A vase Jean made in a pottery class she took one time is broke. The burger's gone. She's got an Ipod, a phone and a wallet too. And it's only later that night I realize that imitation jewelry in the bathroom cabinet's missing.

I got bigger problems though. I can't sleep that night. I wish Jean was here. If she'd a been here none of this would have happened. I never would have admitted it most of the time I was married, but she kept me straight. I don't know why the hell I got involved with this broad. It made no sense. I didn't plan it, and it doesn't seem like nothing I would have done if I'd have thought it through. Guess things just happen, like cancer and death.

But no way do I wanna die. It'd be nice to join Jean, I guess, but I don't know if I even believe in heaven. I never did my whole life. Yet I'm scared shitless, so I kneel down next to my bed and pray to the Virgin Mary, like my wife used to.

In the morning, I decide to take a ride to Long Island, to my younger daughter's house, whether she likes it or not.

I go to my car in a hurry when Mr. Jeffords calls out.

"Hey, Riny!" he yells. I wanna ignore him but I never have, the entire time I've lived here, which is almost my whole life. I've always been polite.

"Yeah, Mr. Jeffords," I say, opening my car door.

"You haven't noticed anything missing from your house have you?" he yells.

I pause. "No," I say, acting my best. Does he mean a burger? "Not that I've noticed. Why?"

"I could have sworn I saw a teenager running out of your house yesterday. Looked like that same girl that kicked your car."

"Hold on," I say. I get in my car and back out, curve around to the right and then pull up next to Mr. Jeffords' porch.

"Really?" I ask, nervous but trying to keep cool.

"Yeah, I could have sworn. Were you there yesterday afternoon?"

"Around what time?"

"Maybe three. Don't recall exactly."

"I don't recall exactly either," I say, wondering which way to fall on the issue. "But I think I was."

"Hmm. Well, check your house when you get back. Just make sure you haven't been robbed. I would have knocked on your door yesterday but I convinced myself I was seeing things. Wouldn't have been the first time, at my age."

I fake a quick laugh. "Thanks for looking out for me, Mr. Jeffords. At your age."

And I'm gone, before he has a chance to ask me where I'm going.

Boy, is my younger daughter surprised when she sees me at her front door. You can see it on her face. When she was sixteen was the last time I think she really, deeply loved me. That's when she stopped thinking of me first and started thinking of herself.

After a quick frown, she puts on a show, like she's all concerned and excited. Then her husband, Mike, comes out in his pajamas and his wife-beater. He's got a twelve o'clock shadow and a beer in his hand, even at this time of morning. And he gives me a hug. I've always detested that. He's a good guy mostly, but I always thought he was kind of fake.

Still, I don't got time to be thinking about these things too much, because I've got other things on my mind. Mary, that's my youngest daughter's name, she sits me down in her kitchen and puts a plate down in front of me and plops pancakes on it. She's been making them for Mike and herself, I guess. There's no doubt, I'm hungry. I didn't have lunch yesterday and for my dinner I had a banana and the rest of that tomato and cheese sandwich I made to carry around in my pocket. And no breakfast. There's no more I could eat. I just wasn't hungry after all that worrying.

But I still don't feel much like eating. Mary keeps on asking me if I'm okay, if I need anything, while she skirts around the obvious question of why I'm here without no notice. When she was sixteen and Jean was alive she'd have no problem saying something off the cuff and straightforward like that. But not no more.

I tell her that I don't want no pancakes but she won't listen, she keeps piling them on, until I lose it and yell at her. She stands there, a spatula in her hand, her mouth open, almost like I was yesterday with Taina. Mike's mouth is full of pancake, but his eyes tell me he's surprised by me yelling out.

"God, dad, I'm sorry...I didn't realize..."

"Just cut the crap, Mary," I say. "Can I talk to you in private?"

She breathes, looks down, then nods. She puts down the spatula. I get up and she leads me upstairs, to her bedroom.

I'm sitting down on the bed, where Mary thinks I'll be comfortable, and she takes one of those rolling chairs from her desk and sits across from me and leans over.

"What's up, dad?" she asks. "What's wrong?"

I swallow. I'm not sure I can say anything to her.

"Come on, you can tell me, dad. Have you been thinking about mom again?"

"Sometimes," I say. "I always think about her. But that's not why—"

"What?"

"Mary, I'm embarrassed. But I have to ask you."

"What dad? What?"

"Mary, have you ever used an expired condom?"

"What?" she asks, laughing a bit.

"A condom that's past the expiration date. Have you ever used one?"

"Dad..." She's thinking now, about what this might mean.

"Are you saying...you had sex with someone, Dad?"

"Your mom's been dead a few years now," I say. "I figure it's time to move on."

She keeps staring at me. She probably never figured I had a sex drive.

She swallows and then she says, "I don't think I've ever done that. But we don't usually check the date." She thinks. "How do you know it was expired?"

"I checked the date. What do you think?"

"But where'd you get them?"

Looking at her I can tell she suspects I got them from her room.

"It don't matter. I just need to know for sure. Can you get AIDS from that?"

"Dad," she says. She shakes her head. "I mean, I'm not a doctor, dad. I don't know for sure. You should have gone to see Doctor Patel—"

"I don't want no one to know. I don't even want him to know. That's why I'm asking you, Mary. I'm not going around asking no one."

"Well, did the condom break?" she asks.

"No."

"Does this lady have HIV?"

"I don't know."

"Well, I doubt she does," she says. I see this as a good sign. She thinks it's a woman my age. "Unless you know for sure," she adds. Then she pauses. "How'd you meet her?" And finally, with a smile, her arms stretched down, she asks, "Do I know her?"

"It don't matter, Mary," I say. "Can we stick with the question?"

"You have to ask a doctor, dad. I'll look it up on the internet. But my thinking is, unless it did break, you don't have to worry. Anyway, she'd have to have it first. And I doubt that she does."

I won't even ask her about pregnancy.

"Ok," I say. "I trust you. I've just gotta put it out of my mind."

"If you're worried, maybe you and her could both get tested, together. It'll be cute. And romantic," she says. She seems happy for me now. I wasn't sure how she would react. I was too scared about the HIV to give it much thought. I figured she wouldn't care, because even though she was crying when Jean died, I'm pretty sure those tears were half-fake and she hasn't talked to me much about Jean for the last couple of years.

I'm looking at her face now. I can tell she thinks I'm asking about sex because I'm old, because I wouldn't know about things her generation took for granted. She's treating me like I'm the child and she's the grownup who has to tell me about the birds and the bees. I always heard that when a man gets old he degenerates into a child-like mentality, but I never believed it. And I'm not about to believe it now.

"Maybe," I say, getting up now. "But I think it was a mistake."

Mary stands up and looks me in the eye.

"It has been a long time, dad," she says. "Mom's not coming back, I know. You're still young, you're still good looking. It is time to move on. I guess it surprised me because I didn't even realize you were thinking about it. And yeah, I'm not completely happy because of mom. But it's natural. It must be lonely in that house. I know Mike and I haven't been by too often, and I'm sorry. It's just been busy here. I guess that's not a great excuse, but...you're welcome to stay..."

"I'll get going," I say. "I don't wanna be a burden."

"It's no burden, dad," she says, but I can tell by the way she says it that she's got no conviction in that statement. That's the problem with this generation. No staying power, no credibility.

I make it down the stairs and to the door. Mike's still

eating in the kitchen and as he notices me passing by he stands up. But I know he's not coming to the door.

As Mary says goodbye to me, she gives me one piece of advice: "Dad, throw away those condoms in my room. And buy new ones."

I don't expect to have sex again, at least not with that girl. But even with my daughter's explanation, I'm feeling uneasy. I'm still thinking maybe I can get something from that girl if she had it. And the next morning, I remember she's starting that new school. I never asked her where it was, but I assume it's closer to her neighborhood, and far from here.

I try to get back to the routine I kept up, picking the tomatoes and basil leaves, walking down to the bocce ball court, hoping I don't run across some other girl beat up in the forest. I try my best to forget about this girl and fucking her. But there's no way I can completely forget.

I'm still surprised. I didn't know what I was thinking, going back there that day. I guess I should feel bad, a man my age taking advantage of a teenager, but on the other hand she's the one who got the real advantages, the things. All I got was to keep some of my makeup and a broken vase and a worried mind.

About six months pass. I'm still on my routine. I did end up getting a HIV test. I got myself to an anonymous clinic in Jamaica. I was more scared about the clinic than the test result, but I went through with it, and it was negative. The nurse told me I could come back in a few months to get tested again, but based on what I told her, she said I shouldn't worry.

I've been calmer recently. The only thing that upset me was Mr. Jeffords. He died a month back, and it was real sad. Even my two daughters came to the funeral, and of course there was all the bocce ball guys, Gino Mellone and the guys from the old days, most who live in Nassau or Suffolk. It was nice catching up with those guys, but too bad we had to do it because Mr. Jeffords passed.

I hate thinking about it this way, but I gotta admit, I was a little glad just because Mr. Jeffords was the only one who'd seen that girl Taina. I hate to think of things that way, but I gotta admit it.

At the funeral, Gino told me about his school again. It's funny that whenever I see him he's talkin' about that retirement, and he always seems to be on vacation too.

I asked him some questions. Somehow it came up that his school is Newtown, the one Taina mentioned. I wondered if he was her teacher, if maybe she was putting the moves on him too, now that she'd learned from me how to get things from adults. But I tried real hard not to ask no more questions. I just agreed with him about how bad the schools and kids are and about how this country is bankrupt in every way.

I'm at my house, peeking out my window during the early dusk and it looks like trouble again. Another group of Hispanic teens are gathered in front of my house.

They're hovering around my Chevy, just like a few months ago. I've seen some kids around since then, but not like this. I feel like getting Mighty Matt but my brain tells me not to get involved. And I don't wanna have nothing to do with the cops neither. So I wait.

I notice they're coming to my door. I'm not sure what to do. Then I realize one of the girls is Taina, except she looks bigger. And the other people aren't teenagers at all. They're short adults.

The doorbell rings. I realize I can pretend like I'm not at home, so I wait around, sweating. Then I hear it ring again, and I decide I'm too old to be hiding. This is my neighborhood, my house. There's no way they're gonna intimidate me.

I open the door. Taina's face don't have scratches no more, but it's a little bloated now. Her eyes light up when she sees me, but I don't pay her no mind.

I recognize one of the others. It's the guy she said was her uncle, who we met on the street. There are two other people too. One guy's short, muscular, wearing a black down coat and a little smirk on his mustached, tan face. The other lady is darker skinned, and her face looks like it's been beat in a few times. They both got triangular faces, while the brother's face is oval. And Taina's face is divine, or used to be anyway.

They look me over without saying nothing. I ask 'em what they want.

The mustached one looks at me funny. Then he says, "Good morning, sir," with a Spanish accent.

"Yes? What can I do for you?" I ask, trying to remain calm.

"I am very sorry to bother you, sir," he says, that little smirk still on his face. "But we have some business to discuss. May we come inside?"

"What kind of business?" I ask.

The mustached man looks at the darker-skinned lady, then at Taina's uncle, who nods at me approvingly.

"It is about Taina, mister," her uncle says. "You know her, *profesor*, si?"

I look at Taina. She's staring at my sweatpants. Then I notice a bulge under her winter coat, and I realize what I thought was just fat might be something else. I get a clue to what this might be about.

I don't know how to respond, what's appropriate. I guess I could just deny I know Taina. It wouldn't be too bad a lie since she looks different enough.

"Sir, please," the mustached man says to me. "May we come inside? The matter is very urgent and we would like to very much discuss this with you."

"But about what?" I ask, though I've already decided to relent. A minute later, they're inside my house. Better in here than out there in the neighborhood, even without Mr. Jeffords around, I think.

I make sure I'm behind them, so they don't make no sudden moves. But they don't act threatening. They look like they're in heaven in here. I don't even remember Taina acting like this when she first came over. They're like country bumpkins who just came to the big city, or something. And my house is pretty ordinary, especially now that that vase is broke.

I have them sit down in a small space next to my kitchen which is kind of like a tiny living room. There's a three-seat black couch there and they all sit on it, men and then women, barely fitting but they're there, like one big happy family. I pull up a chair from the kitchen and put it across from them, next to their coats, which are piled on the floor. I'm so nervous I twitch my thumbs.

No one speaks at first. The mustached man is still looking around, examining my living room and kitchen area, I guess. The other two are taking turns glancing at him, waiting for him to start saying whatever it is he has to say.

Meanwhile Taina, on the right edge of the couch, is staring at the floor. Unlike the others, she hasn't taken off her coat. She's nervous and shy. She's like a completely different person, both the way she looks and acts.

Finally the mustached man stops his personal tour.

Now he's looking at me. He surprises me since I've been watching Taina.

"Sir," he says, with that Spanish accent ringing in my ears. "You know why we are here, sir?"

"No, I don't," I say. "I have no idea."

"But you keep looking at Taina. You know her, si?"

I swallow again.

"Do you know her, senor?" he asks.

We play a staring game, and now I see his smirk come back. He'd hidden it during his examination, and when he started blabbing he had this serious look, almost like he was trying to be professional. But that smirk rear-ends me. I'm down for the count. So I nod.

"Good," he says, in this super-quick, snappy way. "Now we can get to the business. You know Taina has dropped out of school?"

"No," I say. "How would I know that?"

"What do you know then?"

"What would I know?" I ask.

"Don't bullshit me, senor," he says.

"Don't you speak to me like that in my home," I say. "Don't you dare."

"Okay," the woman says, holding her hand out to the mustached man. "Callate la boca."

I can tell he's not amused by this, and he's about to open his mouth to protest. It's probably like the beginning of many fights they've had. But the uncle puts a hand on his shoulder and the mustached man restrains himself. The woman turns to me.

"Mister," she says, reaching over to unzip Taina's coat, with only minimal resistance from her. "We know you and our Taina were together some months before. I think you can see the result," she says, gesturing to Taina's stomach. I can see now that there's definitely a bun in the oven.

"I had nothing to do with that," I say.

"Mister, we know. Taina told us."

"Told you what?" I ask, sweating now. "A lot of kids, they—"

"She's pregnant, mister. Do you think that happened by accident?"

I was wearing a condom, I think. It was expired, but the nurse said that just made it more likely to break. It's not likely my semen had gone through there. And who knows how many guys she had fucked since then without protection. But I can't say that out loud. I may be Italian, but I got American brains. Once you say it out loud it becomes true. But if you keep it in, it's hearsay.

"I don't know how she got pregnant," I say. "I only saw her a couple of times. I found her in the park after she got beat up. I took her home and let her use my wife's makeup. I gave her food, a ride, money to buy a cell phone and a wallet so she could get back the stuff she lost. I helped you," I say to her direct, and she's still staring at my floor. "I just wanted to help you," I say, and I can't help it, I start bawling.

I'm surprised, because the woman, who I'm assuming is her mother, stands and pats me on the back from up top, while I'm bending over. "I was just a lonely old man, trying to help a troubled, helpless young girl," I say.

"Yes senor," she says, reaching into her pocket and offering me a tissue. "We do understand. But you also caused this. It happens, senor. Now you must take responsibility."

I stop bawling, slowly, but surely, rejecting the tissue. Then I'm looking square at Taina's stomach, this monster of a beast.

"I didn't do that," I say aloud, pointing at it. Suddenly I remember Mr. Jeffords. "And you can't prove I did."

The woman laughs. She says, "I am sure the police will have no trouble believing it, when we tell them you had sex with a girl who is underage. Then they will have no problem taking a paternity test."

"You can't prove I had sex with her," I say, standing up now, waving my arms. "Now get out of my house," I say. "Get out and stay out."

"We will go straight to the police," she says.

"Go," I say. "Who'll they believe? An old white man from a good neighborhood, or a bunch of spics from the ghetto?"

They're taken aback by this one, I can tell. The mustached man gets up, but the uncle rises too and takes his shoulders. The mustached man points at me. "This our country too," he says. "We work hard," he says. Then he starts cursing in Spanish. I don't know what he's saying but I can tell they're bad words. Finally he's so angry he's speechless, and the uncle gets him to sit.

Meanwhile, her mother has stood up now, and she's holding a cell phone in her hand. It's open, and she turns it around, showing me its face. I bend down to get a closer look. I see a picture of me naked.

"Where'd you get that?" I ask pointlessly, because I know Taina must have snapped it with the cell phone I bought her, while we were in the room, either before or after we made love. Her mother switches it to a different picture, of me trying to put on the condom. And then there's one picture of her torso, topless, with me in the background, turned away, putting on my underwear.

I start hyperventilating. I slip off the chair and onto my knees. I think I'm having a heart attack, but really I'm just panicking. Taina's mother and even Taina come over to me, but I push them away and get up myself, breathing hard and flapping my hands. My stupidity. I forgot cell phones could snap pictures.

"You still don't know," I'm saying deliriously. "You still don't know."

"What, white man," the mustached man is saying, standing up and pointing at me. "What now?"

"Please sit, senor," Taina's mother is saying, and she helps me sit on the chair. Taina is standing there too, staring. A blank expression is on her face. I don't know what's gotten into her.

I point at the mustached man, who's still mocking me. "How do you know he ain't the father?" I ask.

"Who? Pablo?" she asks.

"Yeah," I say. "She basically told me he used to fuck her in the ass. How do I know he didn't switch to her pussy?"

"Please senor," her mother pleads, horrified.

"He's lying, fucking white man," the mustached man says.

"She used to fuck so many guys. So what if I broke her cherry. After that—"

The mustached man clocks me in the face and I'm down. The room's spinning. I lie there, cushioned by their coats, while a bunch of them hover above me. I lie for a while, and all I can think while I can think at all is how I dug myself into this hole. There's no way I can answer this question. By the time I'm up and sitting in the chair again, I only see the mother and Taina there.

"I told Pablo to go out. My brother will take care of him. I just want to talk business, senor. Pablo, he gets excited," she says. She pauses, then continues. "Pablo is not the father, senor. I know this. He does what he does, but he takes care. I am not here to condemn you, senor, or to ruin your life. I could have already called the police and showed them these pictures, and you would be in jail, the last place you want to be at your age, awaiting trial among young and tough men who want to harm you. You do not want that and I do not want that for you. Senor, we Latinos respect the elderly. There are old men in our country who have sex with young girls. We do not like it but we do not frown either. Some things are natural. But there are obligations. These men provide for

74

the girls. It is only right for there to be compensation. We do not expect much, senor."

I want to protest again that there's no way I can be the father, but I don't really know that for sure. And I'm tired of protesting. "What do you want?" I ask.

"That she can live here. That she can go to school again in this district. If she lives here this will be her zone school. It is not the best but it is better than the other one. She can have her baby here and then she can go to school here. We can make you the guardian. Pablo and me, we have opportunities, in Florida. We will move there. But the schools there, they are not good either."

"Are you kidding?" I say. "I'm retired. I'm old. I live off of disability, social security. It's not much. How can I support her and her kid?"

"Do you think this girl needs much?" she asks, rubbing her daughter's back.

"She stole my wife's jewelry," I say. "I think she needs more than you think."

Her mother looks at Taina in a scolding manner. Taina swallows.

"I know she was bad," her mother says. "That is why I would beat her. Maybe it did no good. But then she became pregnant, and believe me, senor, this baby will save her life. She is different now. You see her now. She is quiet, not rebellious. She is a good girl, and she will take care of her child.

"Do not worry, senor. We do not expect miracles. If things become too hard, we can take her back in Florida, or raise the baby while Taina finishes high school. That is what we Latinos do. Family takes care of family. But we also care about Taina's education and her welfare. At least let her get her GED. What can she do or become in this world without even a high school diploma, senor? We do not expect college for her. But if she can do that, we can help. Please, senor. Do not make me call the police. Work with us. Let the Virgin Mary guide you to do the right thing."

A couple of months later, I look out the window. It's dead of winter, and it gets dark early these days. But it's still the afternoon, and sometimes even in this cold you can see the kids out there, goofing off.

Today, I don't see nobody. The street's empty. Taina's in the bedroom. She's nearing her water breaking. I hope she won't have a tough time of it giving birth, and afterwards when she gets back to school, considering what happened to her when she was in this school before. That's what started this whole thing.

Soon we'll have another kid in here, and things will be different. I won't have time to be a kid myself. It'll be like starting over, taking a fresh jump at life. Mr. Jeffords won't be there to see it, and I doubt I'll be running into Gino either any time soon. Maybe Mary and my other daughter will be part of it someday, but for now, I'd rather them not know. They never come by or call anyway, so why would they care?

This is good for me, I think. And maybe it's good for Jean too. Her jewelry's back now, and her makeup's gonna be used again. I listened to the Virgin Mary. And Jean always wanted to have another kid, but we never did. I hope I can manage it, at my age. I'm hoping that, eventually, we'll be one big happy family.

The Apprentice

*

As Javier emerged from the dimly lit hallway, Guermo regarded him like a butterfly emerging from its cocoon, newly resplendent.

"Mira un hombre de verdad," Li Jiang said, laughing.

"Did you know he spoke Spanish?" Guermo asked, lounging on the sofa.

Javier ignored the question and took out his wallet. May, his masseuse, bowed her head toward him and offered him a small cup of water with both hands.

"Oh," Javier said, smiling. "I forgot."

"Let me handle that for you," Guermo offered, jumping up from the sofa. He grabbed Javier's wallet and began to rifle through it.

"You take much water as you want," Li Jiang said, nodding.

Javier took the cup and drank, keeping one eye on Guermo. May asked him if he wanted another cup. He nodded.

May said something to Li Jiang in Chinese as she took the cup and refilled it at the cooler.

"He speaks better Spanish than he does English," Guermo said. "If only we spoke Chinese."

"Si, if only you spoke less, bro," Javier responded,

accepting and drinking the next cup.

"Please, chico. I bet while I was out here I learned more about this man and this operation than you ever have in the months you've been coming here to get your precious massages."

"So why don't you get off your fat ass and get one?"

"I don't like grimy hands all over my body. Makes me squirm."

Javier handed the cup back to May. Then he realized Guermo still had his wallet. He was lying on the sofa again.

"How much is the tip?" Guermo asked, tossing the wallet from hand to hand. "That's the only question. 40? 50?"

"Shut up," Javier said, grabbing the wallet away from him. Guermo shrieked in delight and jumped off the sofa again.

Javier gave Li Jiang forty dollars. Li smiled and accepted it with both hands, bowing his head. Then he opened the register and looked surprised.

"Oh, no change," he said, putting up his hands.

"This happens every time," Javier responded. "How can you have no change? Not even a few ones?"

"Tell him in Spanish," Guermo said. "He understands that better."

"Oh. Okay, I have two ones," Li Jiang said.

"Now you have some change?"

"Just be generous, Javier," Guermo said. "One hour for..."

"It's the principle, Guermo."

"You give her nice tip, and next time, I have change for you. Much change," Li Jiang said.

"Yeah, sure, next time," Javier replied.

"Mister, this good place," Li Jiang said. "You feel good, right?"

"Sure. I feel good," Javier replied, taking a bill out of

his wallet and palming it. He placed the two ones in his palm too and put his wallet back in his pocket with his other hand.

"You have good time. Look, her name May," Li Jiang said, pointing at May. "She not working Sundays."

"Okay." Javier seemed puzzled. "Not working?"

"Not working. She free."

May had turned red in the face.

"Yeah, okay," Javier said. "Let's go, Guermo."

He placed the money in May's palm and walked out the door.

"Adios!" Guermo shrieked.

"What the hell is wrong with you?" Javier asked as they drove back to the college.

"Just making conversation with your main man."

"He's not my main man. He's a con artist."

"Welcome to America, chico."

"And how the hell does he know Spanish?"

"Says he learned it. He's been here over a decade."

"That girl's been here only a few years, so she says. Says she's got a green card, but who knows."

"They're all illegal, chico. Do you think they'd be working here otherwise? Anyway, on to the main event. Did you get any pu-tang?"

"Shut up, asshole."

"You know that's what's on your mind."

"Usually the girls get pissed off when I give them the tips, like it's never enough. Like they wanna do you know what. But this girl..."

"She's the dating type. That's what our main man Li was telling you. Ask her out, dude."

"Are you kidding? Date an illegal?"

"Everyone's gotta legalize at some point, baby. Didn't you date a Chinese girl at Bowne?"

"Nah, I wish. Most of those Chinese girls dissed me, remember? They seemed more interested in their fellow Asians. And they were all born in Queens too!"

"There was one girl, right?"

Javier thought. "Oh, yeah. Carly Chung."

"Yeah. Big boobies, baby. Even with pancake tits you gotta give 'em props."

Javier thought. "I never liked her," he said. "She was into me, I guess. But I gotta admit, I tend to like the tits small."

"Yeah. Real small."

"Shut up."

"Chico, that girl was mad into you, I remember. She got all obsessive when you stopped talking to her. She was stalking you to math class. We'd be looking out into the hallway, and there she was!"

"She stuck notes in my locker too. Finally I had to be really mean to her to get her to lay off. Man, I still feel bad about that."

"Even though you don't remember her. This is my problem with you, Chico. You keep on talking about how no girl wants you, when there are all these girls around sweating you. You're just too picky, baby!"

"I haven't found the right girl, that's all. It'd be nice if she could cook me an enchilada and some pad thai too."

"No one in our generation can cook, bro. That's why we got restaurants."

"Adjuncting and waiting salaries don't exactly equal eating out every day."

"That's why this May girl works. She's from China, she can probably cook. You'd be eating steam dumplings and lo mein every day, but so what? At least you'll stay away from the Princesses."

Javier was shaking his head. "We'll see," he said.

"Richard Kawata!" they heard. "Richard Kawata! Richard Kawata! Richard Kawata!" The screams came from Pervez Muhammad's office as they made their way to Javier's shared office space, which was empty this late at night.

"What is up with the people in this place?" Guermo asked.

"Tenure. It's like a cancer. A disease I'd like a shot at, not that it'll ever happen."

"Kissing this much ass for this shit? Dude, better to go into finance. At least you'll get something out of it."

"I'm a little too old to be changing course. And how many Dominicans do you know in finance?"

"They got everyone, bro. Anyone who can make that green gets in. It's egalitarian."

"Yeah? You know this how?"

"I saw it on 'American Greed' chico."

They laughed. Guermo made himself comfortable on the communal couch while Javier sat on the edge of Pam Gould's desk.

"This girl's a regular WASP from Massachusetts," Javier said, pointing at a picture of her and her mom. "Not even a snobby JAP girl. An actual WASP. Probably Daughters of the American Revolution or something."

"So why don't you bang her?"

"She keeps hinting she has a boyfriend. I've never seen her with anyone though."

"You're not getting to the point with her, chico. Same old story."

"Why don't you try then, if you're so concerned?"

"I don't need to. I'm a faggot remember? Which reminds me, why don't you join the tribe, chico? Then all your problems will be solved."

"Not so easy. I can't change myself like that."

Guermo began dancing in a circle, holding his arm up and cupping his hand.

"Become a gay Chicano! We party harty! We got no problems getting laid, baby."

"Looks like nowadays you're like everyone else. With your marriages and shit."

"I got to support that stuff, but you're right, those married faggots are boring. It's definitely affected the culture."

Javier settled himself behind his desk and braced for a long night ahead. "I've got papers to grade," he said.

"This late?"

"I'm an adjunct. This is my life."

He heard May rubbing the cream on her hands. When he had entered Li Jiang had tried to set him up with Cora, but he'd insisted on seeing May again, because he suspected Cora did favors. She wore short skirts and sometimes took only 15 minutes with men. He wouldn't have minded getting in on the action but somehow, whenever he turned around, he never had a hard-on and she'd never press it. Anyway, he was paranoid about getting caught. What would it be like? Was it really so great? Why didn't these guys just pay a hooker?

The other problem was that Cora was a bitch. No matter how big a tip he gave her, she always scowled and said "next time" like she was unhappy. He figured it was a tactic she used with all men. He wasn't even sure why he kept going to this place. There were probably plenty of more professional massage places around where the women didn't scowl or wear short skirts. Still, the massages weren't bad and they were cheap, and he felt good being in the company of women who had to attend on him, considering he couldn't get a date in the city.

And he'd kind of taken to May. She'd confessed to him that she prayed to her Buddha and believed in him strongly. Javier didn't believe in anything but poetry, and he wasn't even sure he was good at that, since he kept on getting rejected by journals. He had only gotten his adjunct job through luck, and he wasn't sure how long he could keep it. He wasn't the best ass-kisser, sometimes his honesty slipped through and he could sense the scowls on the professor's faces beneath their gentile exteriors. He tried to kiss ass as much as possible, but he wasn't willing to do laundry at professor's houses like some other adjuncts, or to constantly praise the tenured professors during every phone call like Pervez Muhammad and his ilk did.

May finished up his legs, batted him down and left the room to get a towel. He could hear her arguing with Li Jiang in the main room, and he heard Cora's voice too. Meanwhile, in the next room, he heard giggling and whispers from someone he imagined was an old man. His brain was heavy, almost bursting with tension. Last time May had done the same thing during her massage. She had made the tension go to his brain, and then when he had flipped over, she had rubbed his head to make it go away. He kept hoping she would do the same thing, but the wait seemed to take forever.

Finally May came in. "Sorry, it busy," she said, then applied the hot towel to his back. She batted him down again, then asked him to flip over. He did so and she put the pillow below his head. For a few seconds he was naked. He suddenly realized he was hard, but May put the sheet over him, sat near his head and began rubbing.

"Relax," she said, as she rubbed the sides of his temples in circles.

He closed his eyes. "May, do you really have a green card?" he asked.

"You relax," she said. And she was right, his brain was still heavy. But she rubbed his head harder, and he told her to do it even harder than that.

She began hitting certain parts of his head with a karate chop. "That's good," he said. "Harder."

"I do too hard, you hurt," she said.

"I hurt anyway," he responded.

"You no hurt like me."

He opened his eyes. "What do you mean?" he asked.

"Nothing," she said, now rubbing his neck. It felt good.

"You be quiet now and relax," she said.

He did just that. Finally she finished and began rubbing his pecs. She got up and stood over his left side, and began rubbing his abdomen. He looked down and saw he wasn't hard anymore. He tried to think of sex, but it didn't seem to work.

"May, do you really have a green card?" he asked after he gave up on his penis.

"Why you ask so many questions?" she asked him, smiling.

He put his hand on her leg, but then took it away. "Do you want to have coffee with me?" he asked.

"Coffee?"

"Yes. Outside of here," he whispered.

She smiled and seemed embarrassed.

"You want to?" she asked.

"Only if you do," he said.

She stopped rubbing his abdomen, came around and fixed the pillow behind his head as the buzzer sounded.

"You look handsome," she said, looking down at him.

Outside of the Roosevelt Avenue train station in Jackson Heights, Javier spotted Guermo giving an Indian guy a slice of pizza from his small booth.

"Since when do you sell pizza?" Javier asked.

"Since the economy went broke, bro. We put an oven in here."

"Sick."

"I know. These Indians, they love their pizza."

"Aren't most of them Bangladeshis these days?"

"Wow, you keeping up on demographics? They all look the same to me. 'Hello, my name is Abir, I drive a cab'" he began to mock.

"Shut up, Guermo, and give me a slice."

"Yo, you won't believe who I saw walking by the other day. Your main girl!"

"Who? Maria?"

"Nah. That Chinese chick you dated in high school. Carly."

"Are you kidding?"

"I'm not kidding, bro. I gave her your number."

"You—what?"

"Yeah, I told her about you, she said she wanted to get back in touch. And let me tell you, she looks even better now. She's developed."

"Yeah?" he asked.

"Those tits aren't pancakes anymore, chico. Look out, she might call you up. Be ready. Did you ever ask out that white girl?"

Javier shook his head. "I haven't seen her yet."

"Sticking to the massages, eh? Here's your slice. Hope it doesn't burn your tongue."

Early the next morning, he was grading papers at his desk, across from Pam Gould. He had a picture of his favorite writer, Pablo Neruda, on his desk. Whenever he looked at it he shifted his eyes over at Pam, but she avoided his gaze and seemed to have a perpetual red tan on her face.

The couple of times they'd spoken had devolved into arguments. He knew she was a self-described feminist. Her favorite writers included Adrienne Rich. First he thought she might be a closet lesbian, but then she heard from some of the other guys that she only dated bankers and lawyers who were rough with her. He figured he should always take anything anyone in academia said with a grain of salt, but scanning her now, he figured that assessment was probably correct.

She seemed like the typical hypocritical feminist, spouting ideology on one hand but choosing to subserve herself in her daily life to dominant men. He knew all women were the same, that all they cared about was dating men with money and power. In fact the most self-proclaimed liberated women were the most superficial in their preferences for men. That's what he had learned. He knew he didn't stand a chance with the Pam Goulds of the world, or even the Rachel Goldbergs.

"Doing anything interesting tonight?" he asked her bitterly.

"Just staying in and reading," she replied, laughing despite herself and opening a drawer to act like she was doing something.

"Papers to grade. It's a bitch. Sometimes I do that all night," he said.

"I know. You've got other jobs, other priorities."

"I wonder if we'll ever make it out of adjunct status."

"Doesn't look promising."

"So what's your other job?"

"I'm a waitress at a cafe."

"In Astoria?"

She rolled her eyes. "God no, not in Astoria. In the Upper East Side."

"Ah."

"How about you?"

"Waiting, too, but in Queens."

"Oh yeah, where?"

"It's in Kew Gardens Hills. All Orthodox Jews, in and out."

"Oh. I've never been there. It takes forever to come here, first of all. It's like traveling to the boondocks."

"Yeah." I was born in these boondocks, he thought. Do I think they're boondocks too? "So you come on the subway?"

"Subway and the bus. Taxis are way too much. It's far out here."

"For a pimp," he joked, but she didn't seem to get it. That red tan appeared again on her face.

"So, I'm going into Manhattan," he said. "To the Met. You wanna come along?"

"Hmm....well, I am supposed to meet my boyfriend near there in a few hours." She looked up. "I guess I could stop by."

"Really?"

She shrugged her shoulders. "I might as well, right?"

On the subway he stood in front of the door while she sat on the orange seat adjacent to him. Like a princess, he thought. He gave some change to the homeless guy while she kept staring at another guy's package. Why the hell did I waste my time with her, he thought.

At the museum, he paid a dollar. She paid a nickel.

"I come here a lot," she explained.

"I bet."

"What do you want to see? I don't know if they have any Latin art."

"I like the Europeans."

"Really?"

"Yeah, the Impressionists are kind of cool."

Upstairs they stood in front of Claude Monet's *Bridge Over a Pond of Water Lilies*.

"Kind of amazing he could paint this way. Especially back then. I guess that was special effects for the 19th century. No movies or computers or anything..."

"You think he was gay?" she asked.

"I put my money on Degas. I don't think he ever got married."

"I think he did that for art."

They walked over to Degas' *Stage Rehearsal*.

"If anything he was a pedophile, though he probably just liked to look."

"I guess no one could get away with painting little girls like this today," she said, her face turning red.

"No way, they'd jail his ass for child pornography and put a leash on him for life."

"There is *Dance Moms* on Lifetime," she noted.

"True. But it's different when women do it."

They passed Rodin's *Head of Balzac*.

"You think Rodin was gay too?" Javier asked.

"Look at how good he made Balzac look. Wasn't he ugly?"

"He was a great genius."

"I heard he smelled."

They moved over to the Van Gogh wing.

"He was a looney tunes," she said.

"Balls over."

"He liked God."

"I don't," Javier said.

"Really? I thought all you..."

"That's a stereotype."

She nodded. "Do you like romantic movies, Javier?"

"Give me an example."

"*You've Got Mail?*"

"Are you kidding?"

"I think it was based on a Hungarian play."

"I guess everything's recycled."

"You want to see naked women, Javier?" she asked mischievously.

"Fat ones or skinny ones?"

"There's only one kind in this place."

They saw some of the Rubens and went downstairs.

"Do you think Professor Kawata's going to retire?" she asked.

"Why do you ask that? Did you hear that?"

"Professor Pobbles was gossiping with Professor Gable. You know how they are."

"Busybody express."

She slapped him on the arm. "Exactly! They were saying that Professor Pezran is going to make a play for Chair."

"And that's how Professor Muhammad's going to get tenure?"

"Well, he's got a ways to go."

"Kissing ass for a long time."

"Publications too."

"He's already got that. He gets them like nothing."

"Some people are just lucky. Let's go try the Egyptian exhibit. Go inside the Tomb."

When they were inside the Tomb, he asked her, "Do you ever do Professor Pobbles' laundry?"

She started to laugh. "No, but I hear Judy does. She's her slave."

"But would you?"

She shrugged. "We've gotta do what we've gotta do. I'm not going to law school at this point."

"You went to Vassar, right?"

She nodded. "You?"

"City College. Then straight to CUNY Grad."

"Mmm..." she mumbled.

"I've always wondered what the liberal arts college experience was like. Since I missed out."

"A lot of drinking, doing some pot here and there. Not really four years you miss."

"This guy you're dating? What's he—"

She checked her watch. "Oh, God! That reminds me, I'm going to be late. Sorry, Javier, I had fun, but I've got to go."

"I'll walk you..."

"That's sweet, but I'll talk to you later." She hugged him tightly. He pressed her back and rubbed, feeling her bra strap underneath her soft shirt.

Quickly she let go and ran away from him. She turned around once to wave goodbye again and then she was gone.

"I don't recall you being a fan of fine cuisine, Javier. Not Japanese, anyway," Carly said to him, balancing her chopsticks on top of her bowl.

"You've learned some new tricks over the years," he responded. He scanned her body again. Guermo had been right, she'd filled out.

"Hope you've got more tricks than I do," she said, picking up the sticks again. He didn't respond at first. He was still thinking about Pam Gould.

"Oh," he finally replied, picking up his chopsticks too and holding them awkwardly. She laughed.

"So, what are you up to these days?" she asked. "I was so excited when I ran into Guermo. I haven't seen him in ages. He hasn't changed at all, still has that sense of humor, right? And boy, can he cook a pizza! I told him, you should get a food truck, you know, like on the Food Channel!"

"Yup, that's Guermo."

"So tell me, Javier, what do you do these days?"

He paused for a second. "Well, I'm a Professor of English," he said.

"Oh, wow!" she replied, her eyelids widening. "Are you tenured yet?"

"No, that's a process," he responded.

"Oh, yes, of course, of course," she said, waving with her chopsticks. "So how many years will that take?"

Javier paused, shrugging. "You know, it depends on publications and stuff. I'm a poet."

"Oh, cool," she said, her gaze dropping to her miso soup. "Do you have any publications?"

"No, not yet," he said. "I mean, in college and stuff, sure. But I'm submitting. You know, there are a lot of journals, so you've got to keep sending your work out..."

She faked a smile and continued to nod.

"And I'm only part-time at the college now...I mean I teach two classes. Plus I wait tables at this bakery in Kew Gardens Hills. Kosher, actually."

"Oh, sounds good," she said, nodding, her lips open, stirring her miso with a short, thick spoon.

"So, how about you?"

She resumed the fake smile, but she didn't look at him now. You know, I work a boring job in finance. Nothing like you, Mister Romantic," she said, shaking her head like an Egyptian.

She giggled, then bit her lip and slurped down her soup. She placed the bowl back down, kept looking at the table now, while he kept staring at her breasts, because he wasn't sure what else to do.

"So, do you work in Manhattan?" he asked.

"Yeah, it's in Midtown. Office building. Nothing too exciting."

"Sounds pretty good to me," he said, picking up a lettuce leaf with his chopsticks and munching. The ginger dressing tasted bitter to him.

"I was in Jackson Heights to see a college friend—" she started saying, but he interrupted.

"Do you still live with your parents in...," he asked, but he couldn't remember where they had lived.

"Elmhurst? I did, but then I got my own place, and now I moved in with my boyfriend."

Javier stopped munching. "Boyfriend?" he asked.

"Yup. Over in Midtown West. Not a bad view of the Hudson River, but nothing too special."

"I see," he said. He ate the rest of his salad hurriedly. She continued to don an awkward smile and stare at her bowl. The waitress took it and replaced it with the sushi platter and brought her a Martini.

"He's a financial rockstar too?" he asked.

"Something like that," she said. Her skin had turned red.

"So your parents are okay with you living with a guy out of wedlock?" he asked.

"We've set a date," she said.

"I see."

They ate in silence for a long time.

Finally she said, "How are your parents?"

"My parents moved back to the Dominican Republic. They say they prefer it there. My brother moved to Ecuador. He writes sometimes."

"So you're all alone?"

"All by my lonesome," he replied, chuckling. "I still live in my house in Corona. I guess I kind of prefer it. Having my own place. I mean, I did like having family around. It was cool when all my cousins lived around me, and we'd hang out on the porch and play cards and stuff.

But a few moved to New Jersey and some even out to California. They keep on emailing me and telling me I should come out, that the sun's great. I've been applying to adjunct jobs there but no go."

"I'm sure there are plenty of jobs you can get."

"In this economy? Not so sure."

"Yeah, I guess we're pretty lucky too. I could have been laid off during the crash but I survived."

"Two different worlds, eh?"

"What?" Carly asked, picking up her drink.

"I mean, me being this wannabe academic, and you a high-flying corporate person."

She waved her hand at him. "No, that's in your head," she said, pursing her lips. She sipped her drink.

"Yeah, we've gone on different paths."

"Nothing wrong with that, Javier," she said.

"Nope, nothing wrong with it," he replied.

That night he returned to the college to grade papers. Professor Kawata came in.

"So how's our star adjunct doing?" he asked.

Javier didn't respond. He kept grading a paper on *The Life of Poetry* by Muriel Rukeyser. But when he recalled that no one else was in the office he looked up and saw Professor Kawata still standing there, one hand on the doorknob, the other on his hip.

"What, you mean me?" Javier finally asked.

Professor Kawata smiled. He walked over and sat on Javier's desk, then knocked twice on it.

"Yes, I mean you," he replied.

"Grading papers as usual, Professor."

"Call me Richard. What's wrong with you? Hell, call me Dick."

"Okay, Dick."

"I don't get you adjuncts. I smell such an aroma of fear around you guys. It shouldn't be like that. We all call each other by our first names, used to be that adjuncts did the same, but now, with your class..."

"There's a lot of two-name calling too, I hear," Javier interrupted cautiously.

Professor Kawata rolled his eyes. "Yes, there is that. What is your first name, by the way?"

"Javier," he stated.

"Well, Javier," Professor Kawata said, putting his hand on Javier's shoulder, "you know we love diversity here. Diversity is our middle name. In fact, we've got a couple of people coming in, Dominicans, and I thought you could show them around, give them a good feel of the university. You are of Dominican descent, yes?"

Javier nodded.

"So I thought you would be the perfect candidate, naturally. I hope you don't feel strange about that."

"No, of course I don't feel strange, Professor Kawata —I mean, Dick."

"You're catching on, Javier. Tell me, were you ever a tour guide in undergrad or grad school?"

"No."

"Did you ever host an event?"

Javier shook his head. "No," he said.

"Mmm..." Professor Kawata muttered. "I'm a little bit apprehensive, because these could be big donors, Javier. If we play our cards right, the institution could receive a big reward for our hospitality. You know how important donors are to us, especially in our financial crunch. I want you to give the tour, but perhaps you wouldn't mind some help from a more experienced adjunct? I know Pam Gould has some experience from Columbia, and Judy used to host..."

"Pam is fine," Javier said.

"Mmm...you have a thing for her, huh?" he asked, punching Javier's shoulder lightly.

"No, she's got a boyfriend, Dick."

Professor Kawata shook his head and made a clicking sound with his tongue. "The boring generation. That's what I've dubbed you guys. That scenario would never have stopped me when I was a young buck. Of course, I never had to be an adjunct."

"You got published quickly," Javier said, immediately regretting it.

Professor Kawata seemed to reminisce. "Yes, I shot to fame fast after that. I was only 23. Still managed to end up in this place. I'm not knocking it of course, mind you, I'm just saying."

"It's not Harvard," Javier said.

Professor Kawata knocked on Javier's desk twice again. "No, Javier, it's better. We have the privilege to educate the true Americans, the future Americans. The future of our nation, *that* we are forging at this university. Don't you forget that when you're giving our tour," he said, pointing at Javier.

"Yes, Dick."

Professor Kawata got up.

"Remember, Javier, the better you do, the better you do, if you know what I mean."

"Is it true, Professor," he asked, "the gossip, I mean?"

Professor Kawata seemed taken aback.

"I thought you would be above gossip, Javier," he said. Then his expression changed, and he laughed.

"Well, let's just say this: no matter what happens, I still hold reins here, Javier. If nothing else, you remember that."

"He's using you," Guermo said, heating a slice for a Bangladeshi guy. "He's gonna make you do as much free work as possible for the university or whatever and then he's not going to promote you, chico. You know they never promote upwards for those tenure jobs, they always get someone from the outside."

"Well they already know me. Isn't it about who you know?"

"Yeah, but not for that. They need someone bankable, someone exotic, so they can sell it off to the other departments, not some Dominican kid from Queens. All I'm saying is, keep your options open."

"I'm sick of grading these papers, man," Javier said. "These fucking immigrants can't write for shit."

The Bangladeshi guy gave him a dirty look. Guermo snickered.

"You better look in the mirror before you say shit like that, chico."

"I'm born here, man. I'm American."

"Yeah, like you keep on reminding us lower pueblos. Please, when you walk down the street, they look at you like an immigrant. Hell, an illegal. They think, there's a fucking spic that might mug me if I look the other way. That's what they think, chico. I don't care if you were born in Queens Hospital or in Pakistan. You're one generation removed. You'll never be like them."

"Like who? Pam Gould? Maybe not."

"Don't even think of breathing in her direction, bro. She's too hot for you."

"You're the one who told me to bang her."

Guermo laughed. "I'm half-joking with you, chico. I mean you might as well try. Anything's possible in America, right?"

"How about May?"

"Who?"

"That Chinese masseuse. What does she think?"

"She thinks you're a green card. That's what she thinks of you."

"An American?"

"For her, yes. You are the icon, the pinnacle of the American Dream."

"So it's all relative."

"You still know how to argue, chico, I can see that. How'd it go with Carly?"

"That girl's definitely out of my league."

"Yeah? She seemed so down to earth."

"Wall Street marrying Greenwich, or something."

"Hmm. Those Asians climb fast," he said, handing the slice to the Bangladeshi guy, who left hurriedly.

"Enough with the generalizations, man. I need to get to the bakery and then prepare for my date with May."

"You're a regular dating machine, chico. Get stressed much? Maybe you should get a massage first."

Javier was lucky enough to have a car. His father had left it for him, saying he couldn't take it with him back to the old country, and it was too beat up to fetch a decent price here. The monthly insurance payments put a dent in Javier's finances, but since he didn't drive too far, the gas payments weren't bad, and his metrocard purchases were minimal.

He parked outside of the massage place, waiting for 8:45, when May had said she would get out of work. At 8:36 he was singing along to "Go Your Own Way" by Fleetwood Mac on Lite FM when he saw a figure emerge from the spa. The figure looked similar to May.

He was ready to open the car door when he saw her turn and put her hand out to another individual who was leaving the spa too. He was an older man wearing a suit.

She touched his chest with her hands and they embraced. Then she let go of him and quickly waved to someone inside the spa. The older man put his arm around her shoulder and they walked together down the street, away from Javier's car.

Javier emerged from his car and ran to the spa, eyeing the couple the entire time, believing he recognized the old man.

He opened the spa door and noticed Li Jiang was counting money behind the register. Cora was sitting on a recliner. An older woman lay on the sofa.

"Li," he said, "you know where May went?"

"She out. You take Cora. She good too."

"No Cora," Javier said. "Where's May?"

"She not working right now, amigo. You take Cora."

He cursed at Li Jiang, rushed out of the spa and ran back to his car. He wondered why May had requested meeting him so late after work, rather than on her day off, and then had the nerve to forget about him and leave with another man.

He drove out to the road and tailed the couple down the street. Coming parallel to them now and inspecting them closely, he knew for sure the man was Professor Kawata.

A minute later, the couple stopped in front of a Honda Accord. Professor Kawata unlocked the passenger door and opened it to let May inside.

Javier did a u-turn and waited for them to drive. He followed them onto the expressway and took an exit toward Brentwood in Nassau County, where he had heard Professor Kawata lived. When Professor Kawata's car pulled into the driveway of a three-story home, Javier parked on the residential street and saw the couple enter the house.

He sat in his seat for a few minutes, brooding. Then he got some gas nearby, and drove home.

He arrived at the office early the next morning to teach a class, even though he hadn't slept much that night. Pam Gould was already there, drinking a tall cup of coffee.

"Javier! Listen, I'm sorry I had to leave the other day. But yesterday Dick gave me the good news that we're going to show around those prospective donors! It's so exciting!"

"Yeah. Exciting," Javier said, plopping down on his chair. He emitted a sigh of total exhaustion.

"What's wrong?"

"You ever wonder, Pam, why we're here?"

"What do you mean?"

"You know, why we're slogging through this when we could be doing Peace Corps, or Teach for America?"

She laughed. "Well, I've never thought of the Peace Corps. Teach for America, I did consider. A lot of my friends did that, but they all left after the two years and went to law school. I mean we'd be teaching pretty standard stuff to kids who don't care at all. This way, we can teach what we want..."

"Can we?" He thought. "I guess we can, when we're lucky to get a class. Then we're grading papers all week and teaching for months, just to make $2500 a class. Meanwhile it seems like our main role is to entertain donors and keep the money rolling in."

"That's the only way an institution can run, Javier. It's a team effort. You know that."

"No, I don't know that. I mean, what are we really accomplishing, and who is benefiting? These people will never learn to write poetry. They'll never get a poem published. I might never get a poem published and I'm teaching them!"

"You will, Javier. Just persevere. It's a tough slog."

"It seems so random. Who gets published, who gets tenure, who gets to give a tour."

"Welcome to the humanities, Javier. It is random. It's a crapshoot. Always has been."

"If I was living in the DR, maybe I could till the land, be one with the land."

Pam laughed. "That's a romantic notion, Javier. You could move to West Virginia and do the same thing."

Javier looked up at her. "Maybe I will. I hear land is pretty cheap there."

"Get serious. You're a poet. You're a professor. You'll make it."

"Tell me, Pam Gould, what does your boyfriend do for a living?"

Pam seemed embarrassed. "He's a corporate lawyer."

"If you were single, would you date a guy like me?"

Pam shrugged. "I don't know. Probably."

"Be serious. You wouldn't. I work at a bakery."

"I work at a cafe."

"In the East Side. You're old money. You probably have a trust fund twelve times as large as the price of my house."

"Who told you that?"

"Just a guess. How many generations back are you in America?"

Pam rolled her eyes. "I don't know Javier. Too many to count. I don't know what you're trying to imply..."

"Just asking questions, Pam."

"Well, maybe instead of asking about my life and the size of my bank account, you should prepare for your class, and then afterwards, we can prepare for our tour. Does that sound like a good plan?"

Javier nodded. "I think I'll write a poem before class. And after class, I'm going out for lunch. Some kimchi. I'll meet you later in the afternoon, around 2, before I head to the bakery. We can prepare then."

"Okay, sounds like a plan," she said. "You seemed to have decided on a course pretty fast."

"Seems I can settle down when I'm down for the count," he said.

"Dear class," he said, "I'm going to begin this session in an unusual way. For now, we are going to forget about Ms. Rukeyser. Instead, I'm going to read a poem aloud. My own poem."

Two Muslim women who always sat in the front and obediently called him "Teacher" clapped. Javier began:

Money, we spend so much,
Some for love, some for fear,
Some for beer, some for rule,
Some for ridicule.
Yes, we have money we can throw around
Like confetti twisting in the wind
Landing in the hands of
Some poor, crying boy
Who would rather be watching Barney
Than waving his arm around
At some boring parade.

When he finished reading the poem, he felt flushed. He'd only read aloud a couple of times before. The two Muslim women clapped again. One man had his hand up.

"That from your life, professor? Cuz I got no money."

"Then write about that, Ricardo," he said. "It's all

about finding your voice, transmitting your experiences to the page."

"Teacher, what meter was that in?" one of the Muslim women asked. "I believe we were speaking about meter last time."

"It's free verse," he said. "I didn't think about meter. Honestly, it just came to me."

"Does that mean we shouldn't be learning all this technical crap? That we should go out and party and write about that shit?" another student asked.

Javier sat down. "It's worked for me," he said. "I think your writing will be better if you do that. But 'til then, someone volunteer to write this poem on the board. We're going to analyze its meter."

"Li Jiang," Javier said, walking into the spa, "is May here?"

"Yes, she with customer. You take Cora?"

"How long is May going to be?"

Li Jiang looked at the clock. "One hour. Hombre, you take Cora. Te gusta."

"Fine," Javier said.

Cora walked on his back, using her feet and her knees to pulverize his back. It felt pretty good. She teased him a little on his lower back. The tension rose again to his brain just like when May massaged him, and he would have felt great if she'd rubbed his head. Instead, when Cora turned him over, he removed the sheet covering his body and slapped his penis.

She acted like she didn't understand.

"You know," he said.

"You sure you want?" she asked.

He nodded. She pointed at it. He nodded again. She

put up five fingers. He put up three.

"You give four. And you be quiet," she said, pouting. She covered his mouth. He could hear breathing from the room next to his.

She took it. He grabbed for her breast but she caught his hand and moved it to her butt.

"You be good," she whispered. "You so strong," she said, and he began to laugh under her hand.

She tried for a minute. "You get hard now. You sure you want?"

He heard giggling in the next room now, followed by hard slaps against the body.

"You keep trying," he said as she removed her hand from his mouth. "If you fail, I'll still pay you."

He grabbed for her breast again. This time she didn't stop him. He closed his eyes and listened to the sounds in the other room. He could feel himself getting hard under her hand.

He thought of Dick Kawata fucking May. He came.

She covered his mouth just in time. But instead of grunting in ecstasy he began laughing again.

She cleaned him up with the towel. He was still laughing. She looked at the clock.

"Still time," she said. "I massage your shoulders. You sit up."

He continued to laugh as he sat up. She curled behind him and began massaging his shoulders. She kissed him on the cheek.

"You be good to me. You come a lot."

"Cora, does May leave at the same time as you do tonight?" he asked.

"Why you ask about May? She seeing someone."

"I know. She likes the older guys."

"I like the young buck," she said.

"Whatever. You like anything with a wallet. Let me ask you, do you have a green card?"

"Why you ask me silly question? I be in America if I not have one?"

"I don't know. You know I'm a citizen?"

"You born here?"

"I born here.

"I no believe you."

"Why not?"

"You so dark."

"You have no idea," he said.

"You come a few more time. Then we see. But I have boyfriend."

"So why would I come?" he asked.

"You come more and I see. My boyfriend nice. That's why you not touch me here," she said, touching her right breast.

"But you let me."

"You not come, so I let you. But I have boyfriend."

The buzzer sounded. "Fine. Just rub my brain a little before you go. Then I'll forget about your boyfriend."

Javier went back to the college and met with Pam Gould. They planned the tour together.

After working at the bakery, Javier drove to the spa and waited in his car until closing time. He saw Cora come out first. She noticed him and turned her palms up to the sky. He waved for her to keep going.

Then the couple emerged, arm in arm. Javier exited his car and approached them.

May saw him. She blushed and glanced at Professor Kawata.

He turned and noticed Javier. He squinted at him.

"Nunez," he said. "Is that you?"

"Yup. It's me, Dick. Sorry to interrupt you."

105

"What are you doing here?"

"I frequent this establishment too, Dick. I even speak Spanish with the owner, Li Jiang."

Professor Kawata glanced back at May, then again at Javier.

"He speaks Spanish?"

"Perfect. I habla espanol with him all the time. And I try all the girls. All of them."

"Yes, they are skilled masseuses," he said.

"I had a wonderful massage with Cora earlier today. She told me you were here so I thought I would wait for you to inform you of something."

Professor Kawata swallowed. "And what is that?"

"Well, Pam Gould and I are on board. I think we're going to be a great team tomorrow. We just met and went over the logistics of the operation. But I had an idea. I thought I could bring Li Jiang along. I mean, he's the perfect symbol of Queens' cultural diversity. A Chinese massage parlor owner who speaks Spanish to please his customers. What a wonderful display of cultural border-crossing."

Professor Kawata looked at May. She was staring at the ground. Then he glared at Javier like he was crazy.

"But Li isn't associated with the university. Unless he took a class I don't know of."

"Why don't we ask him?"

Javier pointed at the spa door and began moving in that direction, but Professor Kawata shook his head.

"I still don't see the point of it. I think you and Pam will do a good job of running the tour."

"But you don't mind if I speak to Li Jiang and bring him along if he's okay with it?"

Professor Kawata had become flushed. "Just do what is right in your judgment," he finally stated, pointing at Javier's chest. "But remember that I will be judging you on your judgment."

Javier nodded firmly. "I will remember that. Have a wonderful evening with your lovely companion, Dick. Give my regards to your wife."

Professor Kawata penetrated him with a look of utter contempt. May didn't say anything.

Once they were gone, Javier entered the spa and spoke to Li Jiang.

The next day he met with Pam Gould in the Main Hall. He had Li Jiang with him. Li was wearing a suit.

"A change in plans," he said. "I've got a guest."

He explained who Li Jiang was. Pam looked at him like he was crazy.

"I don't understand. You think this will impress these donors?"

"My friend Guermo told me this guy's story. How he immigrated to America, fell in with Hispanic workers in a fish deli on Roosevelt Avenue. They were all working for Koreans then. He can relate the true immigrant experience in Queens."

Pam was shaking her head. "Yeah, but the donors care about the university, not the immigrant experience. Has he taken a class here?"

"This is the angle, Pam," Javier said, chopping his hand into his palm. "Li wants to raise his family. He believes in the American Dream. He wants his kid to get a top-notch education and receive a six-figure salary when he gets out. And his kid is smart. I mean he goes to Stuyvesant. But can Li afford to send his kid to Harvard or NYU? No, he can't, not today, no matter how smart he is. He'd have to take out another mortgage on the home. But for a fraction of the cost he can still get a quality education by going to this school. That's why the donors should invest here, that's why they shouldn't invest in some private school. I've researched it, Pam, this is a trend for smart kids today in New York City. It's in all the newspapers. I've brought some articles with me. Because of the recession and the high tuition, almost nobody except the rich can afford to send their kids to those schools anymore, outside of receiving some miracle, lottery scholarship. I mean come on, even you're teaching here, right?"

Pam rolled her eyes, but she was smiling now. "That actually does sound like a good plan," she conceded.

"Buena esquema," Li Jiang said, smiling widely, pointing his finger in the air like Socrates.

Suddenly they saw Professor Kawata approach. He marched towards them. Two men wearing pinstripe suits followed him, looking around like they were lost.

"Javier, Pam," Professor Kawata announced, "I've decided to give the tour myself..."

Then he noticed Li and became flushed. Li waved at him.

Professor Kawata gazed scornfully at Javier.

"That's okay, Dick," Javier said. "Pam and I have got it all mapped out. Li Jiang here will help us with the tour. I guarantee your guests will be happy. So why don't you go relax, Dick? I'll come by your office afterwards and give you a full report. Trust me, okay?"

Professor Kawata appeared flabbergasted. He glanced back at the Dominicans, who were talking amongst each other, pointing at the ceiling.

"Fine, what the hell, he said.

Then, cordially, he introduced the Dominicans to Pam and Javier.

On the way back from Professor Pezran's office to Professor Kawata's office, Javier passed Judy Garfield's office.

"Vanessa Pobbles!" he heard yelled aloud. "Vanessa Pobbles! Vanessa Pobbles! Vanessa Pobbles!"

And then Pervez Muhammad's office.

"Reza Pezran! Reza Pezran! Reza Pezran!"

Professor Kawata's door was open. He sat behind his desk. He wore his reading glasses, a copy of *The Waste Land* by T. S. Eliot open in front of him. But he wasn't reading. He was deep in thought.

Javier knocked on the door.

"Good news, Dick!" he announced.

Professor Kawata glanced up. He removed his glasses quickly.

"I don't know what you're trying to pull, Nunez," he said sternly. "But it's not going to work. Close the door."

Javier slipped inside and did as asked.

Professor Kawata rose. His eyes were red and bags sagged under them.

"You know I could have you terminated today," he said.

Javier nodded. "You could do that. You hold many reins, I know. Do you mind if I sit?"

"Yes I do mind," Professor Kawata replied.

"I just came from Professor Pezran's office," Javier stated. "He thought the news that the two Dominicans are going to donate a million dollars each to the institution was pretty great."

Professor Kawata swallowed.

"That is good news," he conceded.

"He called the President of the University himself. He wanted to be the first to relay it."

Professor Kawata swallowed.

"I set up that meeting, Nunez." he said. "I got those

109

donors. Who is he—"

"And you didn't want me to use Li Jiang."

"No one knows about that, do they?"

"Professor Pezran does. So does the President of the University."

Professor Kawata sat down and so did Javier, across from him.

"Don't worry, Dick. He doesn't know anything about Li Jiang's other life. Or yours."

"Make sure it stays that way, Nunez."

"As long as you back up Professor Pezran's account, and give me credit for the tour, it will. Of course retiring early and backing Professor Pezran's appointment as Chair would be nice too."

"Pezran," Professor Kawata muttered to himself. "His criticism couldn't wipe my poetry with a..."

"No one is claiming he's on your level, Dick. Not even your wife."

Professor Kawata looked up at Javier. "My wife is a cheating..." He paused. "I'm going to divorce her. I just need to find the right time."

"And you told May you'll marry her?"

"I show her a good time. I give her money. I give her more than she deserves. I give her more than I ever got for my labor."

"So she doesn't think you'll marry her?"

"I don't know what she thinks. Maybe she does."

He put on his reading glasses. "I need to think."

"I want a tenure-track position, Dick. I want many publications. You have influence with editors."

Professor Kawata breathed hard.

"These things are possible. But they take time. Don't think you have more influence than you do."

Javier nodded. "I do know my limitations, Dick," he said, getting up.

Professor Kawata picked up *The Waste Land* and

fanned himself with it.

"You should've been a hustler, Nunez. You would have made more money, that's for sure."

As he was leaving the building, he saw Pam Gould outside, smoking a cigarette.

"I didn't realize you smoked."

"Every once in a while, to take the edge off."

"What is this edge? I've never understood it."

She laughed. Then she raised her arms in triumph and jumped.

"We did it, Javier!" she screamed. "We made the university money!"

He hugged her.

"Just don't burn my back," he requested.

"You want to celebrate?" she asked.

"Are you okay with kimchi?"

"How about sushi? I like the dinner boxes. Just one thing. You might have to foot the bill this time. I'll pay you back."

"You're kidding right?"

"My trust fund's administered by my uncle, Javier. I can't get any of it."

"What about your boyfriend?"

She dropped the cigarette and killed it with her heel.

"I lied, Javier. I'm not seeing anybody right now. I mean, I was, but it ended two months ago. He hit me for the last time."

"Don't tell me you never go to him for money."

She didn't answer. "Just this once, Javier. I won't ask you again."

"I doubt that." He paused. "But I know you still won't date me."

Pam licked her lip and stared at the ground. "We'll see, Javier," she said.

That afternoon he went back to the spa. Li Jiang was sitting at his desk, still wearing his suit. Javier threw a wad of bills on his desk.

"What this for, amigo?" he asked.

"For helping me," he said. "Don't worry, I won't need change for that. If things go right, I'll be making a lot more than that a day."

"Gracias," he said, stuffing it in his jacket pocket. "I give you free massage. Cora. May. You take pick."

He knew May had been sitting on the sofa the entire time—he'd purposefully ignored her. Cora was dozing on the recliner.

"Let me take May out and talk to her, how about that? I don't want a massage."

Li motioned to May with his head.

She scowled. But she rose. Javier offered his hand to her but she passed him and marched out of the spa.

Javier followed her. "May," he said.

She turned to him fiercely. "You think you so smart," she yelled. "But you stupid. You ruin my green card."

"He doesn't love you. He's not going to marry you. You're the idiot."

She slapped him. He rubbed his cheek, staring at her. Then she tried to do it again but he grabbed her arm and held it tightly.

"You're an idiot," he said again, and grabbed her other arm too when she tried to use it.

"You Americans," she screamed. She began to cry. He released her arms and threw them down. He pointed his finger at her face. "Do I look like an American, huh?

What does an American look like?"

He asked her because he was shocked she had called him one.

"You all liars!" she yelled.

"What are you doing, telling the truth? Why didn't you ever meet me, huh? Why'd you go out with that Kawata jerk instead? I could marry you too. I could give you a green card too!"

He noticed people had stopped in the street and were staring at them.

"You are young guy," she said, jiggling her fingers. "No money."

"You see the wad of bills I gave your boss. You see how I come here. Yeah, sure, I work in a fucking bakery. So what? Does that mean you can lie to me, forget about me?"

"I work hard here."

"So go back to China. What, you won't work hard there?"

She shook her head and wiped her tears. "It is long story. Too long for you."

Javier turned to the people who had stopped to stare. "Get moving, people! Nothing to see here!" he screamed, waving like a madman.

A few of the guys called him insane and said they would call the police. But then they left.

When the crowd had scattered he turned back to May.

"It's too long a story for me to listen to?" he asked. "Yeah, I guess you're right. I'm just not very patient. Certainly not if you're going to leave me for some old guy. Goodbye May, and good luck."

"Check out the scorecard," Guermo said. "Let's see:

Carly, strikeout. Pam, strikeout. Even May, strikeout."

"Guess I'm a .100 hitter."

"Worse. You're a zero hitter. I think you'd do better as a pitcher."

"Already got past the tryout. I'm on the team," he said, biting into a cold slice of pizza.

"The bullpen, maybe," Guermo corrected.

A few months later Professor Kawata announced his retirement. The faculty threw a party for him. Professor Perzan became chair, Professor Muhammad gained tenure, and Professor Pobbles became a full Professor. They advertised a tenure-track position. Javier got it, even over applicants from the outside. In the intertwining months the senior professors had used their influence to get his poetry published in a couple of major journals, so he used that as his credentials on his resume and interview, even though he knew he was guaranteed the job.

Judy Garfield and Pam Gould remained adjuncts.

Pam increasingly came by his office, flirting with him and asking him if he would go out with her. But, focused on his work and remembering her own attitudes towards him in the past, he turned her down. He didn't intend to do that forever, though, just long enough so she could suffer for her insolence. Then he would gain her body, her mind, perhaps her trust fund too.

One day, sitting in his office, his brain hurt from grading papers. He hadn't had a massage since his last visit to the spa. He had resolved to never visit again. But he called the spa anyway, willing to hang up at any moment. He heard Li Jiang's voice on the other line. He asked for May, altering his voice a little.

"May no more," he said. "Cora, Lily, Susan."

"Where is she?" he asked.

"Vacation. You take other girl."

Javier hung up the phone. He took a deep breath. He saw Pam Gould in the hallway. She often looked in while moving from class to class, a smile on her face, mixed with apprehension.

He waved. Then the phone rang. He picked it up quickly.

"Professor Perzan?" he heard himself say. "Professor Perzan!" he said now more enthusiastically. "Professor Perzan!" he yelled now. "Professor Perzan! Professor Perzan! Professor Perzan!"

The Mountain

*

Peter pushed the stick shift to 1 as he approached the Tarrytown train station. He thought he would have to stop the car and track Nilesh down, but there he was, standing in front of the parking lot, hands to his sides and slightly bent. He didn't wear glasses now, his hair was faded in the back and flat on top, he wore blue nylon pants, a long-sleeved green pullover, faded brown backpack and Timberlands whose laces were loosely tied. Perfect attire for a leisurely hike, Peter thought, glancing down at his t-shirt, his shorts, his strapped-on sandals.

"How was your ride up?" Peter asked as he pulled out of the station. He switched the gear to 3 as he accelerated up a steep hill, then put it back into neutral and pulled the emergency brake at the light. Nilesh turned his head and looked through the window, down the slope, feeling like he was at Dollywood.

"Okay," he said, turning back. "I forgot how peaceful a train ride could be."

"Metro-North is peaceful nowadays?" Peter asked.

"Better than the subway in Brooklyn," Nilesh said.

"Yeah, well compare that to a bus ride in Kikuyu."

"Fine. Compare it."

"Are there lambs baying, children screaming, is it so

crowded you have to stick your head out of the window to breath, if you can even get to it?"

"Sounds like India," Nilesh replied as they drove ahead and passed a small diner that looked like it was straight out of *Gilmore Girls*. He gazed at the town's Main Street. They all look this way, he thought. Go over to Greenwich and you've got the same thing: one wide street where it looks like Christmas all year round, surrounded by acres of million dollar homes. One day I'll be in one of these, inside a private gated community. My bratty kids will throw around a football on a large green lawn while I'll be inside, staring out a large window, my paperwork in front of me, my dear wife by my side, holding a teapot, waiting patiently to refill my cup as I try to avoid the most terrifying numbers I've ever encountered.

"I want to go to India," Peter said. "Can you hook me up?"

"I wouldn't recommend going alone. But for you—"

"Yeah, I'm a special case. An adventurer."

Nilesh laughed. "Sure. How was Kenya?"

Now they were out of the car and approaching the woods.

"It was great," Peter said. "I learned a lot, I helped out a lot, had so much fun."

"But in the end, the machetes got you."

"I told you, the principal at the school where I worked, he got attacked."

"My cousin who did a medical residency there, she told me they called Nairobi 'High-Robbery.'"

"There are problems. Otherwise, I wouldn't have been there."

They entered the mouth of the woods. As always, Peter led. Nilesh noticed Peter's sandals as the trail rose steadily higher and he tried to keep up. It wouldn't matter. Peter knew these woods, these trails, like the back of his hand. His father was a park ranger here.

"Main thing I learned," Peter said, "is about life. You have to be resigned to some extent. A lot of life is fate, so why worry or question too much? I worked at a school near Nairobi. I had to teach kids there about AIDS. They didn't know shit, and it made me kind of angry, because a lot of the older people knew about it, but they weren't telling. So I thought, why was I there, doing the work they should have been doing? But I settled down, began talking to them, and I started to understand the culture there. They aren't deceitful, just resigned. They respect the way things work. They have this saying that 'God will manage all things.' They just accept."

Nilesh laughed under his breath, then coughed.

"You had to go to Kenya to learn that?" he asked.

Peter stared back at Nilesh.

"Yeah," Peter said, unsure of himself, continuing on. "I mean here, we're always trying to correct problems. That's why I went there, to change things. But people there don't see things that way. They're okay with foreign aid workers partying on their land. That's just the way it is to them."

"They don't want to learn?"

Peter could feel himself flare up. His face was likely flushed, but he tried to keep his composure. He wasn't used to Nilesh questioning him.

"They just have a different way of thinking. Look, I'll tell you this story, maybe that'll show you my point. There was a farm on the side of the schoolhouse and the farmer was raising goats. I became pretty friendly with him. His name was Paul. His whole family was helping to raise these goats. They weren't bought from some other farm. They were the children of one of Paul's older goats, so they were homegrown. And Paul and his wife and his children, they loved these goats. They'd pet them, and when they fed them, they'd do it like they were feeding their dog. They really did love them. And when one of the goats gave birth, they took care of the little one like it was a person.

"But when the spring came around, Paul's son had a baby, and he told me that as part of the celebration, they'd have to kill one of the goats. Paul had tears in his eyes. He felt sick that he had to do it. But at the same time, he felt a kind of pride. It was a ritual, the way it was always done. And there was no question, Paul would do the killing himself. Because he was like this goat's father, he had raised it, and only he had the right to send it into its next life. That's how they thought of it. They were a community, a family.

"So when the day came, he brought the goat out on a leash, like it was his pet. The neighboring men and women stood around, watching, as he took the leash off. Maybe the goat expected his fate, because immediately, he tried to run. But he was in an enclosed space, like a rodeo, with barbed wire around, so he couldn't go anywhere. The children watched him circle and run and jerk helplessly, knowing the situation could only go one way. The younger ones wept, but the others seemed resigned. There was no gloating, just acceptance of the situation.

"Then Paul ran up to it, and some of the villagers followed. One tapped me and suddenly I was in the fray too. We grabbed the goat and wrestled it to the ground. I was lying on my side, holding onto one of its legs with my right arm. The other guys were crowding in and I couldn't move. My head was shoved into the goat's chest. I listened to the beating of its heart, pounding and then slowing. Then the goat was still.

"I felt a tap again and slowly, I got out from under it and stood up. The other men were standing too. Paul knelt, cradling the goat in his left arm, the knife in his right hand, sad but determined. The goat's eyes were strangely expectant, its baying soft and measured. With one swift cut, Paul slit its throat. Blood gushed out onto the ground. Some of it sprayed on my feet. Paul made sure it was dead. Then he sliced through his stomach and removed his entrails.

"Later that night, when Paul's family and the villagers prepared the goat, they didn't waste any part of it. They used the skin to make blankets, the hoof for glue, the horns and bones for cups and utensils, even some of the entrails to use in tools. We had a huge party, and we ate every part of the goat."

"Gruesome story," Nilesh said.

"Those people, they understand nature," Peter said. "They'd understand these woods, but I'm not sure they'd understand a public park."

The climb was getting steeper now. Nilesh recalled that Peter had taken him on a trail years ago, but he wasn't sure if this was the same one. He remembered it got very steep pretty fast at some point. But until then, it was gradual. He'd done his best to keep up with Peter as he told his story, but he was tired and he wasn't sure he could keep up that pace much longer.

"So that's supposed to illustrate resignation and understanding?" Nilesh asked.

"Yes," Peter said.

Nilesh stepped on a jagged rock and nearly tripped, but he regained his footing. Peter turned aside but Nilesh held up his hand to signal he was okay.

"Well, let me ask you this then," Nilesh said after regaining his composure. "If a father raped and killed his daughter, then ate her and used her skin to make a coat and her bones to create a chair, do you think that would be an example of understanding and resignation?"

Peter was flushed again. "That's not the same thing," he said.

"How is it not?"

"First of all, there's torture involved."

"What, you didn't watch this poor goat run around helplessly, then tackle him to the ground?"

"It's not the same thing as rape."

"Okay, let's take out the rape."

"It's still different because it's not natural. A father kills his daughter for no purpose, with no ritual?"

"Let's say that it was a ritual, in the father's private religion. And what was the primary purpose of killing the goat? To eat it, right? That's why it was raised. And you just said that guy Paul was like a father to the goat. So what's the difference?"

Peter was silent for a few seconds. Then he replied: "The girl is human."

"Exactly," Nilesh said. "She is. That's why you react that way, differently than about the goat. But the truth is they are no different, because they are both creatures of God."

Peter smiled. Nilesh was Jain, and therefore a vegetarian. His religion taught him not to kill even a fly (Peter figured there were cockroaches filling Nilesh's father's motels in Tennessee). Yet in college Nilesh had half-heartedly practiced his religion and even mocked it, while Peter had defended it.

"We might all be creatures of God," Peter said, "but that doesn't mean we all have the same role. Take this trail and this park. There are so many creatures in here: earthworms, caterpillars, chipmunks, deer. Some of them eat each other. Others respect each other. There's a life cycle, a food cycle. Sometimes things are random, other times they're not planned, but usually there is a set way things work. Humans are a part of that, and frankly we're above it. We can feast on God's bounty. But we can't feast on each other."

"Why not?"

"Because, it's written that way. That's murder."

"You mean the Bible. The Old Testament."

"You can consider a lot of things. Or just common sense. Take this path. Would a tiger make something like this? No, humans have made it. Because we do have superior intelligences. That includes superior moralities."

"Exactly. So why eat meat at all? Why kill anything? Why have these crazy tribal rituals? It's animalistic. It's beneath us. It's immoral."

Peter shook his head.

"What's your definition of morality? I think it's more immoral to waste God's bounty. If a piece of cooked meat's in front of you, why not eat it? It's better than wasting it. I just don't get that. And since when did you become all Jain? I thought you hated that."

"Since when did you start talking about God's bounty?"

Peter laughed. "When I was in Africa, I guess."

Nilesh shook his head. He was breathing heavily. Peter was consistently a few strides ahead of him, and increasing his pace fast. Nilesh wasn't sure he could keep up the pace or the conversation.

"So when did you become an animal lover?" Peter asked. "I don't remember you hanging out with the tree huggers at Bedford."

"I did sometimes. I did go to Veg-Eats at Earthhouse, remember?"

Peter snickered. "Yeah, freshman year. That girl gave you a dirty plate to eat on and you said no. She just wanted to conserve a plate, to share, and you wouldn't even go for that. Next thing you knew, no girl there would share anything with you."

Nilesh shrugged his shoulders. He stopped to catch his breath. Peter walked a few strides ahead and turned around.

"Come on, you're tired already? We haven't gotten to the hard part yet."

Nilesh put his hands on his knees and breathed heavily. Then he noticed his shoelaces were loose. He knelt down and tied them, shaking his head as he did. He was thirsty.

"I'm not used to this, man," he said. "I wasn't living on a farm in Kenya."

"You were never used to it," Peter said. Then he paused, and added, "I bet yelling at teenagers all day doesn't get you a lot of exercise."

Nilesh nodded. "I'm glad that's over. Do you have any water?"

"No, I didn't bring any. We're really going to rough it out here."

"Damn," Nilesh said, suddenly remembering. "I left my bag in the car."

Peter continued climbing. Nilesh took a deep breath, rose and followed. It was like old times, like when the tight end on the football team taught the skinny, nerdy Indian kid to lift weights. Peter would wake Nilesh up early in the morning, as early as six, and they'd trek over to the gym. If Nilesh was tired or grumpy, Peter would bully him until he was straight. They'd spot for each other on the bench press, do thigh squats, as if Nilesh would be playing on the o-line too. Then there was the Lat pull, the tricep and leg curls, the hamstring pull, the dumbbell lunges. After the first time, Nilesh could barely walk for a week. Peter wanted him to do it again three days later, and Nilesh almost collapsed. But eventually all that bullying paid off and Nilesh began working out on his own—though when he left Bedford, Nilesh had stopped. That was two years ago.

Now Peter was walking, on average, at least ten or twenty paces ahead of Nilesh, and he'd have been further away if he didn't keep stopping so Nilesh could keep pace. When Nilesh would pause to catch his breath, Peter would turn around and yell at him, telling him to cease the nerdy stuff and keep going. Peter wanted to make Nilesh back into a man.

Then the climb got steeper. Nilesh began stopping more frequently. Peter started to think that his bullying was in vain. They weren't back in college now. It had been a while. At one point, Nilesh stopped completely and sat on the ground. Peter was ahead by about thirty paces. He looked down at Nilesh, through a slit between hickory trees and ferns and caterpillar sacs and he thought, perhaps he should take pity on Nilesh. He wasn't the athlete that Peter was. He didn't know these woods, or any woods.He'd been in New York City for two years, trying to teach the worst urban youth, and he'd probably failed miserably, just as Peter had, essentially, failed in his mission in the Peace Corps in Kenya. They were both failures, so what was the point of continuing this charade?

Peter walked back to where Nilesh was and offered his hand. Nilesh waved it away.

"We can go back," Peter said. "It was stupid of me not to bring water. You could get dehydrated."

Nilesh shook his head. "We're already this far. We started. Let's finish it."

"Are you sure?"

Nilesh nodded.

"Are you going to go any faster?"

Nilesh looked up angrily. Peter laughed.

"I know you were in the city all this time," Peter said. "I guess there aren't any mountains there."

"I was just lazy," Nilesh responded, taking a final breath and standing up. "I guess I could have jogged or joined a gym. My girlfriend did."

Nilesh had told Peter about his girlfriend in an email a year before. Or maybe it had been longer than that.

"Kim, right? Are you guys still together?"

Nilesh looked down at the ground and began walking.

Peter followed him.

"No," he said simply.

"When'd you break up?" Peter asked.

"A few months ago."

"How long were you guys together?"

Nilesh was trying hard to keep up. But soon Peter was ahead of him again.

"Maybe a year and a half."

"That's respectable."

"Yeah," Nilesh said, "but pointless."

"Because it's over?"

Nilesh nodded. They approached a few large rocks that were bunched together. Peter climbed over them easily, using small gaps of grass and moss between the rocks to balance himself. He crouched down like a tight end and leapt like a monkey. Nilesh, meanwhile, placed his foot on the surface of the first large rock. He slipped, and only his hands saved him from falling completely. Peter asked if he was okay; Nilesh, gasping, replied that he was. He tried going up again, but had trouble keeping his footing. Peter told him to place his foot in the gaps, but either Nilesh didn't hear, was incapable, or was too stubborn to do so.

Peter climbed down a bit and put his hand out. Nilesh shook his head, refusing it.

"Come on, take it," Peter commanded, frustration in his voice. Nilesh didn't respond. He crouched back, his right leg behind his left, and leapt upon the rocks. He maintained his grip and sailed over the rocks and onto the dirt, stumbling for a few steps before regaining his balance.

Peter smiled. "Nice," he said. Nilesh didn't look back to acknowledge Peter's praise. He kept climbing, and Peter paused before continuing on.

Now, gazing at Nilesh's back, watching him climb awkwardly up, Peter recalled Nilesh's days at Bedford before he had signed up for Teach for America. Nilesh had never been part of any cause or organization at Bedford, or, as far as Peter knew, in Tennessee either, except for his father's motel, where he had traveled each summer and during breaks and where he had worked, first cleaning rooms, then managing the front desk, then calculating the daily cash intake and the profits, then driving around scouting for other motels to purchase.

But Nilesh had hated the forced duty that his father and the rest of his family expected of him, and he didn't want to go back to Tennessee after college. Yet he had no other plans. He was an economics major, but he disliked it, had only pursued it because his father had insisted. Lying in their beds one night freshman year, slightly drunk and depressed after a night of frustrating parties and failed connections, Nilesh had told Peter that his father had made a deal with him: he would pay the lavish tuition for a blue chip northern university like Bedford if Nilesh would agree to major in economics, work at the motel during breaks, learn the tricks of the trade and use the skills he had learned at Bedford for the motel's advantage. After college, he would return to Tennessee and help his father run one of his motels and scout for the purchase of others. Nilesh had accepted his father's offer, gladly, wanting simply to get away from his family and the Tennessee public school system.

But by senior year, Nilesh had decided that the deal was a manipulative hoax. Peter's father, and other parents of kids at Bedford, were paying their son's and daughter's tuitions without any obligations whatsoever. Even though Peter's father was only a park ranger, he had slaved to pay private school tuition for his son from K-12 and college. Meanwhile Nilesh had been forced to attend bad public schools in Tennessee because of his father's frugality. What did he owe his father for? For being a domineering, controlling cheapskate?

As graduation approached, Nilesh had no intention of keeping his pledge to move back home. But he also had no other plans. He had developed no genuine interests at Bedford, so he was relegated to following the interests of others. Most grads were moving to the Williamsburg or Park Slope neighborhoods of NYC and working in the public service sector, so Nilesh primarily looked in that direction. When Peter had revealed his interest in the Peace Corps, Nilesh debated signing up but he never did, partly because he was afraid of living in a foreign country.

One day, Nilesh ran into a fellow student named Regina who he had worked with at the university publishing press. Nilesh had interned there for a month during the summer of his sophomore year in a warm-up defiance of his father: he held a low-paying, hourly rate position where his main duties involved photocopying manuscripts. Regina was visibly excited about teaching inner city youths and she told Nilesh about a Teach for America meeting the next afternoon. Regina mentioned to Nilesh that, unlike the Peace Corps, Teach for America tended to place you in the area, or at least in the city, where you wanted to teach.

So Nilesh went to the meeting, and he daydreamed through it. But he filled out the application form and attached a resume and letter of intent, putting New York City down as his first and only choice. He didn't really want to teach public school kids, especially after his horrible experiences in Knoxville public schools, but he figured this was an excuse to live away from his family for two years without having to live abroad. Perhaps the admissions committee took his placing down only one choice as evidence of an immense passion to improve that particular community, for they chose his application and rejected Regina's, who, Nilesh had recently learned, became depressed and still worked an hourly-rate job at the college publishing press.

Then Nilesh met Kim, a fellow Teach for America worker. During his orientation in the Bronx, when he was apprehensive about the tough duties to follow, she had approached and befriended him. She was dedicated and passionate about service, and yet she fell for the aimless Nilesh. Their schools and apartments happened to be in two different parts of the city. Kim's school was in the South Bronx and she lived on 145th Street in Harlem, so she needed to take the subway to get to work. Nilesh taught in Fort Greene, Brooklyn, and he would walk to work from his Park Slope apartment. During weekends they would traverse Manhattan and Brooklyn to meet at each other's homes.

Kim adored Nilesh. She told her parents all about him. But he never reciprocated her love fully. And there was another problem. Kim had two boyfriends before Nilesh, and she thought she and Nilesh would have sex pretty soon after they started dating. But Nilesh wasn't comfortable with that—whether it was his religion or his father's voice in his head or something lodged deep in his brain that stopped him he wasn't sure, but he couldn't have intercourse. So Kim decided to satisfy him with oral sex; for her he used his fingers, and sometimes, if he felt up to it, his tongue. Once she had asked him if he wanted to enter her anally. Feeling a combination of lust and disgust, Nilesh had waffled, then turned away.

This was what Nilesh had told Peter in an email, and Peter had assumed that Kim had become frustrated with Nilesh and had found another man who could satisfy her carnal desires.

Now Peter followed Nilesh for a couple of minutes, but soon they were neck and neck. He saw that Nilesh was trying hard. He was beginning to appreciate and admire Nilesh's tenacity. They finally reached an even piece of the path, an alcove of fresh soil and low grass where there was a bench and a view. Nilesh remembered that this was a spot where Peter had stopped on their last outing years before, and he looked at Peter to obtain approval. As Peter waved his hand, Nilesh plopped down on the bench, even though splinters were visible on it.

Peter sat on the ground.

"Where'd you get this fighting spirit?" he asked. "I know you had it sometimes in the weight room, but it's been a while."

"Teaching those kids wasn't exactly easy," Nilesh said after taking a few breaths and moving his hands away from the bench when one of them encountered a splinter. "I mean, it was pretty impossible. I know I wasn't all that enthusiastic in the beginning, but especially after Kim began encouraging me, I tried my best and even got into it. But it was all for nothing. You can't change those kids. They've got their minds set that they'll never be anything and they have no capacity, even at that age, to try any harder to learn. But I kept doing it. I learned about duty from that. And that's why I'm going back."

"Going back?"

"Tomorrow. To Tennessee. I'm flying. I've already got a roommate in for the rest of my lease. It expires in a month. I'm going back home."

"To work in your father's motel?"

"Yeah. To run one of them. And to get married."

"To who?"

"This girl my parents know."

Peter swallowed, then smiled nervously.

"So you dumped Kim when you learned about duty?" Peter asked.

Nilesh closed his eyes. Suddenly Peter wasn't sure he should have asked.

"No," he replied. "She broke up with me. You know why. She couldn't take it anymore."

Peter nodded.

"And that's when I realized that this do-gooder stuff is futile."

"You'd rather work in your dad's motel?" Peter asked. "I thought you hated your dad's motel. And your dad."

"Well, after Kim left, I started thinking about things, about my job at Teach for America, about the pact I'd made with my dad. And I think much of my tenacity, the reason I was able to persevere in Teach for America, was because of my dad. What he'd injected in me through his genes and his work ethic, was this perseverance. And I was never going to get away from that, no matter how hard I tried. So I might as well accept what I am, that I'm Indian and that I'm, essentially, a businessman."

"So you're going to go from Teach for America to business?"

"Honestly it's going to be tough. Not just in terms of practice, but in terms of tactics. Though in a way it's similar because you're always trying to con kids into learning and behaving, just like a businessman cons people. But my dad does some questionable things."

"Like what?"

"Like renting certain rooms to only certain kinds of people. Raising the price to exorbitant rates if he can get people to pay them. Especially uneducated people who don't know any better. Especially black people."

Peter swallowed. "Like the kids you were teaching."

"It's tough after this, to go back to that."

"Did you move to New York, start teaching, because you objected to his practices?"

"That was part of it. But honestly, it wasn't the main reason. I was lazy, first of all. And I couldn't stand him or my family then. I don't know why. I guess I was stupid. But maybe I can change things now. Maybe when I start working with him I'll get him to give up that stuff."

"Or maybe you'll become like him," Peter said.

"Maybe," Nilesh responded. "I can't say you're not

right. Maybe you are right. Maybe it's just fated. Maybe you were right about that goat and that guy too. The way the goat was raised for a purpose, the way it was killed lovingly, maybe that's like me. Maybe I'm the goat and my dad has the knife but all he's doing is cutting out my soul."

Peter swallowed as he looked down at the ground.

"Well, at least you've got a purpose," he said. "That's better than me."

Nilesh nodded. Then he was up and climbing. Peter sat there a moment, amazed at his statement, feeling humbled by it, yet also humiliated. All this time he had felt like he was Nilesh's superior, but now he had made a statement that he thought was incredibly true. His passion for the Peace Corps, his dedication to the people he knew in Kenya, all of it was for nought now that he had fled the violence and didn't know what to do with his life. Peter knew that his father expected him to be in public service, as he was, but Peter wasn't really sure what he wanted.

Peter realized Nilesh was far ahead. He got up and began following his friend, who seemed to have a dogged energy that he hadn't yet seen. Nilesh was leading now, and up a particularly steep stretch of the trail. Peter had to concentrate on the path, with more rocks, jutting logs and slippery green moss in his way. But his mind was still perturbed by what he had said, and thoughts of Kenya and his father flooded his mind—and even of his complacent, non-interventionist mother, who was always annoying him with her shrieking calls for breakfast. He was nowhere he thought, and going nowhere. Maybe he was like that goat, with a knife at his throat, calm and wondering whether he wanted that knife to slice in rather than go on living this controlled yet pointless existence.

He slipped on a rock and nearly fell, but he grabbed a couple of ferns to steady himself. Regaining his balance, he looked up and saw how steep the hill was, how it seemed to go almost straight up. An entire fallen tree was up there, precariously balancing itself. The slope was angled higher than 45 degrees, the steepest hill he had climbed in some time. He knew the trail like the back of his hand, yet this was unfamiliar. He'd been so distracted by his thoughts that he hadn't kept track. He called out to Nilesh, and when Nilesh turned, Peter saw his hand slip off of a rock. As Nilesh scrambled to find another, he panicked and moved his feet. They got tangled and he slid down. Then he started rolling. Dust was in the air and Peter had no time to react. Nilesh's body clipped Peter's legs, flipping him into the air and onto his face. Sliding down too, Peter's head hit something hard, then landed on something softer. He was nearly unconscious.

Peter's vision resembled a fade out in a film. He felt like a goner and was almost at peace with it. But as soon as he faded out, it seemed like the next chapter began, and he was aware again of his sight and his surroundings. He was lying slightly to his side so he could see, barely, that this uncomfortable, bony pillow was Nilesh's body. He could smell blood. But he couldn't feel his own body or lift his head.

He lay there, thinking that this was the end: he was paralyzed, Nilesh was dead. They'd become a feast for vultures and bears. How fitting.

He thought he heard something. He believed it was the wind; no, it was too soft. Maybe it was one of those scavengers, zoning in on its prey. Then he realized it was his own breathing. It was the creepiest sound he had ever heard. Mortality in the face of its opposite. What if that was all he would hear until he felt the sharp beaks and torturous fangs?

He noticed the rising and falling of his own chest, realized he was watching it now, meaning that his head had moved. Then he was able to make the branches above him shift. He couldn't completely feel his head, but he sensed it was moving. A few minutes later, he felt warmth, of all places, in his hand. Slowly but surely, a strength surged through his body and engulfed his senses. Its last stop was his neck.

He carried on a trial of movement. He twitched his legs. Then he was able to move his hands and wave them in front of his face. Finally he could lift his head fully and then his back too.

He sat up. He saw his shirt was bloody. In fact it was soaked in blood, and when he turned back, he realized why: Nilesh's chest had been punctured. The blood wasn't his own.

Nilesh's eyes were closed. When Peter leaned closer, he heard a gargling sound emerging from Nilesh's mouth, and when he placed his hand on Nilesh's chest, he felt a heart beat. Peter had been trained in CPR when he had worked as a lifeguard one summer off from college, and though he wasn't sure Nilesh needed it, Peter opened Nilesh's mouth and blew in, then started pumping his chest. Nilesh coughed. He still seemed unconscious, but he was breathing, so Peter figured he still had a chance.

Peter turned 360 degrees. No one was around. He was on his knees now. He felt pain from the cuts and bruises on his legs and all over his body, but he put them out of his mind and mulled over his options.

He could wait until another hiker stumbled along. That was unpredictable since it was a weekday. It wasn't even clear another hiker would be helpful: he or she might have a million pounds of gear but no walkie-talkie or phone. Which reminded Peter—he hadn't brought a cellphone, just like he hadn't brought any water. In fact, he didn't have a cell phone in this country yet. But maybe Nilesh would have one. Peter ruffled through Nilesh's left pocket, but he found only a wallet. Then he noticed Nilesh's right pocket had a hole in it. His cell phone and whatever else had probably fallen out, and the area was too large and steep to look for it.

Peter was down to his last option: running down the mountain himself, as fast as he could in his injured and dazed state, getting into his car and driving for help. His car key, the only item he had taken with him, was still in his pocket. But it was a long way down, and much of the descent was steep, especially the way down to the regular trail. Peter was not sure Nilesh could survive that long, particularly in this state. And bleeding like this, he really could become an attraction for scavengers, even predators. Was there a way Peter could cover Nilesh? Peter thought this was a good time for a deer to come across him, so Peter could get into his tight end stance, leap on it and kill it with his bare hands, then tear off its skin and cover Nilesh with it so the scavengers would avoid him. A vegetarian like Nilesh would love that.

No. That was not an option. Peter didn't know what to do. So, hunching forward now, he took Nilesh's arms and pulled them over his shoulders, holding Nilesh's hands together with his left hand. Then he curled his right arm behind himself and under Nilesh's butt, getting Nilesh's legs to curl around his torso. He sat on his own butt, on the edge of the leveled space, and began sliding down the mountain. He heard Nilesh coughing. He muttered words of encouragement as he used to do at the gym when they had been weightlifting partners.

The path down wasn't straight. Peter had to screech and stop and use his calf muscles as emergency brakes one second, then as steers the next. But he made it down to the resting stop they'd been to before, with that patch of idyllic grass and the splintered bench.

Peter was tired. He stopped and bent down. Nilesh plopped onto the ground. Peter was having flashes. He wasn't sure if he could go all the way down the mountain with Nilesh on his back. He felt nauseous. He felt like collapsing. But he had to do something. So he decided to take a chance and leave Nilesh. He'd be able to go down the mountain much faster that way.

He made sure Nilesh was straight on his back. Peter thought of placing him on the bench, so that scavengers might think he was sleeping, but he also didn't want any splinters on him. So he left Nilesh on the ground. Then Peter took off his sandals to make it less likely he would trip, and began to run down the trail on his bare feet. But flashes of possibilities went through his mind, and he thought if he came back and found some vulture feeding on his friend, he could never live with himself.

He climbed back up and knelt in front of Nilesh, thinking, despite the sweat and the blood and the flashes, that he had to put his friend on his back again and make a desperate attempt to save them both. He closed his eyes and prayed to Christ.

He took Nilesh's arms again and placed them around his neck. His hands gripped the lower part of Nilesh's thighs, and he breathed in once. He paused for a second, hearing Nilesh's short breaths, and then, without another thought, he charged down the mountain.

He went as fast as he could while at the same time maintaining his footing and avoiding rocks and fallen tree stumps. Normally it would have strained his calf muscles going down, and running would have been nearly impossible. Yet Peter found himself able, as long as he kept his eyes on the ground and his concentration focused.

But he was getting tired. He didn't know if he could sustain it. He reached a relatively level path and slowed a bit. He saw a less angular slope in front of him, and he thought he could make it. He breathed a few times, and with a final burst of energy, he charged ahead.

As he stumbled down the slope, he noticed something moving in the distance. He didn't want to look away from the ground, or he might trip up or lose his focus and faint. But what if it was a bear? It was unlikely, but he had to acknowledge the risk. He looked up, just for a second. He saw it wasn't an animal, but a human. A large, fat, tired, white, male human with a hiking stick in his hand who had clearly been struggling up the mountain but had now stopped, apparently frightened at the sight of a bloody man carrying a bloody carcass down a mountain—a monstrous, two-backed beast.

Peter concentrated on the path. But he was excited, and he began moving faster, changing direction subtly. He could even feel himself smiling as he looked up again and saw the man in front of him, his eyes wide and a cell phone held up to his ear. Peter thought about slowing down, but as he did, he felt a thud on his foot and lost his balance.

Peter opened his eyes. He saw a room tinged with a pink hue. The curtain that covered the only window in the room was orange. And the curtain next to him was white. Directly in front of him, he recognized his mother and father. Then a man in a long white coat, the doctor. And this room, a hospital room.

He didn't know why he was here. His memory wasn't just a blur, it didn't seem to exist. It was like his mind was trying to access his memory but couldn't locate it. It didn't even know what door to knock on. He knew these were his parents and this was a doctor. Yet the history that had led to this point—nothing.

After his parents hugged him, the doctor asked him if he remembered his name, and Peter's memory flooded back like a torrent. He remembered everything, and he demanded to know what had happened, if he was alive or if he had gone to heaven, or hell, was he dreaming or had he woken? His parents assured him he wasn't dreaming or dead: he was lucky, he had made it. He had just been knocked cold. They had worried that he would be in a coma and would never come out. But he had regained consciousness and they were glad. The doctor told him they would need to keep him for several days, to make sure there were no complications from his head injury, but that he'd been stitched up and that most likely, he would recover with little trouble.

Next Peter asked about Nilesh. Peter had tried his best to save him, but as he asked the question, he felt a deep pang of realization, because based on what he remembered of Nilesh's wounds, his breathing, based on the fact that he had probably dropped Nilesh when he had fallen, that Nilesh was dead. And Peter dreaded even more than his own guilt, the prospect of facing Nilesh's family.

But the doctor, patting Peter's hand, told him that Nilesh was fine. He had a chest wound, which was stitched up. He'd lost some blood, but he had been on fluids and was in good shape and might even be leaving the hospital in a few days. Peter breathed relief, yet he also, after his parents left, felt angry that after all he'd done for Nilesh, risking his own life, that he'd probably leave the hospital before Peter.

Nilesh did leave the hospital, three days later. Peter's parents wheeled Peter down, with a nurse's assistance, to the hospital lobby, where Nilesh, both of his arms in a sling, stood with his own parents.

Peter didn't realize Nilesh had hurt his arms too, but there it was, Nilesh's injuries visible to Peter. When Peter got off the elevator and saw Nilesh for the first time in a long time, he wasn't sure what to think—rather feelings of pity, of blame, of jealousy, of guilt, engulfed his heart. Nilesh didn't seem to have anything to say. The two waved to each other. Peter tried to speak but he couldn't. Nilesh didn't say anything. Their parents acknowledged each other with head nods. And then Peter wondered to himself, as Nilesh turned to leave, whether God did have a food chain and whether Nilesh was higher than Peter on it. The sun was bright outside but Peter could barely discern it from that lobby, and the windows were rarely unblocked in his room. A few more days, the doctors told him, and he could be out again, in nature.

Malta: A Love Story

Part I

*

Malta was a transplant from Florida. Her husband had
beaten her up so many times that one day, she flattened
his tires and hitchhiked with a trucker named Greg who
drove up I-95 at all hours, keeping himself awake with
large cups of coffee. He joked that when he stared into
that black abyss and felt the steam rising to his lips, he'd
imagine the night he'd have to face for 8 hours straight
and that, if one day, he suddenly dozed off, he wouldn't
know the difference if he drove straight into hell.
Wouldn't it look and feel about the same? That was a
comforting thought, he said, a feckless laugh emanating
from his throat.

At night she'd lie in the back of the truck, flipping
through issues of *Reader's Digest* that were borrowed
from her local library on her iPad. How could she stick it
out in Florida so long, she thought, when there were so
many intelligent people up North? One woman wrote
about the Christmas she had with her Jewish daughter-in-
law, putting up Christmas stockings with her while they
had the Menorah on their table. Plenty of Jews lived in
Florida but she'd never known a single one who'd
advertised their Judaism. She didn't know why since no
one seemed to give a shit one way or another, but that

was that. Looked like up North people could be what they wanted to be, without retards constantly harassing them to be another way, or suing them for no reason.

When she felt tired she closed her eyes and listened to the sounds of Greg fucking a hooker in the front seat, wondering if he'd slit her throat as she was coming. She imagined the blood squirting straight into his mouth, and him swallowing the hot curd, and she licked her lips and rubbed her pussy, wondering why she was so sick and twisted, why she wanted him to kill her. Or maybe she didn't. Maybe she just remembered it from some porn story she had read online, and in her confusion and loneliness she was dredging up the last remnants of imagination from her former life.

He'd sleep next to her sometimes, in the wide back filled with boxes smelling of disinfectant, because that's apparently, among other things, what he transported wholesale. He'd breathe in her ear, telling her about the products he'd sniff back there when he couldn't find a hooker on the roadsides. She would laugh and tell him to get a life, until one day, he took out a picture of a young girl holding a small kid, and said that was his girlfriend.

"She's 19 years old and I got the pictures to prove it."

"She know you're getting down with the hookers off the road?"

"What she fucking care? I come back to her don't I? I give her the money for the baby, don't I?"

You're giving her diseases, she thought, and pushed him, laughing. He chuckled to himself, thinking about fucking his 19 year old goddess, while she stared at the stubble on his cheek, remembering how she thought Matt Melidos's stubble was sexy too when she let him fuck her on the football field when she was 16.

One day she was coming back from a McDonalds at a road stop and she overheard Greg on the phone.

"What do you mean you lost your job? You think

what I'm bringing in here is enough?" He paused. "Yeah, you better believe you're gonna pay when I get back. But I'm thinking of Gerry. I'll make the money all right. I got a money-making machine right here."

One night, in the trailer off the road, she woke up to find Greg on top of her. Naturally she resisted a bit, but she wasn't too surprised; she knew it was coming sooner or later, so she let him do it, because it was easier than resisting, and why not, it was fun, wasn't it? His rough stubble against his face, his strong hands holding down her wrists, his hefty body on top of hers, having his way. It was pretty sexy, his big dick inside her, even when she wasn't wet. Except she cried afterwards as he smoked, his eyes dead to her wounds. But crying had nothing to do with him, she thought.

In North Carolina Greg paid for a motel room and, as soon as he got her inside, took her by the throat and threw her on the bed.

"Don't think this transport is free, do you? Gerry's gotta eat."

"You gonna rape me again?"

"Wasn't no rape. You wanted it. I could tell. But you don't gotta fuck me no more. I already had that. You gotta ride the brothers now. They pay you, you pay me. Don't worry, I'll feed you. I'm no animal."

"Fucking turd," she said, kicking him. He laughed.

"I know you like it, bitch. Don't be lying to me, or yourself. Now you get some sleep. I'm gonna set up an account. Then get ready to take some pics."

"I'd rather read."

"Suit yourself. I've got some lingerie in the bag over there, so look it over when you're ready."

He set up the laptop on the only table in the room, and got to work. Meanwhile she chucked the bag into the bathroom, and asked him if she could get some ice from the front office.

"You kidding? Why, so you could run away? You're the only meal ticket I got. I ain't letting no other fucker take the cash."

She started smoking one of his cigarettes and tapping her knee, waiting. Then she turned on the TV and started watching a Bible lecture.

"Shit, *Craigslist* works fast," he said. "I don't even know what town this is, and already we got customers."

It went on like that, town after town. Sometimes they stayed a little longer in some places if cash was rolling in and Greg didn't get the feeling the motel owner, always an Indian, wasn't too suspicious, or if he had a look in his eye that he cared. Usually, Indians liked the money. They didn't give a shit about the fucking around if it wasn't too conspicuous. Sometimes, as Greg smoked a cigarette on the sidewalk, the kid watching the desk would come by and ask if everything was okay.

Greg always smoothed the shit with him, talking about the Tar Heels, or any particular university's b-ball team, and usually that diced it. Didn't matter if the night guy was white, Indian, or other, he always had the right words. Still, that was often a sign to move on. No doubt everyone knew the deal, because Greg would always ask for the side of the motel for the local blacks. If the town was racially diverse, no question the motel owner, if he had a light on in his brain, would segregate the motel, because the local blacks came frequently to fuck their mistresses or bring girls home from the bars, while the white truckers and local families just wanted some clean fun or jacuzzi vacs. So if he was a white guy with a white bitch, no question he wasn't there with this wife, and black guys were always coming in and out of the room, a sign in itself.

But sometimes the clients weren't black. If they were driving through a white town, no doubt you'd get plenty of red-faced hicks drinking bourbon and wanting to beat on a woman. Sometimes you got a sweety-pie, but usually he'd be rough. She actually preferred the black guys, because even though they liked the corruption of being with a white bitch, they were straightforward and not too rough, except for the preacher who gripped his bible and yelled "Hallelujah!" while he fondled her in the dark, only to freak out and punch her in the stomach after he accidentally came in her mouth. Greg had to charge in and beat him good, otherwise Malta would have finished him herself, scratching him to death. Turns out they had to leave that town too when the preacher returned the next day, all black and blue, getting on his knees and praying for forgiveness outside the motel room, in the daylight as the cleaning ladies, all fat black women, rolled by, laughing and gossiping with each other. It could have meant death for his business and maybe a jail sentence for both of them if they hadn't checked out and fled as soon as possible.

And then there were the white college students...

Because of the preacher incident and a few others, Greg and Malta started getting along. What else could she do but play ball, and he'd actually give her some of the proceeds too. She even explained to him why she got so freaked out when the preacher had punched her—it reminded her of the time her husband in Florida had done the same when she was pregnant, forcing her to miscarry. In fact, she started counting out the times men had abused her over the years—her various boyfriends, her husband etc.—she was 30 now but the memories still hurt. She went on and on, and even began relating some stories she'd read in *Reader's Digest* that helped her cope, until Greg told her to shut up or he'd rape her again.

But he began trusting her enough, and figured it would be good to keep her mind and body fresh, to let her go out and get some ice from the office. At one of the motels in a college town named Brownston, the desk was often staffed by the Indian-American son of the owner, who was a student at the local university. His name was Kunal Shah. He was brawnier than most Indians she'd met or seen, so she was intrigued by him. She offered him a cheerful hello and tried to engage him in some flirtatious banter. He seemed somewhat official at first, not wanting to engage too much with the white hick clientele, but he became friendlier as she came by more.

"You're a cutie pie," she told him.

"Thanks. You're not bad yourself."

"You mean for an older woman? I'm gonna corrupt you, young man."

"You don't look that old."

"I'm not. But you're what? 20?"

"Almost 21."

"Good age to be. I wish my husband would let me go out more. He's so jealous and protective."

Kunal laughed. "Yeah, I can't judge. So how old are you?"

"Add a decade. But you're not supposed to ask a girl her age."

Kunal closed his eyes. "Sorry, I forgot."

"Especially a young southern belle. Just kidding, I'm 28. You know Kunal, I've read the Kama Sutra. I know what Indians are all about."

"Not these days."

"No, you're business people now. Forced to be by this country. Oh well. So much promise, wasted."

Kunal enjoyed flirting with a MILF, but since he believed she was married, he didn't think much was possible beyond that. He tried to block her out of his mind, but he couldn't. He would think about her in class and on campus, and on his shifts. And Malta began to form ideas too. Business was going well for Greg, they didn't have the black-white issue in this town since their clientele was mostly white college kids. They blended in and the money continued to roll so they decided to stay longer.

But when Malta broached the subject of going out and spending some of her money, Greg balked.

"Are you crazy?" Greg asked, tipsy on bourbon— Malta had noticed that he was a bit more liberal until he got totally plastered.

"I'm getting worn out, Greg. The guys are starting to complain. Give me some air."

"Then we'll move to a different town. Not like we got a Yelp page or nothing. No one's writing reviews."

"It might end up like that preacher. Except the cops'll come this time."

"Bullshit. You want me to let you go out on the town so you can escape? Go to the fucking police yourself? Ain't that candy-colored Indian in that office enough for you?"

"Why don't I just tell him then?"

"He's a young buck, ain't he? I'm sure he'd rather join the party."

"Fuck you, you fucking turd," she said, spitting at him. He slapped her and she hit the bed hard. He picked her up by her hair.

"Now you fucking remember who your benefactor is,

bitch. You clean up and go get some ice for that pretty face. And don't you try nothing, or I'll find you, and I'll kill you too."

When he saw Malta through the glass window Kunal was happy. She didn't enter the lobby but, as usual, went through the alternate door into the little area that held the ice machine. Kunal, from behind the desk, moved to his right so he could see her through the bullet-proof night reception glass.

"It's been a while, Malta. Been out?" Kunal asked. She had told him her real name by accident.

"More like in," Malta said. She pressed the button for the ice machine. It roared but nothing spit out.

"Hold on," Kunal said, "I'll come around." Despite her protestation he came around the desk and entered the ice machine area. He pushed the button and held it down. The machine roared and finally pushed out some ice.

"You've gotta be firm with it," he said. "I guess that's with a lot of things in life, right?" She began scooping out the ice and pouring it into the bucket. Now Kunal saw the outlines of the bruises and scratches on her face beneath her makeup.

"What happened? Your husband did that?"

"Please don't ask," Malta said.

"We've got 911 on speed-dial," Kunal said. "I'll get on it."

He turned but Malta grabbed his shoulder.

"We'll be out of here in a couple of days," Malta said. "There's no point."

"You must be joking, right?" Kunal asked, genuinely shocked.

"It's okay. He goes haywire sometimes, that's all."

"I can't believe you're okay with that."

"I did something bad, Kunal, it's okay. He's a good man, really." She stared at him for a while, and began to rub his chest. He was nervous, and wasn't sure how he should react. He reached over to kiss her but she pulled away and headed for the door.

"Thanks for the ice," she said, and she was gone.

Kunal watched her disappear into her room from the security camera, her husband coming out briefly, leading her in, looking around, closing the door. He normally didn't even pay attention to the cameras, because he didn't work nights and those were the usual times that trouble arose, if there was any.

It was pretty rare here. His father had been blessed with a good location. He'd heard horror stories from other owners who worked in ghetto areas of nearby Wintertown, of constant drug abuse and prostitution, but they didn't have such problems here in Brownston. An abusive husband was the worst he'd seen. He checked the name her husband had registered: Gregory Madsen. He wondered if he should call the cops anyway, but he decided to respect her wishes. He didn't even know her name, if she had one.

University Bar was where the college football gang hung out. Kunal was the starting center on their Division I team, his friend Todd the Quarterback.

The bar wasn't busier than usual. The normal crowd of loud, drunken football players and girls with blonde

150

highlights wearing cheerleader outfits, the obscene smell of spilled Coors and urine emanating from the bathroom, the fools playing beer-pong and doing shots on the edge of the pool-table.

Kunal and Todd sat at a table, drinking beers.

"Lots of honeys out tonight," Todd said.

"Don't see more than the usual," Kunal answered, fingering his Sam Adams.

"What the fuck is wrong with you? Usually you can't lay off."

"I'm thinking about a special girl."

"That's news. I thought you were dreaming about that chop-block you put on Fieldston."

Kunal closed his eyes. "That was sweet."

"Yeah, you know what's gonna be sweeter than that? That Turkey-shoot this weekend. I'm telling you, it'll be the shit."

"Sure, I'd love to drive through hick country. And on a Meal Day? Fuck that."

"You'll be with me, nothing'll happen. You'll be one of the boys."

"I doubt that. I think you forget the color of my skin."

"At least you're not black, dude." He pointed. "Not like this guy."

Thomas, one of their offensive tackles, approached from the bar.

"Am I the subject of conversation?" Thomas lisped with mock elevation.

"Kunal here thinks he'll get lynched on Meal Day."

"Of course he will, man. Fucking confederate flags waving, trailer park rednecks, mountain hicks. What the fuck you think will happen?"

"Redneck's a term of respect. Of lifestyle choice."

"Whatever farm boy. We know you're from Podunk, Carolina."

"All I'm saying is, how we're gonna integrate unless I

151

bring a guy like Kunal to a Turkey-shoot?"

"Would you bring me?" Thomas asked.

"Fuck no. You'll get lynched."

Todd and Thomas laughed. Kunal chugged his Sam Adams.

"Man, is that Argentinian kid Fernandez still rooming with you?" Todd asked. "I wanna ask him to help me with math again."

"You can ask. He's with Crystal now and far as I can tell, they just smoke weed and fuck all day. I haven't seen him in class in months."

"As if you're ever there either. These foreign kids get one taste of the ganja and they're hooked."

"I say it's that American pussy. That white pussy."

"Keep dreaming, Thomas. Maybe one day it'll fall into your lap. Meanwhile our friend here's got pussy on his mind. I imagine it's white. Usually is."

"Who? That bitch Veronica?"

"No one from this school," Kunal said.

"Someone from outside?" Thomas asked. "What, you ran into her on the road or something?"

"Knowing this guy," Todd cut in, "he probably put his dick out the window and told her it was chocolate."

"Certainly looks like it," Thomas commented.

"Why, you've seen it?" Todd asked.

"Fuck off, dickhead."

"I'm talking about yours, dummy."

"She's blonde. She's white. She tells me she's 28 but who knows," Kunal blurted out as he stared at the small TV above the bar, showing a college football game from Tennessee.

"Fucking MILF," Thomas yelled, raising his glass. "I wanna get me some of that too."

"Seriously, where the hell'd you meet this chick?" Todd asked.

Suddenly, Kunal's eyes diverted from the TV to a

figure who was pacing awkwardly around the bar.

"Hold up, man," Kunal said, putting his bottle on the table. "I think I know that dude."

Thomas squinted. "Nah, you're dreaming."

"Yeah, he's staying in my motel. I don't know what he's doing at a college bar."

"Everyone's gotta drink," Thomas said. "I'll be back."

Kunal watched Thomas go over to the bar, then slip into the bathroom. He looked back for the figure but he was gone.

"Where'd he go?"

Todd was texting someone on his Iphone.

"What?" he asked.

"Never mind."

Kunal stood up and marched towards the door. A couple of cheerleaders ran into him, grabbed his hand, and tried to pull him over to the pool table.

"Later, girls," Kunal said.

"Come on, K, we need a tackle."

"I play center," Kunal replied.

"Even better," the girls giggled. But they saw Kunal's look and let go. When Kunal opened the door and peeked outside, he only saw a couple of his teammates smoking.

He charged back to the bar. He didn't see the figure there either.

"Want another beer, K?" the bartender called, but Kunal ignored him and rushed back to Todd.

"You see where he went?"

"Who, bro?"

"That fucking old guy."

"I don't know. Channing's messaging me, man. You think I care about fucking—"

"That's her husband you—" Kunal turned and saw Greg leaving the bar and a black man following him.

"Fuck," Kunal said.

153

"I've gotta admit, this beats a Turkey-shoot any day."

"Shut up," Kunal said, gazing intently through Todd's Iphone at Greg smoking a cigarette outside his motel room.

"Who'd of thought? I figured Thomas would give us a tip, so we could get in on it..."

"Are you kidding?"

"Yeah, you're right. I read somewhere hookers don't like more than one guy at one time."

"We don't even know that's what's going on. Maybe he's buying dope."

"How long's he been in there? No way a dope sale takes that long. Unless they're old friends."

"My ass."

"If this was Podunk, trust me, there'd be a lynching going on right now."

"Will you shut the fuck up?"

The door opened and Thomas emerged. Greg looked back, nodded vaguely at him, took a couple of puffs, then threw his cigarette down and ground it. He moved back to the door. Kunal saw Malta briefly as Greg opened the door and slipped inside.

Meanwhile Thomas rushed to his car and turned on the ignition.

"Which way? Track down Thomas to get the dirt, or go save your girlfriend? Or call the cops?"

"All I have is this Iphone video of a guy coming out of a motel room. And I don't want to get her in trouble before I know the facts."

"And Thomas?"

"We'll deal with him later," Kunal said, giving Todd his phone.

"Can't blame a fellow for getting some tail. I would

have gone younger, personally."

"I'm canceling on that Turkey-shoot, Todd," Kunal said, returning to the wheel. "But hold onto that video. We might need it."

"No problem," Todd replied.

"A black guy, in this town? Are you kidding?" Malta asked Greg as he counted the money.

"They pay, they play. But it's a sign. We should get going."

"Where? New York? I've always wanted to go there. Let's just go straight up."

"I was actually thinking Tennessee. There's money up north, but more risk too. And rent."

"When I got in your truck, Greg, you told me we'd be headed to New York."

"Since when do you get a vote, bitch?"

Greg noticed an expression on Malta's face he hadn't seen before. So when she leapt, he was ready for it, and she met the back of his hand.

"End of discussion," he said.

Kunal asked the night guy, Phillip, to take a breather while he manned the desk. Phillip was an old, reliable worker, dedicated to Kunal's father, and he was taken aback by Kunal's request. But Kunal was firm, and asked Phillip to come back in a couple of hours. He offered Phillip the chance to sleep in their apartment but Phillip declined, saying he'd drive home and come back.

Once Phillip was gone, Kunal monitored the security

155

camera. Finally, after forty-five minutes passed, he saw her come out.

He was ready as she entered the ice machine room.

"I know he's selling you," Kunal told her, grabbing her forearm as she tried to grip the ladle for the ice.

"How?" she asked.

"Just tell me, is it by force, or do you want to? By the bruise on your face..."

"That figures it for you, Sherlock?"

"Come inside my house. I'll call the police."

"They'll arrest both of us."

"Not if you were forced."

"You're so naïve, honey. Once you're a woman of the night, your life is over. People always put that sticker on you."

"But today..."

"Especially today."

"So what? You're gonna let him keep selling you?"

Malta swallowed. "No. But you can hide me until he goes away."

Kunal was shaking his head.

"What? Why not?"

"I can't. My parents won't like it."

"You can tell them what happened. Will they blab?"

"You never know with the Indian community here. It's absurdly conservative. My mom or aunt might be on the phone within the hour, telling someone else."

"So I'm screwed," she concluded. Kunal could see the tears in her eyes.

"Don't worry," Kunal told her, rubbing her shoulder, "you're safe with me. Come on."

When the front door to the motel opened suddenly,

Kunal could sense it was Greg. He smelled the cigarette smoke while he looked through some papers, his back to the desk.

"Guy, you seen my wife?"

He kept rummaging through the papers.

"She was here getting ice," he finally responded, turning halfway around. "Then she left."

Greg's eyes went wide. He turned and looked out the window.

"You see where she went?"

Kunal shook his head. "Nope," he replied.

"You see her cross the street?" Greg asked, nervously. "There's a store with some candy over there."

"Maybe she wanted to get a mink coat from Sears," Kunal suggested.

Greg was so nervous he missed the jab.

"Fuck," Greg said.

"Everything okay, sir?"

Greg rushed out without saying anything. Outside, with his hands on his hips, he stared across the highway.

The next morning, Kunal called Todd's dorm room, but only got his answering machine. When he tried his cell, it was off.

"Just checking in," Kunal said on the voicemail.

He went running with Jacob, a tailback on the team who was much faster than Kunal. One time he came all around the track and back to Kunal.

"Shah, you better be quicker than that when blocking against A&M," he said.

"I got Fieldston on that drive, didn't I? Cleared the way for 75, motherfucker."

"I gotta admit, the way you played that was brilliant.

I'm amazed they didn't throw the flag. But fuck, that was one play, Shah. You gotta be consistent."

"We won, didn't we?"

"Yeah, barely. Without my running..."

"Todd threw the touchdown pass."

"Yeah. But my score made the difference."

"Us..."

"How many times did Todd get sacked? You lucky he slaps your ass, otherwise he'd be blaming you."

"You see how I pull on the wing on The Draw 35? I don't know why you're giving me shit. Blame Thomas for the sacks. It's usually coming from his end."

Jacob slapped the top of Kunal's head. "I'm fucking with you, man. You gotta get a sense of humor."

When Kunal returned to his apartment, he showered and sat down at his dining table to eat his mother's *powa-battaka*. While he squeezed a lime and watched the juice spray onto it, his mother placed some sweet tea next to him, then hovered over his shoulder, massaging a napkin and pondering Kunal's Johnny Unitas cut.

Sensing her gaze, Kunal looked over his shoulder at her.

"What?" he asked.

"You know Ami? Pranavbhai's daughter?"

"Of course. I sat across from her at temple every day. I think I'd remember her."

"She goes to North Carolina State."

"Okay..."

Kunal's mother chuckled.

"What's so funny?" he asked.

"I remember you playing Hanuman and Ami pulling your tale as Sita. It was funny."

"That was sixth grade, mummy. What's up now?"

"Well, the fall break is coming, *dikra*. And I thought since both of you are here..."

"I'm going to A&M for a game, mummy."

"Not the whole week, *dikra*. Just a weekend. But she will be here the whole week."

"Wasn't she into business? I study engineering. And football."

"You must think now. I know it is early..."

"Too early. There are girls at school, mummy."

Kunal's mother made a sharp face and fashioned her claws.

"White girls," she muttered under her breath.

"And anyway, I thought you didn't want me to be distracted from my studies."

"This is important. Whatever career you follow, you will need a girl by your side."

"I'm not taking over the motel, mummy."

"If you become an engineer..."

"Football player?"

She rolled her eyes. "Only blacks become football players, Kunal. I told you, no other Indian parents would have even let you tryout, let alone be on your high school team."

"It's college now, ma. I'm one step away."

"I am letting you know, Kunal, that is all. If you don't want to talk to Ami, don't talk." Kunal began repeating her words under his breath, mockingly. She slapped him on the back of the head with the napkin.

"Idiot," she said in Gujarati. She moved into the kitchen while he finished his *powa-battaka* as quickly as possible.

"There will be a house party at Jayeshuncle's house," she said. "So you will see her."

Kunal cursed under his breath.

He rushed into the front office, where his father was counting some money.

"Kunal, did you finish counting the money last night before Phillip came?"

Kunal slapped himself on the forehead.

"I'm sorry, Daddy," Kunal said. "I lost track."

"Lost track? You are lucky Phillip has been working with us for a while. If it was one of this white trash they would have run away with it. Better than minimum wage, right?"

"I'm sorry, Daddy. It won't happen again."

"In business, you take your eye off the ball once, you can lose everything. Look at that idiot Bush."

"He didn't lose anything."

"Eh. Yes, different story. But you know what I mean."

"Don't worry, it won't happen again," Kunal repeated as he checked the security footage and saw Malta's room locked. He peered into the cubbyhole for Greg's room, and saw the key inside.

"That couple left?" Kunal asked.

"What couple? Are you trying to change the subject, Kunal?"

"No, I just...thought they were staying more nights."

"Fifteen minutes ago this white trash comes in sweating. He says he needs to go, so I let him go. I don't know why we let his kind stay so long."

"Daddy, I have got to go out. I'll be back for the afternoon shift."

"Where are you going, Kunal? To Church?"

Kunal laughed. "I think they already let out, Daddy."

He knocked on Todd's door a few times. Then he remembered the Turkey-shoot.

"Fuck," Kunal said. He went over to Jacob's room.

"You know if Ron's around?"

"He's away for the weekend, man. He's back tonight. Same with Todd. I thought you knew."

"You know anyone else who can open Todd's door?"

"Why? You left some jewelry in there or something?"

Kunal rolled his eyes and stomped down the hallway. He found Thomas' room and noticed him on his bed, scrolling through his Ipod. Fernandez was asleep.

Kunal's entire frame encompassed the doorway, his massive arms serving as anchors for his body.

"Bro," Kunal called out, addressing Thomas, "you notice anything interesting last night?"

Thomas looked up. "Oh hey, what's up, Kunal?" he said. He shook his head. "Nah, same old drunken bar shit. What do you mean?"

"Like maybe you saw the same girl twice."

"What girl?"

"Blonde girl. MILF. My girl."

Thomas scowled.

"What the fuck are you talking about, Kunal? I ain't going after no girl of yours."

Kunal charged in. "Don't give me shit, asshole. You know you paid for that cunt."

Thomas seemed confused. He put down his Ipod just as Kunal jumped him and put his head in a choke hold.

"What the fuck? This is bullshit, dude!" he screamed.

"You know he forced her to do it? You didn't care, did you?"

Thomas could barely get a sound out as he struggled to loosen Kunal's arms with his hands.

"Todd and me saw you," Kunal said. "Just admit it."

Fernandez woke up and complained about the noise.

"Get your white bitch, pussy, before I do the same to you," Kunal screamed. Fernandez said nothing, stunned at what he was seeing.

Kunal loosened his hold. Thomas coughed.

"You got anything to say, punk?" Kunal asked.

"Look, don't tell me you never did nothing like that," Thomas said. "I bet you have."

Jacob and a few other guys were in the hallway now, some watching, some laughing, others shocked.

"Everything alright?" Jacob asked, vaguely bemused.

"Just tell me, did you see her last night?" Kunal asked. "In Todd's room? In the hallway? The bathroom?"

"Why would I see her here, Kunal?"

"You remember what she looked like, right? Check that, yeah, you probably don't."

"I don't know what you're talking about, dude. Why would she be in here?"

"When did Todd leave this morning, Thomas?"

"I don't track his schedule, man."

"You know where his uncle's trailer is?"

"Out in boon country. You know that."

"We're going. Me and you."

"You kidding?" Kunal tightened his hold and Thomas began slapping his arm. Kunal let go again and Thomas coughed.

"You know where Monroe is right?" Kunal asked.

Thomas coughed for a little longer.

"Right?"

"Yeah, but we'll have to ask around for the trailer."

"Guess that's what we're going to do then, partner," Kunal said, releasing his grip, then shoving Thomas onto the bed.

"Black man and brown boy driving through Meal Day, Carolina. We're definitely gonna get lynched, bro."

"Tell me what you did with her," Kunal said.

"Why? To atone or to give you a hard-on?"

"Fuck you."

"Yeah, fuck me. We both had a good time, alright. I treat my women with respect. I didn't realize she had a gun to her head. I asked her and she said she does it willingly."

"Well, she didn't."

"Most of them do. I know finance. It's always about the cash."

"I don't know anything about that."

"Bullshit, boy."

"Who you calling boy?"

They drove past the trailers. The confederate flags were waving and the girls with their ripped t-shirts and their paper plates with barbecued chicken smeared on them were strolling past, and the bearded men pulled up their pants. Kunal noticed some stares as he drove past, but he tried to avoid them.

"A sea of white," Thomas said. "This is what Todd wanted to take you through?"

"What's wrong with that? What are we, ethnic?"

"We've both got white girls, right?" Thomas said.

Kunal glanced at Thomas before the punch flew. But Thomas grabbed Kunal's arm and pulled it towards him. Kunal turned the wheel and the car headed into the field. A couple of men jumped out of the way as the car hurled toward a girl sitting at a table. She stood up. Kunal hit the brake right before the car struck the table.

"Fuck!" Thomas screamed. Kunal stared at the girl, whose eyes betrayed a mixture of terror and exhilaration. All around him, he saw white faces and bodies approach.

Without hesitating, Kunal backed up, swerved to the left and up the highway. He could hear screams of people telling him to stop but he kept driving. A few more guys ran out of the way. Kunal yelled aloud for dear life. He kept driving.

A few miles away they stopped at one of the roadside shacks selling trinkets. The same hag seemed to inhabit all of them. She wore a torn white t-shirt and sweatpants today.

"Look, ya'll gonna buy something or aren't ya?" she asked, slowly walking out onto the road.

"We're gonna get going. Thanks," Kunal responded under his breath.

"That was some shit," Thomas said. "Hope a cop car doesn't come. White people usually do call the cops."

"Those losers aren't calling the cops. Still, we should get moving."

Kunal turned to the woman, who now had a light in her eye.

"Ya'll in trouble with the law?" she asked. "I can call my cousin and he can fix it, no problem. He deals with all kinds of people. Good rates too."

"That's okay, ma'am," Kunal said. "We're riding solo. Just tell us which way's Monroe."

"All these trailers look the same," Thomas said.

Kunal asked one of the kids who'd stopped playing catch to stare at them which way the Winterfield's trailer was.

He pointed across the field to a selection of three.

"Which one?" Kunal asked, but the boy shrugged.

"We can play rock-paper-scissors," Thomas said.

Kunal noticed he was shaking a bit.

"Nervous?"

"Too many poor white people. Good thing we didn't run over any of them."

They walked over to the three trailers. An old woman sat on the dirt ground between them, positioned across folded laundry that was arranged like a shrine on top of a thin cloth. She sewed a Carolina Panther sweatshirt that rested on her lap.

"You know where the Winterfield's trailer is, ma'am?" Kunal asked.

She pointed back with her needle to the trailer on the left. "That's Jed's right there. What you fellas want?"

"We'll talk to Jed about that."

"His business is my business in these parts."

"We wanna hear about the Turkey-shoot. We couldn't make it out."

"He invited you boys?"

"His nephew Todd. We go to school with him."

"Oh, so you're on the football team, aren't ya? A colorful bunch you are. Well, I don't think it'll be too long before he comes back to the nest. Why don't you grab some chairs from around and I can tell you about the old times while we wait."

Kunal wanted to make an excuse to get out of it but Thomas elbowed him, chuckling.

"This'll protect us until they come," he reasoned. "Friends with an old white lady."

"Don't be too sure. In hick country, you never know."

They got some chairs and sat down as Rose, she called herself, spoke about back when she was the daughter of a tobacco farmer a few towns west until her father caught her one day with a hillbilly and beat her senseless. It didn't knock out the baby, though, and she had to still live at home until another hillbilly got enough

165

money together to marry her. Despite the odds she raised that baby and a couple more too. None of them went to college but they did become truckers.

"I tell you, more Northerners are moving down here, the professionals they call 'em, but they ain't never be South. Boy, where you from?" she asked Thomas.

"Town called Redville, just east of Greenville."

"That's good country too. You're true South, boy. But Greenville's been controlled now. That Johnson built that center and now Jew doctors from the North live there."

"I think you mean Jordan," Thomas said.

"Yes, him. That basketball player. You win a million dollars for nothing and think you're a big shot. Boy, see you'll never fall into that trap."

"No, ma'am," Thomas said, laughing.

"Now you, you own a motel, don't you?"

"Yes, I do," Kunal said. "How'd you know?"

"All you Indians own every damn motel and gas station around, I know. Well, at least you speak English."

Kunal laughed. "I'm sorry," she said, "I don't mean to sound unwelcoming. Are you born in Carolina?"

"Yes, ma'am."

"That's good. Now look, I'm not like these others, just cussing and hoping Charlie Daniels comes through and going to the square dances and driving in mud-circles. I understand things are changing. Hell, they done changed and even these parts will change eventually. That Senator of ours talks about bringing the internet everywhere and everyone'll be connected. Well, fellas in the mountains will never understand none of that, and even most folks here won't understand that either. But some folks will, and those will count. I was even telling that nice girl was here about how she could change her life if she just got some internet. I wish I had some."

"Nice girl?" Kunal asked.

"Yes, this pretty little blonde. She was staying with

the Winterfield's, in fact."

"She didn't go to the Turkey-shoot?"

"With those rugged boys? 'Course not. She was out here sewing with me. She shook a lot, that one. One of those legs wouldn't stop twitching, talking about how she wanted to go back to the city and how she couldn't stand it out here. And then that Jessup boy from up in the mountains come down, and she got to talking with him. I told her to watch out for him, but then she got in that truck..."

"Truck? What truck?" Kunal asked.

"Why do you ask, honey? You know this girl?"

Kunal shook his head. He stood up nervously and his mind began to race. He saw the sun was finally setting against the distant mountains and realized he might have to go up there to look for her.

But then he heard a voice behind him. He turned to see three men. One, unshaven, stood in the middle of the group holding a shovel over his shoulder.

"This boy giving you trouble, Rose?" he asked her.

"No, these are nice boys. They're Todd's friends from the football team."

"Ah," the man said, smiling now and reaching out his hand. "I threw around the football with old Todd myself, back when I thought I was good."

Kunal shook his hand. The man's grip was too tight. Then it got tighter. But Kunal's hand was bigger, and he crushed it.

The man yelled out. Kunal released.

"What the fuck'd you do that for, you fucking ape?"

"You squeezed my hand first," Kunal said, firmly.

"Now, now, no trouble," Rose commanded as she got up, but Kunal noticed she had a gleam in her eye.

"I didn't fight for this country to get fucked here by some sand nigger," one of the other men said.

Kunal raised his fists, ready for a fight. He sensed

Thomas shaking behind him. Then he heard Todd's voice call out.

"Guys, you came a little late," he said. Kunal turned to see him strutting up, with two older men behind him, shotguns to their sides.

"Todd, your nigger friends here better watch it."

"That's wrong with you, Shawn?" Todd asked.

"They better be Christians, is all I'm saying," Shawn responded, still shaking his hand.

"Kunal, you do something?" Todd inquired, while his uncles brought their shotguns to the ready.

"He tried to be a wise-ass and squeezed my hand," Kunal explained. "So I squeezed harder. That's all."

"That right, Shawn?"

"I didn't squeeze tight. I was just trying to be friendly to some football guys."

"Alright," Todd said. He placed his hand on Kunal's shoulder. "Let's get you guys out of here. Just a friendly misunderstanding, that's all. No big deal."

Shawn nodded, gave Kunal a final glare, then backed away. "I'll be seeing you around, sand nigger," the other one said. "My name's Mitchell. You remember that."

Rose giggled uncontrollably as Todd led Kunal and Thomas into his trailer.

When they were inside the trailer, Todd made sure his uncles were standing guard and then he locked it tight. When he turned around, Kunal noticed Todd's face had turned beat red.

"What's wrong with you? They're friends but they're trigger-happy like anyone. Even I'm not dumb enough to do that."

"I didn't know who they were," Kunal responded. "I

was just defending myself."

"Defending yourself out here can end your life, bro. Without a badge you're nothing but potential meat. I thought you'd figured that out."

"Sorry."

"I knew that, Todd," Thomas butt in. "That's why I didn't wanna come out."

"So why did you guys come out? When I offered you weren't exactly interested."

"You know why, Todd," Kunal said. "Or at least you should. Maybe you forgot."

Todd seemed confused.

"The girl, you moron," Kunal scolded. "I told you to look after her."

"Oh," Todd said after a brief pause, closing his eyes.

"Instead you brought her to this dump. And then you lost her."

"I told you a week ago about the Turkey-shoot. It just slipped my mind last night when you brought her over."

"You could have left her in the dorm."

"I didn't think, okay? Anyway, this dickhead was over there," he said, pointing at Thomas. "Why'd you bring him here? Redemption?"

"I didn't exactly have a choice," Thomas said, glaring at Kunal. "Look, I said I was sorry for sleeping with her."

"Kunal, honestly, she kinda seemed like trailer trash," Todd said. "So I figured she'd be at home here 'til I got back."

"Well she wasn't," Kunal insisted, balling his fist. He was so incensed his eyes watered and he felt a tear run down his cheek. He wanted to punch Todd, but he held back. "In fact, why am I talking about her in the past tense? She's not trailer trash. She's a human being. She's been abused. She needs our help. And what the fuck are you? A country-club Republican?"

"I'm a redneck, alright? That's a lifestyle choice. My

uncles, they might live with the trash, but they ain't trash themselves. They're good men."

"Whatever. Define shit however you please. I wanna make sure that girl is safe, that she hasn't been kidnapped by some other pimp punk."

Todd stepped up to him.

"So what, Kunal, are you telling me you don't want to fuck her too?"

This time Kunal couldn't hold back, and Todd went reeling from his fist. Thomas had to hold Kunal.

"Asshole," Todd said, holding his jaw. "You're lucky my uncles are outside. Otherwise..."

"Otherwise, what? You'll call them in to do a redneck scum job?"

Todd shook his head. "Oh, so the motel-working dirty immigrant wants to hold the high horse..."

"I'm no immigrant, asshole. I'm born on this soil, just like you."

Todd laughed. "You'll always be what you are, dude. No more, no less."

"And what are you, redneck?"

"An American. That's what I am," Todd said, pointing at his chest furiously.

Kunal stared a long time at Todd, breathing heavily. Then put his palms up in surrender. Thomas relaxed his grip on Kunal's shoulder.

"Yeah, well, be an American, and help me find this Jessup character," Kunal said.

Todd's expression changed. Thomas let Kunal go.

"What about Jessup?" Todd asked.

"That Rose told us she got in a truck with Jessup."

"Oh, fuck," Todd responded, shaking his head.

"Don't tell me he's another pimp."

"He's a hillbilly. I don't know if he's a pimp, but he's worse than trash."

"Great. So let's head to where he lives."

"I don't know where Jessup lives. We'd have to check a large area. None of us go up there. And forget it now, nightfall's come. There aren't even streetlights up there."

Kunal stared at Thomas. "I fucked up, man. I took her away from one lion's den and plopped her in another." He turned back to Todd. "We've gotta call the cops."

"There's a sheriff, Sheriff Picole. I better go myself, in the morning, more likely they'll do something then. But what can we really say? We don't know anything's happened. They might wait 72 hours for her to show up. And you don't even know her real name for sure, Kunal."

"I know she exists," he answered.

A few days later Malta was in Pennsylvania, hiding out on Old Man Sonny's farm. He'd given her the ride up, saying he drove from South to North sometimes just for fun, and sometimes to check out how his fellow tobacco farmers were faring with the decrease in demand. She was suspicious at first of his motives but was desperate enough to take the ride given what she'd escaped, and he seemed a little too old to harm her. He seemed to enjoy her talking about the stories she'd absorbed in *Reader's Digest* and she was delighted when he told her he had a stack of old ones in his barn from the 1980s. When she got there she found them and immediately began to read.

He left to do something and when he returned a few hours later she was scared, but she had armed herself with an ax she'd found inside. Still, he seemed harmless, even laughed gently at her defensiveness. He told her she had the option to stay in the hayloft above the barn or in the house with him. She thought she would still be cautious and take the barn, keeping the ax with her for protection.

She offered to do farm work for him to pay for the keep but he said he didn't need another untrained hand. As long as she needed three meals a day and *Reader's Digest* she was welcome to stay in the barn for free.

She enjoyed living on the farm at first, but soon she got bored of reading and of the bugs and smells of country life. She also had nightmares of Greg coming for her and beating her up—she'd wake up in the total darkness and grasp around for the ax, which was always at hand, and begin wailing, back and forth, until she was convinced nothing was going to harm her. One time when she awoke she was covered in blood. She looked around and realized she'd walked in her sleep and hacked a chicken to death. When Sonny came around he tried to take the ax from her, but she swung wildly at him too, then fell down and cried profusely. Finally she told him what had happened to her, what Greg had done to her, at least. He held her, but when his hand reached for her breast, she pushed him away and grabbed the ax again. He stood with his palms out and begged for his life, insisting he hadn't meant any harm. His quick words had saved his life.

Lying in the dark, Malta began thinking of the bright lights of New York City again, or at least the New York of her mind, filled with runways and beautiful models and talent agents who would compete over her as tall skyscrapers provided the backdrops. She wanted to get somewhere urban at least, but she didn't have a penny to her name. Sonny didn't come around again for a few days —she had to ask the other farmhands to bring her food when she was hungry—then finally she got the courage to go up to the house. He was sitting in the kitchen, a fat cat on his lap.

"You come to apologize?"

"Can you get me to New York City?" she asked.

"Get you there? Sure. But what are you going to do

there? It's not exactly a cheap town to live in."

"Let me borrow some money."

"I'm strapped this season, my darling. I can't afford that." He thought. "But I've got a cousin, Vito, living in Newark. He's fat as this cat and on disability, got no sex drive either, so he's harmless to you. I'll give him a call, see if he doesn't mind taking you in. You can get a job there, make some money, get on your feet, you'll make it to New York City eventually."

"You sure you don't mind?" Malta asked.

"'Course not," he said, letting the cat go. He stood up. "I'd rather you be living here, in my room, but, if things aren't meant to be, then, I guess they aren't."

Malta shook her head. "All you men are the same, I swear. And after all I told you I've been through."

"You can't tell me you didn't enjoy all of that, can you? Can't tell me you didn't enjoy swallowing."

She scowled but she saw his eyes were fiery.

"Well, some of it, maybe." She pushed his chest as he came near. "But not enough for this," she said.

He chuckled. "Why don't you take a knife for the car ride? The ax is a little too big for the city."

He gave her some cash to live off and left her across the state border with his cousin in Newark, New Jersey.

Malta thought cousin Vito was a slob. He left pizza boxes piled up on his living room floor, on the carpet, and lay next to them while watching TV. She preferred walking the streets to staying in the apartment, but after she got followed a few times, she decided to cut back and endure the vulgarity.

She thought of taking a bus and crossing the border into New York. She could settle herself there and maybe become a television actress. First commercials, then the transition to a series. Her husband had always laughed at that, saying she was too old, that they'd take the 18-year-olds but not her. She told him all she had to do was to find the right agent, and he'd set things up for her and she would be golden. Now she thought why not just take the plunge and try to find an agency?

But cousin Vito laughed when she mentioned that, pizza sloshing around in his mouth while he watched Jay Leno. Did she know how high the rents were in New York? She'd have to live in a ghetto worse than this, in a room the size of his closet, and have sketchy roommates, and who knew what their motivations were, and for women? They would kill each other. Given the economy, she'd be lucky to find a retail job, let alone become an actress. He was a postal worker; it used to be the most secure job in America, but now he felt he was federal cut away from extinction.

She told him that was absurd. He asked her to find a job here to pay the rent, then dream of New York. She said fine. She walked the streets, applied at stores and supermarkets, then went on his computer and searched *Craigslist.* She applied for some assistant jobs including house cleaning, homework help, doing laundry—yet she failed to receive a single response. She switched over to *Backpage* and responded to some ads there too, more randomly. Finally she received a response from a writer who wanted a young assistant to help him organize his screenplays. The job paid less than minimum wage.

A couple of days later, she set up a meeting with him. He said he had a lot of applicants but that he was eager to meet her, which set off a bell in her head—she cancelled the meeting by sending him a quick email, and never read his response.

That night she again dreamed of Greg, but this time he didn't abuse her. As she lay in bed, half groggy, he sat next to her and rubbed her head through her hair. He told her he hadn't forced her to sell her body, that it was always in her. Did she not remember how she enjoyed hearing him fucking the other hooker in the front seat, and how she hadn't resisted his initial rape? He'd selected her because he knew she was that type of woman—an adventurer and a fighter, a girl who could change herself at will when the going went tough. Isn't that why she'd left her husband and taken a ride with him in the first place? Hadn't he given her some of the proceeds of their activities? What had happened to them?

When she woke up suddenly she tried to remember what had happened to them. Had she left the money with Greg, or did she have some of it with her? And then she tried to block it out of her mind and asked herself why she was thinking about that money, which she had made on her back?

That afternoon, while searching for jobs, she slipped over to the body rub section of *Backpage*, where women earned about $200 an hour for undefined services. She looked up what that entailed, and read about the specifics of erotic massage. She felt it could be worth doing if she kept it strict. She wouldn't have to do anything that made her uncomfortable or like what she had done before. And anyway, what had been so wrong about it? If Greg hadn't been there, if he hadn't forced the situation, wouldn't she have done the same thing?

As she was thinking about that and what she planned to do, she realized that cousin Vito was standing over her shoulder. He was watching the demonstrations of sensual massage on the computer.

"If that's what you want to do, I've got a safer way,"

he said.

Malta swallowed.

"Oh, I was just looking. It's nothing, just curiosity."

"Look, honey, I know how it goes. I've got another cousin, he's not Sonny. We've got quite the spread in this family. I'll hook you up."

"I swear, she shat on my face, Sheriff, it's no lie."

"I wonder what you did to her that made her do that."

"Nothing, I swear. I was nice to her. Ma was brewing up the tea real good. That's the stuff we got from town."

"So what, she came up behind you, she clobbered you around the neck, got you into the bathroom, took down her pants...God, is that what you expect me to believe?"

"If Ma was here, she'd tell you the same. I'm the last one to admit something like that."

Sheriff Picole glanced back at his deputy, then at Kunal, who was shaking his head. Thomas stood next to him, crossing his arms, while Todd seemed to carefully assess how the Sheriff was acting.

"Yeah, first you swore that she wasn't here at all, 'til I pressed you with that probation," Sheriff Picole said, pushing Jessup on his pecks. "Now you're going on and singing something different. Well, fine, if that's about right, how'd she get out? It's pretty high up here in the woods."

"She stole my truck, Sheriff. I got two."

"I bet you stole that truck first."

Jessup thought.

"I ain't saying where I got it," he said finally.

"Jessup, you're a real good storyteller. So good I'm taking you downtown to tell it. And I'm bringing in a whole crew of diggers. Make sure you don't have that girl buried around here."

"I swear, Sheriff, we ain't that kind of people."

"Just like you aren't the kind of person who would rat on your uncle."

"I did the right thing, Sheriff, like I always do."

"Yup," he responded, putting his arm around Jessup's shoulder. "I'm gonna have a good talk with your ma and your brother when I get back."

"Just don't be telling Jerrie about the shit, now. He won't take it the same as ma."

"Sure, I'll be real discreet."

When the deputy had taken Jessup away, Kunal stood outside the cabin, kicking leaves around, while Thomas pensively paced with his arms still folded. The Sheriff approached Todd.

"In my experience Jessup lies every other sentence," he said. "But I never thought he'd make up something like that."

"What's the likelihood she's alive?" Todd asked.

The Sheriff shook his head. "I honestly don't know. I don't know for a fact Jessup's ever killed anyone, but it wouldn't surprise me if he did. I don't believe his story, or about her driving away in a stolen truck. But I've been surprised before. Won't know for sure until we do some digging. Say, how do you know this girl anyway?"

"Just a friend's friend." Todd pointed at Kunal. "She stayed at his motel."

The Sheriff glared at Kunal, assessing him. "Yeah, I know you Indian folks run a lotta motels," he said finally. "Good, hard-working people."

Kunal swallowed and, avoiding eye contact, kicked a leaf. "I play football for Tech," he said.

The Sheriff smiled and approached Kunal. "Is that right? Never heard of an Indian playing football before. But you're a big fella."

Kunal nodded. "You think Thomas and me can ask

around at some of these cabins?"

The Sheriff shook his head. "I strongly advise you not to do that. This ain't your little college town. We still hear talk about lynchings here. And especially given you're looking for your white girlfriend. A definite no-no."

"She's not my girlfriend," he said.

The Sheriff smacked Kunal on the shoulder.

"Of course not, kid. But you let us do our job."

Todd shrugged. "You don't mind if I ask around?"

Sheriff Picole frowned. "For you? Just be careful."

The club was a few miles outside of Newark. Malta borrowed some money from Vito and took a cab out there. To get to it one had to take a right around a large sign advertising a hotel and drive to the back of a deep parking lot. Its edifice appeared run down but a large sign half-lit by lightbulbs announced *Rizzo's* and the entrance way was ornately done up with a neat desk next to a black curtain. Behind the desk sat a fat girl.

"Yeah?" she asked in a Jersey accent. "What can I do for you?"

Malta peeked at the post-it the cousin had given her.

"I'm here to see Joey," she said.

"He's in the back," the girl said, checking her out. "You looking for a gig?"

"Huh?"

"A job, honey. Or are you some kind of lesbo?" She moved her head like an ancient Egyptian.

"Job," Malta said.

"Jim!" the girl yelled through the curtain. Seconds later a large man appeared wearing a gray, striped suit.

"Yes, what can I do for you?" he asked politely.

"I'm here to see Joey. For a job," Malta added.

178

"You ever strip before? This is all-nude, so you gotta show 'em your coochie. As long as you got something to cover it when you're working the tables, it's alright."

"I thought there was a waitress job?" Malta asked, swallowing.

"Yeah, there's one of those too. That's minimum wage though, only bar tips, and given there's no alcohol here, that's slow in coming. That's why we've got such big turnover in that department. Sometimes the girls'll give you some extra shit, pool together you know, but still, that's rare. You'll make a lot more on the tables and giving dances, believe me. Lot more."

"I just wanna waitress," Malta responded.

Jim shrugged. "Up to you, honey. I'm just giving you the straight dope. You never stripped before?"

"No," Malta said angrily.

"Alright, just wanted to ascertain," he said, giving a sly look to the fat girl. He stretched his arm out and slid open the curtain. "Step this way."

Her heart started racing. She hesitated, then carefully waded through the opening, preparing to be jumped.

She stepped into a dark room lit with low lights. Jim came up behind her. Instead of grabbing her, he passed her and led her forward, past randomly laid out tables and chairs, into a small office in the back, in which a skinny man wearing a polo shirt sat. He had a rat-like face and a skewed nose, only vaguely resembling Vito and Sonny.

"Sit down," he said without looking at her. She sat on a steel folding chair. Jim winked, gave her a playful slap on the shoulder and left, closing the door on his way out.

"So," Joey said, looking through his notes. "You got a resume?"

"Your cousin didn't say to bring one."

He looked up now, into her eyes.

"Vito isn't the brightest bulb. You've gotta bring a resume to a job interview. References or nothing?"

She shrugged. "There's Vito. And Sonny."

"What'd you do for old Sonny? Suck his cock?" Joey laughed to himself. "Don't answer that. I know that old bastard."

Malta swallowed. She felt like getting up and leaving, but she didn't.

"So you want a waitress job," Joey continued. "You got any experience doing that?"

"Yeah. I was a waitress a few years back."

"For how long?"

"A few years."

"Made good tips, eh? Whereabouts?"

"Florida."

Joey nodded with mock pensiveness. "Florida. I like the sun myself. We got the Jersey Shore here, but not a substitute for Miami. You can't believe what you see on TV with those, you know, guidos."

Malta nodded, staring at her knees. She was wearing a skirt.

"Well, I'll tell you, Malta, you ain't gonna make those kinds of tips here. I mean we charge a lot for water but the customers give most of the bills to the dancing girls. That's where the money's at. And it's competitive too. Girls pay a house fee for the nights they work, and it's tough to get in. You've gotta fight for the slots."

Malta swallowed. "How much is the house fee?"

"200 per night. It's flat, not per hour, so make the most of it. I know it sounds like a lot, but you give enough dances, and you'll make it back easy plus some. Aim for the old guys, they're the spenders. Talk 'em into it. Sometimes just getting to know 'em will make you better off in the long run. And if you can get 'em into the VIP booth, you've scored."

"Do you take commission?"

"Lap dance money's all yours. VIP booth we do take 60%. But most clients give tips too. And don't forget the ones you make on the table. Those'll add up. It's a pretty good deal at this place if you ask around. Most of the girls work at other clubs too, so they know *Rizzo's* is the best." He tapped his pen. "So what do you say? Want me to check the calendar and see if I can fit you in?"

Malta examined the office. She saw a picture of Joey and what looked like his wife and two children, happily carousing in a backyard pool.

"I've gotta be naked?" she asked.

Joey rolled his eyes.

"I thought Jim would've explained it to you. Yeah, it's an all-nude club. You gotta show your coochie to the customers, that's why they're here and not the topless bar down the road. You wanna try that place, be my guest. I ain't pressuring you, but I'll tell you for sure, you ain't gonna get a good deal there, and that Tomaso, he's a real greaseball. He'll be trying to get in your pants the second day you're there. I mean I'll have to check out your assets too, make sure they're competitive. And if you can't dance the pole, there's trouble, but nothing we can't get around. As long as you look good, we can train you. Doesn't mean you're gonna be a gymnast like Gina or Crystal, but if you're passable, your coochie and your titties are the main draw. And the lap dance, you've gotta grind 'em good, got it?"

"I don't know. I'm just coming out of something, you know." She paused. "I don't think I wanna be showing it for everybody to see. I'd rather be the waitress."

"You sure?"

Malta nodded. Joey shrugged.

"Your loss. But I'll put you down as a maybe for that. Got any references from Florida?"

Malta's lip began to quiver. "Nothing I wanna share that can get back to my husband. He beat me and that's why I left and came up here."

She began to tear up but she covered her face and

181

tried to hold it in as best she could.

"I'm sorry to hear that, dear," Joey said, offering a single tissue. She took it and wiped her tears.

He began shuffling through some papers. "I'll be in touch. I got Vito's phone number," he said.

He began writing something. She got up slowly.

"I really do need this job, Joey," she said, "I've got nothing else."

Joey looked up, a blank expression on his face.

"I'll be in touch," he said.

"He used to beat me up when I was little just because he wanted to watch *Superfriends* and I was a *Fat Albert* guy. That's the kind of kid he was. But people change," Vito said, ripping a slice of pizza from the pie in the box.

"You really think he'll hire me?" Malta asked. She lay on the floor, staring at the ceiling.

"You're a cute girl. I'd venture that he probably will."

"Is he...you know, connected?" Malta sat up. "Is that what they call it up here?"

Vito laughed, then started coughing.

"They're all connected, I think, to some extent. But I don't know who he's connected to. I don't ask about that." He chomped into his pizza slice. She tried to watch TV.

"We didn't get anything from the ma or the brother," Sheriff Picole said. "They say they never saw her, which contradicts Jessup's account that his mother was there when she attacked him. We've swept the whole place, but without her DNA or even her identity we can't verify if she was in there. I put out a call for a Missing Person named 'Malta' but I haven't gotten anything back on that."

"You can check the motel room she was staying in," Todd said. "Her DNA should be there."

"Along with a hundred other people, unless Kunal is doing really bad business, kid. And anyway, how could we identify it? Plus you must clean the rooms right?"

Kunal nodded. "She was there with a guy. I think he was pimping her out."

Sheriff Picole looked suspicious.

"Now how would you know that, Kunal?" he asked.

"I just figured," Kunal said, looking at Thomas, who had his hands in his pockets. "I saw men coming in and out of the place. So I asked her about it, and she begged me to hide her. I took her to Todd's dorm room. He came out for a Turkey-shoot, so he brought her to his uncle's trailer park. And that's how she hooked up with Jessup and went up to the mountains."

"Why didn't you just call the cops?"

"She begged me not to. She was afraid he would kill her."

"Or maybe you were afraid it'd ruin your business."

Kunal stared at him. "No, Sheriff, I swear, that wasn't a consideration."

Sheriff Picole wrote on his pad. "Okay, I'll put a call into your county's police department. They can check the info he left with you, and maybe do some searching for fingerprints. Maybe even some DNA, who knows. If we find him in the system, then maybe we've got something. Otherwise, I'll be honest with you, I think it'll probably head to the Cold Case File."

On her first day, Malta was introduced to some of the

girls. Most were friendly and seemed to get along, while a few were cold.

Gina, the resident gymnast, jumped on the pole right away and showed Malta some of her moves.

"Getting up high on the pole and twisting around is as simple as it gets," she said, demonstrating. "But I like to do a little extra for the guys. You know how to flip?"

Malta shook her head.

"Well, my move is to turn upside down like this," she showed. "Then put my legs out, stick out my tongue and lick my hand. I crane my back to gain momentum, do a front-flip and land on my feet. Then, I'm going to the ground and getting into cat mode. That's when the real fun starts."

She went through the motions, and in a few seconds, almost like a magician, she'd peeled her clothes off and was completely nude. Now on her hands and knees, she proceeded toward Malta like a lioness approaching her prey, steady and uncompromising.

Licking her lips as she reached the edge of the stage, she flipped her long, luscious hair back, stood on her knees and massaged her tiny aureoles.

"Aren't you ever embarrassed..." Malta started to say, but Gina cut her off.

"These cuties are all I've got, honey, so I've gotta use 'em. Sure wish they'd grow though. I pray every night for it."

"Do the guys mind?"

"Guys tell me they like it. Don't know why, myself."

She flipped on her back and opened her legs and showed Malta her pussy. She began rubbing her clit as she moved her body up and down, balancing herself with her thighs. She put it close to Malta's face, held it for a few seconds, then pulled back quickly, flipped over, and, now on her hands and knees, fed her pussy to Malta's face from behind.

"Then I turn to the side like this," she said.

"How do you do it with those stilettos on?"

"Practice, honey. Everything takes practice. Just like nursing school. Tests take practice too, right?"

Malta laughed as Gina returned to her sitting position. She massaged her tits and moved them toward Malta.

"Then let the guys put a dollar bill between your tits. Give them a little feel. That'll give you a better chance of scoring a lap dance. Who knows, maybe even VIP. And if they wanna talk, talk! Put your mouth against their ear and whisper to 'em." She thought a second and raised her finger. "Oh, and always maintain eye contact. I learned that in all my jobs."

Malta heard a loud voice behind her. She turned and saw a woman with big, curly hair walking towards Joey's office, accompanied by Jim, who spoke to her hurriedly. She wore a suit.

She turned back to Gina, who was rolling her eyes.

"That's Regina. No relation."

"Who's she?"

"Nobody knows. She goes to Joey's office, closes the door, gives him a blowjob, I think. Then she comes out with some cash."

"You think she's—connected?"

"Who knows. Some of the girls call her 'big boss' but she never says one word to us. Maybe she takes it to someone higher up, commission, you know? Or maybe she stuffs it in her bra. Violet says she's not full Italian, she's part Lebanese. I say who cares. I'm full Italian and I don't."

"You are?"

"From South Carolina but yeah. Both sides."

Malta stared at Joey's door, now closed. She realized Jim was inside too.

"Let's go get Crystal from the dressing room," Gina said. "She's a country girl too but she's got the big titties.

She'll show you another angle. And then we're opening."

Most of the customers who arrived at the opening
were old geezers. A few of them sat in the back, at the
small tables. Malta heard the girls complain that they
weren't up front at the stages where girls were dancing.
Malta saw a few of the younger girls jump into some of
the old guys' laps, with the guys hanging on firmly to the
girl's hips and them chatting like old buddies. A few guys
did sit at the stages. Either way, Malta had to approach
each of them to get money for the water bottles. Once she
got the eight bucks she would go to the bar, retrieve the
bottles and the waistbands, hand the bottles over to the
customers and tie the bands around their wrists. If the
customer gave her a 10 or 20 she'd go get the change and
give them back all one-dollar bills so they could give
them to the girls on the stage. Sometimes the customers
made quips about her tits or about her joining the action,
but mainly they were too preoccupied with the strippers
to notice her figure. Joey shadowed her for the first few
customers, and she did seem a little nervous on the first
go, but when she seemed to get the hang of it, he laid off,
only commenting to her before he left, "see, no tips in
this game." She rolled her eyes, then noticed him leave
the club. She ran to the door and saw him meet the big-
haired woman outside and get into a car with her.

As the night wore on, a younger, rowdier crowd
entered. They yelled at the girls on stage, and erupted in
applause when the DJ announced that a lesbian show
starring a white girl named Sugar and a black girl named
Saranda was going to start. Gina whispered in Malta's ear
that both girls were only 18. Malta found herself turned
on by the full-tongued kisses, the sucking of nipples, the

rubbing of oil on each other's bodies and sliding around while the guys cheered on.

Then Malta peeked into the lap dance room and saw the girls, naked except for their g-strings, enthusiastically grinding on the guys' laps, in various positions,while the guys hung onto their waists or asses. Often she noticed the guys observing the lap dances across from them, becoming aroused by communal pleasure.

Later in the night, after she'd grown tired of the stage fun even while the audience cheered on, she went into the back room and hung out with the girls. She found the youngest girls, while sociable, to be arrogant and stuck-up, while the older, more jaded women sat alone. Only the girls in their low-to-mid twenties, like Gina, Crystal, Gloria, Skye and Scandal, were friendly and helped each other out, quipping about the customers, giving each other tips about the big spenders and strategizing ways to get them into the VIP booth.

By four o'clock in the morning, Malta had only made six dollars on tips. Gina told Malta she would drive her home.

"How else you gonna get back, darling? Now let me give *you* a tip. You gotta remind the guys to tip you. No way you're gonna get it otherwise. You keep bugging 'em, and you'll see."

Malta slept until noon. Then she woke suddenly. She saw Sonny's face. He was on top of her.

"Think you can sell yourself up here, without giving me nothing on the farm?"

She slapped him, but he delivered the same to her.

He put his hands around her throat.

"You're gonna take my cock, bitch, just like you did down South. Remember you told me that?"

She tried to scream but no sound would emerge from her throat. She could see Vito in the doorway, examining the situation with cold dispassion.

After practice, before they left for A&M, Kunal drove Thomas up to a hill on top of their college campus called, mockingly, "Bunker Hill" that was used by high school students to make out.

Thomas watched the sun setting against the North Carolina hills. Kunal could hear him breathing hard. He knew it wasn't from the workout.

"What'd you bring me out here for, Kunal?" he asked. "You wanna 'ice' me or something?"

"And lose you for the big game? Why would I do a thing like that?"

Thomas turned around. "I don't know, Kunal. You've been acting crazy over that hooker."

"She was a woman, Thomas. A woman you paid to fuck."

"Dude, if you were me, you'd do the same thing," he said.

"What the hell does that mean?"

"Look at me. I'm a fat black fuck. Don't none of the girls want me, even though I am a football player. The white girls don't want me cuz I'm fat and black and I got a round face, the black girls don't want me for the same reason."

"You see the color of my skin? You see how big I am?"

"It isn't like being black in the South, man. Even in this new South you'll get screwed both ways. You heard how that old white lady talked to me? Like the Klan was still roaming the parts. 'Boy' she says. Nothing's changed in this country. Except you foreign fucks are moving in and taking over everything. And we're still the same here, no improvements. It won't matter if I go to school or get a job and play on the football team. I don't care if I make state senator. It won't matter. I'll still be nothing to the ladies, and you'll still be something."

"I thought you did okay," Kunal said.

Thomas breathed in deeply and turned back toward the setting sun.

"Yeah, well you don't think much about anyone but yourself, Kunal. Except some blonde bimbo you're trying to save."

"You want me to punch you now?"

Thomas turned back to Kunal, and said, "I want you to acknowledge me, Kunal. I want you to tell me I'm your friend. And not just cuz we're partners on the squad."

Kunal put his hands in his pockets and turned away. "It's gonna be dark soon. We should probably head back," he said. He walked back to the car.

Thomas kept staring ahead at the hills.

Malta lay in the darkness for a long time. She heard the door creak open and something slide in. She closed her eyes, assuming the worst, but nothing seemed to stir. When the door opened again, she sat up quickly. She saw Vito with a glass in his hand.

"Just slipping you some grub, that's all," he said.

"You want to rape me too?" she asked coldly.

"Not my thing," he said. "Eat."

While she could dream, she dreamt she was sliding down a water slide, with Greg on top and the old man on the bottom, sliding down and down and wishing she'd hit the lake at the bottom, but never getting there. She could hear Greg laughing and the old man screaming. Putting her hands over her ears, wishing the sounds away. And then in the next image, making love with Greg, willingly, him kissing her stomach with warm, wet kisses. The old man watching and whizzing into the toilet.

This time Joey was by the door. She got up, shaking. She couldn't speak.

"It's alright, Malta. I won't let anyone hurt you."

She heard a woman's voice, and then she saw Regina, the big-haired woman, enter.

"Vito told me about your ordeal. Don't worry, right now my cousin's getting a talk-to, and a work-over, about how he should treat women."

"It's not right," Regina said.

"No, it's not. And we're gonna give you everything you need 'til you recover. Don't worry about the club. The job'll be there for you if you still want it. You mind if I sit down?" Joey asked, pointing to the side of the bed. Malta nodded.

"But your ordeal did get me thinking, Malta," Joey said, ignoring her request. "See, my cousin told me what you told him about your little ride up here from Florida. Seems to me that you gotta have some skill by now in the ways of men. I mean, I can see why you wouldn't wanna strip, that's some gymnast shit, and being on display and everything, it isn't for everyone. But indoors, you could make some bread. See, Regina here, she's my stepsister, and she lives over the river in New York. That's right, big city, where you wanted to go before your little detour here in Newark. She runs a tidy little place near Hell's Kitchen, high class, no losers, no abusers. It's a 50-50 split, good as you're gonna get in NYC. I figure, it's a good *in* for you, gets you out of Vito's place, gets you in New York. No debt, no obligation, nothing like that. You move out when you feel fit. You wanna look at modeling gigs, no one'll stop you. You wanna move onto another job at some point, no one'll stop you. But I bet you, with Regina watching over you and teaching you the tricks, you're gonna get addicted to the cash, and the men, and you won't leave anytime soon. So what do you say? Better than Vito's place, better than waitressing, right?"

Malta examined him, then Regina, who smiled at her.

"Do I really have a choice?" she stuttered, her voice cracking.

Joey laughed, and looked over at Regina.

"Is she serious?" he asked. "This is America, baby. You always have a choice here."

They won the game, 28-24. Todd threw the winning pass to Jacob on The Draw 35 which Kunal created by blocking the strong safety. And Thomas was injured on the play.

Malta: A Love Story

Part II

*

The rooms in the *Boudoir Buttress* weren't too large. Today Malta used a small room with a creaky bed and an air conditioner for these sweltering summer nights.

Malta's clothes were scattered along the bed and on the floor, while the plumber's were neatly folded in the corner of the room, below a black chair.

Usually she received businessmen, but this time the customer was a plumber from Queens named Ted. She could tell most times from speaking to them whether they would return—90% of her clients kept coming back, which paid for her rent and her food. But not everyone did. The trick was to give them the GFE on the first bat, so they wouldn't even question a repeat appearance.

She wasn't sure about the plumber—he was a strange one, and she wasn't sure she'd figured him out yet. He was a fat guy, working class, rough around the edges but not immune to visiting the Met or hiking Bear Mountain. He admitted he had visited "safer" places he'd found on *Backpage* where the girls wouldn't even show their pussies, let alone allow guys to come on their tits. This was his first trip to a massage parlor where sex was sometimes offered. He seemed a little taken aback when she licked her hand before stroking his member—in fact he'd come immediately so she hadn't had a chance to rub her pussy against it, or any of the other things she used to set herself apart and keep them coming back.

"Say, do you ever have sex with the guys?" he asked, leaning back after she had cleaned him up.

"Why, do you want to have sex with me?" she had asked. But he hadn't quite answered.

"Just a general question."

She smiled. "Every girl has their own policy."

"What's your policy?"

She thought.

"We'll see if you come back. Guess you're not getting it up again during this session. Unless you want more time."

He played with himself, slapping his penis back and forth like an unfilled balloon.

She shrugged. "I've got more appointments anyway," she said.

They were silent for a while. The plumber closed his eyes. She rested her head on his chest.

"Guys always wanna nap after they come," she said. "The other girls and me, we've been thinking of making one room a sleeping room, so the guys can nap after they come."

"That gonna cost extra?"

She slapped him and giggled. "Oh, Ted," she said.

He opened his eyes. "I don't wanna go to sleep. I wanna hear about you. Where are you from?"

"Florida," she said.

"And how'd you get here?"

"It's a long story."

"I've got another half-an-hour, don't I? Or do I get the boot?"

"You get the time you paid for honey, no more, no less," she said. That wasn't always true, because she often hurried men out if she had another appointment right after, which was often.

"Ok, so shoot."

"I ran into a lot of jerks," she said. "I got kidnapped. I got raped, okay. I escaped from a mountain hick. Is that what you want to hear?"

"Whoa," he said, laughing. "Are you kidding?"

"I'm not kidding. Do you wanna hear about how I escaped from the mountain hick?"

"That's more interesting than the nap room."

"He brought me up to his cabin. He gave me some pancakes his mom had heated up. So I figured, sure, some Southern hospitality. I even put some homemade maple syrup on it, directly from the sap of a tree. And then, I thought, this isn't right. Are they really going to be so nice to me? Because I was escaping from some pretty bad men at that point, one after another. But I have a way of trusting people, and I was hungry, so I ate them. They were pretty good."

"I see. Some southern pancakes. I've never been to the South."

"It's nice, if you like smiling hypocrites."

"We've got plenty of those here."

"Yeah, well, I think people here are a little more straightforward. Down South they're retarded. Anyway, we got out onto the porch and I get to talking to this guy who took me up, some hick name that started with a J, I can't remember, and suddenly he starts talking really dirty. I mean he's getting all hard talking about locking me in a basement and doing stuff with his axe to my ass. So without even thinking, I slapped him and took him by the hair into a back room. His ma was watching but I didn't care, I was so mad. I punched him in the face, saying, 'I'm not your whore, you're mine, bitch.' And then I took off my pants and squatted and shat a whole fucking day's load on his face."

"Damn," the plumber said.

"I never told anyone that."

"I'll make sure I never get you mad. Or have anal with you."

"You wanna see my asshole? It's clean now." She turned around and opened her cheeks.

"I'll pass. Maybe next time."

"This other guy, he loves—"

"And the ma didn't do anything?" he said, changing the subject. "I remember that old bitch from *Goonies*..."

"You'll love this. She comes in, while I'm shitting, holding her frying pan, and guess what she does?"

"She starts pissing?"

"Laughing. She starts laughing so hard."

"Girl power?"

"I don't know what you call it. It was pretty funny."

"So what, she just let you go?"

"She even gave me pie and the key to her truck."

"You ate it?"

"I didn't trust her that much. But I took the truck."

"She just gave you her truck?"

"No, I lied about that part. But I remembered he kept the key in the ignition. Too bad it only had gas to the highway. I had to hitch a ride from there. With another raping perv."

"Fuck, Miranda. You've lived some life." (She called herself Miranda at *The Boudoir Buttress*).

"Better than a plumber in Queens?"

"That's why I come out here, baby. There are so many interesting lives to hear about. It's better than the sex stuff. Even going around to houses in Queens, I hear so many stories. So many immigrants, you know, from all over the world. It's like the whole world in itself."

"Sounds like an interesting place. I'll have to visit."

"Tell me, are the other clients nice to you, Miranda?"

Malta shrugged. "They're all nice, I guess. Some are weird, that's all."

"Like what?"

"This Orthodox Jewish guy, he just tells me to lie in the dark, and he touches me all over. Guess he's paranoid about diseases."

"We all are, kind of. There's never been a guy who's been nice to you, for real?"

Malta rubbed his head. "Sure, there are nice guys sometimes, I guess."

Kunal got up at 6 AM every morning. His mother still made him his daily breakfast of toast and boiled eggs, but sometimes Ami, if she was going to the office early, would do it instead.

The apartment was crammed now that they were married and his father lay debilitated in his small room with terminal throat and lung cancer, unable to speak because his larynx had been removed. The last stages seemed to take longer than anyone had expected.

"I'm sorry, Ami," Kunal would often say before they went to sleep. "I thought we would get our own place."

"It's okay, Kunal. With your dad and everything, I understand. The motel can't run itself. You're looking for buyers, so it'll work out."

He didn't say anything, because he knew that wasn't true. Actually, he was looking to acquire another property a few miles away, next to a convention center he heard would be built, reputedly from the sponsorship of another major NBA star. That meant the motel's asking price had skyrocketed 200%. But he figured the investment was worth it if he could raise the downpayment; the bank was asking for 50% because of the tough economy.

He'd acquired the taste for running motels from his father, and he had no desire to go into another line of work. His father never had the ambition to acquire multiple properties, and he never directly told Kunal to follow in his footsteps, but Kunal always felt he should. It was in his bones more than some engineering job. He had already married the girl his parents wanted him to, settled down in his hometown and there was no reason he should leave. Plenty of other Indian sons would take over their motels too, so why not him?

Too bad the competition was fierce among the Indian-American community, making it more difficult for him to acquire the property. It was the only motel in town still owned by a major corporation rather than an Indian family, but that would certainly change.

Phillip was the only holdover who still worked for him. He was a retired high school gym teacher who now worked nights to help his professor wife out with the necessities.

He was counting the money as Kunal entered.

"It was a good night, Kunal."

"Really?"

"Yup. Full house, including a party taking six rooms for four days."

"Some kind of town fair next door?"

"Tried to get it out of them, but they wouldn't budge. Pretty secretive bunch. Maybe they're taking a vacation from Langley."

"That would be exciting."

"Oh, we've got plenty of excitement here. You heard about that new convention center? Proceeds are gonna trickle down here too. Ball games, graduations, events—an additional boon to business and property value."

"I know, Phil."

"I'm starting to sound like a dad now, right?"

"A bit."

"Sorry, kid. I know you're smart. Just trying to give you pointers, that's all."

"As always."

"You're like my own son, Kunal."

"You've been loyal, I'll give you that."

Phillip looked hurt. Kunal rethought his response.

"Sorry, Phil, I didn't mean to sound cold. I appreciate everything you've done for us. I guess I'm just tired."

"You guys can't work 16 hours a day, Kunal. You've gotta hire somebody else. Or get that wife of yours to work for you."

"She's got a real job. She's bringing in good cash."

Philip bit his lip and stared at the floor.

"What's wrong?" Kunal asked.

"Listen, kid, I'm not sure I'm gonna be around much longer," Phillip said.

"What do you mean?"

"My wife was offered a good job at the University of Kentucky. Head of the Psychology Department there."

"And you're going?"

"She's still thinking about it. I mean all her roots and friends are here. But she'd be a fool to pass it up, the way I look at it."

"Looks like I'm going to have to hire two new people. Too bad we can never find anyone trustworthy in this town."

"You will. But I won't say bye to you yet because it's not definite. And when I do, I'll see your dad, for sure."

"You can see him now. No one's stopping you. You're family."

Phillip put his hand firmly on the counter and looked like he was about to cry.

"Thanks, Kunal," Phillip said, putting his arm around Kunal's shoulder. Kunal hugged him with one arm.

"Did he give you a tip?" Regina asked, sitting with her back arched on the sofa in the common room next to a girl named Sophie, a short Argentinian girl who never smiled.

"Did he look like a tipper?" Malta responded, coming back from the front door, naked.

"No one ever tips in this place."

"That's because you never ask them to. Anyway, it's good that way. Makes them more comfortable."

"You might move up in this game after all," Regina said. "You know how their minds work now. Took long enough."

"I've been here long enough, bitch," Malta responded, snatching up a towel from a pile on the table.

"Who's fault is that, Malta? Joey told you, first day you started, you can leave whenever you want. You've got no modeling gigs? That's because you don't push hard enough, honey. And by the way, you're too damn old. I'm surprised the guys here still want you."

"Fuck you, you cunt. I look as good as the first day I got here."

She headed towards the bathroom. Regina snickered.

"Yeah? Well your stomach's starting to sag, honey. Even those new pics on the site can't hide that."

Malta stopped in the doorway.

"You've got some nerve, you hag. I'm the most senior girl you got. I've saved so many guys from going to other places."

"Please. All of 'em go to other places, Malta. Even I know that. They just tell you that because you're stupid enough to believe it. Maybe you're not cut out for phones after all."

"I'm cut out. Maybe I'll just join a new agency."

"Yeah, you try that. You know those girls don't even wash the floors every day? Just a bunch of crack whores. Oh, and when's the last time you washed anything for us?

Sophie here's a good girl."

"I washed the laundry yesterday morning, you dumb whore. Go sell that shit to someone with a bad memory."

She shut the door, ran the shower and started scrubbing herself hard like she always did. She thought the same thing she thought every day, about how she'd been there for a few years and still she was barely getting by. She hadn't made a dent in modeling and even with the whore money she only had one CD and a few shares in one stock and her checking account was barely at the minimum. Her rent got paid for her tiny apartment in Williamsburg but that was it. She'd taken a few classes at modeling agencies that turned out to be shams. A math course at a community college she'd walked out on when the professor had hit on her. Well, at least she knew she still had it.

But her dream had never been fulfilled. After seeing so many men, she never got anything. No actress gigs, no rich men willing to marry her and whisk her away to their mansions. Just the same job. At least she hadn't gotten raped again. Maybe she owed Joey and Regina for that.

She could barely remember the days now when she read *Reader's Digest* like crazy. She had bought a new iPad but instead of reading from *Reader's Digest* she downloaded porn on it, which bored her as often as it stimulated her. She would read enough MSN, NY Times and NY Post stories to keep up with current events. She watched streamed movies and television shows so she could keep up with the latest culture and conversation for her job.

And she would browse through other agencies too. She even visited a few, but realized that Regina was right, they seemed filthy or the girls looked like they were just waiting to get money together for their next heroin hit. She never made as much money as she thought she would, and what she didn't put away she would blow on worthless Soho or hotel roof parties, hoping to fit in and be noticed but failing to even charm the girls, let alone the men. Finally she resigned herself to hanging out in Williamsburg, but found the hipsters to be annoying, fake, and absurdly naïve.

A few clients had seemed to be promising. They had visited repeatedly and claimed that they were wealthy businessmen. They had charmed her at first, complaining about how unhappy they were with their suburban or Manhattan lives drenched with boring financial figures, conniving wives and colleagues they distrusted. After a few visits she hoped they would ask to meet her outside of work, and she would hint at it, try to manipulate them into it, but as soon as she did, they seemed uncomfortable and they would balk. Sometimes they would make a joke out of it, but they would never commit to it. She realized she was, to them, their whore-in-waiting. Knowing that she was with other men made her an instant turn-off as a potential wife.

She still had the nightmares sometimes, of various men, from Greg, to Sonny, to others, abusing her. Once she had dreamed that Kunal had pulled off his friend and saved her, and when she woke up she wondered what had happened to him. Had he had gone looking for her, was he thinking and wondering about her? But she quickly put it out of her mind. He was a rich Indian and she was a white trash whore. No doubt he'd forgotten about her as soon as she'd disappeared and some beautiful Indian girl had been introduced to him.

She felt more resigned than ever to learning the ropes from Regina and maybe taking over from her as madam when she moved on, if she ever did. Perhaps that's where her path lay. It was her best estimation from what she had experienced.

Kunal drove around the town, analyzing the quality of different motels like he'd done a million times before. Perhaps there was a better deal than the convention center motel. Now with a couple of new hires and some serious renovations to be done on the existing motel, plus arrangements to be made once his father passed away and the pending payments for his medical care, which had been staved off through loans, he was hardly in any position to be making a bid on any motel, let alone the convention center one.

Finally, he made the round to Ami's father's motel where he sat down to tea with his in-laws. Ami's father had capital and he knew he was one of his competitors for the convention center motel. He could have asked Pranavbhai for the money or for a partnership but then Ami would have found out about his intentions. He wasn't exactly sure what was wrong with that, but he knew he should tread carefully.

"Ami says you are looking for engineering jobs?" Pranavbhai asked.

Kunal nodded. "Yes, pappa. She doesn't want to live in the motel anymore."

"With you in an engineering job, and her healthcare management position, you will make very good money. Buy a house where those Jewish doctors live. I can even help you so you don't have to keep paying the mortgage."

"I think we can manage, pappa."

Pranavbhai was quiet. "We are sad every day hearing about Rajeshbhai. We hope he makes a full recovery."

"Thank you for your prayers, pappa, but I don't think that's likely. He will probably die soon."

Pranavbhai waved his finger. "Never give up hope, Kunal."

"I haven't," Kunal said, standing. "I won't."

Pranavbhai stood too. "I am glad your father made it to your wedding," he said finally, shaking Kunal's hand. "He saw a fine boy grow up."

Outside the motel, Kunal noticed a police cruiser was blocking his car. It wasn't from Browston, however. It was from Sullivan County.

An officer emerged from the seat, wearing a brown hat matching his fatigues. He looked familiar but Kunal didn't recognize him immediately.

"Howdy, partner," the officer called out as he approached Kunal, wearing a big smile on his face.

"Todd?" Kunal asked, taken aback as he shook his old friend's hand limply.

"Do you recognize me?"

"I didn't at first. I heard you went to Canada to try out for football there."

"False promise. Didn't work out. What else is new? I always knew, in the back of my mind, I wasn't cut out for pro ball."

"So you became a cop?"

"Deputy to Sheriff Picole, who handled your bimbo case. Not bad, just domestic disputes, guy drinking too much, taking it out on his wife. Got the occasional Iraq war veteran icing his family. But not often."

"Sounds more interesting than what I'm doing."

"Running your dad's motel? Isn't that what you were doing before? I'm just kidding man. Your mom, she's still nice, gave me a samosa. Spicy, burned my tongue cuz it's been a while. She told me where to find you. Says you've got a nice Indian wife who makes you tea."

"My mom still makes me tea. My wife works."

"Way it should be, right? Listen, I came by because

205

I've got some info on your bimbo case."

"Don't know why you call it that. That's what Thomas called it."

"Speaking of Thomas, he's got quite the rep now, you know? He owns his own consulting business, apparently assisting that guy Davis who's running for state senator."

"Yeah, I've heard that off the grapevine."

"Didn't realize you were still on the grapevine."

"I know more about the town now than I ever did growing up here."

"Funny how that works. Same thing with my county. I'm even respected by the mountain hicks now. Nobody messes with me. About your case, though..."

"That was a while ago."

"So you've forgotten it?"

Kunal swallowed, intent.

"Tell me," he said.

"That perv, we finally found him. His name's Gregory Melville of Florida, he's in the system now for rape and battery. The DNA match finally came back. Soon we'll be adding kidnapping and a whole host of other charges."

"That's nice to know. But did you find Malta?"

"Well, I paid a visit up to Jessup and his mom. He hasn't changed, but unlike usual, he's sticking to his story. And then the mom laid a big one on me. She says she saw Malta take the truck after she took the shit on her son's face."

"And she never told Sheriff Picole that she stole her truck?"

"She says she thought maybe evidence from the truck might implicate Jessup in something else, so she kept her mouth shut. I figure that she might have been afraid for herself. But whatever."

"So what are you saying? That Malta's alive?"

"I don't know. We found the truck at a used car dealer. Owner says some mechanic found the truck ditched on the road. It wasn't working so he towed it up to his shop, fixed it up good, stripped it of the plate and sold it to the dealer. We tracked the guy down and just so happens he's still got the plate, and it matches Jessup's truck. And he says that his buddy saw Malta get out of the truck after it broke down, that she walked up a bit to the highway, and that then she got picked up by a guy with a Pennsylvania plate. He even wrote down the license number. Amazing how these guys work."

"He still has the number?"

"It's amazing how these guys work," Todd repeated, hitting Kunal's shoulder.

"Yeah. It is amazing," he said, smiling.

Todd followed him back to the motel. Kunal got out of his car and went over to Todd's vehicle.

"I'll check with the county up in Pennsylvania," Todd said. "If we do get a hit, we can get the FBI or the U. S. Marshals involved, if they care enough. Though it might be more fun if I take a trip up myself."

"Mind if I come?"

Todd shrugged.

"It wouldn't exactly be legal. But we'll see if I can fit you in. Just don't get too emotional if we find her."

"I'll be professional. I've learned how."

Todd shook his head. "What would your wife think of your little obsession?"

"I'm not sure what she thinks period," Kunal said to himself.

"Say what?"

"Nothing."

"Well, I'm still a free man myself. But I've got a lot of ladies bring me baskets."

"Of condoms?"

"Ha ha. I'm holding out as long as possible. No doubt I'll get bit soon."

"Thanks for telling me about Malta," Kunal said.

"No problem, partner. I figured you would hear about it anyway, so I might as well bring you the good news myself."

"Listen, you know where Thomas' office is?"

"Sure. It's by where they're building that convention center. I hear he's even got a stake in it."

One night Malta got drunk in her apartment off some Jim Beam and took a stroll around Grand Avenue. She walked by some hipsters hanging out on the sidewalk and figured a block party was near. When she went a little further she located the warehouse, and through a slit in the wall, saw the strobe lights and women dancing while the men stood aside drinking beers.

In a split second, she decided to be one of them. Recently she'd felt self-conscious being around young partiers. Though she'd probably gone to more New York parties than all of them combined, she felt old now, too old for these hipster types. She should have been hitched to a rich guy and her modeling career should have risen, then plateaued and ebbed, instead of never happening at all. The low self-esteem that had plagued her periodically throughout her marriage and during her captivity had returned. She felt more isolated than ever and pessimistic about her future, and now she had to drink to go out. And yet, this very desire to believe she was beneath the crowd was also freeing to the point that tonight she no longer worried about the opinions of others and just wanted to escape the dungeon of her existence.

She approached one group and asked them where the door to the party was. As if from another sensory orifice she heard laughs and observed points and followed their fingers to a guy wearing a glow stick around his neck. He asked her for 12 dollars; she searched her pockets and gave him 20.

Inside she went directly toward the crowd of dancing women and gyrated to the beat. She didn't recognize the song but they always played the same songs in New York, whether in Soho, Midtown or Williamsburg—Rihanna, Kanye, Jay-Z, same shit they probably played everywhere in the world except down South, where country still reigned. But this song was different. The relentless beat was matched with no words, just an insistent rhythm that bobbed her head to the flow. She felt it played for her alone, that only she was privy to its machinations, as the other lithe women, the rich half-Jews, the liberal arts graduates, the Midwestern casualties of the false ambition of independence, moved like bright, hungry silhouettes across from her and against her. She didn't even fight them off. She decided to ignore them and focus only on whether they defied her movements, in order to eventually one-up them.

They differentiated her, made her unique. She ignored the pokes, requests for drinks, guys whispering into her ear. She continued to bob her head. At some point she remembered going into the narrow hallway, then pissing into the toilet in the tiny excuse for a bathroom, pressing her hands against the walls as she squatted, hoping she could blame some gonorrheal attack on the seat's germs. Then she recalled another snippet, speaking to a girl who had a mohawk, or maybe it was a guy, short and stocky, about Brazil and soccer, but didn't they call it football? And then the South reared its ugly head in the mouth of some tall girl, a bitch with a red cup, blabbing like most girls who blabbed about nothing, except she was dissing the South, as if she knew something about it. Then she remembered a bigger guy, muscular, taking her by the hand to the front of the dance floor, and the music taking over again, this time in her head, because she ignored the generic garbage being played; now the music played over and over again for her alone, rhythmic, rambunctious, and rising to a sustained chorus, until it steadied and then let out into a furious blowing, like the deflating of whoopee cushion.

"Looks like someone's finally awake," a voice rang into her ear. Malta awoke with a start. A brunette with an anorexic face stared back at her.

"Who are you?" Malta knew her apartment, her bed, from the pink shade of sunlight that emanated through the red curtains.

"I'm your guardian angel, baby."

"Guardian what?"

"Don't you remember? I brought you home."

"I think I'm gonna puke."

She began to get out of bed but the girl pushed her back in and held her.

"We already have a bucket for that, remember?"

The girl grabbed her by the neck and pushed her head down between her legs and over the edge of the bed where she saw the bucket she usually used for mopping encrusted with white foam. She felt the vomit come up. She opened her mouth and tried to release, but nothing would come out. She began gagging and suffering that agonizing feeling where nothing is coming but one hopes in vain that it will. Finally only saliva slithered down into the bucket. She felt slaps on her back and then her head being pulled back by her hair.

The girl kissed her on the cheek. "Isn't it fun?"

"Yeah, load of laughs," Malta responded, wiping her mouth. "What time is it?"

"It's Stacy," she said. "Cindy at the apartment."

"What?"

"I guess you don't remember last night at all. We're in the same industry. You know, hush hush."

She shook her head. "No, I don't remember."

"Don't worry, I made you breakfast. Good old milk and Special K. Great for your figure."

Malta rose on her knees and, pulling the curtain aside, looked out at the brick building across from her, and at the sun above it. She'd learned in Florida how to tell the time from the sun's position, even though she rarely saw much of it these days. She figured it was around 11 AM.

"Same industry?" she repeated, just for the sake of it.

"Yup. I'm from Jersey too. South side. Small town."

"I'm not from Jersey. It's just where I worked last. I'm from Florida."

"Cool. I've been to Disney. Just went down there last weekend."

"Disney?"

"Disneyworld."

"Oh. I've never been to Disneyworld myself. Daddy was in and out of jail when I was little, my momma was working all the time to pay the rent. We didn't have much time for trips."

"Even now? With all the cash the guys give you? Our girls are going to California, Europe..."

"No time. I barely can pay the rent now."

"What, your place isn't busy?"

"It's okay. I don't know, with the split, I don't find it amounts to much if you count groceries, eating out. And I go to modeling agencies and sometimes they ask you to pay for leads. With everything, I don't know, a trip's the last thing on my mind."

She walked over to the dining table and, after rubbing her stomach and coughing once, picked up a spoon and started eating the Special K. Stacy followed her and sat across from her, leaning her elbow on the table while cupping her chin.

"Next time, make me some oatmeal from whole oats, it's better for the complexion," Malta said.

"Yeah, don't you hate it when you break out? You've gotta miss days and all that cash. Sometimes you can fool them with makeup. But a lot of times you can't. Then a client brushes his stubble against you, and makes you break out even more."

"My boss checks. Even a little cut on your finger and she makes you put on the liquid band-aid."

"If we had bosses, they would send us home."

Malta glared at her sharply.

"You don't have bosses?"

"Well, we've got a head girl, Shirley. She's been there for a while, even took over for the old lady, Fernie, who started it. I mean she wasn't old, she was one of the girls too. *Sensational Souls* is a business run by women. And we get a 60% cut."

"60? I thought 50 was the best you could get."

"We get 60. We don't exactly advertise it, but that's it. Best in the business. And we don't have a strict boss. I mean Shirley runs it, but she's not always there."

"Regina's our main boss, but we get a lot of ladies coming in to run things. I've been there longer than most of them."

"We could always use more girls. You want me to put a good word in with Shirley?"

"You've gotta take the STD tests too?"

"Every few months. Not too strict."

Malta nodded. "I wonder if Joey will let me go."

"Who's Joey?" Stacy asked.

"Nobody," Malta replied, swirling around the soggy

flakes of the cereal. "Remember, make the oatmeal next time."

Stacy smiled. "Next time?" she asked.

"Long time, no see, Kunal," Thomas said, holding out his hand. He was sitting behind his desk. Kunal noticed he'd lost a tremendous amount of weight. "How are you doing?"

"Not as good as you are. How's being state senator?"

"I'm only the assistant for a candidate. But I've got this consulting thing."

"Who do you consult?"

"Anybody who needs to trim their fat. That's what we do. If you need to cut some employees at your motel..."

"Actually I need to hire some."

"Yeah? You're looking to expand? I can advise you on that too."

"I'm afraid I need capital."

"Then maybe you shouldn't be expanding."

"I want to."

"Will isn't a good enough reason. You've got to think these things through logically. Why do you think that credit loan crisis happened? People have dreams but they don't necessarily have the means to implement them. They might never. We put false hope into people's heads. Often it's for the purpose of ripping them off. Guess that's the American way."

"How'd you get this smart, Thomas?"

"I broke my leg in that game against A&M. I had to get smart fast. My daddy was a fixer of things. Just went along fixing things for whoever wanted it. He probably would have done shit for your motel, if he'd lived. He was a lazy fuck, slow like the South. Well I'm not slow. I use my mind now. I realized I needed to, sitting in that hospital bed. Football, women, college degrees...all false dreams."

"I want another motel. No one else knows I want one, but I do. Hell, I want the convention center motel, and I hear you've got a stake in it."

"I see. So you didn't visit me for old times' sake, or for my business mind. Just old-fashioned connections."

"It is the South, isn't it?"

"That's the language of the world, my friend."

Thomas stood, and began limping over to Kunal. Kunal stared at his leg.

"What, you never recovered?"

"Amazing, with all these scientific advances, you'd think they could cure anything. But seems I got hit in a specific spot where science is dark. Lots of darkness, and lots of light too in this world. An amazing balance the Lord has provided."

Kunal swallowed. "My wife might know a doctor."

"I've gone to plenty. With my money?" He laughed. "I've made my peace. I've got to work out, eat less, lose weight to complement my situation. And with my cash, I landed a beautiful wife. Maybe even more beautiful than your own."

"I'm sure."

"Tell me," Thomas said, bringing out a couple of glasses and bottle of brandy from his drawer, "how do you expect my stake in the convention center to help you with your motel purchase? You want me to lean on some bankers? I guess I do know them all."

"I want you to invest with me in the motel. The better the convention center does, the better the motel does, and vice versa. It's a great investment for you."

"You want to be partners with me? I mean we weren't exactly stellar on the football field together. Or even on the friendship field."

214

"I thought we were fine. Except for the Malta thing."

"You never saw me or spoke to me after I broke my leg. You never forgave me, and for what? Something that you wanted to do too. Something that I could do, that you couldn't..."

"That's bullshit," Kunal replied.

"Don't lie, Kunal," Thomas said, pointing his finger at him. "Accumulation, lust, power, these things rule the world, not love. No, there's none of that. Now listen, why would I need you if I really wanted the motel? You don't think I have the cash for that?"

"On the surface, you don't need me. But with your stake in the convention center too, the board might see too much control there for one man. They could vote you down. Not to mention that you're black. But with me as the visible partner..."

"They wouldn't vote you down for completing the Indian domination of the motel industry? Please. They care about money, nothing else. It's the New South. That has changed."

"Not sure about that, dude."

"And why don't you just ask your Indian buddies to loan you the money or go into a partnership with you?"

"We seem to be better at competing than sharing."

"I've heard differently. Didn't you marry one of their daughters?"

"That was a love match."

"Love. You Indians are crafty, I'll tell you that. Not as smart as the Jews though. But I'm smarter."

"I didn't say you weren't."

"Let's face it. You could get a partner with one of them. Your wife's father. But I've got the political future, and that means, making nice with me, being in with me, gives you a bigger edge in the long run. You were born here, you grew up here, unlike most of them, so you think that gives you an advantage. Well, it does, but only if you're with me."

Kunal thought, and after a pause, said, "So?"

Thomas sat down and began writing something. "So I have a lot more to offer you than you have to offer me."

"I offer you my partnership, my support. I'll bring the Indians together, they'll vote for your candidate. They'll advertise him in their motels. You don't think that will sway people?"

"You just said Indians are better at competing than sharing."

"We still meet for social events, religious functions. I have sway with them."

"What are you, and by extension me, offering them for their vote and their persistent advocacy?"

"Your promise to give tax breaks to motel owners in this state? Or in this particular county? Which will make motels here more profitable and make outsiders want to purchase them because the property values will go up?"

Thomas nodded. "Good. But what if it isn't in my candidate's ability to pass such legislation?"

"I'll lie and pretend that it is," Kunal said, shaking.

Thomas lifted his pen and smiled. "Now we're getting somewhere, partner."

Malta arrived outside of the apartment on the Upper West Side and called the cell number again.

"Hello?"

"It's Malta. I'm downstairs."

"Okay, honey. You're right outside the doors?"

"Yup."

"Can you call back in 60 seconds? Shirley will take your call then. I'm Rhonda, the phone girl."

"Okay." Malta walked half a block and turned back.

She called again, and this time the woman from her first call picked up. "I'll buzz you up, honey," she said. "It's 7 flights up, on the right."

She made the long trek up, huffing and puffing by the time she got there. She waited outside the door, or what she thought was the door, her heart racing.

Finally the door opened slowly. She saw it was dark inside but no one was on the other end. She entered.

The door closed behind her and a short red-haired woman was behind it. She wore a red dress.

"Hey, sorry, we've gotta take some precautions. Lots of LE around, you know. I'm Shirley," she said, holding out her hand.

"Malta. I thought that you would meet me at a cafe or something."

"Normally, I would, but it's busy today. You know, so many clients, so little time." She giggled. "Okay, so first, let me show you around," she said, leading. She pointed towards a room that was draped off with a red curtain, and Malta heard a man's voice and giggling behind it.

"That's one of our rooms there. Being entertained at the moment. We've only got three. Then there's another room over here," she said pointing toward another. Malta saw it was bigger than the rooms they normally used at Regina's place. The windows were curtained over and a dim light protruded through the red shade of a lamp in the corner. On a single bed covered with maroon sheets was a pillow and additional sheets, folded neatly.

"We run a clean establishment here. Our girls clean the place and themselves constantly," Shirley said, her arm still in the air, leading her left past another curtain. "That's our home base," she said, "but to that later. First, past our bathroom," she continued, pointing toward a restroom with shiny porcelain tiles, a Listerine bottle on top of the sink and cracks in the sink basin, "and onto our last room." Malta looked in and saw the last room was bigger than the other two and contained a king-size bed with two pillows on it. "For doubles and triples," Shirley explained. "That's probably where you will be trained, if we get that far."

She turned back and stopped in front of the curtain, opened it ceremoniously, and let Malta inside. Malta saw a small den with a green sofa, a tiny table stacked with CDs, and a fat girl sitting in front of a laptop computer, sipping iced coffee through a straw.

"Rhonda, Malta," Shirley said, giggling. "Is that your code name, or your real name, Malta?"

"My real name," Malta said, shaking Rhonda's limp hand as Rhonda continued to concentrate on what looked like Solitaire on the computer.

"You have a dazzling name, Malta. Was your mother from Malta?" Shirley asked, floating down into the sofa and gesturing for Malta to sit across from her now on a wooden folding chair.

"No," Malta responded, "I think she just wanted to make life difficult for me."

Shirley didn't respond at first, then faked a giggle. "Well, I doubt that name would do that."

"Funny, not too many people make a big deal of it. I don't even think they know it is a country."

"At least you know, Malta. We'll have to find another name for you of course. How would you like Sicily?" She giggled. "I am joking, of course. Now listen, Malta, I want you to know that we run a very sophisticated establishment here. Only the best of the best work for *Sensational Souls*. This isn't some hole-in-the-wall full of crack whores. Far from it, we are professional masseuses, who offer the finest sensual experience for discerning gentlemen. Now, tell me Malta, do you happen to have any professional degrees?"

Malta hesitated. She nodded.

"Good. From where?"

"University of Florida," she said.

"The Gators. Excellent. What did you study?"

"Psychology."

"You sound better every second!" Shirley shouted, raising her arm like a cheerleader. "And you can speak about Freud, Adler, Jung? Many of our customers love literature. Do you know books, current movies? Do you go to Film Forum, the Met?"

Malta nodded.

"Excellent. Well, you are beautiful, blond, and all the rest. I'll need to check out your assets. Please stand and disrobe."

Malta hesitated. "Now?"

"Why yes, now. This is an interview. You'll have to be naked for the men. And, I thought Stacy said you already worked for some establishment."

Malta nodded and stood up. "Sorry, it was just abrupt. I'll do it."

She began removing her top while Shirley examined her face.

"I should have asked you about your experience. Got away from me. Tell me, why do you want to leave that place for this one? Do you work there full-time?"

Malta nodded as she removed her pants. "A better percentage here. Better atmosphere." She paused as she unhooked her bra. "It is 60%, isn't it?"

Shirley was transfixed as she stared at Malta's breasts.

"What wonderful titties," she said, tiptoeing up to her. She took the two balloons, which jutted out like small pears, and suctioned onto one with her lips. Malta reacted with surprise, then began to feel aroused.

Shirley spit the tit out, then licked Malta's nipple with the tip of her tongue.

"Damn," Malta said, feeling a rush into her brain, like a mini-orgasm.

"Delicious," Shirley said. "The men will adore them.

Turn around. Let me see your ass."

Malta pushed her panties down and they fell around her ankles. She turned around. Shirley slapped them hard. "You do work out, I see. How horny are you?"

"What?"

"How horny do you get? Is this something that you'll enjoy? We all need the money, but I need to see passion too."

"I've been doing it for years," Malta said.

"So have bureaucrats. Look how passionate they are."

"I want to work here," Malta said.

Shirley regarded her closely.

"Ok, come next week. I'll set up a double for you with Stacy, so you can learn the ropes, what's acceptable and what isn't here. Plenty of clients will want to break in the new girl. We'll have to lie about your age, of course. Can't have a girl past 27, officially."

"How'd you know?"

"I can tell. Thankfully, most men can't."

Kunal, lying in bed, was unable to sleep. Ami sensed his unease and turned toward him.

"What's wrong, baby?" she asked.

"I was thinking about daddy."

"Oh, Kunal," she said, taking his head in her hands. "Don't think about it. It will be okay."

"Not about him dying," Kunal said. "About following in his path."

"What do you mean?"

Kunal sighed. "I want to run motels like him, Ami. I don't want to be just another engineer."

Ami didn't say anything. Then she sat up and turned on the lamp in the cramped room.

"That's what you've been worrying about?"

"Yes, Ami," Kunal said, sitting up too. "That's it."

"That's pathetic, Kunal. And crazy. You want to work 16 hours a day forever?"

"Your father doesn't do that."

"My father runs a Howard Johnson and a Hampton Inn. He's a little more set up than you."

"So why doesn't he help me out then? We're family."

"I don't want to live in a motel. I'm just putting up with this because I love you, and I know how much it meant to your father. But when he passes..."

"That's what you're waiting for?" Kunal asked.

"Of course not. Don't even try to suggest that."

Kunal began crying. Ami held his shoulders.

"We're not like these white people," Ami said. "We don't get divorced, we don't separate, we don't blame other people for our problems. We'll get through it. But I know what kind of life I want. I'll ask my father to help you out, as long as you promise to get an engineering job. Then we can hire people to look after this motel, and live somewhere else, in a nice house, where those Jewish doctors live. And your mother...well, we'll see."

"She can't live with us?"

"We'll see, Kunal."

"Look Ami, there's another property..." Kunal started to say, but Ami shushed him.

"Shhh. Let's talk about this in the morning," she said.

Todd drove up to Pennsylvania. He didn't tell Kunal.

At the first Turnpike rest area, he bought some coffee and flirted with the black girl behind the counter.

"Wanna come on a ride with me?" he asked. "Just the two of us, trip to New York City."

221

"I don't think my boyfriend would be okay with that," she responded, rolling her eyes. "Or my boss."

"Alright baby, your loss. Down south, we don't get cute, healthy girls like you."

"So isn't it your loss?" her co-worker, a pimply white boy, said.

Todd drank his coffee fast, burning his tongue in the process, but he swallowed it down anyway. He pointed at the white boy, winked, then turned around and marched out.

"I don't know what girl you're talking about," Sonny said, giving Todd back the license plate number he'd scratched on a pad. Todd noticed that his ring finger was missing.

"That is your number? You are Kenneth Russo, aren't you?"

They were standing in Sonny's barn. Sonny picked up some hay and played with it.

"So what? Someone could have written that down out of spite."

"What were you doing in North Carolina?"

"I don't remember. That was years ago." He thought. "I've got family down in South Carolina. I was driving up from seeing them, probably."

"Okay. So write down their names and I'll follow up."

He handed Sonny the pad, but Sonny wouldn't take it.

"Why not?" Todd asked.

"I don't want you prying into my family life, okay? I live on this farm for a reason. I'm estranged."

"That finger have something to do with it?"

Kenneth looked nervously at his hand.

"None of your business."

"For all I know you kidnapped this girl, raped her and threw her in a ditch in Virginia Beach."

"She's alive!" he shouted, then realized his mistake.

Todd began laughing. "Give it up, old man. Where is she?"

Sonny swallowed uncomfortably. His hand twitched. He sat on a upside-down bucket. "Look, she works for my cousin Joey, okay. Last I heard she'd moved to New York City, but I don't know where."

"Your cousin Joey moves around?"

"He lives in Jersey. But he's got many businesses."

"And what business does Malta work in?"

Kenneth stared at him dispassionately.

"What business do you think?" he asked.

Malta climbed up the long flight of stairs again. She hadn't said a word to Regina about quitting, and it had been months since she'd seen Joey.

The door opened again. She snuck in. This time Stacy was behind the door, wearing a red negligee.

"You're on time. Let's start the party."

She followed Stacy down the hallway to the back. She passed another girl wearing a white corset and heavy-set makeup. "This is Courtney. Another busy day," Stacy said, taking Malta by the hand. Malta could hear Rhonda munching on something in the other room as she entered the big one. Inside, lying naked on his front, was a tall white man. Malta saw a yarmulke on his head.

"This is Judah, one of our best customers." Judah raised his hand and shook Malta's. He looked familiar to her, but she couldn't place him. Malta laughed.

"Strange way to shake someone's hand," Judah said. "Nice to meet you."

Malta giggled and rubbed the hairs on the bottom of Judah's head.

"Let's get Milly here more comfortable," Stacy said. She took Malta by the hand and they left the room. Malta could hear Courtney greeting a customer.

They entered the living room. Rhonda was playing solitaire again, and was pawing through a bag of Lays.

"Have the phones been ringing off the hook?" Stacy asked, opening the closet.

"When aren't they?"

"These guys have to get a life, huh?"

"This is their life," Rhonda responded, deadpan.

Stacy laughed and addressed Malta. "See, you're in the right place. What do you wanna wear? Judah doesn't really care. Some of the other guys are more particular."

"How about a matching negligee?"

"Sure. We've got this cream one," she said, pointing to one in the closet.

"You're fire and I'm ice."

"Wit! You're perfect. Doesn't matter, because as soon as we get in, we get topless."

"So why don't I just go in topless?"

"You can do that, I guess. It's just a formality. Maybe something legal, I don't know. But I won't tell Shirley if you won't."

Malta took off her clothes, keeping her panties on.

"Do you wanna try a g-string?" Stacy asked.

"Sure."

Stacy whipped a black g-string from the closet. "Here you go. Now why do I need this thing either?"

She handed Malta the g-string. Then she took off her negligee, revealing her 32 C tits.

"Nice," Malta said. Stacy giggled, then got serious.

"Okay, now remember, you go slow, follow my lead. We'll tease and massage. When I give the cue, he can turn around. Judah's usually hard. Not every guy is. If not, we might need to try some manual or extra teasing. Just so you know, he's more of a tits guy, and he likes to suck, so be prepared. I'll start with his head and you take his feet, we'll criss-cross, then when we get him around, he'll have one arm around each of us. You can rub his inner thighs. He likes licking on his nipples. For the massage, follow my lead. Just do the opposite side of his body that I'm doing. How'd you do the massage at the other place?"

"We didn't have a standard procedure. Mainly I'd just get naked and we'd kiss, then I'd give him a massage if he wanted. If not..."

"Okay, this is a stricter place. He can't kiss you, touch your pussy, he can't turn around until we say it's okay. He gets a soft but real massage. We're in control, remember that."

"Should I take off my g-string?"

"After he turns around, yeah. He just can't touch it."

Malta nodded, curious. This place seemed more legit, and she worried that her massage skills weren't up to par.

"Ready?"

Malta took a deep breath. "Yup, nothing new."

Stacy took her by the hand again.

"By the way, why Milly?" Malta asked.

"M & M," Stacy explained. "Shirley thought it was funny."

Malta smiled. As they entered the hallway, Malta thought she heard someone crying, but just as soon she was inside the big room. Then she heard the phone ring inside the living room.

She noticed a wad of 20 dollar bills next to the lamp on the table.

Stacy went to his head and Malta to his feet.

"Nice of you two to join me again," Judah said.

"Nice of you to come on by again, Judah," Stacy said, giggling. She took some oil from a bottle, rubbed it in her hands, then spread it down Judah's back, arching over, rubbing his back with her breasts simultaneously.

"Mmm," Judah said. "I know all about your titties, Cindy. How about the new girl? I like the name Milly. The boss lady pick it for you?"

"You know there are no boss ladies here, Judah."

"Yup. Woman-run, I know."

Malta began rubbing Judah's calves.

"You ever done this before, Milly?" he asked. "Are you new to the city?"

"I'm from Florida. But I've been here for years."

"Judah's a curious cat," Stacy interrupted. "He's a rare customer who actually is from New York City."

"This is the city of 'everyone from somewhere else' I'm told. But there's a base of us. So Milly, what have you been doing in the city?"

"Similar stuff," she said.

"Really, so you're pretty experienced?"

Milly began to think of a response as she stared at Stacy, but then she heard a commotion in the hallway and lost her thought. She heard a bunch of voices, both male and female.

Then the curtain opened. A group of men and women wearing blue jackets entered, holding walkie-talkies.

"Put your clothes on, ladies and gentlemen," one of the officers said. "You're under arrest."

Thomas entered the motel just as Phillip was leaving.

"Hello, sir," he said to Phillip as he stumbled inside.

"Good morning to you," Phillip replied.

"Nice to see you, Thomas," Kunal said from behind the counter. "I didn't expect you."

"People rarely do," Thomas replied. "I've come by to speak to you."

226

"I see," Kunal said. "In private?"

"It's early in the morning. I don't see anyone in here."

Thomas stared at Phillip, who said his goodbye and left.

"A loyal soldier."

"Used to be. He just told me he's moving on. So I've gotta find another guard for the night."

"How about me? I'm pretty sure I can hold down the fort with this gimp-leg. Won't any hookers get past it."

Kunal laughed, but stopped when he noticed Thomas' grave expression.

"I don't like being kicked around, Kunal," he said.

"What are you talking about?"

"I've heard off the grapevine you've been making deals with other people."

"Who's on this vine?"

"Not the issue. My issue is when you come to me for money, we set a plan, and then you go behind my back to get money from the same people we're plotting against."

"You're not reading it right. Where I get my funding from isn't relevant to you. You'll still be the 50% partner on your side."

"It is relevant when we set up a plan."

"And this will help us because now more people are invested in the convention center's success and in your candidate. How does that hurt us?"

Thomas smirked. "It doesn't. But it bothers me when someone plays the game better than me."

"Well, maybe I'm learning. Or maybe I just got lucky. I told Ami, my wife, about it and she suggested we get her father involved. And it went on from there. See, she doesn't want to live in a motel. And while I want to run one, maybe I don't want to live in one either."

Thomas was silent, seemed to think. "Your wife. A love marriage, or arranged? Tell me again."

Kunal didn't respond immediately. "Love," he finally

said. "Our families weren't exactly unhappy about it, but yeah, after the whole Malta thing, I met her like my mom had suggested. I already knew her when we were kids. But damn, she had grown up. So we hit it off. I never expected we would. And then my dad got sick, and things just kind of clicked in place."

"Does she know about Malta?"

"No. Why would she? There's not much to know."

"Except for your secret pining for another woman."

"There's no pining. I love Ami. Sure, I'd love to know Malta's okay, that she survived Jessup and everyone else trying to fuck her in her life. But I never knew her."

"You wanted to. You blame yourself for letting her slip away into the darkness."

Kunal nodded. "I do. It was my fault for leaving her with Todd. I should have just kept her in my apartment. If I wasn't scared of my dad..."

"Yet, Todd's gone looking for her up in Pennsylvania, and you're here, minding the store and making deals with your wife's family."

Kunal's chest contracted. "He already left?"

"Sure. He came by to tell me. I guess he missed you."

"He told me I could go with him. Why would he go alone?"

"Maybe he changed his mind. Or maybe he wanted to tease you with the possibility, and for me to see your face when you realized you got fucked over."

Kunal shook his head. "I'm sure he'll call me when he finds her."

Thomas shrugged. "Personally I've never understood Todd's motivations. Now he walks around with this air of arrogance, not unlike his football days, but more so, with a devil-may-care attitude. Like one of those..."

"What's your game, Thomas?"

"Sorry..."

"Why are you fucking with me like this?"

228

"I just thought your wife might be interested to know about Malta."

"Why?"

Thomas shrugged. "Your business partners should be informed of all things."

"What, do you want me to give the money back? To break up the pact?"

Thomas slammed his hand down. "No, I want you to understand who's the boss, bitch."

Kunal swallowed, taken aback. "Who is the boss?"

"I am. And if you're going to do something where my interests are at stake, then tell me about it first."

"I told you..."

"I've got shit on you, Kunal. I'm sure your wife would love to hear about your obsession with Malta. Why don't I..."

"And I've got shit on you," Kunal said firmly. "You fucked a prostitute in my motel, remember? This motel. And Todd took a picture of it. That's right. Why don't I text him and have him email it to me, and to the local police department too? You're right next to that douche bag they arrested. I wonder what they'll think of that."

Thomas shook his head. "Todd wouldn't do that..."

"Really? Is he better friends with you or me?"

"These days? I'll take the cake."

"Fine. Gamble."

Thomas swallowed, his lip trembling as he gripped the counter.

"Fuck you!" Thomas yelled suddenly, pointing at Kunal. "That's it. I'm taking my fucking stake back. And to fuck you over, I'm gonna buy that motel myself. No partners necessary."

"Fine, Thomas," Kunal replied. "You can forget about support for your candidate by the Indian-American community."

Thomas snickered. "You don't have influence, Kunal,

you just wish you did. And we don't need these weak-kneed Indians. We've got the Jewish doctors, the blacks, plenty of business owners and the university. They're benefiting from the center the most. And you know how the university goes, this town goes too."

"We'll see about that, Thomas."

Thomas turned and began to limp out. "This is war, Kunal," he said. "You better go get your shit together, because I'm gonna hit you hard."

Kunal didn't respond.

Jim was putting the chairs upright after a wild night went later than usual when Todd came in, holding up his badge.

"Are you the owner of this establishment?" he asked.

"No," Jim said. "But close enough. What can I do for you?"

"Do you know a Malta?"

"Um, yeah, I think so. She worked here for a day or two. Just waitressing. She wasn't a dancer or nothing."

"You know what happened to her?"

"No. I just know she didn't show up to work again."

"Where's Joey Russo?"

"He's out. You wanna see her employment records or something?"

"That would be helpful."

"I don't know if I can, though. Joey owns the place."

"I can wait. When's he coming back?"

"Not sure. He doesn't show up until the afternoon, usually. We don't open 'til 4. And even then...he doesn't keep regular hours."

"Does he have a cell?"

"Sure. Let me get it for you."

Jim walked to the back office.

Gina, wearing a leather jacket and carrying a duffel bag, was walking out when Todd showed his badge to her.

"You know a Malta?"

"Who's asking?"

"The law, that's who."

"Jersey Law usually have southern accents?"

"What's it to you? Answer my question or I'll bring you in for hindering. Or worse. I could shut this whole place down by talking to the right people."

"Be careful who you talk to." She looked into Todd's eyes. "I don't know what happened to Malta. She worked here for a day. I showed her my moves. I could show you too if you want, cutie," she said, changing her tone.

"Yeah, what do you I get for that?" Todd asked.

Gina paused, taken aback. "What do you want for it?"

Jim came back with a cell phone number written on a piece of scrap paper. Todd took it and Gina by the arm.

"Come on, I'll walk you to your car," he said to her, winking at Jim.

At the arraignment, Malta was shaking. Being inside one prison cell with prostitutes, purse snatchers and murderers had shaken her up. She thought smiling when they took her mugshot might take the edge off, but the officers had discarded that one and made her take the picture again.

Her lawyer, a public defender named Alvin Bennett she'd met only moments before, was putting his papers together.

"Look," he was saying, "normally, I'd just plead this out, get you a misdemeanor, you do some community service, and that's it. But they've got nothing here. Just another pseudo-vice bust with no evidence except they say so. The mayor's getting desperate, just wants numbers for his baloney nanny state. I'm going to get you off. But first we've got the bail hearing to survive."

Malta nodded to everything he said. She was nervous and jittery. She turned around and saw Joey behind her, sitting in the second row, next to the aisle. She didn't see Regina or Shirley.

Joey got up and approached her.

"Don't worry, baby, I've got you covered. They give you bail, I'll post it."

"I'm sorry, Joey," she responded, almost crying. "I got greedy."

Joey winked at her. "No problem, honey, we all make mistakes. You'll make it right."

She turned around again and faced the judge, who pounded her gavel. The other girls in the cell had told her that this particular judge was tough.

The bailiff read the case number aloud and called out "The Honorable Judge Joan Jimenez presiding."

After Malta's name and charge had been read, the judge asked, "Ok, what do we have here?"

The prosecutor and Mr. Bennett started to argue about her case. Mr. Bennett told the judge Malta should have never been arrested. She was just an alternative masseuse doing her job.

"Erotic massage isn't illegal, your honor. There must be sexual contact specifically for payment. Paying for a massage isn't illegal. He must pay for a sexual favor. That didn't happen here."

"Topless massages in private apartments? There's clearly intent," the prosecutor countered.

"*Craigslist* is filled with these services," Mr Bennett responded. "It's honest work for honest money. We know the rent costs. The economy's crap. I don't see anyone talking about that."

"Save it for the media, counselor. Is the defendant a flight risk?"

"Yes, your honor," the prosecutor said. "We've got a confession by another prostitute that this defendant has been working in the sex industry for years, that she's been a prostitute in Florida, North Carolina, Pennsylvania and New Jersey. She could easily flee the state and resume business as usual."

"I imagine this other 'prostitute' was a mole used by the Mayor's office, your Honor, to carry out this unlawful sting and arrest," Mr. Bennett countered. "I don't know enough about my client's history to say anything about that, but I do contend that someone else's testimony is hearsay. My client is a resident of New York City. She's got an apartment and she pays rent on it. She has to work two jobs to support herself. I don't see how she would have the funds to flee."

"Your Honor, if I could add just one more bit of hearsay," the prosecutor interjected. "I just heard this gentleman behind me say he was going to post her bail. I previously overheard this gentleman telling someone else he owns a strip club in New Jersey. If he were to post her bail, wouldn't she go back to New Jersey?"

"More hearsay, your Honor. In a bail hearing? This is appalling."

"And this is my court, counselor. I can consider what I want," Judge Jimenez said. Malta whispered "bitch" under her lips.

"Sir," the judge said to Joey, "can you stand and state your name?"

Joey looked around, then stood awkwardly and did as commanded. "Joey Russo, your Honor."

"Do you intend to pay this defendant's bail?"

He hesitated, then said, "Yes, I do your Honor. She's an old friend."

"And an employee?"

"Yes, your Honor."

"Is it true you own a disreputable establishment in New Jersey, sir?"

"A Gentleman's Cabaret, your Honor. But I also have business interests in New York."

Judge Jimenez peered at him over her glasses. "I'm sure you do."

"What I mean to say is, your Honor, I'm just paying her bail to be helpful, not because I intend for her to work for me."

The Prosecutor laughed.

"Anyway, I'm saying, I'll make sure she comes to court, your Honor," Joey insisted.

"I can pay my own bail," Malta said.

"Can you?" Judge Jimenez replied. "You don't know yet how much it is going to be."

"Neither does Joey," she said.

"That's true," Judge Jimenez agreed.

"Your Honor," another voice from the audience called out, "I can pay her bail and make sure she comes to court."

Malta turned and saw a tall white man wearing a yarmulke. She recognized him. He was the Jewish man who had visited her at Regina's and made her lie in the dark while he touched her all over.

"Who are you?" the judge asked.

"Jonah Cohen," he said. "I'm brother to the man who was arrested with Malta, Judah Cohen. Prostitution is abhorrent to me, your Honor. I have posted my brother's bail and will make sure he will come to court. I will do the same with the young lady."

"Do you own any disreputable businesses, sir?"

"Only a diamond business in Manhattan."

Judge Jimenez shrugged. "Very well. Tell me, do you still want to pay your own bail, ma'am?"

234

"How much is it?" Malta asked.

"I object to this entire farce," Mr. Bennett said. "The charges should be dismissed. There's no evidence..."

Judge Jimenez rolled her eyes, then cut him off. "I will set it at $1,000, as long as you agree to be in the custody of Mr. Jonah Cohen and appear in court."

Malta looked at Mr. Bennett, who seemed puzzled. She nodded. "He can pay it," she said.

"Very well," Judge Jimenez declared, pounding the gavel.

Malta turned around. Joey was gone.

Malta got out of the backseat of the Lincoln Towncar and looked up a hill at the side of a house covered with vines.

"Are we in the suburbs?" she asked.

"Forest Hills. Close to Kew Gardens," Jonah said.

"Sounds like the suburbs."

"If that's how you want to think of it, be my guest. Come on," he said, waving her on. She followed him to the side of a large orange wall which looked like it was made of clay. But Malta knew better. She ran up half of a long staircase before she stopped and panted for breath.

"Don't die of a heart attack," Jonah said, looking back. "I'll lose $1000 on you."

Malta laughed, unsure if she was supposed to. She continued her trek and at the top of the hill, she saw, to her right, a slight dirt path between short bushes. Zig-zagging through it, she ended up at a marble staircase leading up to a porch, which led to a large wooden door.

But her benefactor was nowhere to be found.

She looked around, and noticed many of the tree trunks in the yard, instead of being thick stumps, were huge roots like veins criss-crossing each other. They were competing for honors, rising to branches that dipped to the ground like luscious vines. They must have been centuries, even more than a millennium, old. She recalled trees like that from her childhood in Florida, which she would climb with her male friends, back when she was a tomboy chasing jack-rabbits and didn't have a care in the world, when she didn't worry about anything but catching who was "it." A long time ago. Distant memories.

She climbed the stairs and approached the door. She was about to knock when she heard sounds coming from the window. She tiptoed to it and listened.

"A shiksa, and a prostitute on top, in our home!"

"It's temporary. It's for Judah," she heard Jonah say.

"Judah. Judah. You didn't care about him at all until he inherited Abba's fortune. Now suddenly everything he wants he..."

Malta heard a slap. A long pause, a woman's screech, and a man's stiff and sudden roar.

"Don't you dare..." she heard him say, and then she heard running. She wondered if she should follow suit. She stumbled to the edge of the hill and peered down at the bottom of the street. A single car drove past.

She wanted to run away but something stopped her. She couldn't do that. Could she?

The door opened. She saw half a man in the doorway.

"This way, Malta," he said. "Don't be afraid."

She froze, but she saw his hand beckon, and naturally, she responded as she had done so often before. Beckoned to a man's call. Except usually he had money in his hand. Then again, this wasn't much different. The money had already been paid, as usual.

She entered and the door closed behind her. She was in a large rotunda with a ceiling taller than any she'd ever seen. A staircase led up to another floor, and another passageway led left and up. In front of her was another opening that was better lit.

"Go straight ahead, it's the kitchen," Jonah said.

Malta hesitated, then gravitated towards it.

"We've got some spaghetti in the fridge. Or do you mind matzah?"

"You know, when I was young I wasn't too good with the ladies," Todd said, lying in bed.

"Yeah, you couldn't take command? Use your badge like a weapon?" Gina taunted, buttoning her shirt.

"I didn't force you into anything."

"Really? You didn't use some old-fashioned coercion? I do the same thing, except I don't have enough authority to make people. I just talk them into it."

"Even in college when I was quarterback and captain of the football team, I didn't get much play. The charm worked sometimes, but it was always on the ugly girls. The ones you really wanted, even the slutty cheerleaders, somehow you could never get them."

She stood up and began putting on a pair of pants.

"Even as quarterback? What were you, in some junior league or something?"

"Nothing like that." He glared harshly at her. "Bitch."

Gina studied him. "Why do you want Malta anyway? You got some interstate warrant on her or something?"

"Yeah, something like that."

"Or is it something more personal?"

"For a friend," he conceded.

"Really? Because you don't seem like the kind of guy who would do something for a friend."

"I was quarterback. Everything was team to me."

"As long as you were the star, right?"

"I won games."

"Yeah, like I said, as long as you were the star."

Todd stood up. He was stark naked. He marched over to where his clothes were folded below a wooden chair. He took his pistol out of the holster and pointed it at Gina.

"Am I the star now?"

"You wouldn't dare do it."

"You're getting a little too curious, baby."

"You're freaking me out, officer. Just put the money on the bed and go."

"Money?"

Gina looked perplexed. "What, you think this is free or something?"

Todd approached her, holding the gun with one hand, and his penis with the other. It was growing again.

"I don't pay, baby," he stated. "I never have."

"Who the hell is this Malta?" Ami screamed, standing across the bed in their tiny room.

"Nobody. Thomas is just trying to tear us apart. It's part of his master plan to get back at me and break up the Indian coalition to buy the convention center motel."

"Coalition? I'm not talking about some coalition. I'm talking about some blond bimbo whore you're apparently obsessed with."

"Obsessed? Thomas is the one who fucked her. I tried to save her. Who's obsessed?"

Ami was silent. "You cared enough," she finally said.

"Yes, I care about people. That's what sets me apart from a guy like Thomas."

Ami was breathing hard. "It's just all these things at once. First I find out you want to keep the motel and expand, that you never wanted to be an engineer, and now this thing about some hooker you knew. It seems like everything you've said has been a lie. You lie when it suits you."

"I didn't tell you about Malta, Ami, because it wasn't important. It was a short incident that happened over a few days before I met you again and we fell in love. Why would I tell you about that?"

"Do you still think about her, Kunal?" Ami asked, folding her arms.

Kunal shook his head. "Rarely."

"So sometimes."

"It's something that happened. It's not every day I try to save some abused girl."

"How do you know she was abused?"

"She told me."

"And you believed her?"

"Yes. What, I wasn't supposed to? I mean she shit on some guy's face to get him away from her. In the fucking mountains."

"How do I know, when you're fucking me, that you're not just thinking about her," Ami said. She began crying. "That maybe you always have been."

She began to walk to the door but Kunal grabbed her arm.

"What's gotten into you, Ami? I love you. I'll do what I said. I'll become an engineer, we'll move out, we'll own businesses on the side. I've made that deal. Thomas wants to destroy that. He deliberately put this in your mind. I mean I wouldn't do that to his wife. What do you think she'd say if she found out he fucked a hooker?"

Ami finished crying, then wiped tears from her upper cheek.

"Maybe you should. Find out I mean. I'll call her."

Kunal thought. "Maybe she won't care. It was a long time ago. He was a different man."

Ami nodded. "I think she will, at least temporarily."

239

"What'll really hurt him is the town's perception," Kunal reasoned. "It'll ruin any political ambition he has. But I need evidence for that. I need Todd's picture."

"So get it. Thomas told me Todd went looking for this Malta. Why?"

"To get the case settled. To find a missing person."

"For you?"

Kunal smirked. "Well, I didn't ask him to."

Ami put her arms around Kunal's neck.

"Promise me that if he brings her back, you won't see her."

"Why would you ask me to promise that?"

"If you love me, please promise me."

Kunal thought. "Okay. I promise."

Ami kissed him, then pulled back and touched his nose. "This is one promise you're going to keep, mister."

Thomas sat in his bed, his wife lying by his side. Staring at his gimp leg, he recalled the day he'd injured it, on the game-winning play against A&M, as they had rolled out on The Draw 35. Unlike most teams who ran a quarterback draw, where only the guards pulled out of the line and assisted the fullback with blocking for the tailback and quarterback, their system included the center pulling too. They used that system because both Todd and the tailback, Jonah, were fast enough to outrun the defensive linemen, and the guards and Kunal, the center, were fast enough to keep pace, meaning they could take out the linebackers. The fullback played either/or, reading the situation. But that meant the tackles, at the line of scrimmage, had the added duty of blocking the defensive linemen immediately after the snap. Often that involved blocking more than one player at a time. Teams often preferred playing a 3-4 defense against an offense that specialized in the quarterback draw, employing more linebackers for versatility to defend against the run or pass, and also using a nose tackle to defend quarterback sneaks and runs up the middle.

On that crucial play against A&M, Thomas had the thankless duty of blocking their nose tackle, a massive creature named Socratum who was drafted in the first round by the NFL later that year. Kunal would normally have blocked him on a drop-back or run up the middle. But on a tailback roll-out or quarterback draw, it was Thomas's responsibility. Because Thomas got a slow start up (only by a split-second, but it was significant on the line), he only managed to get a hand up on the defensive end's shoulder while Socratum had rushed into his side. Then Thomas had slipped on the sludgy dirt. His right leg had gotten crossed under his left, and the nose tackle had fallen upon him, crushing him and twisting the leg. He recalled lying on the ground, being in excruciating pain while his teammates had celebrated the dramatic victory in the end zone, and for months afterward while he lay in the hospital, only Todd and a few other teammates and coaches had visited him. Kunal never did.

Now Thomas shuffled around and got out of bed. His wife awoke and blindly threw out her arm out to touch him.

"What's the matter, honey?" she asked.

"I'm thinking about that fucker Kunal. He's screwed me so many times in my life it's not even funny. Just once I want to crush that fuck."

"You will, honey. No one messes with you now."

She seemed to wake up a little. She sat up on her elbow, her eyes still betraying drowsiness. "Not since I've known you has anyone tried to mess with you, Thomas Campbell."

Thomas turned to her. "Let me ask you something,

baby, honestly. If I didn't have all this capital, would you be with me?"

She shook her head and rubbed her hair.

"Of course, baby. You know I would."

"Even with this gimp leg? You wouldn't care if you didn't have the BMWs and the shopping money? Come on, are you serious?"

His wife opened her eyes wide now.

"You trying to start with me, Thomas? What's up with you?"

Thomas stared at his door, at his large window, at his the carpet, at the cupboard filled with jewelry.

"If you hear anything from Kunal, from his wife, or anybody else about me, don't believe a word, okay?"

"I don't even know this Ku-nal," she repeated nastily, closing her eyes again. "What kind of name is that?"

"Even if it's in the papers," Thomas said under his breath. He realized she wasn't paying attention. She was sleeping. "Not that you'll notice, anyway," he said.

Malta had a nice spaghetti meal and a banana split with chocolate ice cream. She couldn't remember the last time she'd had the latter.

"Do you want to watch some TV, or head up to your room?" Jonah asked, taking her plate.

"I think sleep would be good after some kosher ice cream," Malta said, sighing. She looked around.

"Where's your wife?" she inquired.

Jonah didn't answer at first. "In our bedroom," he said finally. "She'll probably greet you tomorrow."

"I hope I haven't caused any problems," Malta said, winking flirtatiously.

Jonah stifled a grin and entered the adjacent kitchen

to deposit and wash Malta's dishes.

"It's a strange coincidence about your brother and you," Malta said.

Jonah shrugged.

"You couldn't bare making love to me before," she continued. "Has something changed? You keeping me here for some other reason?"

Jonah kept washing the dishes. He didn't turn around.

"To touch me some more?"

She stood up and began to unbutton her shirt. Jonah turned his head.

"I didn't bail you out for myself."

She stopped and held onto the button.

"So you don't wanna touch me?"

Jonah shook his head and kept washing the dishes.

Afterwards, he led her up the staircase and down a wide hallway to a room. The door was shut. He knocked two times, then opened it.

"Is someone inside?" Malta asked as she entered.

She didn't say anything at first, seeing the man sitting on the edge of a king-sized bed.

Then it came out of her. "Judah?" she asked.

"The one and only," he said, standing and opening his arms. She hesitated, then let him approach her and engulf her. She was delighted, although she wasn't sure why.

"I didn't even think to ask where you were staying," Malta said.

"I'm under Brother's custody too."

"Yeah, but I didn't realize you were staying here. How about Stacy?"

Judah looked up at Jonah, who immediately left the room and closed the door behind him.

"You mean Cindy? I think she was the mole," Jonah said. "Either her or Courtney. We haven't heard from her. We think Shirley bailed her out, maybe thought she was a more valuable commodity."

Malta stared at the door.

"Something wrong?" Judah asked, arms around her.

"Let me ask you something," she said, "could I leave this house if I wanted?"

Judah cleared his throat. "You could, but you'd get arrested. And my brother would lose $1,000."

"How about this room?"

Judah swallowed. "What are you suggesting?"

"I think you know."

"You're not a prisoner anymore, Milly."

"I never was a prisoner. Well, once I was, but not in New York."

"You're not here either. But I don't think my brother would like to lose $1,000. And I wouldn't want to lose you, Milly," he said, putting his hands on her butt.

"My name is Malta," she responded, not moving, and staring him down.

"I prefer Milly. Like you were at *Sensational Souls.*"

"As a masseuse? Will you pay me for that?"

"I'll do more than that, honey. You can be my girl."

Malta began laughing. She wiggled out from Judah's embrace and approached the door.

"Where are you going?" Judah called after her, angry and bewildered.

Touching the knob, Malta turned to Judah.

"I guess I wonder what Jonah's wife thinks about this arrangement? The shiksa masseuse in her house."

"Who cares what that bitch thinks? She might have to worry about a shiksa wife soon enough. Then she'll have a lot on her mind."

Malta laughed. "You want to marry me? Why? You barely know me. I barely know you."

"I know you like money. That's all you girls. I've got that, in loads."

"You don't know anything about me. I was married once. Beaten, abused. Raped, sold. Didn't seem to be a difference, being married or being a hooker. The only freedom I've ever had is in being a masseuse, strangely enough. That's as much freedom as there's been."

Malta started to turn the knob, but she stopped.

"There's nothing out there but slavery," Judah said. "No matter what you do. You basically said it."

Malta snickered. "Even if we were married, you'd still go to the massage places and sleep with hookers. You'd probably wear your wedding ring for all the girls to see too. Slimebag."

"I'm not that bad. Give me a shot."

"You'll probably kick me out after tonight. Then I'll wish I took the money up front," she said bitterly, letting go of the knob and turning back to Judah. "But you're right. What else can I do? Where else can I go?"

At three in the morning, Kunal got out of bed, went into the hallway and entered his father's room. He didn't turn on the main light, just felt around for the stool that was always there. He sat slowly upon it, then waited for a couple of minutes, listening to his father breathing, waiting for his eyes to adjust so he could see his father's face in the darkness.

When they did, he began speaking. "Daddy," he said, whispering, "I am about to betray your vision, and maybe even your values. No matter what happens, I won't be living at this motel, running it the honest way. I'll be somewhere else, doing some other job. But it will always be in my heart, Daddy. I know life changes you, you get married, you buy houses. I'm not really sure what you wanted for me. I thought I knew what I wanted. Now it seems like I want more, and I need to compromise too. I don't know. I'm about to betray an old friend, to crush his chances at success, all for the chance to own motels. I wonder what advice you would have given me, Daddy. It seems like the unity of the Indian community in this town was something you would have wanted, but would you have wanted me to behave in this way? I know Thomas did wrong once, but was he right when he told me that time, that he was disadvantaged? Should I work with him rather than side against him? Is there a way to work with him? God, I wish you could speak, so I could get your advice. I never sought your advice when you could talk."

Kunal paused. He listened for a good minute, trying to figure out what else to say. He felt around for the lamp switch and struck on the light. He saw his father's face clearly now, in the low lamplight against a maroon shade, wan and expressionless. Kunal felt like that face wasn't so different from the one he recalled while growing up, a hard and demanding face. But now he realized it always betrayed a soft interior. He wondered if the face would have been as hard if his father had stayed in India and worked there at a government job, instead of making the trek to America for the good life of 16 hour work days, worries over taxes, health insurance, lawsuits, vandalism, crime, and all the rest. He wondered how he, Kunal, would have been in India, growing up, or if he had been born there, how he would have been different if he had come over to America on a H-1 visa, or even illegally. How his values, his demeanor, his stance, his sense of composure and dignity, would have differentiated him, if he would have been liberated from within. If he hadn't played football, had lived a traditional Indian life, eating *powa-battaka* every morning for breakfast and drinking tea and taking siestas in the afternoons. Would he have had large ambitions, or would they have been balanced with another life of meditation, contemplation, a oneness with God and a worship of others?

He looked back at the corner of the room, where the

miniature temple was, where his mother prayed and meditated every morning. She had forced him to pray there when he was little, but the force had become less pronounced as the years had passed, and other than his birthdays (opposite from the American way, Indians gave thanks to God that they were born, rather than thanking themselves) his mother had laid off from her criticisms since he'd become a man. His father had never been a big worshipper either, though he did believe in God. Kunal had never believed. He had rarely thought about God or spirituality since he was a young teenager.

Now, though, he went over to the temple and sat in front of it. Even in the low light he could see the images of Shiva and Parvati, the tiny Shiv ling and the miniature Yogeshwar. He closed his eyes and tried to meditate, but he realized that he had not practiced enough, that instead of focusing on the divine, his mind began to wander to business, to Thomas, to Ami.

He opened his eyes now. He looked back toward his father, then turned again, straightened his back, placed his hands in his lap and tried to focus on other aspects of the temple. He saw the picture of Krishna and Radha in the background. He noticed the brass thali smudged with gray ashes from his mother's ceremony the day before. Inside was a candle holder of blackened ghee and a tin tub of bright red kum-kum powder. He dipped his ring finger in it and dabbed it against his forehead, then dipped his ring finger inside another tub of sesame seeds and pressed them against his forehead too.

Worshiping intelligence, he remembered. A blessing from God. Was he using his intelligence now?

Suddenly he realized something strange. He wasn't sure what it was at first. He felt a pang of dread that he hadn't felt since he'd realized Malta was missing years ago. He tried to listen and to concentrate his senses as acutely as possible. But he couldn't discern anything. He

247

couldn't hear anything either. He attempted to adjust his attention back to the temple, but then he realized that the nothingness was exactly what had caught his attention.

Then he knew. He got up suddenly and ran over to his father. He bent over and placed his ear over his father's mouth. When he didn't hear anything, he stood straight up and placed his hand over his father's heart. He felt nothing.

All morning members of the Indian community came over. Kunal sat on the recliner in his tiny living room, a brahmin and his mother doing a small pooja on the floor, while families, dressed in their best saris and kufni pajamas, sat on the sofas next to him, speaking of the old times, of when his father first came to America, many of them living together in an apartment building in Passaic, New Jersey until someone's errant ghee offering had accidentally burned it down.

"We lost many good people in that fire," one motel owner, Suman, recalled, sipping some whiskey. "Your father was the first to move down here. First he worked in a gas station, and he told me about the opportunities of owning it. Then when he heard a few Patels had bought motels, and that other Patels were buying them across the South and Midwest, he said, this is where the business is. By that time many of us had heeded your father's advice and moved down here to Brownston and began working towards the same goals. Even though he only owned this motel, he put his heart and soul into it."

"Tell me, Sumanuncle," Kunal asked, "why didn't Daddy buy any other motels? I know this wasn't the most profitable motel, and he had enough saved to put in a downpayment. So why not?"

"I wish I could tell you for sure, Kunal," Sumanuncle answered. "Your father wasn't always the most talkative man, nor was he the most religious man, but he was very well-respected. He walked into a room and commanded respect. Perhaps he felt secure in the knowledge he was doing the most important thing, putting you through college, and making sure you had learned and absorbed the values that were important to him and to any Indian —family, justice, duty, righteousness. I mean look at this America we live in. We give rooms to prostitutes, drug dealers, adulterers, we are surrounded by broken families. Even some of our people come with black prostitutes and stay at Jasi's motel.

"We say, we are Indian, we are business owners, we have our own culture, we do not judge the actions of others. So be it. But you are born here, Kunal, so you are easily susceptible to their culture. You are part of their culture and of our culture too. I think your father believed that he had to make sure you didn't fall too much into one or the other. He let you play football, but he still wanted you to marry an Indian girl like Ami. Perhaps he was secure knowing that if he could transmit these values to you, then you would go ahead with the next phase of your lives. That you would expand your motel empire. As, I have heard, you are doing."

Kunal nodded. "I always knew that's what my father wanted, that he worked every day to ensure that I was raised right. But I never acknowledged it myself, I was too concerned with football, and women, and who knows what else. I was lucky to find Ami, to have family here," he said, nodding towards the kitchen, where Ami was helping some other aunties make food. His mother was crying in her room. "But Ami wants me to work as an engineer, and run the motels from the side. I know that's the practical thing to do, that's the sensible thing to do, but I feel guilty, Sumanuncle. I feel like I'm betraying my father's vision."

"He has already raised you right, Kunal. You are not like these white people, or these black people. You are an Indian, first and foremost. You have those values inside. So your next job is to expand on it. It is like they say in the Scriptures. First comes the control of pleasure, that grounding, that education at the ashrams. And then, after marriage, the making of money, until duty takes its place."

Kunal laughed. "I didn't know you were a religious man, Sumanuncle."

"I am not so religious, like some others. But I have done some reading in my time."

"So you're saying that it is right for me to buy the convention center motel with Pranavuncle?"

"Right? I want to be a partner too. With my money we can expand it. I have looked at the motel property. I believe with the approval of the community board, we can buy a side property too and expand it to add 200 rooms."

"The community board..." Kunal mumbled to him.

"Yes. That is the main problem. It is run by these American people."

Kunal stared at the small fire, the *yagna* the brahmin was starting. He swallowed and pondered his next action.

That night, Malta, laying in Judah's arms, dreamed about Greg again. But this time she wore a dominatrix corset and had a whip and he was bent over a log. She pounded his ass good. Past a raging fire, another rapist was tied against a tree, screaming as he realized his fate. And from behind the tree, emerged Kunal, advancing steadily towards her, holding a single rose.

"Honey," he said, "I've never stopped thinking about you. I've come to save you."

She teared up, holding out her hand. But as the rose came near, she noticed the thorns on the stem, and she pulled back.

"I don't need saving, silly," she replied, smiling. "I've got me, don't I?"

Todd had given Joey Russo a good talking to on the phone and got him to divulge information about Malta's benefactor. Then Todd had called Judge Jimenez's office to confirm it and the library to look up the address.

In the morning, he drove to the house in Forest Hills and parked on the street. As he got out of his car, he saw a text on his phone. It was from Kunal. He explained the situation with Thomas, and said that he needed the photo.

Todd smirked. After all these years, he had kept the photo. Leaning against his car, he flipped through many albums until he got to it. He laughed, shook his head. But he didn't send it, or delete it. He closed out of the photo app and put the phone back in his pocket.

After the steep climb up to the house, he crept around it, checking for vulnerabilities and noting ways a person could escape. Then he calmly walked up to the porch and rang the bell.

When Jonah's wife answered, he showed his badge.

She let him inside and began to call for her husband, but Todd told her to be quiet.

"Is there a girl staying here with you? Malta? Or she might go by another name?"

"Milly, I think," she said. "She's a hooker."

"She is, ma'am, though she's wanted in Carolina for some things worse. So if you could be quiet and tell me

251

where's she at, I'll inch up and nab her and take her back. Before you even know it, she'll be out of your hair."

Jonah's wife smiled. She pointed up the stairs.

"Can you lead me up, ma'am?" he asked.

She climbed up first and he followed, unclipping his holster and removing his pistol while climbing. At the top of the staircase she pointed out the room. He thanked her.

"Knock on the door and pretend you want something from her. Might surprise her, might not. But just in case, I want you to run downstairs like hell after you knock. We don't know what'll happen after that."

She agreed. But as they approached, the door opened. Malta stepped out. She wore pajamas and a pink t-shirt. Both sides paused and assessed the situation quickly.

Todd raised his gun. "Freeze!" he yelled.

Malta rushed inside and closed the door, blocking it with her body.

"Judah, that's the guy that raped me down South," she said. "He's got a police uniform on. He's in the hallway. Oh my God, he's gonna kill me."

"What are you talking about?" Judah asked, getting out of bed and putting on his pants.

"He's outside. Do you have a weapon?"

"Are you kidding?" Judah said.

Outside, Todd had commanded Jonah's wife to run downstairs. Now he was outside Malta's door, gun drawn.

"Come out, Malta, you're wanted," Todd said.

"I've got a gun!" Malta screamed.

"I've got a warrant to take you to Carolina. Just give yourself up peaceably."

Malta scurried from the door and hid behind Judah, who was shaking.

"You're not a cop!" Malta yelled. "I'm going to call 911!"

"I am a cop. Just come out, I'll show you my badge. You call 911, and it's the same thing."

"Sir," Judah said, "we know you've got to go through the courts for jurisdiction. You can't show up at people's doors."

Todd paused. "Who are you?" he asked.

"Judah Cohen," he said. He had since grabbed a bat from underneath the bed. Malta was still behind him.

"Judah, you are harboring a fugitive. I want you to open this door for me. Can you do that?"

"My brother paid the bail. You can't come here."

"Judah, you're hindering prosecution. You could go to jail for this. Now I'm the law. I showed your wife or your sister-in-law or whoever my badge. I'm legit, a sheriff from the South. I've come to take Malta. She's a fugitive from the law down there."

"Liar! Rapist!" Malta yelled. By this time Judah was by the door, holding the bat, and Malta stood a few feet behind him.

A second later, the door came down. Todd burst in, but his head met Judah's half-hearted swing.

"Ah!" Todd yelled. He grabbed Judah's shirt; Judah pulled his hair in return. A shot rang out, and Malta was blinded by splattered blood.

She screamed, wiping it off. When she opened her eyes, she saw Todd's horrified face, holding Judah's body up. In a split second she leaped and got by him.

Todd pushed Judah's body to the ground. He reached out and grabbed Malta's t-shirt, but she was running so fast it ripped off in his hand. She was pulled back a bit, but, turning and yanking forcefully, she ripped it away from the torn end.

Todd fell onto his knee and kept himself up with his left hand on the ground, his right still holding the gun. Charged by pure adrenaline, he lifted himself up and into the hallway. He saw Malta running full-steam down the hallway toward the staircase. He raised the gun up, aimed carefully, and shot her straight through the chest.

She felt a huge force hit her back and blow her body straight through. The force of the shot arched her back, but then she fell naturally forward, her face hitting the marble railing of the staircase. Her body spun and rolled down the stairs, hitting the wall, twisting up and ceasing at the edge of the second landing, her head resting on the first stair going down, her face up towards the ceiling. Her eyes were closed.

Todd heard one loud, pitched scream, a woman's, and then a man's voice too, asking what was going on.

Breathing hard, holding his head, Todd limped down the hallway and saw the body at the bottom of the second landing. Below, on the first floor, he could see an outline of Judah's sister-in-law, and a man holding her shoulders.

Steadily, he descended the staircase until he reached Malta's body. He took his Iphone out from his pocket, pointed it at Malta's bloody, slashed face, and snapped a picture. Then he sat down on the first landing and sent the picture to Kunal. He sent the picture of Thomas too.

Malta: A Love Story

Part III

*

Kunal sat at his polished wooden desk. A small splash of tea lay in the saucer next to him, and the matching cup next to it, decorated with gold-clovers, was half-filled. A solid brown island of fat floated on top of the light brown tea, while a trembling foam clutched to its sides, unsure.

He had been busy calculating the mortgage payments on the house. They had moved to Durham so they could be close to Kunal's job at an engineering firm. Ami had also found a new job in a marketing firm in the Triangle.

Ami was working late today. He did expect her home soon. He had cooked eggplant and potato shak as well as he could, letting it sit in the open pressure cooker and allowing it to simmer at low heat, the rice in the tall pressure cooker next to it, still closed, and the dal in a pot on low heat too. He knew Ami hated it when he burned the pot; he knew he shouldn't let it sit for too long, but the calculations needed to be done.

His mother's funeral costs had added to their financial burden. He didn't want to think of it that way, but he had to. She had passed away a couple of months before. She had been devastated by his father's death. She had kept it inside, but Kunal had noticed the progressive withering of her face. One day she had died suddenly in her sleep of a stroke.

It had been, in a way, the final break with the past, of his parents and motels and his old life in Brownston. Now Kunal felt he could concentrate on his new life, in his spacious home with his wife, Ami, who he loved and who would eventually bare his child, once their finances were stable enough, or at least enough to appease Kunal's anxiety.

When the doorbell rang he believed it was Ami, home early. He threw his pen down in frustration and yelled "I'm coming!" like any American would. He descended the stairs. He almost tripped but he regained his balance and opened the door, preparing to be hit by the gentle, warm wind of Carolina's early summer air.

But it was not his wife standing there. Instead, it was Thomas, dressed dapperly in a suit, balancing himself on a polished brown cane.

"Hello, old friend. Remember me?" Thomas asked.

Kunal breathed the air in, nervously.

"Of course. To what do I owe the pleasure?"

Thomas laughed. "So courteous, Kunal. May I come in?"

Kunal shrugged. "It's a free country."

"Yes, but it's your home."

"The bank's home. In reality."

"Rates are so low these days it's absurd. Refinance, refinance, refinance and it'll be yours in no time. I have heard you make plenty of money," Thomas said, limping in. He stopped by the staircase.

"Do you mind if I sit down somewhere?" he asked.

"Our dining room is right here," Kunal said, pointing to the left. "We never use it. We can sit in there. Or in the back, there's a living room, if you want to watch TV..."

"Awfully big house for two people. I heard your mom passed away. I'm sorry about that."

"Who did you hear that from?"

"News travels fast in a town like ours. You remember, don't you? I'm fine in the dining room. I feel less lazy and more majestic in there."

He limped over and sat at the table engraved with Sanskrit characters.

"Nice wood," he said, punching it. "If you never use this..."

"We basically live upstairs."

"Got rugrats?"

"We will. But no, not yet."

Thomas settled into his seat. "I've got one. Another on his way. My woman works fast."

"Good to know you're securing your legacy," Kunal responded bitterly, sitting adjacent from Thomas, at the head of the table.

"I'm glad you approve."

"I'm surprised you heard about my mom, since you've pushed out half the Indian community, encouraging the corporations to buy out their motels."

"Plenty remain. The ones willing to listen to reason. Your father-in-law is still there."

"We know why that is."

"Yes, Kunal. I have to say, I am grateful. I know you could have ruined me, but you didn't. So we are friends once again, aren't we?"

Kunal nodded. "The shock of everything hit me," he said. "My father. Malta. Ami's insistence. I wanted to get away. And I'm glad I did. I wasn't really meant to be a business tycoon. I like a simple, professional life. There's nothing better than that in America, is there?"

Thomas smirked. "You know what I like?"

"Yes. I do know. I imagine you'll run for state senator now, and you'll win."

"Basically a guarantee."

"You own the town with only a few years of work on it. I should congratulate you."

"You won't?"

"I just imagine that's why you're here. To negate any liabilities. You want to buy the picture or something?"

"You've always been the cynic, Kunal," Thomas said, reaching over and touching Kunal's forearm. "I can never get over you and your...multifaceted personality. I know I can buy it, but how do I know you won't keep a copy? Or that Todd won't? It's not worth it. I value your friendship more. Can I count on that?"

"Assuming you don't do evil things, I suppose you have my silence."

"I do prefer friendship. In fact, that is why I am here. I've heard from our old friend Todd. He wishes to make amends with you."

Kunal's face changed to one of anguish.

"Amends? After he murdered Malta?"

"He says it was just an accident. He tried to bring her in for you, and to make sure justice could be done for her. She freaked out and things got out of hand."

"He shot her in the back while she was running away. How could that be explained?"

"The New York jury acquitted him."

"I hear New York juries will acquit any cop."

"He's still living in Sullivan. He gave up his badge. And I've got news, Jessup and his family disappeared. No one knows what happened to them."

"You mean Todd's responsible? That's an even better reason to go team up with him."

"He's trying to make things right. He's too ashamed to contact you directly. He wants to explain what happened in New York to Malta. He wants to be friends again.

"I don't know," Kunal replied, shaking his head. "At best, he better explain well."

They heard the door knob jiggle.

Thomas looked unsettled as Kunal got up and moved toward the door. It opened swiftly and Kunal heard Ami call his name.

"Yes, I'm here!" Kunal exclaimed.

"Wow, you're downstairs!" Ami said.

"To greet my wife, anytime," he replied, hugging her.

"What a welcome. I was going to say that the garbage needs to be..."

She saw Thomas in the archway to the dining room, leaning against his cane, staring nervously at the floor.

"What's he doing here?" Ami asked hatefully, turning to Kunal, placing her hand on his chest.

"He came by," Kunal answered, "as an old friend, to see how we were."

"Nothing is ever that simple with you," Ami said to Thomas.

"I'm sorry you're not a fan, ma'am," Thomas replied. "But your father does think well of me."

"Maybe that's what he tells you," Ami snapped back. She handed her purse to Kunal and headed up the stairs.

"I would appreciate it if you could say your goodbyes quickly and leave our house," she added.

"You're wife's got some spunk," Thomas said. "More than mine. I kind of admire that."

"I guess I'll see you around," Kunal said, holding the purse in his right hand and offering his left to Thomas. "Or maybe not."

Thomas laughed and wrapped his arm around Kunal instead, slapping his back hard.

"Think about what Todd's offering. My office number is still the same as before. It might be good for you to make amends." Then Thomas continued, in a whisper, "Because, despite what your wife might think, I know you've never gotten Malta off your mind."

260

While Kunal finished up his calculations Ami came into the room. She wore a nightgown and held a glass of white wine.

"Are you going to eat? The delicious food you made is going to get cold."

"Sorry, Ami. I thought I would get these calculations done but Thomas interrupted me."

"I can't believe you let that creep inside our house."

"It's been a long while since I've seen him. What was I going to do, shut the door in his face?"

"He ruined the Indian community in Brownston. He basically exiled us. We came here to get away from him and his ilk."

"Do you ever wonder why your father's still around?"

"I don't wonder. I know. He tried to buy the picture, didn't he?"

Kunal shook his head. "I thought he would try but he didn't."

"Strange," Ami said. "I'm surprised he would waste the gas then. Maybe he had some other business meeting in the area."

"Maybe, Ami. Yeah, you're probably right," Kunal said, pretending to concentrate on his calculations.

Ami didn't say anything at first. She drank some wine and tried to read her husband. "There's something else, isn't there? He did have some purpose. Is he trying to recruit you back into his game? Because if he is..."

"No, Ami."

"You should have released it, Kunal. We could have still moved away and..."

"Well I didn't want to move away!" Kunal screamed, rising so abruptly that Ami dropped her glass, shattering it.

Breathing heavily, Kunal stared at the table, shocked his outburst.

Ami was frightened but she controlled herself.

"I'll go get something to clean this mess up," she said, walking away.

"I'm sorry, Ami," Kunal said. She stopped and turned back to him.

"No, it's my fault," Ami replied. "You wanted to get something off your chest. I get it."

"I mean I did want to move away, but only..."

"What, Kunal?"

Kunal rubbed his head with both hands.

"Look, Ami, I need to go somewhere this weekend. I know we said we'd visit the Pattersons, but..."

"Are you going to tell me what it's about?"

"No. I need to do this myself."

"Do what?"

"Look, Ami," Kunal said, staring at her intensely. "I could have just lied now, or made up some excuse. I've got something to do. Just don't pry, this one time."

Ami was shaking her head. She had tears in her eyes. "Somehow, I know exactly what this is about, even after all these years. I don't know how that's possible, but it is. You're amazing, Kunal." She wiped a tear away. "I'll be at my dad's place, praying for you, Kunal. That's not something I normally do. Then I'll consider whether I'll give you a divorce."

"Shut up, Ami," Kunal said, pushing the papers to the floor. "And pick up the glass."

Kunal drove his Lexus past the Meal Day campers for the first time since his trip with Thomas years before. Strangely, being alone made him feel more calm when he saw the trailers and the confederate flags waving, and the streams of white people moving down the street with corn ears, steaks and beers in their hands and Jason

262

Aldean blasting in the background. He hoped that nobody would remember him from the incident years before, and thankfully, he didn't get into an accident. He stared at a few guys drinking beers; their red eyes didn't readily distinguish merriness or madness.

Todd had asked to meet in the same trailer park where they had met the last time. Apparently his uncle hadn't moved, and Todd, after returning from the trial in New York, had settled there with him.

As Kunal drove in, he saw Todd standing with his two uncles and a crowd of other men Kunal recognized vaguely as those who had threatened to attack them years before. Next to them was Thomas, sitting in a wheelchair.

He didn't see Rose.

He pulled up by the trailer and parked. As he got out, he noticed some of the men had guns.

"Kunal, good to see you," Todd said, walking up to him and holding out his hand.

"What's up with the party?" Kunal asked.

"Just a welcoming party. Like in the old days with the Injuns," Todd answered.

"What is this, a joke or something? You said that you wanted to explain about Malta. To be contrite."

"I do, and I will. But the boys want to go on their weekend Turkey-shoot, and who am I to say no? Even Thomas is coming along, and he brought his turbo-chair for it. Didn't you, Thomas?" he asked.

Thomas tipped himself up in his chair, then turned himself around. "Technology can't fix legs, apparently, but it'll move me around faster."

"I've got a shotgun for you too, Kunal. You always wanted to come along, right? To see what it was like. I can explain while we do the old male-bonding thing. Old football buddies."

Kunal stared at him. "You don't seem sorry."

Todd didn't reply. He turned to one of his uncles, who

handled him his rifle. Todd offered it to Kunal.

"It's got bullets and everything. You can check. You can even shoot me, if you want."

Kunal took the gun. It was heavy.

"I don't know the first thing about guns."

"Remember those shooting ranges we went to when we were at Tech? You told me you went when you were younger too."

"That was a long time ago. It doesn't mean I know anything about it."

Todd reached over to the shotgun. He removed the magazine from the fore-end and showed Kunal the shells inside. Then he slipped it back inside and stepped back.

"That's the best rifle we have, by far. The Remington Sportsman. I'm letting you handle it."

Kunal offered it back to Todd.

"Thanks, but that's not what I came for," he said.

"Look, Kunal," Todd said. "I am sorry about Malta. Things just got out of hand in New York. I think every day about her, wishing I hadn't fired on her. I just thought someone else had a gun. That guy who was with her, he attacked me with a bat, so I had to shoot him. And then I thought that lady, his sister-in-law, yelled "Gun" and I freaked. I shot, and Malta happened to be running. It was a big accident."

"Your aim was that bad?"

"I didn't aim or think. Just fired."

"But why'd she run? You'd come to save her."

"That Jewish guy, he was holding her captive. He was like Greg, except he wanted her for himself. He was a john, he had his brother pay the bond so he could enslave her, and have her all for himself. I don't know if she was brainwashed or what, but when he attacked me and I shot him, she freaked and started running. Maybe she'd never heard a gunshot before, I don't know. I'm sorry, Kunal, I didn't mean for it to happen. But it did. So if you wanna shoot me..."

"Will you stop suggesting that I shoot you?" Kunal asked angrily. Some of the other men laughed. Todd held up his hands. "Alright, Kunal."

"Tell me about the picture."

"What picture?"

"Why'd you send me the picture that she was dead? If you were so sorry, if it was an accident...it seemed pretty cold and heartless."

"That's because I wasn't thinking, Kunal, given the circumstances," Todd insisted. "After I fired I felt like I was in a trance. And I still haven't completely recovered. I still wake up in the middle of the night thinking about it. You know they put me in jail in New York? On Riker's Island?"

"I hear they put you in the cop ward."

"It was still jail. No fun and games. And a cop in jail? I'd watch my back every day. That's why I gave it up once I got acquitted. I just come back here to be a good old boy, to help my uncle out in his work and to go on these shoots. That's what makes me feel Carolina. So I understand if you don't want to partake, but I'm offering you a chance to come as a gesture of goodwill, and to make you one with your home country. All of it. I know Durham's not the same as these parts, nice buildings and sophistication and all that. But this is the real Carolina. This is where I'm at. I'm hoping you'll be the same."

Kunal turned to Thomas.

"And you? What's your excuse? You know he sent me your picture too?"

"I'm hanging out with my people, Kunal. The real Carolina people," Thomas said.

"A new constituency?"

Thomas smiled. "I've gotta be one with the people to represent them," he said.

"I don't see any cameras around."

"Not every moment is a photo shoot, Kunal."

They rode on the bed of Todd's uncles' pickup truck to the Fallon's farm due south about fifteen miles.

"Fallon's been letting us use his range for about 15 years," Todd yelled against the noise of the motor and the wind, his brown hair waving. "A lot of the neighbors complain to the cops and try to get ordinances passed, but nothing ever comes of it. We've got a right to hunt and it's his land. That's the way Carolina sees it."

"And the way you see it too," Kunal said, smiling at Thomas, who seemed perpetually amused, holding his own Remington 870 in his lap, the choke separate, his wheelchair secured to the truck with a rope.

"I'm just saying, man, we've got our rights. I told you when we were on the team, this Redneck shit, that's a lifestyle choice. That's about honor and the traditions of the South. We're not scum like those mountain hicks like Jessup. That's a whole 'nother category."

"So whatever happened to old Jessup and fam? I hear they haven't been heard from."

Todd glanced towards the mountains in the distance. "Who knows with these hillbilly scumbags. They up and move all the time. They fuck their cousins and then they kill each other. All the time in Sullivan there's crimes that are never solved."

"Really?" Kunal asked, vaguely recalling Todd telling him something different.

"But obviously I'm not sorry," Todd added. "And I guess you aren't either. I just wish that when I was deputy we'd got something solid on them."

"I remember you telling me you only got domestic disputes in Sullivan," Kunal said.

"A guy fucking his cousin isn't domestic? Anyway, I wasn't counting the hillbillies. They got their own police force: themselves. It's kind of like in the old days, like in that story, *The Lottery*. You can ask Sheriff Picole, he goes up there only once a blue moon. Only went there for Malta because we'd called it from below."

"Sheriff Picole's still here?" Kunal asked.

"The old dog's still the master. He would have given me my old job back, didn't hold anything against what happened in Yankee heaven, but I said no, I didn't want it. He still respects me. He knows I worked hard for him."

One of Todd's uncles yelled from his seat that they were approaching the farm. They turned right and went under an old, large archway. They drove along a narrow path through rows and rows of tobacco plants.

"Look, I've gotta explain the rules of the game to both of you," Todd said to Kunal and Thomas. "Every Turkey-shoot's got different rules. Most don't have a smidgen of authenticity. Usually they just use some PDF file paper turkey and you get points for who shoots closest to the head. Now it's a skinny target, so it's a tough bet still, I'll admit. Then others got some rough and thick boards made of oak. We've used those too. But that ain't nothing like using a real live turkey, is it? I know, you're thinking, why waste an entire turkey, and a real live one, let alone a bunch? But the prize for winning is usually bacon, beef, or some other meat, so why not just use a turkey? When it dies, the one that shoots the head gets that meat. Thankfully Farmer Fallon doesn't just grow tobacco, he also raises stock, and that includes turkeys and chickens. So first we'll take out the chickens, that'll be the warmup. They're secure, don't worry none, they won't run away or nothing like that. Once a round is over, it's shot up pretty well, and we throw it in the bin and the runner takes it up to Farmer Fallon's and his wife roasts it up. A few of those go. Then the turkeys come and the same thing. So the winners get the turkeys and the losers get the chickens. Sure we lose some money on the stock but hey, Farmer wasn't gonna use them forever. And we feed the folks in the trailer park, not like these other leeches and selfish assholes. That's real Carolina style."

They pulled up to a large open field and stopped. Kunal noticed posts sticking up out of the ground. They were equally paced.

"These are the posts we'd use if we were going for the typical shoot, or just doing target practice," Todd said, pointing at them as he jumped out of the back of the truck. "But since we've got the real deal..."

"How do you figure out who wins?" Kunal asked. "Shooting a chicken isn't like shooting a target with defined benchmarks."

"That's why we've got a judge, Kunal," Todd said. "My uncle Jed has been judging Turkey-shoots for going on 25 years. If anyone's got a good eye—"

Uncle Jed approached. Apparently he was the uncle who'd yelled out earlier from the front of the truck.

"You're sitting on my chair, young man," Uncle Jed said to Kunal, pointing.

Kunal looked down and noticed a folded steel chair beneath him.

"Oh, sorry," he said, jumping off the truck too.

"And your other friend's on my table," Uncle Jed continued, pointing at a distressed Thomas.

"How am I gonna get off this truck?" he asked. "This chair is fast but it can't fly."

"My uncles'll help you," Todd said. "And then Jimmy here is gonna drive the truck up to Fallon's place to get the livestock. Meanwhile, I'll explain the shooting rules to you."

Todd's other uncle got on the truck bed and pushed Thomas's chair forward. Thomas closed his eyes as it appeared he'd be tipped over, but Uncle Jed grabbed him and let him down gently with Todd's other uncle stepping down to assist.

Once he was firmly on the ground, his shotgun and choke on his lap, he zoomed over to join Todd and Kunal a few yards away, though he had to stop abruptly because the speed of the chair zoomed him past his target. Meanwhile Todd's uncles unloaded the chair and table, and Jimmy drove away with the truck. The other men yawned and laughed and horsed around in the middle of the field.

"Now normally," Todd said, "no one is allowed to have shells in their guns until the range is set up and we're ready to fire. You're the only one who's got shells in his gun, Kunal, because I wanted to make that point. My Uncle Jed has got the rest sitting in that box he set down right there."

He pointed to a small box in the grass next to the tire track of the truck.

"Alright, now for every round, we've got shooters, the judge, and the runners. That's the setup. My Uncle Jed is gonna lay out a string, and that's where we've gotta stand behind while the runners put down the target. We can't have no shells in the guns while they're in the way. That's safety. Safety first, always. The runners are gonna yell "clear" before and after shooting, to make sure no one's still got shells in their guns. My uncle tells when to fire and when to cease, and he judges who hit the chicken in the head. Usually one fellow blows it clear off, if we're lucky. But always safety first, so let me have your shells, Kunal."

Kunal examined his Sportsman."I'm not even sure I know how to take them out," Kunal said.

Todd shook his head and grabbed the gun. Kunal thought he pointed the gun at him for a second, but then the muzzle quickly hit the ground.

"This beauty's got four in the magazine, one in the

chamber. You take out the magazine from the fore-end here, you take out the shells. And one in the chamber, theoretically. You don't need one in the chamber, so you don't have one in there. "

Todd took out the shells from the fore-end.

"Is there a rule for how many shells we can have in the gun when we're shooting?" Kunal asked.

"Obviously, it makes sense to have one. Because no one's guns can be loaded after we fire, and everyone's got one shot per round."

"Except when you're playing cop, right?" Kunal said. "Then you've got to have a loaded weapon."

Todd stared at him for a second, but he didn't respond at first. He went back to unloading. "Obviously, Kunal," he finally replied, putting the shells in his pocket and handing Kunal back the shotgun.

"Now, let's get everyone in a line," he continued.

"Tell me, Todd," Thomas said, "how's this fun for folks?"

"Out here, winning a chicken, or a turkey to take home, that's a big deal. I mean it's a fun time. Some guys like to drive around in circles in the mud. That's pretty big in Virginia, especially. Here it's Turkey-shoots. That's a Redneck thing. It's good clean fun. You remember that when you're running for office. That's why we like our guns."

"I'll become a member of the NRA," Thomas said.

"Black Republican, baby!" Todd shouted. "We need that for sure."

"I didn't say I was going to become a Republican."

"We gonna start this shoot anytime soon, Todd?" one of the other guys asked. Kunal thought he was the jerk who had squeezed his hand tightly years before, but he wasn't completely sure.

"Shawn, we've gotta wait until Jimmy gets back with the chickens to start firing."

"I brought some cardboard targets just for practice. We can use them 'til Jimmy gets back."

"Yeah, I'm ready to start shooting," another one said, and now Kunal recognized him as the war veteran who'd called him a sand nigger.

"Alright, Mitchell, I guess we can practice a little bit. Just put one of the targets up after I yell clear."

Todd cleared his throat. His uncles were still putting up the table.

"Clear!" he yelled. Mitchell rushed over to one of the posts and latched on a cardboard picture of a turkey and a big red circular target around the middle.

"Todd!" Uncle Jed called out. "You should let me yell clear. What are you doing?"

"It's alright, Uncle Jed," Todd said. "We're just gonna practice." Uncle Jed shook his head at Todd's other uncle.

Meanwhile, Shawn came over to Kunal and stuck out his hand.

"Howdy, partner," he said.

"You remember what happened the last time you did that?" Kunal asked, bowing instead.

Shawn looked unsure, then withdrew his hand.

"Oh, I remember you now. Can't believe I forgot."

"It was a long time ago," Kunal said. "Let bygones be bygones."

"That's what today's all about, ain't it?"

"What do you mean?"

"We all heard that talk between you and Todd. Don't worry, partner, we're just here for fun. Good old Carolina fun."

"Your war friend feel the same way?" Kunal asked.

"Who? Mitchell? Don't know. I guess you better ask him yourself."

Mitchell rushed up in a giddy mood, rubbing his gun.

"Let's get this party started, baby," he said to Shawn.

"You remember royalty, here?" Shawn asked.

271

Mitchell looked Kunal over. "Sure, guy who thought he was tough. That's alright. I love brown folk. You got a look lickin' over in I-raq. Your womenfolk will never be the same."

"They're not my 'folk'," Kunal replied.

"Sure, sure," Mitchell said, slapping Kunal's arm and chuckling. "That's fine. There's plenty to go around. Now let's get this party started."

Kunal looked over at Thomas, who swallowed and steered his gaze to the judges, who were sitting down now and writing on some paper.

"This here's Byron," Shawn said to Kunal, pointing to the third man. "He's pretty quiet."

Byron nodded at Kunal.

"Alright," Todd yelled, "my Uncle George is gonna give every man a shell. He's gonna be the runner for this round. So you listen when he and then my Uncle Jed says 'Clear.' Uncle Jed's the final judge."

The three white men lined up next to each other. Todd asked them to move over a little to the left. He positioned Kunal next to Mitchell, Thomas next to Kunal, and then himself.

"Alright, let's go. Ya'll ready? Clear!" Uncle George yelled. He began making his way down the line, asking for the shooter's type of shotgun, giving the correct shell to each man.

When Uncle George made it to Kunal and asked him, Kunal was silent.

Uncle George, deciding to answer his own question, said, "Sportsman" and forced the shell into Kunal's palm. Kunal fell it hot to the touch and almost dropped it. Then he watched Mitchell as he took out the magazine and loaded the shell into it.

Kunal copied Mitchell and he did the same with his weapon. He'd shot a handgun before but never a rifle. It was heavy in his hands but he felt good taking out the magazine and loading it. Then the shell was inside and loaded. He pointed the rifle at the target.

"Always point the muzzle away and never put your finger on the trigger until you are ready to shoot!" Uncle George called out. Kunal felt a pang of embarrassment. He quickly pointed the gun at the floor. He heard the other men laughing. When he looked, he saw they had their rifles over their shoulders. Thomas was still fixing his choke onto his rifle.

"Is everyone loaded?" Uncle George called out.

"Jimmy's gonna be the runner when he gets back. But meanwhile, Uncle George'll do it," Todd called out again, reminding everyone.

"I'll call out the firing," Uncle Jed said.

"You've gotta judge. I'll call out the firing and I'll run too," Uncle George insisted.

"Okay," Todd concurred. Kunal saw Uncle Jed give a mean glance to Uncle George. Then Uncle George said, "If everyone's loaded, come up to the line."

Kunal noticed that everyone was already at the line. Thomas had screwed in his choke and was pointing his rifle towards the target.

"Alright, now aim everyone, and wait 'til I give the word," Uncle George said.

The others aimed. Kunal pointed his gun straight ahead. He wasn't sure if he was aiming correctly. He put the barrel at eye level, closed one eye like in the movies and tried to align the barrel with the target.

"Now you need to fire one at a time, first person on the left, and then the next person. I will yell 'Fire!' each time. You've gotta remember where you are on the line. This way we can tell which shot is which."

Uncle George cleared his throat.

"Fire!" he yelled. Quickly Kunal felt like he heard an explosion next to him. He closed his eyes and fell into a squat position.

273

"Damn!" he heard a voice yell. "Uncle George told you, one person at a time!"

Kunal opened his eyes. He was holding the rifle, his finger on the trigger, and he was squatting down low. He saw Uncle Jed was up now and walking out to the firing range.

"Clear!" Uncle George yelled. "Hold your fire!"

Uncle Jed checked the board.

"Now how can I tell who won this round? The bullet holes don't have names on 'em."

"Uncle Jed," Todd yelled. "I didn't fire."

"You're a good boy," Uncle Jed said. "Who else didn't fire?"

Kunal looked around. Then he stood up and raised his arm.

"Point that muzzle away from Jed!" Uncle George yelled. Kunal, in a panic, pointed it at the ground and pulled the trigger.

He heard a screech as the ground exploded and dirt flew into the air. Everyone hit the ground or went down on one knee and shielded their faces. Kunal could see Uncle Jed on the ground.

"Oh my God!" he yelled. He heard another screech, and Kunal realized it was Thomas next to him.

"Fuck, Kunal!" Todd yelled back. "You could have killed somebody!"

"I didn't?" Kunal asked.

Uncle Jed got up. "I'm okay. Just a false alarm."

"That's your own fault, Jed," Uncle George scolded. "You shouldn't be strutting out there when there's rifles loaded."

"No one's following instructions," Uncle Jed insisted, making his way to the table. "That's why we couldn't stay the course in I-raq. No one fucking listens."

"Sand niggers can't shoot," Kunal heard Mitchell say. "That's why we couldn't stay out there. Nothing to do

274

with instructions."

"Alright," Uncle Jed said from behind the table now. "We've still got two shooters, Todd and Ku-nal. Uncle George, you do your duty and give Ku-nal another shell. And we'll finish this judging based on their shots."

Kunal noticed Thomas was shaking. "I'm not staying anywhere near you when you've got a loaded weapon," Thomas said, and zipped backwards.

"Me neither," Mitchell said. Kunal could hear Shawn and Byron laughing.

Uncle George approached. "What weapon?"

"Uh, Sportsman," Kunal said, and Uncle George put the shell in his palm firmly, like the first time.

"Remember, son," he said, "don't put your finger on the trigger until you've got the target in your sights and you're ready to fire."

Uncle Jed watched Mitchell and the others walk back to where Thomas was.

"You fools messed up and you're trying to stay away from this fella," he said. "Amazing."

"He could've killed you, Jed," Mitchell yelled.

"And that would've been my fault," Uncle Jed said. "I walked into the line when I shouldn't have."

Uncle George leaned back on his heels. Meanwhile Todd approached Kunal and stood next to him in the line.

"I guess it's me and you," he said as Kunal took the magazine out and loaded. "Should we put up another target?" he asked Uncle Jed.

"No, I'd have to go back out, and I don't wanna waste time with you reloading. Anyway, I think I can tell if you stick to the rules and fire one at a time."

"Half the target's blown out, Uncle Jed."

"Looks fine to me, boy. Don't worry. Your friend will be first. Remember to wait for the second prompt."

Todd nodded.

"I guess this is a piece of cake to you," Kunal said to

275

Todd, sticking the magazine back in, the muzzle sticking up toward the sky.

"We'll see. I don't know how good of a shot you are."

"You've had practice, and experience," Kunal said.

"Are we talking about something else?" Todd asked.

"I don't know, you tell me."

"You started the conversation, Kunal."

"You threw the passes. I was just your blocker."

"Oh. That something else."

"Blocking for your ass, guiding traffic for blocking, running in front of you, sacrificing my body."

"You were a good center. A great center. We couldn't have done anything without you. And I wouldn't have been half the quarterback without my bodyguard."

"I'm glad you feel that way, all these years later."

"I was slapping your ass, you were snapping the ball. You should know something about accuracy."

"I was never the long snapper."

"You guys done jabbing, and ready to shoot?" Uncle George asked.

"You told me if the blitz was coming, where the linebackers were, if the DTs were leaning one way or the other. Let us change up the play. That was big."

"A bond," Kunal said.

Todd nodded, his eyes focused on Kunal. "A bond."

"Shooter number 1: aim!" Uncle George yelled aloud. Kunal turned his attention away from Todd's eyes and toward the target. He saw holes in it but mostly the board was still intact, unlike what Todd had suggested. He tried to aim the barrel towards the bullseye.

"Bond that was a long time ago," Todd said, as Uncle George yelled "Fire!"

Kunal paused, processing what Todd had said. Then he fired.

When the smoke cleared Kunal saw a new hole that had gone clear through the target. Through the head of the turkey. He smiled, raised his hands and screamed. Then he was silenced by a loud crash.

"What in the hell was that?" someone yelled behind him. Then he heard a rush forward. He saw the shooters running past the table over to a tree on the edge of a hill against the horizon.

Kunal followed. Then he saw the smoke, and a truck smashed against the tree.

As he approached, he heard the screeches of what sounded like birds. And then he saw Jimmy slumped in the driver's seat, his eyes open and a clean, red line of blood descending from his temple.

"Fuck!" Todd yelled, clearing the way to Jimmy. He opened the passenger side door, hurled himself inside and checked Jimmy's pulse. Jimmy's eyes were fixed open. The verdict was already clear.

Mitchell turned to Kunal, who was shaking. "You've done it this time, sand nigger," he said. "Can't believe it."

"What are we gonna do?" Shawn asked.

"We're gonna turn in this murdering sand nigger to the authorities, that's what!"

"Stop calling him that," Kunal heard from behind him, and saw Thomas zooming up.

"Fine. I'll call him a murderer from now on."

Kunal looked at Uncle Jed. He was shaking his head, but he was looking at Uncle George, who seemed to be shocked into stoicism as he pondered Jimmy's fate. Meanwhile the birds were crowing; Kunal realized they were roosters. One had been dislodged from the truck and was jumping up and down.

Todd descended from the truck, slowly, still holding his rifle. He looked at Thomas first, then Kunal.

"This is hell. What are we gonna do?"

"It was an accident," Kunal said. "Completely."

"So we're even," Todd said.

Kunal felt his stomach tighten. "You set this up. You

277

set me up," he said, pointing at Todd.

"How could I set this up?" Todd asked angrily. "It was completely random."

"We can lynch this—" Mitchell started saying but a strong voice stopped him.

"Shut up, you hick!" Uncle Jed yelled. "This ain't no antebellum South, is it? Who do you think we are, them mountain hicks? If I ever hear..."

"I take responsibility for it," Uncle George mumbled. "I should have cleared the back like I cleared the..."

"Ain't no one taking responsibility for it," Uncle Jed insisted. "This was an accident. We'll tell Sheriff Picole what happened. We need to stick to the right story. The truth."

"We should call Sheriff Picole," Thomas said firmly. "But give it a few. Remember, I was never here."

"And what about Jimmy's momma?" Mitchell asked. "And his grandma? No way we're gonna..."

"We need to stick together, Mitchell," Uncle Jed said. "There ain't gonna be no accusing or..."

"Just like on the football field," Todd said, handing Kunal his shotgun. "We stick together. Through thick and thin. We're teammates, right, buddy? Bodyguards."

Kunal looked over at Mitchell. His face was red but Uncle Jed's hand was on his chest.

Kunal turned to Todd. "Yeah, bodyguards," he said.

A few months later, Kunal sat in the dining table, which he now increasingly used, eating Ami's cooking. She came downstairs.

"My father called," she said. "Thomas just won the election. They've projected a landslide victory. You want to watch it on TV?"

Kunal shook his head. "What's the point? We already know what the result is. And there's no other election I care about. Not even the President."

Ami sat across from him. "Landslide victory for a black candidate here. That's unheard of."

"Yup," Kunal said, continuing to eat.

"Looks like things are finally changing."

Kunal muffled his laugh. "Yes. Changing."

"I guess you don't plan to ever use that picture against Thomas?"

"That's all over. I don't even have it anymore."

"What?"

"The picture. I deleted it. I destroyed everything."

Ami was shocked. "And he knows?"

Kunal nodded. "I told him."

Ami shook her head. "Why would you do that? Now we don't have any leverage. What if he decides—"

"He won't," Kunal said. "He won't try anything like that. If nothing else, he'll help us."

"Why? Does this have something to do with the boy who got killed last spring? That was—"

"An accident, Ami. Don't worry about that. It has to do with everything. We're at peace now."

"And Todd?"

"I think he destroyed his too. He's living his life."

"And Malta?" Ami asked, finally.

Kunal broke his rotli and folded it over his shak.

"Malta was a part of our lives," he said. "And now she's not."

Bridget's Brother

*

    .

"When is your brother coming over?" Helen asked, eyeing the cake in the oven.

Bridget was looking out the window.

"Hopefully in a half-an-hour," she replied. "He called an hour ago from Cambridge. He went over there to visit a friend. Is the temperature right?"

"Quite right. Let me check."

Helen pulled the oven door open with her mitt and examined the cake.

"We'll let it sit for a bit. Maybe about 3 minutes."

"Shouldn't we put it in for longer?"

"Don't take the mickey out of it!" Helen exclaimed, slapping her mitt against the kitchen counter. "If we leave it in too long, it'll be burnt and Fred won't like it at all. He won't even be able to eat it!"

"And we won't either."

"Yes, you won't either and you won't like that, will you? You've got a taste for cakes. I remember from hall. That and strawberry tarts. And especially that vanilla stuff you Americans like so much."

"Yes, I don't know why. In Germany, I never did like chocolate. Everyone else did. But I always liked vanilla." Her eyes darted to the window.

Helen hopped over and shook Bridget's shoulders.

"What is with you? You are so pensive tonight."

"I'm sorry. I'm just worried about Fred."

"Why?"

She looked up at Helen and smiled.

"I've always loved your hair, Helen. Have I ever told you that? I've never had a friend with red hair before."

"And the tomboy cut?"

"I love it."

"It's lovely, isn't it? Don't you adore it?"

"I ADORE it, madame!" she replied dramatically.

"We'll make you British yet, my dear."

"I bike on the left side of the road, don't I?"

"You won't buy fish and chips from the kebab van."

"I don't know how you eat that crap. They deep fry everything."

"If you joined crew, you could work off the fat."

"FAT chance. Ha!"

The doorbell rang. Bridget darted to the oven.

"He's here! We need to take it out. It's burned. Oh no!"

"It isn't burned," Helen replied. "I'll get the door."

Before she reached it, the door cracked open. A tall young man entered the home. He had a dark complexion. He examined Helen for a second, then turned his back to close the door.

"Fred?" Helen asked, smiling.

"No, that is Marco," Bridget corrected her. "How was your day, Marco?"

He grunted, locked the door and went up the stairs.

Bridget crossed her arms, then uncrossed them. She removed the cake from the oven and proceeded to spread vanilla frosting on it with the large butter knife. Helen scurried to her side.

"The Spanish grad student?" she whispered.

"Yes, what a dick."

"Maybe he's shy."

"He's not."

"How do you know that? Have you ever bothered to have a conversation with him?"

"Why don't you go upstairs and have a conversation with him? Then you can find out whether he is shy or not and you don't have to rely on my opinion of it."

"Lord, don't get so uptight. I was just asking you a question, darling."

The knife in her hand, Bridget said, "Did you notice, for example, how he rang the doorbell before he used his key? He knew someone was home so just like a Spanish prince he wanted to be served. But right before you open the door, he uses his key! Who does that?"

"He's from a different culture."

"You're from a different culture too, and you don't do that."

"It's our Anglo-Saxon affinity."

"Well, I'm a hodgepodge of two cultures and I don't do that."

"Just don't be too hard on the boy now."

"There's only one boy I'm worried about."

"Tell me something about him."

"He's a raving homosexual and he's brilliant. At least he tries to be both."

"He goes to Harvard, doesn't he?"

"The Oxford of America. A senior but he's applying to the business school."

"The Saed business school of America."

"With blood balloons and all. There are two things that define my brother. He thinks that he can lay any boy he wants, and that he can out-wit anyone he wants. He's arrogance defined."

"Sounds like an interesting chap."

"Indeed."

Helen stepped back and created an imaginary camera

with her hands.

"You seem to have cheered up considerably. Making wisecracks about your brother, who you seemed to be so nervous about."

"Oh, I am still nervous. Look at my hands. They are shaking."

Helen did notice that they were shaking slightly. But they were stable enough to put away the frosting and take out the candles and yellow paste from the drawer. Bridget carefully spread the paste upon the frosting to spell out "HAPPY BIRTHDAY, FRED!" Then she put two candles on the left side of the cake and three on the other. Helen broke off a small piece. Bridget slapped her hand away, but Helen tasted it anyway. It was crisp for Helen's taste, but close to what she expected.

Before they made it, Bridget had explained to Helen that Fred's birthday had been two months before, but since they celebrated it every year, she felt obligated to do so this year even though they had been an ocean apart on the actual day.

Fred had no idea. It was a surprise.

The cake was finished and Fred hadn't arrived yet, so the girls entered the living room and sat on the recliner, Bridget on Helen's lap. They made fun of each other and told funny stories about Helen's acquaintances at Christ Church, particularly the girls she rowed with.

Bridget was jealous of Helen's close relationship to her crewmates. The students in her study abroad program weren't so cohesive. They were self-absorbed, involved in their own projects. Elan the Turk from Connecticut had become a master debater at the Oxford Union; Katya, the Ukrainian-American from Chicago, a neuroscientist

285

and musician; Christine, the JAP from New York, was so superior in her high heels that she wouldn't even speak to most of the girls; Elaine, the naïve girl from Nebraska only wished to sit in Starbucks and stare at Chelsea Clinton, converse with her secret service agents or read and write philosophy.

Bridget was most envious of Julie, who was adept at infiltrating high society. She actually knew a very good friend of Chelsea Clinton—it was rumored that he had attempted to kiss Julie *despite* the fact that he was engaged—and it was possible that she would actually get to meet Chelsea Clinton one day and obtain numerous opportunities once she returned home. Bridget wished that she could be as socially ambitious as Julie, but she considered herself too shy. She didn't even know any of the boys on the program well except for Thomas, her other housemate. He was the sweetest boy in the world, but he was always away on his excursions across Britain.

Bridget had met Helen when they had gone on a trip to Dublin. One of the boys had decided not to go, and in his place Katya had invited Helen, a friend of hers from her orchestra. Katya played the flute and Helen the oboe, and they complemented each other nicely. Bridget was friendly with Katya, but she wasn't sure that they were friends.

Katya was fairly odd. She was extremely industrious and only needed a couple of hours of sleep a night. She was already a medical school acceptee, and her pursuits in neuroscience and music made her a prime candidate for a Rhodes or Fulbright once she returned to America. It was a double jab to think that Katya could return to Oxford while Bridget could only dream about such an opportunity. Bridget was an excellent student and a very hard worker but she had contentious relationships with her tutors and was too insecure to believe that she was on Katya's intellectual level. She would definitely apply to the Rhodes but she doubted she could trump Katya's talents or Julie's connections.

Katya did have much in common with Bridget: they both immigrated to America from foreign countries when they were teenagers, Katya from Ukraine and Bridget from Germany. Katya didn't like Germans—as a Jew, she associated them with Nazis on one hand, and capitalism on the other. She was a moderate leftist (the communists had killed her parents, so she couldn't be too leftist), but she disdained all aspects of the American right due to her perceptions of its effects on their society. Bridget had told Katya she was a liberal, but Katya saw only her German exterior.

At gatherings Katya would constantly refer to Bridget as "The German." At first Bridget had laughed at this reference, believing it was in jest; but soon she noticed a sneer in Katya's voice when she uttered it, and the two became more estranged.

Bridget could not bring herself to understand Katya's attitude. The Nazis were in power long before they were born, and Bridget hated the Neo-Nazis. Her supposed admiration of capitalism was more ludicrous. Bridget had grown up in Dresden, which had been part of Eastern Germany until 1989. Though her parents wanted to rebel to some extent against the communist ethos in their move to America, neither they nor she had developed the hard right perspective that many immigrants who had escaped from tyranny had. She was a leftist. She was, after all, attending a liberal arts college.

The tension between Katya and Bridget reached its breaking point on the cruise to Dublin. There wasn't any spectacular event or trigger. They just stopped talking because they realized they had little to talk about. They still smiled when they passed each other, but an actual friendship was not in the cards. Then Bridget met Helen.

The cruise was the first either Bridget or Helen had

been on, though Bridget's brother had told her about one he'd sailed. While Katya was preoccupied with the paper on neuroscience she had to read to her tutor when she returned to Oxford, the two girls had a wonderful time running around the floors. They ran through the casino and played the slot machines, watched *American Pie II* in the theater and laughed hysterically, and tried on jewelry at the duty-free shop. And while everyone else dozed on chairs in the lobby, Bridget and Helen managed to climb to the deck of the ship, where it was so windy they had to force the door open.

They stared at the small islands that they passed and speculated where Ireland was. They selected one of the grassy islands and imagined what it would be like if they lived on it, using the fruit, sparse wildlife and fish to eat, and the trees to build fires and shelter. They discussed who they'd bring on the island if they could each take one person: Bridget would bring her brother Fred, and Helen the boy in the Christ Church choir she had her eye on. Helen's wild imagination conjured up a *Lord of the Flies* scenario, where she would rally the occupants around her, only to kill them off, one by one, in a frenzy of bestiality. She would use the fruit and the mud to make war paint and rub her face with it and proclaim herself the Supreme Conqueror of the island.

Bridget was delighted by Helen's imagination and her spunk. She hadn't had a friend like Helen since she was a little girl in Dresden in the public grammar school. She barely remembered the girl she used to play house and dolls and run around with, but now she had Helen.

The doorbell rang. Bridget jumped up and ran to the kitchen to check on the cake a last time. As Helen undid the lock, Bridget scurried to her side.

The door opened and there stood a tall, skinny white male with short black hair and a very pale complexion. He wore designer eyeglasses and was blessed with small, blue irises. He also wore a black blazer and black pants.

Immediately, he hugged Bridget. He stared at Helen.

"How's it going, Midget? Who's your friend here?"

"Fred, this is Helen. Helen, this is Fred."

"Friedrich..." Fred corrected as he held out his hand.

"Hi Fred, it is so nice to meet you," Helen said. "I've heard great things about you."

"Not too great I hope," Fred replied.

Helen shook his hand once. Then Fred dropped it and approached the cake. He placed his palms above the cake and vibrated them in mock awe. Bridget's face reddened.

"Damn, I forgot to hide it," she muttered volubly, her hands clenched below her waist.

Fred laughed, turned and hugged Bridget again, extra tight.

"Don't worry about it, sis, I was surprised." He began to cackle, staring at Helen.

Suddenly, Fred became serious. He released Bridget and perused the house.

"Aren't you going to show me around?"

"Oh yes, of course," Bridget stuttered, then stomped hurriedly into the living room.

"This is the living room..." she started.

"The common room, as, I believe, the British like to say," Fred said, staring at Helen.

"Oh yes," Helen said.

Fred paced around majestically, his chin jutting out, his hands in his pockets.

"Nice color. Could use a few paintings other than this Renoir, though."

"It's better than your room at Harvard," Bridget said.

"I have some paintings in it now," he retorted. He

plopped onto the recliner and crossed his legs.

"Helen, please, tell me about this country."

Helen had stood awkwardly by the kitchen, but now she inched up, waving her hands excitedly. "Like what?"

Fred turned his attention to Bridget. "B, I saw the most disgusting thing on my way from the bus station. You know that little island in the middle of the road a few blocks away? Well, I was standing on it, waiting for the light to turn red. A car pulls up, and this mom gets out with her kid. She tells him, 'Okay, do it here.' He pulls his pants down to his ankles and starts pissing on the cement! I mean, this wasn't some butt-fuck bush in the Appalachians, it was the middle of the street in the most educated city on earth. So I guess I'm just wondering, Helen, are all the British this…" He glared at Helen. "…uncouth?"

Bridget yelled something at her brother in German. He laughed and replied gently, though the roughness of the language echoed in Helen's ears.

"My brother didn't mean to be so rude," Bridget said to Helen. "Did you, brother?"

"Oh goodness, no, not at all," Fred replied in a badly imitated British accent.

He waved his hands in the air and jumped up from his seat. "Let's do something. Go party or something. Aren't there any parties in Oxford?"

"You're impossible," Bridget scolded.

"Were there any parties at Cambridge?" Helen asked.

"Sure, great parties. Not as good as Harvard, but…"

"Fred loves talking about Harvard," Bridget said.

"Yup. Greatest school on earth. The smartest people, coolest environment. This place is a little like it, with the river, but the people don't seem all that sophisticated."

"What would you know about people here?" Bridget asked.

Fred cackled.

"How was Cambridge? I've never been," Helen said.

"Oh, it was fine," Fred replied. "I just met a couple of boys, you know..."

"You went to visit a friend there?" Helen asked.

"Yes, a former lover, if you will."

Helen stared at the floor.

"That's boring though..." Fred said. "Tell me about you two. Are you roommates?"

"You know we're not," Bridget replied, her arms now crossed.

"Oh yes, you've only got male roommates. I'd like to meet these roommates of yours."

"One's not here and the other's an uncouth mute," Bridget said.

"Just the way I like 'em. Is he here?"

"Do you really want to meet him?"

"Why yes, I would love to, sister."

Bridget smirked. She got up and slowly strolled to the staircase.

"Really, brother?"

"Hell yeah, sis. Bring him on."

Bridget hesitated. Then she called out Marco's name.

No one answered her first call, so Bridget called his name again. Slowly a bed creaked. Then a door opened. They heard someone approach the staircase and grunt.

Bridget sighed. Helen saw Marco's legs descending.

Without waiting for Marco to land on solid ground, Bridget introduced him to Fred.

"Marco, I'd like you to meet my brother. Fred, this is Marco. Marco, this is Fred."

Fred swaggered up to Marco, who rubbed his eyes like he had just woken up.

"Nice to meet you. I'm Fred. A nice name you have. My, you have big hands. So I hear you're from Spain..."

"Yes, I am."

"How's it over there? I want to see a bullfight. Ever

291

seen a bullfight?"

"No, I'm not from that part of Spain."

"So where are you from? Basque country?"

"Barcelona. A bit more cosmopolitan than the rest of the Basque."

"Of course. I hear they have nudie beaches there. Do the men strip too?"

"No, but some of the women are topless. It is not a nudie beach though."

"It's all about comfort, that's what I say. What about the Gaudi? You're into him, right?"

"I don't know much about him. But yes, much of his architecture is there."

"I thought all of it was there."

"I don't know. I don't study architecture."

"What do you study then?"

Marco wiped his eyes again and looked at Bridget, who still had her arms crossed.

"Your brother asks a lot of questions," he said.

Bridget shrugged. Helen laughed. Fred smirked.

"That's just the way I am. I'm very social. So what do you study?"

"I study chemistry. I am trying to get my Mphil in it. I also teach Spanish at a local public school. All bratty boys in uniforms, you know?"

"How old?" Fred asked.

"Excuse me?"

"How old are the boys, I mean?"

"Okay," Bridget said loudly, "I think we should start cutting the cake now."

She headed to the kitchen. After jumping on Bridget's back and off again, Helen followed her.

"It's K through 5th," Marco said as an afterthought. He moved toward the kitchen.

Fred grabbed him by the arm. "That's very young. Ever thought of moving up into the big leagues?"

"What do you mean?"

"You know, just fucking around in the big leagues."

"No, I don't think I have."

"Just wondering. Don't worry. No doubt you'll get around to it. You want some of my cake? I'm hankering for some."

He led Marco by the arm to the edge of the kitchen. Then he let his arm go and skipped up to Bridget's back and placed his hands over her eyes.

"Peek-a-boo. Who do you think this is?"

"Really, Fred."

"Come on, you've got to play along and answer the fucking question!"

"I think you better do it," Helen advised, taken aback.

"Okay," Bridget said. "I think it's a silly skinny fruity wannabe who acts like a kid even though he's twenty-two years old…"

Fred removed his hands and focused on the cake. "Good enough," he said.

Marco started walking to the staircase. Fred spotted him and ran over.

"Come on, man, you've gotta stay. It's my birthday. You'll see. We'll have a blast."

"I have work," Marco replied.

"Don't worry. There's plenty of time for that. I'm here now and leaving tomorrow. This is a celebration."

"How long will it take?"

"Few minutes. Fifteen at most. Nothing in a lifetime."

Marco scowled. "Okay, I will see the cake cut."

"Great! Awesome! Let's go."

Fred approached the cake. Bridget stood beside it, holding the knife taut and tapping her foot. Helen was beside the door, amused by Fred's behavior.

"Okay," Fred said, waving his hands above the cake. "Now, a tribute to all the fags and dykes. Of course that's everyone here, including Bridget…"

Bridget slapped him on the arm.

"As if I'm supposed to be insulted by that," she said.

"Insulted? You should be ecstatic."

"I'm not a lesbian, okay."

"What about you and Mary Poppins over here? Don't tell me you weren't smooching on the couch before I came strolling over."

Bridget clenched her fists, but her arms were low.

"You don't know anything," she pouted.

"Your friend here has a boy cut. If that doesn't make her a fruit, what does?"

Helen bit her lip. "That doesn't mean much," she said. "It's just a hairstyle."

"That might be, but I still think you were doing a helluva lot more than talking before I came in here."

"How would you know anything about that?"

"I'm leaving," Marco said. "Thanks anyway."

He turned and disappeared.

"You cost me another boy. Now what am I gonna do tonight?" Fred asked Bridget.

"You can suck on it, that's what!" Bridget yelled.

She slapped the knife on the kitchen table and headed for the staircase. Fred grabbed her arm and pulled her towards him.

"Where the fuck are you going?"

"Let go of me, you monster!"

Helen tried to intervene, but at some point her arm got twisted. She screamed and smacked her back against the front door.

Fred had both of Bridget's wrists gripped in his left hand and was using his other hand to spank her bottom.

Bridget screamed and Fred laughed crazily.

"That's what a bad girl gets! That's what a bad girl gets!" he was saying. Bridget began to cry. Fred laughed harder, then released her wrists. "Yeah, cry. Go ahead. You were always a baby." Helen was still holding her arm. "See how she behaves. It's ridiculous."

Before he could say another word Marco was by his side. Bridget was now near the cake, sobbing in a fetal position.

"What happened here?" Marco asked.

"Oh, nothing, just a little horseplay between bro and sis," Fred answered.

"Is this how you play with your sister?" Marco asked.

"We come from a long line of sadomasochists," Fred replied.

Marco examined Bridget. Helen bent over her and relayed words of comfort.

"Very strange family," Marco commented, and went back up the steps.

"Can I have my cake now, please?" Fred demanded, approaching the two women.

"You are such a—fucking bastard, you know that?!" Bridget yelled.

"No," Fred replied in a very moderate tone, "you just refuse to admit your true nature. I mean look at you girls. You're a regular Jane and Jill. What need is there for men in your world?"

Helen stood and faced Fred.

"That's just the way girls are. They're there for each other"

"Oh, is that it? Pussy pussy...Well, maybe you don't realize it because you're an uptight British lady. If you were, say, American, you wouldn't have issues. You'd be in lezzie heaven, with all the other goddesses."

"Listen, you snide fart, there are plenty of lezzies in Britain and they don't make bones about it. You're just trying to rile us up for no reason besides your sadistic self-amusement."

"And it is working, isn't it?" Fred said, taking some cake frosting on his finger and licking it. "I'm ready for some cake. I'm gonna dig in."

He ground his fingers into the cake and ripped out a piece.

"Do you know what I think, Fred?" Helen started. "I think you're just a little brat who's looking for attention wherever he can find it. When he can't snog the chap of his choice he attacks the closest person to him, like some child who steps on his mother's foot because he can't build a sand castle."

"That does remind me," Fred said, chewing the cake, "that's twice you have thwarted my attempts to seduce Marco. I'll have to deal with you later."

"I did no such thing," Helen retorted. "Besides, he's not a bloody gay fucker like you."

"Ah, so the homophobia finally surfaces."

"How can I be homophobic if I'm a lezzie?"

"You're a self-hating homosexual. There are plenty of 'em. Look at me." He said something harsh in German to Bridget. She started to rise. Fred chuckled lightly, licking frosting off his fingers.

"Come on, now," he continued in English, "let's put this whole episode behind us and celebrate my birthday. It's a feast we're having after all."

Helen stared him down. "Not me, I'm leaving," she said and approached the door. Bridget held her back.

"No, please, Helen, stay. I promise he won't be like this the whole night."

"I really do need to go," she said. She thought, her face glum. She spoke in a low whisper. "I only came to help you bake the cake. I said I would stay to meet him. Now I've met him. I have work to do so I better go for now. But I'll see you soon, okay?" She tapped Bridget on the head, then gave her a brief hug with her left arm. She opened the door and shut it behind her without looking back.

Bridget faced the door, transfixed on the cracks in the wood. Her face was devoid of expression and her eyelids drooped.

"Good riddance, what I say," Fred said, breaking the silence. "Let's get to the real party, me and you. Let's get at this cake together."

But Bridget didn't move. She still stared at the door, this time at the knob, and then further down, all the way to the floor, until finally she turned her body and started moving very slowly toward the dark living room. Fred opened his arms as if to say, "what?" but elicited no response. Bridget, staggering like a zombie, reached the sofa. She lowered herself onto it. Fred tailed her and turned on the light.

He glared at her quietly, standing over her, then sat on a sofa adjacent to Bridget's.

"What's in your head?" he asked. "Are you mad?"

Bridget stared at the floor. After a short silence, she stated, "She won't be back."

Fred rolled his eyes.

"Why do you want her anyway?"

"Because I like her."

"There are plenty of fish in the sea."

"She'll go back to Katya. I know she will."

"She's a nice girl, she likes you, she'll be back. She just couldn't stand me."

"Who can?"

"I don't know. Who can?"

Bridget sighed.

"You do not understand, Friedrich," she said to him in German. "I am lonely here. There is no one for me here. It is always cloudy. There is nothing but my study. I can't understand what anyone says."

"That's ridiculous," he replied in English. "You can adapt. You adapted to America. We both did, didn't we? What's another foreign country to you?"

"It's different here. Everyone is so talented."

"People aren't talented in America?"

"I hate it, Friedrich, I hate it!" She began to weep.

Fred sat motionless.

"And I can't rely on you anymore," she said. "It's not the same."

Fred focused on Bridget's lap.

"So is that it?" he asked after a silence. "It's goodbye me, hello misery." He smirked at his linguistic brilliance.

"It's just that...you can't do it for me anymore, I'm much older now."

"So find a man. Or a woman. What are you accusing me for?"

"You know you'd flip out and scare them away."

"What do you care what I do and say? You haven't in a while."

"That's so unfair. You know I always do."

Fred rolled his eyes, stared at the wall for a second, then rose.

"Where am I sleeping anyway?" he asked. "I've gotta get going in the morning."

"Where are you going?"

"I'm traveling to Paris and the continent, remember? Down to Munich and flying out."

"Why don't you just stay here?"

"You said you don't need me anymore. And you're right. That's why I'm leaving you. I'm going off into the sunset, leaving you without your golden parachute."

Bridget thought. Then she said, finally, "Okay."

"Good. So where do I sleep, Marco's bed?"

"No. You sleep where I'm sitting."

"How about your bed?"

Bridget shook her head.

"Okay, so I'll sleep on the couch. It's settled. Now for some cake before bed."

Fred entered the kitchen. Bridget heard drawers open and dishes rattle. She sat for a while, then went upstairs. She found the extra sheets, blanket and pillow they both knew so well. She descended the stairs and placed them on the sofa. Then, without entering the kitchen, she re-ascended the stairs.

Good Americans

*

When Tom called me, the semester was over. I was in Queens again. I was on the phone with Alison. She lived in Massachusetts, but we talked every day so things weren't bad.

Tom's voice was low and he seemed lost at first. But when I said "Hello, Tom" for the fourth time, he perked up. He told me he was back home and asked me to come over that night. It was a Saturday and I had plans in the city. He told me to cancel them.

"Something wrong, Tom?"

"Just need to see you."

"No problem. What's the rush?"

"I need to see you now. Can you come?"

"Um…sure. What've you been up to?"

"I'll be expecting you," he said, hanging up.

I was apprehensive to say the least. I hadn't seen Tom in almost a year. He lived in Highlands, the town where West Point was. It was a long ride up from Queens, about an hour and fifteen minutes.

I had driven up there a few years before, the summer of 2001. We had been roommates at Bedford for a year. I never understood why Tom had attended—Bedford was well-known as a PC liberal haven for everyone from the transgendered to vegan activists; Tom kept a dartboard above his bed covered with snapshots of famous liberals he thought enemies to the country. He treated me like dirt, slapping my ass with wet towels, heckling my political beliefs, even pretending to rape me, and all my friends urged me to move out or tell the administration about his behavior. But the day I decided to ditch, I found him lying naked on his bed, curled up and crying, and I felt so bad for him that I abandoned my plan and took his abuse for the rest of the year—when he dropped out.

I can't completely explain my fidelity to Tom. He was everything I wasn't, believed in everything I was against, yet I must admit, I was attracted to him. Not in a sexual way, but with a camaraderie that I didn't feel with my other male friends: pot-smoking, wealthy hippies who hadn't known a real problem in the world, who waxed philosophical about helping people but who in reality wouldn't lift a toothpick if it didn't serve their needs. Tom was violent at times, but his aggression always hid a need for companionship whose potential he must have seen in me. He didn't hang out with anyone else and was shunned for his beliefs, so it was natural he would cling to the person closest to him, and I shouldn't have been surprised when he called me up that summer after he dropped out and told me I was his only friend and he needed to see me.

What he needed was a weight-lifting partner, and I was glad to oblige. I realized that the skinny look wasn't working around the ladies and I needed to buff myself up. My pothead friends could get the girls all right just by smoking the reefer with them, and one of my buddies, a visual artist named Jake, told me all I needed to do was have some cocaine stashed away and a girl would definitely sleep with me for it. It worked for him. But for some reason, it never worked for me. Sure, I smoked like the other guys, but I held my joint awkwardly and I coughed more than usual after a hit. The girls would just look past me at the taller white dudes with long brown hair and cheap rock and roll t-shirts of bands I barely recognized, and they'd flirt, while I'd be sitting in the corner on a dirty pajama bottom that my roommate had thrown down carelessly, actually listening to the Sublime song that was playing. I wasn't sure if it was because I was timid or because I was brown, but for some reason I always felt dissed and rarely recognized. It made me feel like I needed to go in another direction to obtain the companionship that I so desperately craved, and I thought perhaps, if I was too intimidated to attend frat parties, maybe lifting with Tom would give me the muscles and confidence to finally try. Plus there was no one else who could help me—potheads were overwhelmingly lazy.

When I pulled up to Tom's house that night, it was almost 9:00 PM, day had faded into dusk, and an orange-red streaked veneer seemed to pervade the town. The house was old, decrepit, faded, more than I remembered it. The exterior had been painted yellow but was now brown where the paint had chipped off. I remembered the first time I had driven up to it that summer. Tom's father had been sitting on the porch, a shotgun on his lap, and he had taken me aside, with Tom nowhere in sight, introducing himself proudly. He asked me what I thought of America. I hadn't known how to respond, and before I could, he slapped me hard on the back and told me that he sensed I was a true patriot. Then he showed me his 12-gauge and said that if a "soul brother" ever came around, he'd be ready.

Maybe I should have ran then, but I didn't, because Tom came out, more excited than I'd ever seen him, and

304

then the two of them showed me his basement, which his father had furnished as a part-time bedroom and full-time gym for Tom, complete with a bewildering combination of workout equipment. Tom and his dad showed me nearly every conceivable weight lift, including the squat. When his dad left the room, Tom had me try them, wearing me out with his constant pushing. The next day, I couldn't stand because my thigh muscles hurt so much. I cursed Tom, vowing never to go back. But I did go back, because I realized that pain was in the cards no matter what, that it was an inevitable part of growing into the man I wanted to be.

Now Tom sat on his porch instead of his father, and rather than a shotgun, a tattered American flag lay on his lap. The last time I had seen him, at a diner following his first tour of military service, his head had been so shaved and clear that I could almost see my brown face reflected on it. Now his hair had grown back—a wave of blonde protruding through his skull like a skunk's mane. I waved to him as I exited the car, but the way the light hit him I couldn't see his response. He just seemed to stare out into the vast expanse of the Hudson River, a block beyond.

As I came up the steps, he spoke suddenly, his voice hoarse and somewhat aimless, as on the phone. "You know," he said, "I should have forgotten about Bedford and gone straight to West Point. Done some kind of ROTC in college and just gone straight in for officer's training. That's what my daddy told me to do, but I didn't listen. Thought I'd be a well-educated boy of the family, for some reason."

"We all make mistakes Tom. You still did what you wanted. Got what you wanted, didn't you?"

He turned to me, seemed to see me for the first time. His face seemed worn and used, the skin simply hanging. He snickered and laughed inaudibly, under his breath, then it came out somewhat, like a hyena's. He slipped the

American flag from his lap, rolled it up quickly. Then he wrapped it around his neck.

"I got what I wanted all right," he said, staring at me.

I saw what he wanted me to see: his right leg was missing below the knee, only a stump left where it once had been. He wore shorts, so I could see the bottom of the stump: it seemed round and clean, from a distance.

There was another chair on the porch, the only other seat, so I sat down on it, and tried to focus on Tom's face.

"How'd it happen?" I asked quietly.

"Roadside bomb. That's what you hear about, right? That's what I see on TV. Funny thing is, we were going over to help some of these brothers in Sadr City. The ones supposed to be on our side. They got us good. Don't ride around in a Humvee in sand nigger country."

"The others?"

"All dead. One had shrapnel lodged in his stomach, survived for a coupla weeks, but he passed on too."

He sighed, staring still at the horizon beyond the river, the sun sinking into the water yet illuminating it splendidly despite its destruction. Then he appeared to focus, put his arm around the chair, and tried to pry something. I saw something drop. Tom cursed, twisting around. Then something else dropped. He closed his eyes. I rose and picked them up. They were crutches. He reached out and grabbed them.

"I don't feel anymore like staying around here," he said, getting up with the crutches, slowly. I stood there, so I could lend a hand if he faltered, though I could tell he was offended by the gesture. "I need to be on the road, man. Feel like a drive? Nothin' like good ol' American air. Wisp o' the sea instead of the desert."

I nodded. He was steady with the crutches now and hopped on his right foot to the steps. I saw the front door to the house was open. "You want me to close that?" I asked.

He seemed confused at first, then looked around his shoulder.

"Yeah, doesn't matter really." He paused. "My keys to the truck are hanging in the kitchen. Go get 'em? My truck's much better for traveling."

I nodded. I stepped into the house. It was dark, quiet, yet light enough to see: that point at dusk when any internal movement is suspect, and the entire atmosphere is of depressed twilight. The inside of the house was familiar structurally, yet disturbing in detail. There were clothes, furniture, shards of glass, old family pictures all over the floor, like the place had been ransacked by midnight thieves. I decided not to focus on it. I marched into the back, curved into the kitchen, where I smelled mold and saw a stack of unwashed dishes in the sink. But I saw the hook and grabbed the keys. As I stepped back in the hallway though, I shuddered and almost screamed. A figure blocked the entrance to the house, the twilight hitting the body and giving it the appearance of a shadow. It was Tom, who had climbed back up the steps.

"You got 'em?" he asked.

"Yeah," I said. "Let's go." As I marched toward him, confident in my movements, he slowly turned.

Following my summer visits in 2001, Tom had been motivated by the September 11th attacks to join the Marines. He called me up the following day, asking me to wish him luck. I had mixed emotions that day, reeling as I watched people jumping out of buildings to their deaths in a city I thought unassailable, my city, and there was nothing else I could do but wish him luck in plastering the "sand niggers" which I forgot I was a part of. It was only afterwards that I began to be told that my feelings of patriotism were either wrong or misguided, that I should hope for or work for peace no matter what the reaction from the other side. My friend Jake's father, for example, had nearly died in the Towers, yet after a few days of catching his breath even he was thinking of practical solutions of "reforming the region" rather than the blunt action of revenge. And on the streets outside my college campus, I saw an even different sight, vans of brown people driving around, for what purpose I didn't know. I remember walking with a white girl to a bagel shop and feeling that a white van was following us, and upon looking at the driver, I saw that it was a brown man in sunglasses glaring right at me. I didn't know if they were there to kidnap and brainwash me into action against my country, to kill me because I was Hindu and not Muslim, or because I was with a white girl, or if they were trying to protect me from harm. I only knew that I was so terrified that it took over a half an hour of persuasion from the white girl to convince me to leave the bagel shop.

That event and others left me nearly paralyzed for weeks, and it effected me for the rest of the year. I began using drugs more, cocaine more, and for some reason, even my dour state couldn't stop from attracting women who wanted the cocaine that I had purchased. While Jake stopped using and sleeping around, I took his place, and I found that it wasn't half bad, except for the random nights when I would cry myself to sleep, those mornings when I would wake up with a random slut next to me, feeling filthy and empty, wishing I was dead. Some nights I couldn't sleep, my coke high was that strong, and then I would walk around the campus, lost and confused.

Upon falling on the ground and nearly fainting, I would wish that I believed as my parents did so a god could come down from the sky and grant me a boon to end this chaotic life. But I went on, sniffing, fucking, licking, no matter what the cost, and by the time summer came around, I missed Tom and our weight-lifting. I wanted to continue it, despite his random bullying and constant insults. I wanted to be a man, not a sniveling, juvenile boy.

In September 2002, nearly a year after the attacks, Tom called me and we met up at a diner in Westchester, a midpoint between Queens and Highlands. He came dressed in his uniform: he was so proud of it that he wore it all the time. He told me he had received basic training in Ft. Jackson, South Carolina, where he had met a girl and "started something." Tom had expressed interest in women often but I never saw him pursue one, so this was a healthy shock. But Tom said that both of them had been reassigned—after six weeks, he had landed in Georgia and she ended up in Alabama. He never saw her again, but he was still happy, because he was promoted to PFC and then Lance Corporal, and was told that he could be assigned to a team in Afghanistan any day. But Tom said that opportunity never came, and instead, he was shipped off to Saudi Arabia to man a base there. He had never seen combat, but seeing how things were going, he hoped to see some in Iraq or somewhere else one day.

I told Tom that he looked well, that he seemed to be living his life with a purpose. On the other hand, I was directionless. Even outside of drug use and promiscuity, I had picked an anthropology major I wasn't sure about, and I had no idea what I was going to do with my life. I didn't tell him about the specific things I had done, I just said that I had battled temptations and that I was losing, in a kind of bible-speak that I thought perhaps his military-oriented conservative mind would appreciate.

But he chuckled and replied that there were plenty of temptations in the Marines too, and that no one was immune to them.

Then he grew silent. He flipped over his pancakes with his fork. He said there was another reason he was back home. His father had died. He had heard only a few weeks before he was to come home, so he had waited while his lone uncle had driven up from West Virginia to take care of the funeral and had hired a lawyer to advise on the handling of his father's estate. But Tom would have to handle the estate himself now, because he couldn't afford to give the lawyer a percentage or a fee. Tom was alone in this endeavor too: his uncle had business in West Virginia and Tom's mother had died of jaundice when he was a child.

Before I could ask Tom more about it, he wiped away what appeared to be a tear that had trickled down to his lip and asked for the check. He didn't talk much after that, and I didn't bother pushing it. Outside the diner, he saluted me, and marched to his pickup.

I had never driven a pick-up before, and it was a hell of a time to start up. I kept fearing that when I braked I would crash into somebody, because I wasn't used to that huge jut in the back. For a few years I had only driven a small Honda Accord.

Tom was speechless. I asked him if he wanted to visit the military base.

"Nah, that's behind me," he said. "No point in staring at a bunch of officers with feathers in their caps. You know what I really need?"

"What's that?" I asked.

He glared at me. "Some action," he said.

"Action?" I asked, though I sensed what he meant.

"Woman action."

"Like the Strip?"

"What do you think? You think I could get anything else with this?" he asked, slapping his lap.

I didn't say anything. Then I offered, "I'm sure you could, with some practice."

He scoffed at that. "Practice? What, with the other cripples?"

"Have you even seen a woman in a year?" I asked, trying to attack it from another angle.

"Not any good ones."

"I'm sure there were some at the military base."

He laughed. "You joking? You must have got some sand in those ears from those sand nigger genes. A lot of butch babes, yeah. Black ones. But not anymore. I need paid action, now. I need a big, bad, black broad to do my thing. That's what I need."

"A black broad?"

"Black, baby. I got a taste for it now."

"How?"

"Marines baby. Marines," he said.

We had gone to The Strip one time before, after Tom and his father had gotten into a fight. After a weight-lifting session, Tom and I had sat in Tom's living room with his dad. Tom had an old, 1981 Hitachi television, with only network channels working. Tom's father had flipped to Channel 7, which happened to be covering the Gary Condit case. Then he switched over to Channel 5, where *America's Most Wanted* was profiling a black criminal. Tom's father shook his head.

"Goddamn soul brothers are at it again," he said.

"Ruining this country, giving us a bad name. They ever come around here, I'll be ready for 'em."

"They're American, daddy," Tom said. "They're not as bad as the foreigners who wanna kill us."

"They're even worse," Tom's father said. "At least those foreigners have a reason to compete with us. But these black assholes wanna kill each other and when they don't got no one else to kill, they'll come after us. So fine, let 'em kill each other, then we'll get together and we'll kill them. Better for all of us that way."

"They're American, daddy," Tom said.

"They're bad Americans. Hell, they're even worse than the dirty spics who cheat welfare. They've been here longer and they should no better."

"Dev's an immigrant," Tom pointed out. I sat there, speechless.

"That's different," Tom's father answered after a few seconds of clear discomfort. "He was born here. And he's a perfect example, in fact, because he's done something with his life, he's going to an excellent school, instead of robbing and killing people or having his hand out. That's what an American does. He makes something of himself. And that's what the Indians and Pakistinians do. They don't whine and complain about things that happened years ago to their ancestors."

"Still, Daddy, they're American."

"I don't wanna hear another word out of you, son. Not another word."

At that, Tom stood up. He didn't say anything. He marched into the hallway, down the stairs and into the basement. I was paralyzed. I watched Tom's father stare out into the hallway. Then he turned off the TV. He got up slowly, lifting his pants up to his waist, then walked into the hallway, following Tom down the steps. I sat there, listening. I heard the steady creak of the stairs, a short yelling match, then a few screeches. The house was silent for a second, then I heard the stairs creak again. Tom's father emerged from the basement and headed straight to the front door. I heard it slam. A minute later a car engine started, then a car pulled out.

I stood up. I crept cautiously to the stairs. I listened for a second. I heard breathing. I called Tom's name, but he didn't respond. So I climbed down.

Tom was lying on the bench press, lifting without a spotter. He was lifting far more than his usual, and his face and body were beet red. He was wearing only his boxers, and was lifting so hard that his penis had sneaked out of the piss-slit, so I turned away. But when I saw through the corner of my eye that he was struggling to lift on the final try, I ran over and helped him. As I pulled up and rested the bar on the stand, he jumped up and yelled at me furiously.

"Why the fuck did you do that? Can't you see I had it?"

"It was falling, Tom," I said.

"I had it, asshole!"

"It was falling…"

"I had it!"

He marched over to the other side of the room, then back, his hands on his head, breathing heavily. Then he sat abruptly on the bench press and bent down, his head in his hands. I saw a large welt straight across his back.

I went over to him and almost laid my hand on his back, but stopped myself. He raised his head. I could tell he was muffling tears.

"Let's go somewhere, Dev. I'm gonna take you to a place where we can relax."

"Where?" I asked.

"You'll see. Believe me, you'll like it."

He got dressed. I wasn't sure about it at first, since he wouldn't tell me where it was, and the whole ride there in his pickup I wanted to ask him, but I didn't have the nerve. Anyway, I kind of enjoyed the suspense, though I also wondered if I should jump out of the car to save myself. For all I knew, it was a ruse and at the end of it I would be tied up and tortured to death. But when I realized it was a strip club, I was both excited and guilt-stricken. I had never been to one.

Inside I saw a side of Tom I had never seen. He was extremely excited to be putting dollar bills between girls' breasts, while I sat on the side, both titillated and guilt-stricken about being part of a clearly sexist endeavor that my liberal arts education had taught me to abhor. But that guilt soon evaporated when a fully nude girl jumped on my lap and asked me if I wanted a warm-up. At first I didn't know what she meant, then she told me about a lap dance. Tom came over and said it would be better to wait until we had a full view of the options. It was a weekday, so the place was nearly empty, and only one girl danced even though there were three stages. Even after the rejection, the girl continued to sit on my lap, asking me if I thought the girl on stage was pretty and whether I went to any other clubs. Soon after she left, though, I was sitting around the dance table too, putting dollar bills between girls' breasts, thrilled when I got to touch one or when they squeezed especially hard around my fingers and I got to graze the nipple. By the end, Tom got his lap dance, while I took forever to pick mine, not being sure which girl would be the special one. I had two options, a lithe brunette and big-breasted blonde, but I must have waited too long, because one was already taken and another had disappeared. So I ended up going with a voluptuous girl, to put it nicely, and even though I wasn't too excited about her, it was the first time a girl had ever rubbed against me like that, so I quickly came in my pants. She kissed me on the cheek, but I felt so empty and dirty that I pushed her off me and forgot to pay her. She tugged me on the arm, then violently asked me for the money. I apologized, putting up my arms to calm her. I paid her and she smiled back, told me to have a nice week. Outside, Tom was ecstatic about the experience, and told me we could go there every time I came up if I wanted. But the summer was nearing an end, and I didn't come up anymore.

After meeting with Tom at the diner in 2002, I had turned myself around. I had stopped hanging out with the hippie crowd, had ceased doing drugs and drank only occasionally. I began to lift weights again and focused on studying. Eventually I started to hang out with a more responsible crowd dedicated to community service work and public interest legal professions. That is when I met Alison. She completely changed my world. She was the first person to truly care about me, and I was suddenly happy for the first time in a long time. I had started the transition after seeing Tom at the diner, but she was the icing on the cake. And I really didn't want to lose her.

By the time we got to The Strip, it was almost 10:30 on a Saturday evening, so the place was packed with people. The manager, the bouncers, and the customers stared at Tom, but he acted like he didn't care, and refused my help for support. He hopped all the way to a chair on the side of the room. The girl came and took our money for water, and gave us wrist bands. He claimed he didn't need a band, but the girl insisted. I was afraid he would get hostile but he let her put it on.

We stared out at the scene. This time, all three stages were in use. All the girls were white, all girls I hadn't seen before. I felt uncomfortable, tried not to make too much eye contact. Now that I had a girlfriend I really didn't want to be in there. But girls kept coming up to me to ask for dances. So I steered them over to Tom, though I wondered if it would be okay for me to get one.

He didn't want them though. Not even one girl who offered plainly to "ride his cock." Not until a black girl strode by. He tugged my arm and ordered me to get her. I got up and ran after, telling her that my friend wanted something. She smiled, asked me to give her a minute. I thought I had lost her. But a few minutes later, she came back, and whispered something into Tom's ear. Tom smiled slightly, the first time all day I'd seen him smile. He nodded and took his crutches. While getting up, he stumbled a bit, but was quickly aright again. I told him I would help him get to the lap dance room, but he refused my assistance.

Still, the stripper asked me to accompany Tom to the lap dance room, just to make sure. Tom said he would be fine, but didn't object as I tailed them. When we got to the lap dance room, I saw it was crowded. Every seat was taken except one, the room was lit up, and all kinds of girls were in all kinds of positions. I was almost sorry that I had decided not to get a dance myself. Tom seated himself and gave me a fierce look to get out of there, so I did.

I left the building. I needed some air. The whole thing was too much. I'd never seen an amputee before, and I certainly never thought the first one would be my own friend, that I would have to drive him around, and take him to the last place I wanted to go.

I paced around the parking lot for a while, absorbing the relatively cool summer air. I must have lost track of time, because by the time I strode back to the entrance, Tom was leaning by the door, his left crutch in his hand.

"C'mon, let's go," he said flatly.

Tom asked if we could drive to the diner we had gone to last September. I knew the diner was a 24-hour place so it sounded good to me, but it would take half-an-hour to get down there. He said that was fine with him, he had all the time in the world. He took out a CD from the glove compartment and put it in the player. It was a Charlie Daniels album, one he used to listen to when we were roommates. He had tried to educate me in Daniels and country, but I hadn't cared. He didn't try to educate me this time. He just lay back, closed his eyes and listened.

By the time I pulled into the diner parking lot, "Still in Saigon" was playing for the second time. The first time it had played, Tom had teared up, but this time he seemed to be asleep. I poked him. He opened his eyes, though not in a startled way—perhaps he had just been resting them. Tom took his time getting out of the pickup. The waitress smiled at me but seemed distressed when she saw Tom.

"Can I ask you something personal?" I asked once we were seated.

"Sure, what is it?"

"Well, I guess it's not really that personal. It's mainly curiosity. They…didn't give you an artificial leg?"

Tom laughed. "They had one. Expensive as hell."

"They made you pay for it?"

"VA ain't what it used to be." Tom chuckled. "I'm

joking. They gave me one, but I don't use it. I like my body natural. A fake leg seems like cheating."

"You'd be able to get around easier."

"I get around fine. I've got one good leg, don't I?"

We ordered. I had scrambled eggs, he had pancakes, the usual for him. He also got a beer.

I asked him about his father's estate.

"Settled, finally. It ended up going okay because the only benefactors were me and my uncle, but still, it was a lot of work. When I was redeployed, it wasn't completely finished. So when I got back, I had enough saved to pay a lawyer to settle it for me. Now it's done. I'm the main heir, not that I care."

"You don't care? Won't that help with your—"

But I stopped myself.

He looked over at the waitress.

"Can I get some butter?" he asked. He turned back to me. "No amount of money in the world's gonna help with the problem, cowboy."

I cleared my throat. "So what are you going to do?"

"Go to tittie bars. Waste my daddy's money. Get a job where I can work the register and I don't have to move around. Hell, maybe at a tittie bar. Don't think the mob's too happy about the guy who's working there right now."

"The mob?"

"Yeah, you know the mob owns all those places. In New York City and up the Hudson."

"How'd you find that out?"

"Talkin' to a stripper. Way back when, before I took you. She coulda been lying, though. I wouldn't be too surprised." He drank some beer. "I was far more gullible then."

We sat in silence for a while. Tom took his time with his pancakes, much longer than he normally did. But he finished them and ordered another batch. He also ordered another beer.

"So what about you, man?" he asked finally. "What you been up to? We haven't even talked about you. Still tackling those temptations?"

I was surprised he remembered our last conversation.

"No, they're tackled. I've got a girlfriend."

"You? A girlfriend? Wow. No wonder you ran outta that tittie bar."

"I didn't want to go. I went for you."

"No problem going to tittie bars, whether you got a girlfriend or not. Go and then fuck your girl at home. Is she Indian?"

"No, she's white."

"Huh." He drank some beer. "Well Dev, I'll tell ya, normally I wouldn't approve of that, but since it's you..." He shook his head.

"Are you serious?" I asked.

"Damn right I'm serious," he said.

"But back then you said..."

"I don't wanna hear about shit I said years ago!" he shouted. I looked uneasily around the diner. People were staring at us. I signaled the waitress that all was okay.

"Look, point is my daddy was right. He was a hard man, a stupid man, true, but right on the fundamentals. Now, it ain't even racial. It's a matter of hierarchy, of respect. It's a matter of knowing your place on the chain of command. Now you know that I respect you as an American, Dev, and especially during a time of war we are all equally American. But that doesn't mean we have the same *rank*. Now you know my mommy's family were old school Scotch-Irish, came over in the late 18th century to Virginia. But I'm a mutt, my daddy was a goddamn Pollack whose family come over turn of the last century. So I'm not a pure-blood, but I'm a lot higher than you. Yet when the war cry came, all kinds of people were dying in the towers but a whole buncha natives were going off to fight. Where were you, Dev, in the fight?"

I didn't say anything.

"It ain't your fault, Dev, I'm not saying it is totally. The system's fucked up. Tradition's gone to shit and soon we'll probably have sand niggers running for President. I'm telling you, Dev, it's not far off. And I'm not saying no immigrants put up the good fight, some did. But you didn't Dev. And most Indians and Pakistanis didn't either. And it's not right that you can stick your dick in a white girl and I can't get mine up for a black one."

He finished his beer. He yelled at the waitress. He wanted some ice cream and another beer.

I wasn't sure what to say or where to tread. He kept fidgeting his hands as they lay on the table, folded. We both looked out the window and I saw some interracial teenagers approaching the diner. A black guy and white girl were holding hands.

"Are you going to do something about that?" I asked, sarcastically.

He snickered. "Of course not. It's not my place. I'm just saying."

"So things didn't go well in the club, huh?"

"They went as fine as could be expected."

"So…are you impotent?"

"It's not a side effect. But I've been having trouble… getting it up. I can't even jerk off. When I try…I guess it's psychological. Maybe I should see a psychologist."

"Maybe."

His ice cream and beer arrived. He ate and drank quickly. Now I observed the interracial group staring at us, quietly amazed.

I heard a ring. I looked at my cell. It was Alison. I excused myself and picked up. I said the normal hi, how are you, this is where I am. Tom stared at me the entire time. Alison wanted to say hi to Tom. I asked him if he wanted to, but he declined. I didn't mention the strip club, of course, just hanging out at his place and the diner. I said I figured I'd be heading home soon.

I asked Tom if he wanted any more to eat or drink. He said no. I ordered the check. He rummaged around in his pockets. He looked at me, then at the table, funny.

"What's up?" I asked.

"Shit," he said quietly, thinking, "my wallet's gone."

"Are you sure?"

"Yeah. Unless it fell out." He looked around his seat. I bent over and scanned the floor. Then I searched around Tom's seat and on the floor along the route to the door.

Nothing.

I sat down again. "Are you sure you didn't leave it in the car? Or at home?"

"No, I had it when I left. I think I know where it is."

"Where?"

"In that bitch's purse."

"Who?"

"That black bitch. At The Strip."

"How?"

"She pick-pocketed me, that's how."

"Are you sure?"

"Why you keep asking me that? No, I'm not positive, but it's a good guess. She was pissed in the club when I couldn't...you know. I was more pissed than her. So I didn't pay. She was mad, but she didn't really pursue it. Now I know why."

"The guy at the register didn't do anything?"

"She didn't say anything to him. I thought she just let it go, considering. Now I know why she didn't."

"I'll pay the bill. I've got some extra cash I didn't use at The Strip. And my father's credit card."

"Thanks. But what about my wallet?"

"Call the cops?"

"About a wallet? In a place run by the mob? Here, pay the bill," he said, getting his crutches. "I'll tell you in the truck."

321

His plan was to stalk the Strip, then tail the stripper home and make her give the wallet back. I didn't like it. Why not tell the guy at the register that he lost his wallet? Tom said they'd find out he didn't pay, and it would be a whole mess. Only thing to do was to stick to the plan. Or go home and cut our losses. Which he wasn't willing to do. He was a soldier. And I was his recruit. Would I do my duty?

"Of course I'll help you out, man," I said. "I wouldn't leave you."

"I know you wouldn't, Dev," he said. "You're a good man."

While I pulled out of the diner parking lot, he bent over and took the tattered American flag, which he had put under his feet, folded it and placed it on his lap. Then he took another CD out of the glove compartment, removed Charlie Daniels and put it in. It was Bruce Springsteen.

"You like Bruce?" he asked.

"Generally," I said.

"Well, you're gonna love him before the night's out."

It was a nervous drive for me. What was I doing agreeing to help Tom out with this plan? We were going to stalk somebody? Outside a strip club? Yet I couldn't say no, certainly not to someone in Tom's state. And I had to admit, there was something exciting about it.

It was 1:30 when we left. By the time we got there, it would be 2:00. The Strip wouldn't close until 4:00. That meant two hours of waiting and staking out the place. For all we knew, the stripper had finished her shift and was gone. Tom said that was unlikely on such a busy night, and we didn't have anything to lose by waiting.

I thought about Alison. How she would kill me if she ever found out about any of this. Yet this was my guy's night out. I hadn't had a steady male friend since Jake, and he'd reformed his ways long ago.

We pulled into the lot a few minutes after 2, the CD playing *Born in the USA* for the third time, because Tom kept restarting it. After the initial bickering over the plan, he had become quiet, not sleeping, but calm, collected, concentrated on the road and I assumed on the plan. The parking lot was still crowded, but I was able to find a spot in the middle of the cars, so that we had an excellent view of the front door but weren't so close that anyone would get suspicious.

After a few minutes of waiting, Tom started clearing his throat. But he didn't speak, not at first. Finally, he let it out: "I need to piss, man."

He placed the flag on the dashboard. He opened the door and turned his body with his hands, slowly. He grunted a few times, shifted around in the seat. I heard an unzip, then a slight wiz, then silence, then another. I heard the piss hitting the gravel, as Tom let out a sigh, lifting his head and blowing his breath against the car ceiling. He breathed heavily a few times. Then I heard him turn around.

I kept my eyes concentrated on the doorway to The Strip. A few guys in their 20s had left the club, but I didn't see anything else.

I heard the door close. I kept watching the entrance. After a few moments, I turned back to Tom. His gaze was concentrated on his lap. His penis had slipped out of his fly. He was trying to pump it with two fingers, attempting to get it up.

"Must be some way, man," he said.

I had an urge to say something but I didn't. I just kept glaring at his attempt, until I remembered our mission and shifted my view to the entrance.

Finally I saw her. The stripper. She rushed out of the doorway, wearing a tiny tank top, tight black pants and carrying a duffel bag over her right shoulder. She hurried to a dingy black car and opened the door.

Tom noticed my eyes moving and saw her too. He adjusted himself and closed his fly. Then he pushed my shoulder.

"C'mon, let's follow her."

"No way, man," I responded. He sighed loudly. Then I heard his body twist and his arm swing. I closed my eyes, but then I realized he had reached into the back of the truck. I had a split second to act, but I didn't, and a second later I had a shotgun in my face. A slight glance and I recognized it vaguely as the one Tom's father had showed me years ago.

"Look, do what I say or I'll fucking blow you away."

"What's so fucking important about a wallet?"

"Do it, asshole."

She started pulling out of the parking lot. I turned on the engine and followed. She took the highway. I took it too. We drove in silence. She took an exit. I asked why he was doing this, that I thought we were friends.

"Just do what I say, man," he ordered.

I followed her along local roads, trying to be discreet, not getting too close, and I thought if she had any brains she would get suspicious about the one car behind her around every turn. But she didn't speed up or slow down. Finally, she pulled into a path in the woods. I slowed the truck and pulled over to the side of the highway, about 10 yards beyond the path. That's when I realized the path was the driveway to a trailer home that I could see now brightened by her lights.

Tom told me to back up and pull into the adjacent driveway. I turned off the truck's lights and did as told. When I was close enough to see the trailer, I parked the car and turned it off.

He pulled the shotgun off me and rested it in his lap.

"I'm sorry I had to do that, man," he said. "You're my friend. But I need that wallet. And I can't let you get away tonight."

"I don't get it."

"You will," he said.

I breathed, tired. "So what now?"

"You've gotta sneak in there and get that wallet for me. I can't do it."

"How the hell am I going to do that?"

"You went to Bedford. Use your brain."

I thought. But I couldn't think.

"You want the shotgun?" he asked.

"No," I responded, after considering it.

"Good. Cuz you could use that to get away, and that wouldn't do me any good."

"So how…"

"Alright," he said. "Alright. Here's the plan. You go there and stake it out. I'll follow you. After you tell me what's what, that there are no obstacles, you go knock on the door. I'll stand behind you, and when she opens it, I'll show her the gun and make her give it back."

"Are you sure she even has it?"

"It's my best guess."

"She's gonna call the cops."

"She won't. She's a thief and a stripper."

"I'm not gonna hurt anybody, man."

"You're not going to. Just follow the plan. We'll be okay."

So I got out of the car. I could have made a run for it, but Tom had the shotgun, and where could I really go? I stepped into the woods. Then Tom said, "Go ahead and stake it out. I trust you. Come back and we'll do the job. I'll take my time."

I was shocked at his suddenly relaxed attitude, but I nodded. I crept through the woods, occasionally glancing

325

back to make sure Tom wasn't aiming at me. Instead, he was limping back toward the truck. So I continued on to the trailer.

I could have made a run for it, again, but there were only highway and pitch-dark woods about, and I didn't feel like getting lost in the woods for an entire night, or hitchhiking with someone who was driving by at 3 in the morning. The other option was to tell the stripper about my dilemma and have her call the cops, but apparently she had stolen Tom's wallet and I had no idea whether I could trust her. So I chose to stake the place out for now, then decide what to do later.

When I approached the trailer, I noticed one window was lit, but it was too high for me to see who was in it. But after searching around, I found a bucket and a brick. I put one on top of the other and climbed on top. Now I could see the stripper talking to a black man wearing pajamas.

No other lights were on in the trailer except for that room, so I figured it was only the two of them there. But I jumped off the brick and circled the trailer to make sure, glancing back at the truck to see if Tom was watching me as I went behind it—but it was too dark to see anything. I made a full circle around the trailer and didn't see any other lights on or people but the two talking through that one window.

But now, standing on the brick again, I could only see the top of their heads, so I assumed they were sitting down. I waited for a few seconds, then saw the man rise and walk away, and then another light in another window went on and I saw that the black man was in that room now. There was no way to be sure that no one else wasn't in that room also, so I kept watching.

I was enjoying this now. There was a thrill to it, and I felt exhilarated, as if I was spying on the enemy and waiting to report back to my commander. I glanced back.

I could see the truck, but no sign of Tom. I returned my attention to the window again, hoping I hadn't missed anything. The man was still there, but now he seemed to be looking down at something. He was talking too, so suddenly I was intrigued. Perhaps there was someone else there. I looked back at the last window, and still saw the top of the stripper's head. When I switched back to the other window, the man had switched directions, and now I could see his left profile. He also seemed to have an object in his hands, but I couldn't see what it was at first. Then he lifted it to his face. First I thought it was a bundle or a bag. Then I realized it was a baby.

I felt sick to my stomach. What was I doing, out here, spying on a family? I didn't get a chance to ponder my dilemma for long, because I heard my name called. I turned back. I heard it again. I recognized the voice as Tom's, but I wasn't sure where it was coming from. Then I heard it a third time, and noticed a flicker of light that seemed to die as soon as it was lit. I hesitated. But my curiosity got the best of me. I jumped off the brick and followed the fourth holler into the woods.

About 100 feet away, a light revealed Tom. He stood, crutch in one hand, a small flashlight in the other. He turned it up to his face, then to me again, then to his immediate body. I noticed a shovel leaned against his left leg, and the shotgun against his right stump.

"What's up?" I asked.

"You stake out the place?"

"Yeah. There's a family in there."

"How many?"

"A man, a baby, and her."

Tom breathed deeply. "That's fine. I need a favor."

"Leave me out," I said. "I'm not holding up a woman with a kid. I don't care that much about your wallet."

Tom laughed. "Uh-huh."

"And...if you want to shoot me for that, then shoot

me," I said, amazed at my words.

Tom snickered, low and knowing. "Well, you're an honorable man, Dev. More than me. Only difference is, you haven't proven yourself in battle."

"I guess I haven't," I said.

"You haven't," he stated firmly.

"But it's not as important as you say."

"Is that right? Well, that's where we differ. You know, over in enemy country, in *that* country, they're breeding people to kill us. We can stop that, easily, by destroying their brood. It might not be right, but it's necessary."

"It's not right."

Tom seemed to think about it. "You're right. It's not right. None of it's right. But it goes on anyway."

I didn't respond. "Look, Dev," he continued, "I'm not gonna shoot you. You're a civilian. But you can prove yourself a soldier, and shoot me."

He picked up the shotgun by the muzzle and held it out. I didn't move.

"What?"

"That's right. Shoot me. That's my order to you. You can prove yourself now, today, by doing that."

"Why?"

Tom laughed low. "Why? Look at me. I'm a fucking cripple. You think I wanna be like this? Just end it for me. Do me a favor."

"Are you kidding?" I asked. "I'm not going to shoot you."

Tom seemed to think for a moment. "Well, you're probably a lousy shot anyway. So how about this: I'll shoot myself, and you just cover me up after. Look," he said, twisting around and swirling the flashlight behind him. I saw a large hole in the ground, with the dirt mounted up beside it, as if it had been recently dug. The tattered American flag carpeted the hole. "I'll fall back into this grave here when it's done, and just cover me up.

328

It'll take maybe five minutes. I've muzzled the shotgun so the shot won't be too loud. And if someone does hear it, you can run, and they'll probably blame the niggers."

"Are you serious? You're gonna set them up because they're black?"

"Not because, asshole. She stole my wallet. I wasn't making that up."

"So you didn't plan it from the beginning?"

"I had ideas. But not this specifically."

"I don't believe you. I can't believe this."

"Believe what you want, or what you don't want. Will you be a soldier, though?"

"Why are you doing this to me, man? If you wanted to kill yourself, why not do it yourself, in your place, without involving me?"

"I'm giving you a shot to prove yourself, you fucking sand nigger, that you're an American. Will you take it or not?"

I breathed heavily. "No, man. I can't. I'm not a killer. I'm not an accomplice either."

Tom stared at me. "Fine. You can desert if you want. But there are two shells in this gun, and I can't promise I won't take a shot at you if you run. So you can stay here and do the deed I asked for or make a run for the truck. But either way I'm gonna join those folks in Sadr."

He lifted the shotgun and pointed the flashlight at me. I turned and ran. A few seconds later, I heard a muffled shot. I jumped to the ground and stayed there, my eyes closed, fingers gripping the dirt, paralyzed, for what felt was like a good five minutes. I heard a door open, some voices in the distance, and then a door shut and silence again.

A few more minutes passed. It seemed like an hour. I opened my eyes and got up. I didn't see or hear anything but the occasional chirping of crickets. The lights in the trailer were off now, and I didn't see the light from Tom's flashlight either. I thought that I knew which way Tom had dug the hole and began to creep toward it. There was a chance he was hiding in the hole, waiting to pounce on me. But I decided to take the chance, creeping up, my knees bent, my arms close to the floor. Then my foot hit something, and I snapped back, fists up, waiting for a confrontation. But nothing happened. I kicked the spot again, and the object moved. I put my hand on it. It felt like the flashlight, and it was hot on the bulb.

I picked it up, stood up, investigated the darkness. I listened. I still couldn't hear anything but the sound of crickets. I turned on the flashlight and searched the area with it. I observed the shovel and shotgun on the floor. I moved up to the hole. I saw Tom's body inside it, on the crumpled American flag, half of his face gone, barely recognizable.

I turned off the flashlight. Then I closed my eyes and covered my face with my right hand. I considered what to do. I could call the police and tell them this crazy story, but would they believe me? I'd seen enough shows and TV media coverage to know that they could suspect me just the same, of participating in Tom's death or in the stalking of the stripper.

I decided to follow Tom's advice and cover him up.

I opened my eyes and stood there for a few minutes, getting used to the night vision. Finally I could see the mound of dirt in the darkness. I turned the flashlight on again for a second to locate the shovel and I noticed that Tom's crutch was half in the hole, half out, so I kicked it in. Then I picked up the shovel, turned the flashlight off again, and started covering the hole, turning the flashlight on occasionally to make sure I was covering it right. By the time I was done with it, I was glad that I had started lifting weights again, because my muscles were tested but not too weary. I smoothed the hole over a few times to make sure it didn't seem out of place. I grabbed the shotgun, looked around to see if I was missing anything else. Then I used the flashlight to locate the truck and cautiously went toward it.

I placed the shotgun in the bed of the truck, shook the shovel to get as much dirt off it as possible, then put it back there too. I noticed that Tom's other crutch was in the backseat, so I opened the door and put that in the bed too. Then I looked around again one more time, started the car and pulled out.

I drove the way we had come. I had no idea where I was, but I had a concept of the route the stripper had taken so I tried to do the opposite. I took a few wrong turns, flinched when a cop car passed me, but eventually I made it to the highway. Once I was there, it was much easier to navigate.

By the time I got back to Tom's house, the sun was coming up. I parked near his house, next to the river. I took off my shirt and rubbed down the shotgun, crutch, shovel and flashlight. Then, after making sure no one was watching me, I flung them into the river.

I drove back to Tom's driveway, making sure no one came out and saw me, and parked the pickup. Leaving the keys in the glove compartment, I got in my Honda and pulled out. I drove by the river and stopped my car. I thought of Tom and our times together, of what could happen now. I saluted to the sun, and drove away.

Dhan's Debut

*

I've always been attracted to great personalities: Elmo on Sesame Street, Martha Gomartri in the sixth grade, Lauren Tobelman in high school, Edna St. Vincent Millay and Dorothy Parker in college. When I moved to New York City after attending Oberlin, I planned to follow in their path. I wanted to live in the Village, pen poetry and eventually wiggle my way into a job at *Vanity Fair*. Instead I was forced to live in Jackson Heights, intern for a travel magazine (I didn't even get to travel) and endure perpetual writer's block.

When my new friend Jose referred me to Mr. Davis, a literary agent, I was intrigued but cautious because hope had been struck down so often. I can't tell you how many networking events I'd attended and how many promises I'd been made that hadn't materialized as a friend on Facebook.

We met at The Voice, a bar in the Lower East Side, apparently renamed after the raspy tone of a cabaret singer/burlesque dancer who used to hang out there in the 1990s before and after her gigs at the club down the street. She'd reminded the patrons of Kim Carnes in "Betty Davis Eyes"—something *I* was reminded of constantly as I perused the articles pasted on the walls.

I was scared as I stood around the bar, being leered at by drunken leches, my knees shaking. It was my first meeting with an agent—I had never conceived that such Gods would ever answer emails, let alone meet you in person, and the fact that I was able to procure the meeting through someone I had randomly befriended in my building was an even greater miracle.

When Mr. Davis came in, grasping a wooden cane and gliding in an almost aristocratic way, I was even more intimidated—I'd colored half my hair green and I figured the alternative look wouldn't exactly work in my favor this time. We lived in the age of conformity after all, and I supposed that even translated to the arts.

But I was quickly put at ease by Mr. Davis' kind manner, polka dot suit and thin goatee that reminded me of an uncle back in Ohio. We sat at a table and ordered beers—I a Heineken ($7) and he a craft beer ($10). He told me he was from Indiana, that he specialized in gay fiction and celebrity nonfiction, which made me at least more comfortable with him than the men around me. While conversing about the horrors of socializing in the Midwest, I recounted the story of an erstwhile friend telling me, while sitting in a dorm room at a gothy anti-frat I'd joined at Oberlin, that it paid to be nice to people. Mr. Davis' eyes lit up and he revealed that not only had he attended Oberlin too but that he had resided in the very same anti-frat there, just 20 years earlier. Suddenly I felt a sense of utter connection and I knew this would be my agent.

Not so fast. It turned out that Mr. Davis wasn't too interested in my writing, which he admitted he hadn't had time to read. But he did tell me, rather excitedly, about a remarkable young man named Dhan (spelled with a "h" he specified) who was writing the text of our time (his words) and that he was looking for an assistant who could help edit the book, as well as to perform all other office duties as required, for a minimal, industry-standard salary to be discussed later. While I was grateful for the offer, I suddenly felt that the conversation had taken on a manipulative character and felt uncomfortable. Anyway, I was expecting a promotion to an official Staff Writer position at the magazine, which I believed I had earned, so I politely declined, and we left on amicable terms.

A couple of weeks later, I realized that I had missed out on a golden opportunity. The Staff Writer position at the magazine was never posted. Instead, it was gobbled up by the owner's niece, a recent community college graduate with no magazine experience.

I was depressed for a while, often sitting on my floor without showering, drawing doodles and refusing to see Jose when he knocked, despite his earnest inquiries of concern. I realized that I was terrible at the only skill that could sustain me in this city. I had no true connections and I was so bad at networking it wasn't funny. I guess I had written poetry too long, gazing at trees and breathing spring air. With print mags going the way of the dodo, I figured I was lost. I had applied to Conde Nast online but I had never heard back. I had sent a few proposals for stories on occurrences in the Lower East Side and in Jackson Heights, but *Vanity Fair* wasn't interested in the little people.

I realized that, because of Mr. Davis' connection to celebrities and his ability to put on airs and manipulate, he was probably my best, and only, bet for getting stories and achieving a publication that could finally put me out there. So finding him and seeing if he was still interested in an assistant was my best chance at survival. Otherwise, I might have to move back to my parent's place in Ohio, which wasn't exactly a tempting option.

I needed to get Mr. Davis' contact information from Jose, so I went over to his apartment, but when I knocked on his door, a short, stocky woman answered.

Speaking in Spanish, she said, "Jose no vive aquí ya."

I responded "¿Dónde vive él ahora?"

But she kept repeating "No sé."

I considered searching for Jose on the streets of Jackson Heights, but I knew that I didn't have the street smarts or the looks to get far. Knocking on doors in my fluffy cheap skirts wasn't going to cut it with the mareros or the Muslim clerics. I did not know Mr. Davis' first name. A search on agent databases didn't produce much. All Davises were either female or first names. I figured his client list was so exclusive that he preferred getting them through referrals rather than being inundated by queries from wannabe writers like me.

I decided to frequent The Voice, hoping either Jose or Mr. Davis would show up there one day. They didn't, but I did begin feeling more at home there. The expensive beers and dirty old men continued to annoy me, but I met some great characters and learned to love playing darts. I was lonely, being new in New York, living far away in Queens, uninvited to parties because my head was always in books or writing. Most Oberlin people had settled in Williamsburg and Astoria, but I didn't know them well and I'd never been to those places. I had stayed in my own corner, and I might have died there completely alone until I met Jose one day when he dropped his cervezas down the stairs and I picked them up for him. We got to talking and he began coming around my room, and when he realized I liked to write he had set up the meeting with Mr. Davis, who he knew from the "gay" world.

Now Jose was gone, but I had met a new friend at The Voice—a transsexual magician named Kieva. He was thirty-three years old and performed magic tricks at the burlesque club a few blocks away. He had a strange habit of winding up with a raised foot then sidearming his darts, which almost always hit the bullseye at an upward angle.

He "picked me up" when he told me that he loved my hair. I'd never had anyone say that to me before. If he'd been one of those creepy old guys tapping his fingers at the bar I would have told him to get lost, but he wore a cape, had long, thick black hair and looked enough like a woman. If I had to guess I'd say he was Asian, probably Vietnamese, but he told me he had lived in England and Australia during his childhood.

One day I let him come to my apartment. While he braided my hair, I mentioned that I was frustrated trying to get stories about celebrities in New York City since I was too shy to become a paparazzi or to send random emails to people and way too unconnected to get set up. He sympathized with my difficulties, considering he was a struggling artist himself. He said that I should just keep on pushing and that I shouldn't let anyone detract me from my ambition. We were in New York after all, and there was no going back. Then he got this gleam in his eye and said he was going to tell me a story that might intrigue me.

A week before, he had been performing a bird trick at the club. In this act, Kieva randomly selected an audience member from the crowd, who stood on the stage and held up a balloon he had been given. Kieva pointed up to the balloon and said a word in Swahili: "Kugeuza!" The balloon suddenly popped, smoke appeared and a bird seemed to fly from the balloon, prompting applause from the audience and segueing into the next act.

This time, Kieva picked a tall Indian guy. "Get this," Kieva said, "he was wearing a purple tux, orange shirt and green tie, just like the Joker in *Batman*.

"When he held up the balloon, dear, I swear to God

he snickered like Two-Face. That distracted me, so I didn't look at his face as I yelled "Kugeuza!" Usually the smoke almost blinded me but this time nothing happened. No smoke at all. I wondered if Dougie, my assistant, had been dosing off. Then I glanced at the Joker's face and I noticed he had stopped snickering. I could see a gleam in his eye. He took the balloon down and started twisting it. When he held it up again it was shaped like a bird. He flipped it into the air, it popped and there was the real bird, flying.

"The crowd cheered, thinking this was part of the act. But I knew better. The bloke was trying to one-up me, dear. He disappeared right after, as if he was rubbing salt on the wound. I didn't let it deter me, of course. I'm a professional, so I finished the show in stride, but he was all I could think about. After the show, I went backstage to find my assistant, Dougie, who was responsible for the bird trick.

"But instead I found the Joker standing backstage, waving me over with his index finger. I was mad as hell, I wanted to get him back, but I had to be cautious too, because some men want to hurt women like me. It's a sad case but you know how some men are about that. It's one thing if you're fighting with another woman but a man's a different story. But I didn't get a chance to do anything because suddenly he left the club through a back exit that led into an alley. I hesitated at first but I decided to follow him.

"When I got into the alley I saw Dougie. The bastard was in front of the door, arms behind his back. I yelled, 'You back-stabbing, nipple-twisting wanker!' Then the Joker came out from behind a garbage can and told me to leave Dougie alone, that Dougie wasn't at fault and if I would allow him the privilege he would explain the reasoning behind his deception. Well I gave him the old 'whatever,' a finger snap and head roll and I faked like I was turning to leave.

"At that, he opened the right flap of his jacket. I turned back when I noticed a half-cross, half-sickle sewn into the side. I remembered it from Yale. Back when I thought I was a man, that I was headed to some career in investment banking, believing that my international connections and Asian looks would help me. Did they? No, I had decided on a different path, a better path for me, dear.

"Anyway, I recalled reading about this secret society in the Yale Daily News, even though it was supposed to be secret. Some blokes invented this new society when they couldn't get into Skull & Bones. Repressed queers, dear. One of the great ironies of our elite institutions, eh? It was called Saints of the Far Union. I had no idea what that meant and I still don't. I said to The Joker, 'So what if you joined some wannabe society? What does that make you?'

Then he grinned that devil grin.

"'Of course, I can't talk about that. That isn't the point. What I am saying now is, don't blame Douglas for his transgression,' he said. 'He might have gone to Yale with us, but he's not like us. He'll never have what we have. But that's why people like us exist, to assist and to give. He needed some money. I made him a deal and gave him some. That's the nature of us fortunate ones. We can give, we can assist, we can *serve*."

He examined me, like he was checking me out, but I wasn't sure why.

'Do you think that's funny?' he finally asked me.

"I stared at him. 'Duh!' I thought. I wasn't sure why I would think that was funny. I didn't even know what he was babbling about. Dougie had gone to Yale recently, on a scholarship, but he wasn't able to finish his work and he had dropped out. But he had found me on an alumni listing and had contacted me. I could have used a steady assistant since the last one ended up becoming a heroin addict. So I took him on board, and he'd been pretty loyal and steady. But I didn't say that to him, darling. I didn't say anything to this Joker.

"So he kept on talking: 'I've learned not to get mad when you get beat, to keep your mind on the prize,' he said. 'And try different things, master what you can. I put my money today on trickery and illusion. I just needed to learn to tie a balloon and get to one person. Which means I can get to more if I can get to some. Don't you think?'

"'I guess,' I said. 'But I don't remember you and I still don't understand why you fucked up my act.'

"'When you were a senior, I was a freshman,' he said. 'I came to see you perform at Nick Chapel with the Entrance Players. You were in that improv group and you played, in successive fashion, a deadbeat dad, a lazy couch-potato, and a retarded kid. Then, after the show, you performed this bird act. Even then, you were a skilled deceiver, and your act made a deep impression on me. My primary challenge was to understand how you pulled it off.'

"'So you did this to one-up me? Or you just don't like women, dear?'

"'I'm beyond that,' he said. 'Well beyond that. In fact your transformation into a woman only sealed the deal and taught me that you were someone I needed to revisit, and to beat.'

"The creep took something out of his pocket and put it in my hand. Before I could examine it, he was gone, and so was Dougie. When I checked it out, I saw it was a hundred-dollar bill wrapped around a business card that read 'Dhan Duval'—Dhan spelled with an 'h'—and listed a law firm with a string of Jewish and German names I can't remember for the life of me.

"I wiped my ass with it and threw it in Dougie's mailbox in Brooklyn," Kieva concluded. "Then I took the money and burned each corner of the bill with lighted incense. This witch doctor I talked to in Alphabet City told me it could ward off evil spirits. I still have it in my drawer at my apartment, but I'll never touch it again and I'll never spend it either. That wanker was dodgy, dear. Personally, I never want to see him again. But I thought you might want to hear about what kind of people you would be 'reporting' on if you truly want to continue in that line."

I pretended to agree with Kieva—what else could I do while he had control over my hair—but I must admit, I was intrigued. It was the second time I'd heard about Dhan. Maybe it was a coincidence. But if I found him, I might be able to locate Mr. Davis too.

I decided to wait for a few days to ask Kieva if he could remember Dhan's business address. Meanwhile, I drafted a proposal for an article regarding Dhan's book. If I could find him and edit it, maybe an article pitching it could be my *in*. Plus it could be a PR boon for both of us.

When I returned to The Voice, I didn't find Kieva, but the dirty old men (it seemed like the same few guys every time) reminded me he was out performing. The burlesque club was only a couple of blocks away. I'd never been inside and as I walked down the narrow hallway with red velvet carpeting and walls lined with black-and-white pictures of a bygone past, my heart beat with excitement to see what it had to offer. But I never got a chance to peek in at a performance, or even to see the stage. Kieva paced around outside the performance room, sweating, muttering that he wasn't sure he could act after being shown up by Dhan. Maybe it wasn't such a great time to ask for Dhan's address, but I couldn't wait any longer. I had to strike while the iron was hot.

Kieva looked at me strangely. Then he reminded me about the fate of the card.

"What about Dougie? Do you have his address?"

He asked me if I truly wanted to pursue this story. He regretted telling me about it, but I said I had to do what I had to do. So he gave it to me, and right after, he seemed to change entirely. He became fired up.

"Lay him a big one, dear," he said.

The address was in East New York, about as far into Brooklyn you could go without leaving New York City. A guidebook had advised me to avoid it. If I had to go to Brooklyn, I should visit Brooklyn Heights, Park Slope, maybe Coney Island if I was adventurous. But Bedford Stuyvesant and beyond were off-limits.

My heart beat fast as I rode the dilapidated subway car, but I figured that it couldn't be worse than Jackson Heights. Sure enough, the building was a lot like mine. Graffiti, denoting some signature, or perhaps a gang sign maybe, was sprayed on the walls and next to the doorway the names on the resident listing were scratched off. I rang the apartment bell anyway. Two seconds later, I was buzzed up without a word.

Inside, the building smelled like stale marijuana. I decided to forgo riding up the cranky elevator and instead climbed the dirt-grimed marble stairs. I could hear my worn shoe soles clack on the marble as I ascended, round and round the landings until I reached the fifth floor.

As soon as I knocked on the brown door, it opened.

"Shorty, my nigga—"

A stocky man stepped out, wearing a down coat. A black pick penetrated a hacked afro.

"You not Shorty." He ducked into the apartment, then stepped out again.

"You from the agency, ma'am?" he asked.

"No," I replied. Kieva had written his assistant's full

name and address on a piece of scrap paper torn from a club flier. "I'm looking for Douglas Forrester," I said, reading off it.

"Oh," he replied, glancing back into the room. A large woman appeared next to the door.

"She looking for Dougie," he said to her.

"Dougie ain't here," she said, putting her hands on her hips. "What he done?"

"Nothing," I said. "I need to speak to him."

"You PD?"

"No," I replied. "I need to talk to him about someone named Dhan."

The short man said, "Dhan the man. My nigga."

Immediately they escorted me inside. Decorating the living room were oriental curtains that covered the windows (which I believed were arched), impressionistic paintings that filled the walls and plush sofas with fluffy cushions that were numerous and inviting. I was offered a big couch while the woman sat on a love seat and after trying to join her but being slapped away, the young man lounged on a recliner.

"Dougie live in Park Slope now," the woman said, "he gone to the big time. But we don't mind, cuz we here. Mister Dhan done it. Like a Messiah born, praise Jesus."

"Dhan got you this apartment?"

"We from down the street. Ain't nothing but trouble over there. Brothas thieving, dealing, killing. But Mister Dhan, he Yale-educated, like Dougie. Ain't no one like that around here. I mean we got them medical school brothers a few blocks down, but they do nothing for us unless we got a gunshot lodged. Anyway, a few months back, we sitting on the steps, watching the girls jump rope, hoping them brothers around the corner don't get the cops called, when Mister Dhan comes over and gives us his card. Says he's a big-time lawyer and he give us a hundred dollas just for our time. I tell him, don't let them brothers on the corner see it, or they'll want a piece, and they'll kill you too. But he not scared. I never seen a man like that not scared of the brothers. Figure he make his money some way not legit, but he says he legit. Says he come to help people. So I says, well, I need some help!

"He laugh and he say, 'I know a way to get you out of the project.' And I say, 'Really?' So he lay it on me. And lo and behold, here we are, across the street and nice and set."

"How'd he do it?"

"Damn if I know. He tell me to sign some papers. So I sign 'em. Junior here, he tell me watch out, white folks always trying for a sucker. But Mister Dhan, he the tribe. Ain't no way he gonna rip us off. What we got to rip? A few weeks later, he come back, tell us we gotta come to court, and say nothing. So we go and we say nothing, and when we done, Mister Dhan say he come back in a week with a check. So when he don't show in a week, Junior going around saying he gonna pop off if he sees another Indian man in the projects. But a week later, Mister Dhan back for sure, and Junior ain't popping nothing, because with that check, he got this key."

"And the decorations?"

"Here already. Like Jesus done descended."

I noticed now that etched in gold on an oriental rug was a half-cross, half-sickle.

"How do you know Dougie?" I asked.

"He used to come around too sometimes, but it wasn't to give us no hundred-dolla bills. No, it was to buy from the brothers. Most of those we don't like none, we don't associate with that kinda trouble, but he was a kind one mostly, so I let it pass, and Junior here become friends with him. He always got a good word from folks around the neighborhood, and that counts for a lot. And a school like Yale, that counts too."

"Did he say anything about when Dhan put up these

furnishings?"

"No. Don't know if it was recent or past but, looks nice enough to be recent. Say, what you want Dougie for anyway?"

I told her that I was a journalist writing an article on Dhan. Did she happen to have his contact information?

"Junior," she said to the short man, "you still got Mister Dhan's card?"

"Think so," he replied. He jumped up and ran into another room. I saw three young children, each smaller than the last, line up near the doorway, like Russian dolls. While Junior searched, the woman showed me around her apartment which included a new stove, shiny tiles and a blow fan. When Junior returned, he said he couldn't find the card, so I asked if they had Dougie's address.

"Sure," she said. "Junior go to Dougie's when he wanna live the white folks' life. We got that all right."

The Park Slope apartment was in a brownstone walk-up. "Karan Sanghvi" was listed on the panel for what was supposed to be Dougie's apartment on the first floor. When I rung the bell, no one answered. I rapped on the window once, but no response.

As I went down the steps an Indian man of medium height and build walked up. He looked about my age, but his hair was already thinning. He wore frameless glasses and a look of permanent contentment.

"Hey there. Looking for somebody?"

"Yeah, Dougie," I said. My heart started beating.

"You're in luck, I'm his roommate, Karan," he replied, and held out his hand. I had hoped he was Dhan, so I was disappointed.

After a handshake that he held longer than he should,

he brought me inside his apartment. The room contained a futon, a low table and a TV in the living room, and another futon and bookshelf in a tiny bedroom.

"I'm sorry, Dougie's not here," he explained after closing the door. "He had to get ready."

"For what?"

"We're off to a party tonight. Can I get you a drink?"

"When will he be back?"

"I don't know. He can take a while to get ready."

"I need to know whether I should wait."

"Why don't you?"

He moved into a small kitchen alcove next to the futon. The door wasn't locked. A laptop was open on the table, an Evite prominently displayed in the web browser. Dhan's name was printed in it.

"That's the party," Karan said, tracking my eyes, a tea kettle in his right hand. "Are you going too?"

The Evite read:

Come One, Come All, to Dhan's Debut! The Outing of a Maharajah, a Housewarming for a Kid from Queens, the Hailing of A Great Benefactor, A Warm Soul, The One. The Party of the Century if you Arrive with Style

Then it listed an address in the West 70s, today's date and a time of 9 PM.

"What is this?" I asked. "Did his book already come out?"

"No, this is my friend Dhan's housewarming party. He just bought a brownstone in the Upper West Side."

"He's not writing a book?"

"Not that I know about. He could though. Getting up there from Queens, and making it like that, it's a great story. He's gonna do it for all of us. What was your name again?"

I gave a fake one. He offered me tea. I said no.

"Aren't housewarmings normally for close friends?" I asked.

"Yup, but Dhan's the man. If you come like you mean it, there's room for you. He's got a big tent. I mean, there are important people coming, yet he's inviting everyone. Who else does that? Now why don't you sit down?"

I asked if he could print out the Evite for me. He said sure. He put down the tea kettle, went into the other room, and came out a minute later holding a large printer and two cables. He sat down in front of his laptop and connected the printer and the computer and the electrical cord.

After he handed me the printout and grazed his finger against my wrist, I thanked him and bowed slightly. Then I turned and left. I heard him call me, but I needed to be quick.

This party was the perfect opportunity to convince Dhan to let me edit his book, assuming he was writing one.

I had to pause and ponder this phenomenon, though. In our time you would think a great text would appear on the internet, in a blog, a webpage, a wikipedia entry or application on Facebook or even a twit. This was a Text, meaning a book, and though books still sold occasionally and might still sell, whether in hard form, online or in ebook readers, it's questionable whether a young person today could write a seminal work in book form. But maybe I could use that as my angle. I could press Mr. Davis to consider alternate forms of dissemination for the work. Maybe it was already in his mind, or maybe the form of the book was already radical.

Really, Dhan intrigued me more than the book itself.

Karan had hinted that Dhan rose from nothing to become a contender for partnership at a law firm. My dad had once been rejected for partnership in Columbus, so I knew something about that. Dhan had a kind of Horatio Alger story. He had political inclinations. He had diverse talents and interests from magic to decoration. He had helped at least two groups move into better housing. He was not only on the precipice of achieving success, but had actively exercised power for good.

I had to admit that I was attracted to this man without ever having met him. When I got home, I wrote another proposal for *Vanity Fair*, this time about Dhan himself. If I didn't get one article, maybe I could get the other.

I didn't know what "arriving in style" meant. If I had better social skills, I would have asked Karan before I left. I don't know why I feared him. I guess I didn't want to take a chance. I had been in compromising situations before. Kieva was safe. But Karan, I wasn't too sure.

I called Kieva and told him about my plan. He hated Dhan but he did acknowledge that he seemed like an interesting guy. I googled "Dhan's Debut" and found a plethora of blogs extolling Dhan's social events. I didn't see anything about the dress code, but the info would help me write about Dhan's phenomenon on the internet.

On Facebook, I found Dhan's name, but it was a fan's-only page, listing that he was a "people person." Some users had written on his wall things like "Dhan, you're the man!" I even saw a post by Junior. The event's invitation was there, but the list of invitees was hidden. Dhan Duval had over 8,000 subscribers. The number of confirmed guests to the event was 126. A few people had asked about what "style" meant on his wall, while others responded that if they didn't know, they couldn't go. One person said it was whatever you wanted, as long as it was true to you.

I decided to take his advice and I wondered what was true to me. Kieva claimed my person was goth. I told him I didn't want to appear too conspicuous, but he said if everyone was going to dress in a different way, why not me? I hadn't exactly been a social butterfly, so I didn't know how to dress in the city, really. So I let Kieva lead me.

He painted my eyes with black mascara, eyeliner and blue eyeshadow. He placed foundation on my skin and skin-toned lipstick on my lips. He dressed me in a scoop neck and a black bustier on top of a frilly black skirt. I put on black stockings and fuck-me heels. Kieva blow-dried my hair until it was puffy. When I looked in the mirror I resembled one of those pathetic girls trying out for *America's Next Top Model*, except I wasn't pretty enough to make the cut.

"Dear, don't worry, you'll be the life of the party!" Kieva exclaimed, fingers on his chin, admiring his work.

"I hope they don't make fun of me."

"Are you kidding me, darling? If they do, I'll commit harakiri."

He stuck his tongue out and imitated it. I stared at him strangely. I laughed. Then I put inside my purse the things I needed: a pad, a couple of pens, a small recorder I had bought for interviews but never used. I'd never been to the Upper West Side but I calculated how to get there on the subway. I realized it would take me about forty-five minutes. Since it was nine, I'd be late, but I knew, and Kieva confirmed, that would be fashionable.

When I emerged from the subway, I was astonished at the neighborhood's quiet atmosphere. I was standing next to Central Park, yet all I heard were a few cars driving past. When I rounded the corner to walk up the street, I heard only crickets chirping. It felt so different from Jackson Heights or the Village, and the brownstones were more majestic than Park Slope.

I tracked the addresses and as I neared the designated one, I heard blocked sounds of music that reminded me of college parties. On top of a steep staircase stood a black man in a black tuxedo coat with a back flap, like some vampire on an old TV show. His face was painted with pale white foundation and his lips were bright red.

"Are you looking for something, madam?" he asked, shouting in a firm voice.

"Yes," I said. "Dhan's Debut."

"Are you on the list?"

"I don't think so," I said. I had forgotten to RSVP on Facebook. I held up the print out. "I have this. It says all are welcome."

"Yes," he said, smiling. "All who arrive with style. Where is your style, madam?"

"My style is goth," I said.

"I see that, Madam. But is that the right style for Dhan's Debut?"

"I thought all were welcome," I said. "I thought he had a big tent."

His smile widened. "He does, Madam. But he doesn't determine entrance. You do. All are welcome, as long as they arrive with style."

"Then what is this?" I asked, pointing to my bustier.

"You tell me, Madam."

The door behind him opened. Another man stepped out. He wore a similar outfit. I recognized him, but the pick was gone. His hair had been curled into cornrows.

"Junior," I said. "He's not letting me in."

"Oh, the reporter lady," he said a few seconds later. "You talk to Dhan yet?"

"No," I replied. "I'm trying to get in."

"Dougie," he said, "this lady's a reporter. She wants to talk to Dhan."

Dougie examined me again like I was a mouse. "Oh, a professional," he said with disdain. "I didn't realize."

He opened the door, releasing a rush of air. I heard Michael Jackson's *Billy Jean* blasting on the first floor. Upstairs hints of Benny Goodman resonated. I turned to Junior.

"If you knew his address, why didn't you just give it to me?"

"I didn't know about this 'til after you left, miss. Dhan called me up. Said he needed a favor, so I get up and go. Shorty or no Shorty. I don't know about Dougie."

Dougie, who I had searched for long and hard, stood motionless and mute like a soldier at Buckingham Palace.

A limousine pulled up, one of those big white ones you see on W. 4th Street sometimes that look more like an armored tank. The door opened and some older people stepped out, dressed in tuxedos and glittery dresses. I nodded at Junior, then stepped inside. Immediately the door closed after me.

A crowd of people had already packed the hallway and the first-floor apartment, making it difficult for me to get through. People were hanging out on the stairs too, like at a college frat party, except they were all ages, ethnicities, genders, sexual orientations—though I didn't see any trannies. No women were dressed with any risk. No cleavage showing, just bare legs emerging from conservative skirts. Even the older women weren't fans of stockings. I was the only goth there, getting stares from the ladies and the queers.

The old and young people didn't mix. The latter drank exotic beers and cocktails in martini glasses while the older people sipped champagne from flutes or red wine in bulbous glasses. A soldier approached and gave me a cocktail list printed on cotton resume paper.

The drinks were new to me. Sazerac and Brandy Alexander were mysteries. Even my father had limited himself to scotch and bourbon back home. The soldier waited patiently, keeping his hands behind his back, until I decided upon an order. Underneath his cap was a jheri curl and I could tell he had just shaved a goatee. His rank insignia on his shoulder confirmed he was a lieutenant (my dad had been in the army, so I could tell), but his servility made him seem like a foot soldier. I struggled with the menu, reading it over several times. Finally I closed my eyes, repeated "eeny-meeny-miny-moe," and picked one at random. It was the Sazerac. The soldier bowed, grabbed the list and left.

I made my way into the first-floor apartment, looking for a tall Indian man who could be Dhan. I didn't find any. I left the room, "excusing" my way to the staircase. As I tried to go up, someone grabbed my arm.

"Look who it is," Karan said. He pulled me over to a small group headed by an Indian girl wearing a red halter dress. She was texting something on her smartphone. The others dispersed.

"This is Dhan's sister, Kenali," Karan said. "I'm sorry, I don't remember your name."

I told him the fake name again. It was Avril, a name some kids used when I was little.

"Oh, it's so nice to meet you," Kenali said when she seemed to finish her text. She checked me out. "Can I get you anything?"

The soldier returned and handed me the Sazerac in a rocks glass.

"Oh, you already have a drink, don't you?" Kenali said, laughing. "Tell me, how do you know Dhan?"

I was puzzled. Considering Karan had introduced me,

wouldn't she ask how I knew him? And if everyone with "style" was invited, why would she assume I knew Dhan personally?

Karan got me off the hook. "She's Dougie's friend," he said. "She came by the apartment earlier looking for Dougie and I told her about this party. I guess you met him outside."

"Yeah," I said, thinking about what else to say, what to reveal and what not to. They were waiting to hear something else about Dougie, about our conversation or relationship or something, but I didn't deliver.

"I see," Kenali said to break the silence. "What do you do for a living?"

"I'm a journalist," I said.

"Really?" Kenali said, smiling now. "Me too. Who do you work for?"

I told her the name of the travel magazine. She acted like she had heard of it, but I could tell that she hadn't and I was annoyed about that. I told her I also freelanced, that I was writing an article for *Vanity Fair*.

"Wow, that's ambitious," Kenali responded, suddenly impressed, and clearly envious. "What's it about?"

"It's a profile," I said. "And a search for a text."

"That's nice," she said, though I could tell she was annoyed by my ambiguity. I assumed a fellow journalist would press me to reveal more details but she didn't.

"Where do you work?" I asked.

"*Self.* I'm a junior staffer. But I'm trying to move up."

Her concentration wavered. A girlfriend approached, pointing to her blackberry. Soon they were off and I was alone with Karan. He looked down at me, his chin raised.

"How do you like this party so far?"

"It's okay," I said. "Do you know where Dhan is?"

His awkward grin turned fully wrought.

"You wanna get to the head honcho right away, huh? No one knows, at the moment. Before he was making the rounds, like he usually does, meeting everybody. Now he's probably upstairs, on the top floor. That was a dressing room for debutantes in the 19th century. It's beautiful up there, with a huge bed, mirrors all around, little private closets and peepholes. No one's allowed up there except for close friends. I think that he's planning something special, trying to give these guys a show. He was worried that these partners, the ones who've shown up, might be offended or something. He shouldn't worry. He's been planning this for weeks. He's been emailing me about this and that."

"Can I ask you something? How'd you end up in that apartment?"

"That is my apartment. If you're referring to Dougie, I let him move in with me."

"And he pays rent?"

"Dhan arranged it. I don't know who pays, but it gets paid. I'm a civil engineer for the city. I love Park Slope. Dougie never told you?"

I shook my head. I felt my hand itching to get my pad and pen out of my purse, but I realized that might seem rude. I said, "You told me Dhan is from Queens. Did you grow up with him?"

"I've known him since he was a baby in a cradle. I was in the cradle with him."

"I've never been to Queens," I told him. "I don't know anything about it."

"It's a dark place. It's full of ghouls and goblins." He laughed. "I'm kidding, but when we were growing up, it wasn't too safe. It was a place you wanted to get out of. Dhan's made it beyond our wildest dreams. And he's done it the right way. Not just by attending the top institutions and making pay, but also by helping people. That's his main goal. To help people."

He paused, looking strangely at me. Then he laughed. "Oh, now I get it. I don't know why I didn't put two and two together before. You want to profile Dhan. This has got nothing to do with Dougie."

I swallowed.

"Don't worry, that's awesome. We can try to find him. He'll be glad to talk to you."

He took me by the arm again and we headed to the staircase, exactly where I was going before I ran into him. On the way up we passed a man wearing a hood. From a brief glance I could have sworn it was Jose. When I turned around he had run out the door. Karan was pulling my arm, so I continued up the stairs. He stuck his head into the second-floor apartment, then took my arm again. We headed toward the next pair of stairs, but I recognized someone on the landing, and this time I was sure. It was Mr. Davis.

I shrugged off Karan's arm and approached him. He was speaking to an old man with a big nose, bald head, owl glasses, wearing a striped shirt and gray bow tie. Mr. Davis didn't recognize me at first. But when I told him my name (my real name), he remembered.

"Oh, the girl with the green hair." He examined my get-up. "I see you've graduated."

I chuckled, not knowing how to take this comment. The other man glared at me, a wide smile revealing half-blackened teeth.

"You're dressed like a China Doll, aren't you? What's the occasion?" the other man asked.

"I thought this was a theme party," I replied.

"Why it is. But I don't believe they had Harajuku girls in the 1920s."

"It didn't mention a specific theme in the Evite. And I don't see any flappers."

"No, but it's a debut," he said. "When I was young, they still had debuts. They are rarer today, aren't they? Have you had one?"

"No. Though I guess I am wearing a kind of corset."

"The 19th century. Of course."

I could sense Karan standing behind me. Mr. Davis said, "Do you know Dhan somehow? Or did you just fall into his orbit, as everyone is liable to do?"

I told him I had reconsidered his offer but couldn't find Jose and couldn't contact him, so I had gone on a search which led here.

"Jose has had some troubles," he said. "And I run a very exclusive agency. I don't list it, because there are so many crazies out there. I get clients through referrals."

"Was Dhan a referral?" I asked.

"Dhan was a triple referral. Mr. Sandman here; then Ms. Skidmore, through Dhan's sister; and of course Mr. Kloesterman."

"Yes, Dhan is an incredible young man. Hungry and energetic," Mr. Sandman added, pumping his fist. "He's a welcome addition to New York society. I helped him get into the University Club, you know. He was already a member of the Yale Club, so I couldn't help with that." He laughed.

"Are you his boss?" I asked.

"Lord no. Mr. Kloesterman is a partner at his firm, and he has certainly taken Dhan under his wing. Not that a dynamo like him needs it. But I met Dhan at the Yale Club. I'll tell you, there are advantages to joining a club, and that is one, my dear. Did you attend Yale too?"

"No, she went to Oberlin," Mr. Davis replied for me.

"Ah. So you may be eligible for the University club. Unfortunately, the Yale Club is closed to you."

I didn't tell him that I had no desire to join clubs or societies. I just wanted my article on "Dhan the man" and then I wanted to leave. But I couldn't say that. I wasn't sure now whether Mr. Davis or Karan would be better in getting me access to Dhan. I asked Mr. Davis if his offer was still open.

"That's up to Dhan. I couldn't find anybody qualified,

so his sister found someone instead, and she's been just as good with the office duties. It doesn't seem like he needs any more help with the book, but we can't be sure unless we ask."

"Can we?"

Mr. Davis grinned at Mr. Sandman. "She's feisty, isn't she?" he said.

"They say young people these days don't have the fire that our past generations had," Mr. Sandman said. "This girl and Dhan prove our top private institutions still churn out the best talent. We can still compete with the Chinese, with the Japanese. Especially the immigrants, especially the Indians. No matter what, the Indian parents, they get their children well-educated. Isn't that right, young man?"

I turned around. Karan looked embarrassed.

"Yeah," he said, his head down.

"Also a humble people," Mr. Sandman said. "That is what I love about the Asians. There was a time in this country when Asians weren't even allowed to immigrate here. Yet they persevered. You know, I was stationed in China during the war, and later I became an ambassador to Japan. I've been all over, but I never forgot the Asians. Such a competent people, a reliant and resilient people. Dhan is one of these, but he doesn't just demonstrate these qualities. He has a foot in everything. Doing your job well and with honor, but also being able to master other skills, that's the path to true leadership. I have to say, our children, they aren't equipped with that. Dhan's generation and the immigrants, they will lead us."

"Is that what Dhan's book is about?" I asked.

"Part of it, yes," Mr. Davis said.

A moment later, Kenali descended the stairs. She asked people on the second floor to move downstairs because Dhan was coming out soon. She wanted space so everyone could see him and express how much he meant to them.

There was an exodus from the second floor, but many people hung out on the stairs, making it difficult for people to get to the first floor. Kenali waved her arms, trying to get them to move down, or at least to make an alley. But many stayed put, determined to get a glimpse.

It was like a raucous wedding. Everyone was dressed in tuxedos, suits and elegant dresses, beautiful and brilliant people who had gone to the best schools and had the best jobs, except the servants who served as the gatekeepers, the feeders, the drug givers, the entertainers, and me, the self-designated recorder-in-chief.

But I wasn't the only one. Someone shone a flashlight on the staircase, and people took out their digital cameras and smart phones. I took out my recorder. I had forgotten to bring my cell phone. I wish I had brought it, though all I needed to do was to friend Karan, or Dhan, or Kenali on Facebook, and I'd be able to get somebody's pictures of Dhan and his debut.

Karan was watching me. He had seen me take out my recorder. I didn't see Mr. Davis or Mr. Sandman. I had to find Mr. Davis again before I left to get his information. The landing was getting crowded. People were squeezing me. I felt someone's hand touch my butt. I figured it was Karan. I didn't care though, because my focus was on the staircase above.

I noticed that someone had placed candles on the top and bottom ledges of the staircase railing, and on the side of each stair, which seemed pretty dangerous to me, but it produced another light source than just the one flashlight some random person held up.

The music stopped. The crowd became jubilant one second, expectant another. If Dhan had enemies in this crowd, they were submerged. Almost any crowd I'd been part of had included people who bad-mouthed the person being honored. Here, I heard nothing.

A door creaked open. People were silent—you could

hear crickets chirping outside. I almost expected a hand to go up my skirt, yet Karan's hand stayed on my butt. Maybe he was transfixed. Then the stairs creaked again, and I saw four legs descending. One set were female: light brown, bare, branching out of a lithe body in a white dress. Her face was round, coy, superficially pleasing. The other person was tall and skinny too, dressed in a white suit and a black bow tie. His face was carefully structured. He had a Roman nose and a cleft chin, and his cheekbones protruded in perfect proportion to his eyes, which were well-rested within the sockets of his face. His sideburns were even and down about to the middle of his ear; his hair was scissor-cut and his neck well-shaved. On his head lay a large Rajasthani Crown, wrapping around the upper half of his temple and rising; on top was a peacock feather.

The couple descended the stairs in lock step, their arms hooked, donning automatic smiles. They stopped at the bottom of the stairs. Flashes blew from left, right and center. An older white man dressed in a blue striped suit approached, shook Dhan's hand and had the couple pose for pictures. He had a wireless microphone in his hand. Everyone on the second floor cheered. The people on the first floor cheered too, though some were shouting that they couldn't see him. I heard Kenali pleading for people to make room on the second-floor landing so the couple could move forward, but the people didn't listen. They gawked, flashed photos and struggled to move closer. I was pushed to the railing at the edge of the landing, scared I would tumble to my doom. I couldn't see Karan anymore, but I did see the older man waving at Kenali, telling her it was okay, that he would make his speech where he was. She asked the crowd to quiet down. That didn't work either, but the older man started speaking.

"I want to speak on this solemn occasion," he started to say, then repeated, because the crowd was still loud, though they had started to listen. "I want to say that I am fortunate to have met Dhan. He calls me a mentor, and that I've tried to be. But the truth is that Dhan didn't need a mentor. Sure, maybe it would have taken longer for him to learn what he's learned, but the fact is that he's got it, and he's probably always had it. He's been a boon for our firm, bringing in new clients through his contacts, even though he's not yet a partner, and mastering every aspect of his job, from briefs to trial work, to the careful reading of contracts and beyond. This has led to our being able to increase bonuses across the board, for all our associates. His hard work and skills have resulted in everyone at our company benefiting, and I think that all of the associates who are here need to give Dhan a well-deserved round of applause."

A sonorous ovation sounded from a small, dispersed group. Who knows if every employee clapped. But I did realize how many people weren't work associates, how many people Dhan knew in many ways.

"But that's not what has most impressed me about Dhan," the man continued. "It is his pro bono work. He wrote a brief for a Somalian woman who was raped and marked for death for being a Christian, persuading the judge to grant her asylum in the U. S. He helped a poor black family living in a violent housing project sue the government for bad living conditions and resettled them in a proper apartment. These are the things that we look for, in New York. People who go beyond their expected duties and help people. That's why we are throwing this special party for Dhan, why we have helped him buy this building. We have invested in his future because he has invested in us. For too long we have gone the other way, investing in ourselves while shortchanging and turning away the future. No more. Today, we will lift those who will one day lead our land. Enjoy your brownstone, Mr. Duval. And congrats to you too, Miss."

He shook Dhan's hand, then the girl's. Dhan took the microphone from Mr. Kloesterman, who descended the stairs.

"Thank you, Mr. Kloesterman. And thank you to all the partners and other great men of this city who are here today, who have been kind enough to befriend me and guide me and sponsor me in so many ways. I am not me. I am you. You have built me up, you have made me. I would be nothing without your support, and I hope you will continue to support me because I will need it. But it's not just about you gentlemen. It's about everybody who has been a part of my life, everyone I have touched and everyone who's touched me, from the newspaper guy on the corner who I buy my morning coffee from, to the custodian who cleans our floors and the guys I've helped sue their landlords. I'm telling you, I wouldn't be doing everything I've been doing if it wasn't for you guys. That inspires me more than anything. Growing up a poor child of Indian immigrants, in Queens, I know what it's like to struggle. My parents couldn't find work half the time and sometimes I didn't know if I'd be able to eat when I got home. I got free lunch at school. I'm one of you. But I've achieved my dream, and Mr. Kloesterman, you and the other partners and the members of the Yale Club and everyone else who has pitched in, thank you for helping me purchase this brownstone. I always wanted to be a 'new money' guy, and now, finally, I am. But that's not all. I called this my debut because it is. I plan to be on the front lines to help people and do my duty as a new aristocrat in these tough times. I'm going to continue my push to serve this great city. And I need all of you to help me do it."

People clapped, but not as many as before.

Dhan continued.

"I would also like to use this occasion to announce another great event." He put on his wide smile and turned to the girl, holding out his arms. "This is Mal. We met through friends, and we immediately fell in love. Tonight, I'm announcing our engagement." Dhan smiled even more widely at Mal. She had her hands over her mouth. Then she put them in the air and hugged Dhan, who kissed her cheek. Mr. Kloesterman ascended the stairs again and led a more passionate cheer.

A few hours later, the party appeared to be winding down, based on the amount of music and noise I could still hear through the wall while lying naked in a third-floor cubicle next to Karan. I'd given in, finally, to his advances.

Dhan's dressing room was cut up into sections, consisting of one main room and a bunch of smaller cubicles filled with futon beds and Christmas ornaments. A peephole in the cubicle let you look into the main room, which was extremely bright, lit simultaneously by a yellow-bulbed chandelier and a white florescent light with three bulbs. An old-fashioned dining table was next to the wall, supporting an oval mirror bordered by small, unlit light bulbs. Across the floor were tall, red cushions. In the other corner was a gold-colored brass rack covered with metal and plastic hangers. The clothes draped were diverse—for a sample, a little black dress, a suede suit, a thong, a slip, a studded strap. The colors of the collection ranged from purple to sepia, the styles from 1890s to 1970s and beyond. It appeared that Dhan's commitment to diversity didn't just include his political base.

While we were making love, I had teased Karan with a blowjob, delaying the finish until he told me more about his friend. Dhan's real name was Dhananjay. and Mal was really Malini. Recently Dhan's sister had exerted greater influence over him, convincing him, for example, to settle down to make him appear more mature. She had discovered Malini, a registered nurse and graduate of Harvard's nursing school. Karan wasn't sure what Malini thought of Dhan, but like everyone else Malini believed it was in her best interest to follow him.

I could tell Karan was somewhat jealous of his friend. As a child Karan's parents had told him constantly to be like Dhan, who had excelled at everything Karan had failed at. Karan was cautious and defensive; Dhan ran full-steam ahead. Dhan held his friendship with Karan in high-esteem, yet he also dominated and bullied Karan. When Dhan had encouraged Karan to follow him into corporate law, Karan had resisted and done the safe thing, attending a cheap city college and becoming a civil engineer. He had resented it when Dhan had gone to Yale, but once Dhan finished law school and gotten into a top firm, Karan had accepted Dhan's superiority.

As we lay there, Karan's head on my chest, his hand caressing my stomach, I heard stairs creaking and voices laughing. I sat up and gazed through the peep hole. The door to the dressing room opened and Kenali walked in, followed by Dhan. He had taken off his shirt, but he was still wearing his jacket and pants. His chest was hairless and bony, containing little strands of muscularity. He was also shorter than I had realized. He had towered over Mal on the staircase but seeing him now, he looked stocky and compact.

He also seemed sweaty and drunk. Sighing loudly, he plopped down on a cushion. Meanwhile Kenali marched around, her hands on her hips.

"That was a success, right?" Dhan asked, laughing.

"It would have been if people had moved back like I told them to."

"Plenty of people shot the footage. There'll be plenty of youtube videos."

"I know, but there could have been a lot more if they had moved back."

"Stop worrying," Dhan said. "The mob doesn't listen. They gravitate towards instant gratification, you know that. Did you talk to Mr. Davis about the book?"

"Yeah. He talked to Mr. Sandman." She paused. "He still wants me to cut out that chapter."

Dhan shook his head, standing up suddenly.

"But that's my best idea. And Mr. Sandman said it's achievable."

"You need to learn to withhold, Dhananjay. You don't just tell the people everything. No one is ready for what you're suggesting."

"All these years I've been a tool," he said. "I haven't been advancing and learning, but only copying, not really inventing. And now I have an idea, a real innovation, and people want to stop me?"

"No one's ready for it," Kenali responded. "And you don't have the capability to develop anything yourself. That's why you need Mr. Sandman. You need Mr. Davis to sell the book. Appreciate the people you have."

"I know, dammit," he said. "But it's frustrating."

He flipped off his shoes, slid off his pants. I glanced back at Karan. He looked scared. I chuckled silently.

When I turned back to Dhan, he'd taken off all his clothes and was standing in front of the lighted mirror, hands on his hips. He admired himself. His penis and testicles were huge, larger than I'd ever seen. He lifted his genitals and underneath appeared to be labia lips. Then he rubbed the clit area.

"Will you stop touching yourself?" Kenali requested, sitting on a cushion. "It's annoying."

Dhan stuck his tongue out at her, turned to face her and began rubbing it even faster.

"God, you're sick," Kenali said, giggling.

The door opened. Dhan dropped his hand and closed

his legs. Mal entered. Dhan closed his eyes with relief.

"You scared me," he said.

"Maybe you shouldn't march around naked like that."

"Is it wrong to be proud of our work?"

"You don't have to show it off."

Mal plopped down on Kenali's lap. Kenali wrapped her arms around Mal's waist.

"Did you talk to Mr. Sandman?" Dhan asked.

"Are you going to pay me?"

"Since when do I need to?"

"You've got to be a man of the people," Mal said.

"What did he say?"

She sighed and stared at him for a few seconds, her head tilted disrespectfully.

"He said," she exclaimed loudly, "they've done more testing. But it's still a long way away."

"How long does it take to switch this shit around?" he asked, grabbing his penis. "So one can go in the other?"

"They have to insert another reproductive system that the person's body won't reject, and mix genes so people with both systems can be made. Even after that, who knows if the same genes can mix and produce a person who won't be a retard."

"By the time I'm thirty-five," Dhan said to himself, as if he hadn't been listening. "If I play my cards right I could be the youngest person to ever run for mayor. After some preliminaries, we can implement the strategy."

"What about City Council?"

"By that point, if I run for comptroller, some other positions, we can get them on board. This isn't just about me. It's a concerted effort. That's why we'll need Mr. Sandman, Mr. Kloesterman, and who knows how many people down the line. I still don't get why I can't write about it in my book. A lot of great figures have written about what they would do. Who doesn't want immortality for the human race?"

"It won't guarantee that," Mal said.

"People will still die. But once we can fuck ourselves, we can control productions of children. It'll cut out the middle man."

"We could have a population problem if people fuck themselves as often as they jerk off," Mal said. "They'll have to wear condoms all the time and we might need to enforce a one-child policy."

"Once people realize they don't want to constantly become pregnant, they'll stop fucking themselves. The people won't tolerate mandates. They're individualists to the bone. But if we spring this on them like it developed naturally, people will self-select and limit themselves to their own offspring because it's in their interest to reproduce themselves. You can produce little yous, like amoebas, you'll be asexual and in total control of your destiny, your progeny. It's completely American. There won't be sexes anymore, just individuals. If someone is raped, we'll know it's a crime because no one would want to fuck anyone else when they could fuck themselves."

"They could still fuck others."

Dhan rubbed his chin. "True. I guess I hadn't thought of that. It'll create diversity."

"It won't eliminate rape," Mal said. "It won't control procreation. It'll give the people who have both systems the ability to reproduce themselves if they choose. They can still reproduce with others."

"But will they?"

"Opposites attract. Think of chaos theory. And sexual people could ostracize asexual people, even kill them."

"Christians were persecuted too, in the beginning," Dhan said. "Later they dominated the world. I won't live to see the full ramifications. None of us will. But I think it'll work. Like Mr. Sandman said, ultimately we need a controlled population to lessen the number of people in the world and to purify the gene pool without genocide.

Then we can target and get rid of AIDS and cancer more easily. Once people realize that, I think asexuality will win out. And I want to get the credit for it."

"We're still a long way," Kenali said. "Let's get you married, a partnership, get a campaign together."

Dhan sighed. He returned to the mirror. Meanwhile I had taken out my pad and was scribbling furiously. Then I noticed Karan wasn't behind me. When I peeped back through the hole, Karan was telling Dhan something, and all four were gazing in my direction.

You can come to this city planning to get into one game and instead, by knowing the right people and being in the right places, you can get involved in something completely different. That's what I learned that night. When I felt those eyes on me, I thought it was over. I assumed my sentence for overhearing would be death. But I had underestimated Dhan. He was a compassionate politician, a true believer in bringing people together and finding them work. He took me under his wing, and I got more than I wanted.

I completed my article on him, keeping out what I'd overheard, but being honest about other things. It wasn't without criticism, but it announced Dhan to the city and to the world. Mr. Davis became *my* agent and he got it submitted and published in *Vanity Fair*. I got my name out there, they got the press. A few months later I became head of Dhan's publicity for his City Council campaign. As long as I remained loyal and Dhan kept afloat I could be employed in this city.

A month after I got my new job, a neighbor told me he'd seen Jose in the same apartment as before. I knocked on his door. He was glad to see me, though morose. I sat in his living room, filled with unpacked boxes, and drank chamomile tea. When I told him I thought I had seen him at a party in the Upper West Side a few months before, he became distressed and left the room. When he came back undressed I saw why. Around his loins were bandages, and they were soaked in blood.

Made in the USA
San Bernardino, CA
01 February 2014